THE SHADE

MIDDY GLENN

The Shade
©2021 Middy Glenn

Print ISBN 978-1-66781-859-7 | eBook ISBN 978-1-66781-860-3

Dedicated to Dotty.

CHAPTER 1

NORAH GRABBED HER COFFEE AND STEPPED OUT OF THE rusted truck camper onto the dewy, pine-needled earth. She breathed the cool mountain air into her lungs while the night sky waited for the sun to rise from behind the snow-capped peaks. The campground was unusually silent for a busy long weekend. Her ears registered a faint humming in the distance, and the sound was met with an uneasy twinge inside her stomach. *A quad or chainsaw?* When her eyes had adjusted to the dim light, she wrapped herself in her oversized wool Siwash, walked to the small creek a few steps away, and dipped her toes in the glacier water. Her toes numbed while she took a sip of her coffee, steam dancing around her face. The hot and cold sensations relieved the mental exhaustion of yesterday. She walked to the picnic table, opened her tattered journal, and scribbled a poem by the light of the moon.

> *Clawing out her insides, they now lay at his throne*
> *This offering, the sacrifice, she kneels on shattered bone*
> *Lifting off his blood-soaked crown, both eyes an empty hole*

The guts are spilling over as he fills his hollow soul

What shit, she thought, her usual consensus after creative musings. *This poem belongs in a hole.* She flipped a page back. The pang of yesterday crept into her stomach as angry words exploded off the page.

Every trip, every goddamn trip. Why? Why do I stay? Is it possible to be happy with someone miserable? Is it me who's miserable? All this shit about changing yourself, well, I've tried and tried and tried, and where am I now? Angry. And my poor son probably ingesting all this pain of the said and unsaid, the heavy air and words. My guilt overcomes me, like this pit in my stomach, a combination of too many things—anxiety, shame, pain, so much hurt. I know I can't fake it till I make it out of this. I feel lost and stuck, responsible for my life but out of control. His righteous, condescending voice enters my eardrums at an unbearable frequency. Over the years, they've become so sensitive that even the slightest pang triggers an over-the-top reaction. His inability to recognize or hear himself is so messed up. But once again, I'm not supposed to focus on him but me. How can I not focus on something so disturbing? More disturbing is that I've allowed being taunted, triggered, and gas-lighted for years. God help me I love him, ignore him, leave him, accept him, be like Mother fucking Theresa in putting up with his shit. If there was a painting that encapsulated this relationship, it would be The Scream.

She breathed out an audible sigh, crinkled her toes into the pine-needled dirt, and walked to the woodpile beside the camper. She lifted a small log but lost her grip, it fell onto her big toe and landed on a string of profanities. She slumped onto the cold ground and cupped her throbbing toe. Tears rolled down her cheeks. She lay back onto the rough earth floor and allowed the last few tears to fall.

Strange, she thought, *not a single bird singing.* Not once had she been camping without awaking to a choir of chirping. She raised her hand to the air. It was still, not a single leaf blowing on the massive oak trees. No squirrels jumping from tree to tree.

"What are you doing?" said a voice.

Startled, she shuffled to her feet. Seamus and Theo were staring at her. She knew her eyes were puffy and red, her messy bun tangled with twigs and pine needles.

"Here…" Seamus reached out and brushed the debris from her hair. She subtly pushed him away.

They had looked forward to this trip for months. Norah had tried for years to secure a coveted spot at Shady Oaks, the impossible-to-book, swanky, celebrity-visited campsite in the Rocky Mountains. Two hours into the four-hour drive, Seamus, distracted by his phone, had swerved into the other lane and almost caused an accident before Norah yelled to get his attention. He flipped out and blamed her for his erratic driving. An old story at this point—him blaming her for everything under God's green earth.

"Mom, why were you lying on the ground?" Theo smiled, his cute freckles scrunched into his round cheeks.

"I was meditating," Norah replied with a half smile, self-conscious about her puffy eyes. "Where were you guys?"

"We got up early. Went fishing in the creek. Beautiful morning." Seamus looked at her, his beard scruffed over his dimply smile. It was that exact smile that had initially drawn her in. He put his arm around her.

"Stop," she said under her breath and slinked away.

"Holding on to it, hey?" he said.

Norah changed the subject. "Catch anything?"

"Nope," Theo said. "Dad thought I had a bite, but I didn't."

"I think it was a nibble, Theo." Seamus smiled.

"No, Dad, it was a weed." Theo's voice cracked.

Norah's heart sank. *Where did the time go?* Her son was already eleven years old. His frame now filling in stocky like his dad's. She refused to let anger sour another trip and scolded herself to snap out of it. She wrapped her arms around Theo and gave him a big hug.

"Love you, Mom." He hugged her and headed inside the camper.

"Norah," Seamus said, "can you just let it go?"

"Is that your idea of an apology?" she snapped.

"I'm sorry, okay? I know it wasn't your fault." He piled some wood inside the firepit, on top of the skeleton of an ashy log still smoldering from the previous night. He put his arms around her again.

She didn't push him away or return the embrace, just let her head rest on his shoulder. Twelve years into the relationship. She loved him. She hated him. The cycle wore her down. What she hated most was the uncontrollable ugliness it brought out in her.

"Did you notice anything weird? It's super quiet." She shuffled out of his arms and sat by the fire.

"Wasn't really paying attention." He shrugged and grabbed more firewood. "Now that you say it, when we were out, I didn't see a dirt bike or a hiker." He paused. "We should take a walk and see if we can find someone. We need to check in anyway."

"Mom," Theo shouted from the small window of the old camper, "can I have Ichiban?"

"No, it's too early."

"Why, Mom? We're camping, I'm allowed to have Ichiban. Please?"

"No, don't ask again," she said, prickling with a tinge of irritation. "Grab a granola bar, we're going to the office to check in."

A moment later Theo jumped out of the camper. "Look who I found!" he said, a half-eaten granola bar in one hand and his stuffed llama in the other.

"No way, where was he?" Norah asked.

He grinned. "Tucked inside a couch cushion."

Norah looked at Seamus. "How long has it been since he went missing?"

"Has to be at least five years. Theo, you cried about Llama for months. I was sure he got left somewhere."

Theo hugged the stuffie to his chest. Norah smiled at the sweet reunion. She slipped on her shoes, and they all walked down the path to the office. With every step, the hairs on Norah's neck stood at attention. Everything from tents to giant motorhomes filled the sites, but not one person or animal could be seen. Fires burned unattended. Not one kid at the park.

"Dad, where is everyone?" Theo asked.

"Don't know. It's still really early, probably sleeping."

Norah squeezed Seamus's hand as they reached the office, a stunning modern log building. Stained glass windows with etchings of bears, deer, and other wildlife adorned the massive windows, and oversized hanging baskets of flowers surrounded the front beam. Far from the typical camp-sites they'd visited. But what had caught Norah's attention was that the automatic door stood wide open.

"Hello?" Seamus yelled and glanced at Norah.

"What the hell?" she murmured under her breath.

"Hello?" he yelled again.

"Hello!" Theo screamed at the top of his lungs.

"Jesus, Theo," Norah gasped.

"The till, it's wide open, full of cash," Seamus said. "And whoever was here left their phone."

"Is it on?" Norah asked.

"No, it's dead."

"Does the landline work?"

Seamus lifted the receiver to his ear. "Nope." He walked to the camping supplies, grabbed two crowbars, and passed one to Norah.

"Nice, leave the child unarmed," Theo said, his face red.

Seamus laughed.

"Dad, it's not funny!"

"Here," Seamus said as he passed a third crowbar to his son. "Be careful."

Theo gripped the crowbar in his shaky hand and held it up, ready to strike. Seamus smirked at Norah and shook his head.

"What is that sound, like a humming?" Norah asked, stopping outside the closed office door. "Do you hear it? It's louder now."

"I don't know," Seamus answered. "Let's just get going."

The room brightened and Norah's uneasy feeling morphed into dread. She looked outside. The moon filled half the sky, shining enough light to clearly see the surroundings. "Seamus. The moon. Have you ever seen it that big and bright? I swear that's where the humming is coming from. And shouldn't the sun be out by now?" She put her hand on her chest, trying to steady her breath.

Seamus just stared at the massive moon, speechless.

"Mom, what's happening?" Theo looked at her for answers.

Her mind raced, thoughts disorganized. *Could something actually be happening? This is sci-fi shit, not reality.*

"We're getting out of here." Seamus's voice was shaky.

They hustled back to their campsite and checked their phones. All dead. Theo scurried to sit between them in the truck and leaned on Norah.

"Shit," Seamus said, rifling through his pockets. "The keys, they're in the camper." He jumped out of the truck and slammed the door.

A shriek pierced Norah's ears, like nails on a chalkboard magnified to infinity. She pulled Theo to her chest and covered him with her hoodie, cupped her ears, and screamed from the pressure inside her head.

It stopped.

"Are you okay?" she yelled at Theo. Deafened. Unable to hear her own voice.

He nodded, his face white as his shirt.

"No, no," Norah whimpered as her gaze fell on her husband. She nearly fell out of the truck as she went to Seamus and kneeled beside his lifeless body slumped on the ground. Blood dripped out of his ears.

"Dad!" Theo screamed.

She put her ear up to his mouth. She couldn't hear anything. *Shit*. She pressed her shaking fingers against his pulse. "He's alive, get some water and paper towel."

Theo returned a minute later. She wet the paper towel and wiped the blood from his ears.

Theo trembled. "How do we get him in the truck?"

She didn't answer because she didn't know.

Seamus coughed, turned to his side, and threw up bloody mucous.

"Seamus!" She lifted his head. "We gotta get you in the truck. Theo, grab his arm."

Seamus murmured. They managed to slump him halfway into the truck before he passed out. They each grabbed an arm and pulled the rest of his body into the truck.

Norah stifled her tears. Her breath stopped. Sweat beads moistened her brow. Panic waved into her body. *Breathe deep, don't go there*, she thought while she tapped two fingers on the steering wheel. *One two, one two, one two*, she counted as she wiggled her toes and stared at the vanilla air freshener dangling from the mirror.

"Mom, what are you doing?"

"Shut up, Theo," she snapped, "give me a second to think." She rested her head on the steering wheel. "I'm sorry," she whispered.

He leaned his head on her shoulder.

Her thoughts raced. *Where to go? What to do?* It made no sense to stay at the campsite, and home was far. She hoped the event was isolated to the region but knew in her gut that wasn't the case. She glanced back at Seamus. He was slumped over the back seat, in and out of consciousness.

"The hospital," she blurted, "we'll head there." Her nerves frazzled as she started the engine and looked in the rear-view mirror. She had never driven the truck with the camper on top, and now she realized it blocked the entire back window and made the rear-view mirror useless. Seamus had told her to practice driving it but she never bothered.

"Where, Mom?" Theo asked quietly.

"I know where it is—about an hour and a half from here, close to a mountain resort village on the outskirts of Trumlin."

"Trumlin?"

"It's a small city. There's a new hospital there. Just trust me."

Bright lights flashed in the side mirror, startling her. A dark-green Grand Marquis pulled up behind them, and two well-dressed young men in matching suits stepped out.

Mormons. She pressed the door lock and cracked the window an inch.

"Hi, ma'am," said the smaller man, smiling kindly, "I'm Josiah, this is Peter. Any idea what's going on?"

"No clue. We were camping. You?" Norah asked.

"Us either," Peter answered. He was tall and muscular with a deep bellowing voice. "We've been on a year-long mission, staying up at Toromin Flats for the last week. Woke up this morning and everyone—*poof*—disappeared. You're the first folks we've seen."

Peter's eyes seemed kind, but a tinge of unease rested in Norah's stomach.

Josiah tilted his head in Seamus's direction. "He's in rough shape, are you all right travelling on your own?" he asked, his voice soft-spoken.

"We're fine, thanks."

Josiah smiled at Theo. "What's your name, son?"

"Theo," he answered quietly and squeezed Norah's hand.

"Where are you headed?" Norah asked.

"No plans for us," Peter answered. "Guess we'll try and find other people, figure out what happened."

"Do you think this has something to do with your book?" She glanced down at the holy book gripped in his hand.

Josiah shrugged. "Nothing about this in our book."

"Well, looks like none of us know," Norah said. "Thanks for stopping. We're going to carry on."

"You take care of yourselves." Josiah's nervous laugh was out of place.

Norah's stomach churned. She chalked it up to her senses being on overdrive and pulled the camper away. She looked down at the gas gauge. *Three quarters.* She let out a sigh of relief. More than enough to get to the hospital. She glanced in the side mirror. Josiah and Peter stood in their polyester black suits and continued to wave until she lost sight of them.

"Weirdos," she whispered under her breath.

"What?" Theo asked.

"Nothing." She fiddled with the stereo buttons and searched for a signal. Every channel emitted the same white noise.

"How is the moon shining without the sun?" Theo asked.

"I don't know."

The highway had a few cars on the shoulder, some in the middle. She didn't stop to check, just weaved through. The drive passed in silence. Her eyes manically glanced at the side mirror every few seconds from a sense of being followed. But no one was there.

"Mom." Theo pointed at a large sign: Trumlin – 5 miles.

She nodded quietly and continued to drive down the winding mountain road. A ball of concrete hardened in her stomach. She had only ever experienced pretend fear. Rabid mosquitoes living inside her brain, infecting her mind with disordered thinking, anxiety, and neurosis. It was a foreign sensation, this real and raw fear suffocating her body. In a moment of crystal clarity, a knowing settled into her bones.

Life, as she knew it, would never be the same.

CHAPTER 2

THE LIGHT OF THE MOON GUIDED THEM THROUGH THE DES-
olate city. It was as if God had snapped his fingers and the entire population
vanished. Norah wondered if she had entered some wormhole alter reality,
another dimension. Then she pondered the Bible.

The rapture, is it possible? She organized her thoughts. *No, Theo
would be gone; kids would go too.*

She followed road signs to the new state-of-the-art private hospital
outside of Trumlin. Months ago, she had read a headline about its grand
opening. Protesters had picketed the injustice of privatized healthcare for
the wealthy, as well as the hospital's environmental impact. It was built into
the side of a mountain on untouched forested land and bordered the river.
It had taken over fifteen years to complete.

She drove down the winding road tucked inside the mountain
walls, relieved to be out of the eerie and unsettling city and grateful for
tiny moments of ordinary, untouched by whatever catastrophic event had

transpired. Unlike the giant oak trees blackened and dead as if winter had visited overnight.

Norah gasped as the hospital came into view. "Holy shit, that's a hospital?"

"More like a fancy hotel," Theo said as he stared out the window.

She pulled up alongside the security booth and up to the lowered barrier arm at the hospital entrance. The booth was vacant. She shifted the truck into park, checked on Seamus, then went outside to see if she could raise the barrier arm. She reached inside the booth and pressed the buttons. The system was dead.

She heard splashing water and looked over. "Theo, for god's sakes." He was taking a piss right beside her.

"What do you want me to do, go into the forest?" he asked seriously and finished his business. "How are we gonna get through?"

"Get in the truck and buckle up."

They hopped in, she cranked the truck into drive and gunned it, and they blew through the arm.

"That was awesome!" Theo shouted.

The hospital was an architectural masterpiece made up of brick, metal, and concrete buildings, along with stained glass windows and green spaces. A blend of ultra-modern and historical.

"Look, Mom." Theo pointed at a quaint historical hotel with a sign that read River Rock Seniors Home. It was actually old, not a replica. She considered stopping but continued driving around the bend. *The hospice unit.* It felt right.

"Dad needs a stretcher," she said.

"How will we get him on?"

"We'll figure it out. Stay with him, I'll be quick." Even at this moment, she resented Seamus for no good reason.

The hospice unit was quiet and dark with no signs of life, but a stretcher leaned on the wall by the front desk. She brought it out to the truck and fumbled with the settings until she had lowered it to the height of the truck door, then she reached her arms under Seamus and pulled. He didn't budge.

"Theo, help me," she gasped.

He grabbed an arm while she supported Seamus's neck. They managed to hoist his body onto the stretcher. She turned to close the door.

"Mom!" Theo yelled.

She turned back around. The stretcher was rolling downhill towards the river with Seamus not strapped on.

"Jesus Christ!"

She bolted after him, caught the sidebar, and almost lost her footing while the stretcher gained momentum down the hill. She kicked the brake down. It stopped. Seamus nearly fell off, his head and arm dangling over the side.

Short of breath, Norah sat on the pavement and fell into a *Wrong place, wrong time* fit of laughter.

Theo caught up to them. "Mom, it's not funny!"

"I'm sorry." She heaved in laughter as the ridiculous situation played in her mind on repeat. Indeed, the lines between horror and humour blurred. She and Seamus were a funny couple, telling merciless jokes with not much off-limits.

Theo slumped beside her on the ground and wept. She stopped laughing. The gravity hit her. She stroked his curly hair and let him cry.

"Let's get Dad inside."

Theo wiped his eyes, stood, and reached out his hand. Norah squeezed it and nodded.

*　*　*

The stretcher wheels squeaked down the hall, which smelled of fresh paint and new construction. Rapid-fire thoughts peppered Norah's mind: *What is the plan? Did I think there would be a medical team waiting for us? Are you a doctor, Norah? Jesus Christ, what am I going to do, find a snuggie and put some earmuffs on him? He's probably going to die.* She wanted to yell, "Hey, Siri, what the hell am I supposed to do? It's the end of the world, I have a kid and a dying husband." Or ask Alexa, "How do you save an idiot with bleeding ears?" She was no longer able to lean on her robotic crutches, the false technology gods who had reigned only moments before now perished.

They found a room with a couch, a double bed, and a cupboard full of medical supplies. Norah straightened Seamus on the stretcher and put a pillow under his head. With limited knowledge of medical care and zero recollection from any first aid course, she fumbled as she wrapped Seamus's head with gauze and covered him with blankets.

She laid her head on his heart. A waterfall of tears gushed. The thought of losing him was agonizing.

*   *   *

Norah was startled out of sleep by distant sounds. Unsure if the noise was out of the ordinary or the building's regular creaks and groans, she laid her hand on Seamus's chest, reassured by his breath.

Theo woke, tremoring and drenched in sweat. "Is Dad, okay?" He sniffled.

She wrapped her arms around him and rubbed his back. "He's still breathing."

"What are we going to do? What about Nan, Pops, Auntie Brie, and Auntie Sarah?" He sniffled again.

Norah hadn't allowed herself to think about her family. "I don't know. We have to deal with what's in front of us. Dad needs to get better before we think about anything else."

Images of her family flashed before her and stabbed her heart. *Where are they now? Have they vanished? Or are they, too, fumbling inside this nightmare?* She remembered the last time she saw her dad and cringed. They'd had a heated argument about some human rights issue and his far-right opinions.

"I need to get food and clothes out of the camper, you have to stay with Dad."

"I'm not staying here by myself."

"We can't leave Dad alone, Theo. I'll be quick."

He grabbed her arm. "No, Mom."

She sighed. "Okay, we'll find another room. One that locks."

Theo nodded. They pushed Seamus into the hall and explored. Most rooms looked sterile and unoccupied, others were cluttered with personal affects, clothing, and decorations.

"Here," she said, pointing to a door. "Staff sleeping quarters, it locks. Look, there's cupboards, probably some food." She pushed Seamus inside as Theo started rifling through the cupboards. "Do you feel safer now?"

"Thanks, Mom." He opened a box of Oreos and shoved one in his mouth.

"Don't open this door for anyone but me."

"Mom. I'm a chicken shit, do you think I'd open it?" He shook his head.

She couldn't help smiling. She left the room but waited until she heard the door lock.

Paranoia vibrated into each step away from her son. The air was dense and the faint hum still beckoned in the distance. When she reached the camper, she filled a backpack with food, supplies, clothes, her journal, a crowbar, and a bunch of random shit they probably didn't need, then lifted the heavy pack over her shoulders and started heading back to Theo. The hairs on her neck lifted as lights reflected on the window. She turned around and watched a car pull up. *The Grand Marquis.* Her heart pounded, mind raced. *They seemed okay. Weird, but okay. They followed us?* Her mind was scattered.

The car doors creaked opened and the men got out. She thought about running but froze.

"Hello," Peter said. His suit jacket open. Shirt unbuttoned.

"Hi." She could hear her own voice in slow motion. "What are you doing here?"

Josiah smiled. "Nowhere else to go."

Gut punched, her mind raced back to their earlier encounter. *Did I tell them where I was going, what did I say?* They stared at her. She backed up slowly. "I better get back, you guys take care." She turned and walked away. A hand clasped her arm gently.

"Can we help you with anything?" Josiah asked.

She glanced down at his hand and then at him. "No, we're okay."

He let go of her arm and lifted his hand to her face, brushing her cheek. "You are beautiful."

Her heart pounded, throat tightened. "Thank you," she said quietly and walked inside the hospital, her mind racing. *Shit, shit, shit.* As soon as the door closed behind her, she dropped the backpack and pulled out the crowbar, ran into the room with the medicine cabinet, and rifled through the pill bottles. Nothing she recognized. She remembered seeing a locked cabinet behind the front desk, ran over, and slammed it with the crowbar. Syringes and vials with medications—OxyContin, Vicodin, morphine— lined the small shelves. *Why the hell have I been giving Seamus Advil?* she thought and proceeded to fill a large syringe with a cocktail of all three.

Armed with a syringe in one hand and a crowbar in the other, she headed toward Theo and Seamus. No time to think about the lunacy of it all. Three days before, she had been binge-watching Netflix.

"Hey," bellowed a deep voice from the front door.

She hid the syringe up her sleeve, gripped the crowbar, and turned around. They were walking towards her. Sheer panic enveloped her. *Should I run?... Theo, fuck.* Her throat closed.

"What do you want?" Her voice shook.

"Thought we could stick together." Peter scanned her body.

"I'd rather go at it alone," she said.

"What fun would that be?" Josiah laughed, his holy book gripped in his hand.

She backed up. They walked faster. She turned and ran into a vacant room and waited against the wall beside the door. Within a second, a boot stepped an inch past the doorframe. *Smash.* She walloped Josiah in the face with the crowbar. He backhanded her before she could stab him with the syringe. The syringe dropped and she fell to the ground, ears ringing, head pounding. He crawled on top of her. Norah squirmed and spit in his face.

His eyes turned rage-black. He stopped and grabbed her hair. His warm, putrid breath misted over her face. He started unzipping his jeans. She went still and inched her fingertips toward the edge of the syringe. Stretched again and rolled the syringe into her hand. Stabbed it into Josiah's eyeball and emptied the liquid. He screamed and barrelled to the floor. Her hands grabbed the crowbar and walloped Peter in the face over and over until he slumped to the floor. Josiah squeezed her arm. He struggled to stand up. Her hands jabbed him with the syringe until the tip broke off inside his cheek, then she picked up the crowbar and slammed his face.

She stared at her bloody, shaking hands and stood. Dizzied, she stumbled to the shower, turned the knobs until warm water poured down, slid down the wall, and dry heaved. She pulled herself up with the shower handle and caught a glimpse of her reflection then turned away in disgust and dressed her sore body in a clean jogging suit. Limping to the medicine cabinet, she filled another syringe and held it up to her neck. She closed her eyes, pushed the needle in, and slowly pressed down.

Her mind flashed to Theo alone with Seamus.

She dropped the syringe and punched the medicine cabinet over and over until her hands were raw. Stuffed her sweater in her mouth and screamed. Downed a few Tylenol 3s and limped back to the staff room.

"Mom?" Theo's voice shook.

"It's me."

"What happened?" His voice cracked. "You're bleeding."

"I'm okay." She held her side in pain.

"Can I come out?"

"Not yet, I just came to check on you. I'll be back soon."

She returned to the scene. The vile bodies were slumped on the cold tile floor. Her eyes watered from the stench. She pressed two fingers into their cold, rubbery necks in search of a pulse. Nothing. She kneeled and tucked a blanket as far under the bigger guy as her arms would reach then shoved her hands underneath him and rolled his heavy and uncooperative body onto the blanket. She gagged. Her arms and legs nearly gave out with each pull down the long hallway. *Where the hell do I leave them?* Her mind scrambled to find a place where the stench and horror could disappear. She stopped and leaned against the wall to catch her breath. A sign at the end of the hall said PARKADE. *That's it.* She gripped the blanket and pulled the heavy industrial doors open, then slid the body to the top of the steep concrete stairwell. Kneeling down, she pushed as hard as she could, then fell back and watched the body slam down the stairs.

A micro sense of relief.

Until she remembered the other guy and doubted her body's ability to do it again. She returned to the room. Rolled him onto the blanket, pulled him through the hall, and sent him down. Her emotions numbed while she stared at the bloody bodies twisted and mangled on the concrete floor.

Her lungs struggled to take in air. She slid down the wall, hugged her knees, and trembled. She'd never experienced sexual violence. Like many women, she'd had questionable encounters that left her feeling used or empty. Lines had been crossed but not enough in her mind to warrant *victim status*. She now knew what it meant to drift away from her body. Lose a piece of herself.

She shelved her pain.

After filling a bucket with soapy water, she cleaned the bloody scene, intermittently cleaning up her own vomit.

*   *   *

"Get off me," Norah yelled. Her face was drenched in sweat.

"Mom, it's Theo." Fear etched his face.

She shuddered out of a dead sleep. "Theo—sorry, I was having a bad dream." In and out of sleep for the past few days, her body waffled between excruciating pain and total numbness.

"It's okay, Mom. "He passed her a bottle of water and some Tylenol. "Dad woke up for a second and passed out again."

"Oh good," she murmured, then shoved the pills in her mouth.

Theo smiled. It stabbed her heart. His eyes were lost. She willed herself out of bed and stumbled to the shower. The freezing water needled her body and stole her breath. She gasped at her reflection in the mirror, at her half-closed swollen black eye, her bruised arms and chest. She bit down on her arm and cried.

"No more hot water," she shouted to Theo from the bathroom.

"It only holds for a while once electricity stops."

"How do you know that?"

"YouTube. I watched what would happen during a zombie apocalypse."

She shook her head, dried off, dressed in clean clothes, and stepped out of the bathroom. "Let's go for a walk."

"What about Dad?"

"He'll be fine, it'll just be a short walk." She reached out her hand to him and half smiled. Outside, she inhaled a deep breath. "Do you feel that?"

"What?"

"The air, it's minty." Her lungs cooled as she inhaled another deep breath.

"Weird," Theo said. "Isn't that the same car as those guys?" He pointed at the Grand Marquis.

Her stomach sank and flooded with rage. "Let's go the other way."

"What if those guys are here?" He sounded worried.

Norah stopped and stared into his eyes. "Those men are not here."

"Are they—"

Norah grabbed his arm and shook her head.

Theo nodded, his eyes wide.

They continued walking in silence, stepping off the concrete sidewalk onto a small forest path.

Theo broke the silence. "Why didn't you wear shoes?

Norah didn't answer, just planted her bare feet on the ground. It, too, felt different. The soil vibrated with a magnetic pulse as if gravity now pulled harder.

When they came to a river, Theo grabbed a rock and threw it in.

Norah sat on a bench and stared at the crashing water. "Does the water look indigo to you?" she asked.

Theo shrugged. "Kinda."

Norah couldn't tell if it was an effect from the moonlight casting off the water or the actual colour. She emptied her water bottle and dipped it in the river.

"Don't drink it, Mom."

"I'm not. Just want to take it back to have a look."

"Look, Mom." Theo pointed at a structure in the distance.

They approached the unique patio space shielded by a thick glass dome. Inside, the area was quaint with tables, a small garden shed, lanterns, games, couches, a washroom, and books. Norah decided it was a better place for Seamus to recover than the room he was in now. They returned, collected Seamus and their few items, and moved into the new space.

Norah opened the bottle filled with river water and transferred it into a glass cup. She shone a wind-up flashlight under the glass. It wasn't an illusion from the moonlight—the water had a deep indigo hue.

*   *   *

Days passed. Norah was unsure of how many. She guessed ten, maybe. Her bruises were now a faint tinge of brown and the aches in her body were barely detectable. But the wounds of her spirit and mind were still wide open. She wondered when or if they would scar over.

"Mom, what are you doing?" Theo was staring at her in disbelief.

"Smoking." She took a drag of the cigarette and stared at the paper in her hand.

"Why?"

"I smoked for years before you were born. Found a few cartons in a patient's room." Norah loved smoking. Another point of contention with Seamus. He hated it. Eventually, she decided to quit on her own, due not to the impending health issues but to the fine lines etching around her mouth.

"Can I try?" Theo asked.

Norah passed him the cigarette.

He pursed his lips around it and inhaled deeply. He coughed and gagged, his face turning a pale shade of green. "God! How can you enjoy that?"

Norah took another drag and smirked.

"What are you reading?" Theo asked, then coughed again.

"A letter I found in an old man's room. He was ninety. It's where I found the smokes."

"He was ninety and smoked cigarettes?" Theo scrunched his face in disgust.

"Lucky guy." Norah smirked." Do you know what the hospice unit is?

"Isn't it another word for hospital?"

"No. It's where people go when they are dying."

"Really? So, they would stay here until they died?"

"Yes."

"Can you read me the letter?"

"Sure, I haven't started it yet."

Theo plopped on the couch beside her. He pulled out an unlit cigarette and pretended to smoke like a fancy lady.

Norah smiled. "Theo, put that down. I shouldn't have even let you try. When Dad wakes up, keep it to yourself." She paused. "Do you wanna hear this letter or not?" When he nodded, she began to read. The words were written in neat handwriting.

"I didn't know how to address this letter. To your friends you were Flip. To strangers, Harry. To me, nothing. You were not a friend or a stranger. I have struggled with what to call you and have landed on a few different titles throughout my life. Asshole. Deadbeat. Liar. Cheater. Broken. But never Father.

"As many titles as I have struggled with, I have equally struggled with questions. Why? How? Who? When? You know, the usual questions a child has when they are never chosen by their father. This letter isn't another tear-soaked humiliation or another attempt to make you see me or earn your love. It's goodbye. Someone told me once to write a letter to someone who hurt me and even if they were dead, it was still powerful. Well, you're not dead yet.

"It's funny. The pain is always on the surface. I couldn't build the armour I needed, even with the beautiful life I created. When I heard you were dying, it all came back. As if I was seven years old. But I'm not seven. I'm seventy.

"My mind is sharp. My life has been blessed. When the pain resurfaced, it was different. It didn't own me anymore. I don't know when this change happened, but I know why.

"I chose myself. In your absence, I chose myself.

"Thank you for nothing and everything. You gave me the strength to find myself despite you. To know who I am and who I'm not. When I say thank you, I mean it.

"Rest easy old man.

"Love, Poppy."

Norah wiped her eyes with her sleeve.

"Are you crying, Mom?" Theo blurted.

Seamus murmured. Norah glanced over and he was propped up on the stretcher, his legs dangling over the edge. He started to stand.

"Seamus!"

Norah and Theo helped support him. He took steps towards the bathroom.

"Let me go, I'm fine." He walked slowly on his own.

"Theo, get him some Gatorade."

Seamus came back from the bathroom with a wet towel around his neck.

"How long have I been out?" He sat on the couch.

Norah sat beside him. "Around ten days."

"Here, Dad," Theo said, passing him a drink.

Seamus guzzled the entire bottle. "Are we alone?"

Norah nodded. "Yes, it's just us."

"What happened?" he asked, staring at her face.

"Nothing, I fell down at the river."

"M—

Norah shot a death glared at Theo. "I fell at the river," she repeated. She looked at Seamus. "How are you feeling?" Her throat tightened. Her heart filled with hatred and rage. She knew it wasn't his fault but struggled to reconcile what she had gone through with now asking him how *he* was feeling. Their relationship had already been hanging by a thread.

*　*　*

Norah grew quiet over the following week, and not in a stonewalling way— genuinely quiet because words seemed meaningless. She didn't try to hide the smoking and it felt freeing to not care.

It didn't take long for Seamus to attempt to figure out what had made the world go dark so he could fix it, but his attempts were in vain. He entered a borderline manic state as he researched possible theories. It reminded her of a deranged patient in an insane asylum. He had news articles strewn all over and pictures plastered on the walls. He found white-board markers and took over an entire window to write theories and events he recalled. Norah didn't share the same obsession, but with little else to do, they brainstormed.

She studied the window, dripping with the dread of the world: the political unrest, racist uprisings, wars, injustice, inequality, violence, climate change, poverty—an endless list. They refuted theory after theory and scoured religious books. Nothing lined up or made sense. They considered the commonalities between the three of them. They were a mix of males and females, children and adults, different ethnicities. What did they have in common? They focused.

"Norah." Seamus had gone pale. "We're all AB negative. We all have the rarest blood type."

"Jesus," she said, something resonating.

"Remember, only 0.6% of the population has our blood type—what if that's it? What if only our blood can survive the shift in the earth?" The possibility could not be refuted or proven but had some weight. "Trumlin was a city of around fifty thousand people. Just think, if only AB negative survived, there would be three hundred people left. Some would have offed themselves, and others—the elderly, children, and sick—would have died too."

Norah thought about it and felt an instant pang in her stomach. If the theory was correct, her loved ones were all gone.

"We need to head home; I can't stay in this hospital anymore." She glanced at Seamus with desperation. "You might be right about the blood type, but we'll probably never know. I just want to get out of here."

Seamus sighed. "I know. But I don't even know if gas stations will work." He put his head in his hands as if at that moment the reality of the situation had settled.

"We have to try, move, do something. I'm certainly not staying here until I die."

"Dad, I want to go too. Something bad happened here."

Norah's eyes shot daggers at Theo. She felt betrayed, put on the spot. For a moment, she hated him.

"What happened?" Seamus asked.

"Nothing." Norah snapped.

Theo stared down at his feet.

Tears welled in Norah's throat. She stuffed them down.

Seamus stared at her but let it go. "We'll leave tomorrow." He put his hand on her shoulder.

She jerked away. "Don't touch me." She walked to a bench outside and bawled, overcome by the guilt of feeling hatred towards her own son. Of hating Seamus. The rage occupied every cell in her body.

"Mom." Theo's voice shook. "I'm sorry." Norah looked at him, her face soaked with tears. "I'm sorry, Mom." His face scrunched into sobbing.

She pulled him close. "No, I'm sorry, Theo." He leaned his head into her neck. "Something did happen, but it's mine to share, not yours."

"I tried to start the truck, it's dead," Seamus announced. "I'm going to the parkade to see if I can find a car for a boost."

She let go of Theo, lit a smoke, and inhaled a deep drag.

The parkade! Her mind raced, and she scrambled to her feet. "Seamus, stop!" she yelled.

He continued walking.

"Seamus!" she yelled again.

He pulled the parkade door open.

Shit shit shit! Her heart pounded. She ran towards him.

Halfway through the door, he looked back and waited.

"Don't go in there. I…" She leaned on the wall and tried to catch her breath. "I heard noises before."

"What? Noises? What the hell are you talking about?"

"Just don't go in there!" She breathed heavily and clutched her side.

"Norah, what is going on? It's the parkade, I need a car." He shook his head.

"Please, listen to me. I'm begging you."

"Okay, okay, I'll look somewhere else. Calm down."

He reached over to hug her, and she let him. She turned to walk back. In a split second, he reached out to close the slightly open door.

"What is that? It looks like—"

"I told you not to," she snapped. "Why can't you listen to me one fucking time!"

"Jesus, Norah, it's a bloody blanket, maybe I should check if someone's hurt down there."

The expression on his face was obliviousness. She grabbed his shoulder tight and peeked down the stairwell. The twisted blanket lay at the bottom. No sign of the men. An image of their mangled bodies flashed in her mind. *They were dead*. Her thoughts became panicked. She fell to her knees and struggled to breathe.

Seamus kneeled beside her. "What is it, Norah? What happened?" He rubbed her back.

She dried her eyes with her shirt. "Nothing. Promise me you'll never go down there."

"I promise," he said gently.

"I just want to go home."

She returned to the dome and lit another smoke. Seamus left to search for a vehicle and returned an hour later, exasperated.

"Every single vehicle I tried won't start. I tried over fifty," he said, his voice raised.

"What?" Norah snapped, still shaken from the stairwell. "How is that? They worked before? We drove here."

"Is it my fault none of the cars will start?" he said, his voice angry.

"Just shut up. Even in all this, you can't get rid of that shitty tone. What are we going to do?"

"I don't know!"

Norah glanced at Theo. She saw pain and fear behind his eyes and felt sick from the guilt of him once again witnessing their bullshit. She hadn't factored in his feelings since all the shit went down. The horror he must have gone through seeing her all beaten and bloody. Left to make up his own stories about what happened. Losing nearly everything, including a mother who could be there for him.

Norah sighed. "I'm sorry, Theo."

Seamus nodded. "I'm sorry, bud." He tousled Theo's curly hair, gave him a hug, and pulled Norah in. "I'm sorry, okay?"

"Okay," she whispered.

"I saw people," Seamus blurted.

"Where?"

"At an old building, looks like a hotel."

"Did you talk to them?" Norah asked.

"No, I spotted them and left."

"Why? We should go there. Maybe they have answers?"

"I think we should settle in somewhere else first. If winter comes, we'll need to hunker down and keep warm. We can always come back and see what's going on. I found a residential area on the map—Raven's Ridge. It looks to be around an hour trek. We can leave now."

Her stomach twisted. She wanted to go see the strangers in the hotel but didn't have the energy to fight.

"Okay." She sighed.

CHAPTER 3

THEY COLLECTED HER FEW ITEMS AND VENTURED OUTSIDE. The minty air poured into Norah's lungs as she breathed in a rare moment of awe, the dark sky wrapping around them as they walked the path towards the ridge. The moonlight glowed bright, dead trees scattered the ground, no birds or squirrels skitted about. The only sound was their feet hitting the earth and the crashing indigo river. No wind, only warm, minty air.

"Holy shit," Norah gasped. *WELCOME TO RAVEN'S RIDGE* was etched on a wrought iron and brick sign. They walked through the open security gate.

"These lots must be at least two acres," Seamus said.

Norah had never been in an area this wealthy. Even now she sensed she didn't belong, her pilot light of unworthiness burning dimly. Norah, a government clerk, and Seamus, a tradesman, they lived the indebted blue-collar life and constantly scrimped for moments of freedom. It was a never-ending fight around the stress of money.

"Mom, look at that yard!" Theo shrieked. "There's a trampoline and a pool!"

"Take your pick," Seamus said with a smile as they continued up the path.

Norah stopped dead in her tracks, her eyes fixed on two massive cement lions guarding the gate of a Victorian castle. "That one," she announced.

"I'll go check it out first," Seamus insisted.

She shot him an irritated look. "Let's just all go."

"Just wait here, I'm going first."

She shook her head and was about to argue, but one glance at Theo and she decided to let it go. "Come on, Theo, we'll wait over there." They sat on an oversized wrought iron bench flanked by ornate antique streetlights. Theo leaned his head on Norah's shoulder.

"How are you, honey?" she asked.

He sat in silence for a few minutes. "I don't know, Mom."

"Me either," she said gently.

"I miss everyone and feel bad because I'm relieved," he continued.

"Relieved?"

"I hated school, those guys always bugged me."

"What guys?"

"Just these older guys in grade seven." He looked down sheepishly.

Norah tried to remember her recent conversations with him. *How did I not know this?* She had been struggling with her weight, her relationship with Seamus, her purpose in life. Thoughts of suicide had amped up in the months before the camping trip. Her heart sank with the realization that she had checked out long before her attack.

"I'm sorry, Theo." Her voice shrank. "I didn't know."

"It's okay, Mom. I know you were having a hard time."

Tears of guilt welled up in her eyes. "It isn't an excuse. I'm sorry I wasn't there for you." She squeezed his hand, and he squeezed back.

"Come on," Seamus yelled from across the street.

Theo pulled her arm. She smiled at him and kissed his forehead, and they walked across the street together.

The concrete lions reminded her of the sphinxes from *The NeverEnding Story*. She nervously imagined their eyes open as she slinked past. Her jaw dropped when she walked through the massive wood doors into her dream home.

"I'm going to check out the garage," Seamus announced.

"Mom, look!" Theo pointed inside a room. Boardgames were piled ceiling high, alongside art supplies, toys, and a hanging swing.

"Wow." Norah shook her head.

"Mom, let's play." Theo went over and grabbed Monopoly off the shelf.

"Get the game ready, I'll play in a few minutes. I'm going to look upstairs. And don't shortchange me." She smiled and winked. Theo loved playing Monopoly with them. It always ended in a big uproar with Norah jokingly cheating. Seamus would catch her and lecture her about setting an example. She loved to mess with him; he could be so goddamned serious.

Upstairs in the master suite, she found a bed like one from a five-star hotel. The bedding and sheets felt luxurious, infinity thread count. The ensuite was the size of her old bedroom, with a clawfoot tub, old farmhouse-style wood floors, and double sinks. The walk-in closet was packed full of hoity-toity designer clothes, jewellery, and shoes. Norah tried on a black Versace sweater and Balmain jeans; the sweater fit, but the jeans barely squeezed over her thighs. Her self-hatred chatter screamed at her reflection in the five-way mirror. She wondered where the disdain for her body came from, the aching unacceptance of her own flesh. She shoved the clothes and chatter inside the closet and closed the door. Then she laid her head on the pillow in the centre of the king-size bed and snuggled into the fluffy feathered blanket.

*　*　*

She opened her eyes. Her body felt like it was coming out of anesthetic. She didn't know how much time had passed.

"Theo," she called groggily.

Silence responded.

"Seamus? Theo?"

She walked down the spiral staircase. With every step, her stomach churned. In the kitchen, she found the Monopoly game set up on the table, Theo's sweater slung over the back of the chair, and his backpack leaning against the leg. *Seamus would've left a note, and where would they have gone anyway?* she thought. She unlocked the patio door and slid it open, then scanned the massive treed yard. Her stomach tightened and her breathing shallowed. She walked down to the river.

"Seamus, Theo!" she screamed as she slumped down onto the sandy beach. Her body clenched in the fear of being alone, in the eerie feeling of someone being there but not. She walked back into the house. Every creak of her feet on the hardwood floor pressed more fear into her body. She carefully searched the house. They were gone. She rifled through Theo's backpack and pulled out a small journal. She always encouraged him to write, to get his feelings out, but he resisted.

Nowhere safe. At school, those assholes tease me. I hate them. Wish they were dead. Mom and Dad hate each other. Sometimes I hate myself.

The words stung. Her body lay paralyzed on the couch while she waited for their return.

She woke drenched in a puddle of cold sweat. Hours had turned into days. With scattered sleep and little food or water, she was confused and alone, unable to decipher dreams from reality. Hallucinations became vicious intruders. She had felt lost and broken her entire life, but this was different. Stifled inside her aloneness, she needed something—anything—to take the edge off.

She willed herself off the couch and scoured the mansion, medicine cabinets, underwear drawers, desks, and closets. Not one bottle of pills except for Tylenol. She entered a massive rounded library at the end of the long hallway. Wall to wall and ceiling to floor with books and a moving ladder, it reminded her of something from a movie. Moonlight shone through the glass ceiling and reflected off the marble-tiled floor. Even in her state of despair, a hint of awe crept in.

She climbed the moving ladder and touched the spines. She pulled a book out and sent it crashing to the floor. One after another, she threw them down to create a small mountain. She placed her hand on the first book of an encyclopedia set and realized it was stuck together in a cluster. It was not a set of books. To the left she spied a small key lying on the dusty shelf. She pushed the key in and opened the small chest. A painkillers paradise. She nearly fell off the ladder, then braced herself and brought down the box. As she climbed over the mound of fallen books, she slipped and fell.

"Fuck!" she screamed.

The pill bottles fell out and rolled down. She gathered them back into the box. The last bottle had landed on top of an antique book: *Love Letters from Death, by Torsy Smeegendon, 1811*. She flipped it open.

> *Born into my first agonizing breath*
> *You took my hand, leaned in close, and whispered*
> *I breathed in familiarity; I knew you*

Comfort dispelled the agony
My eyes opened to loving faces
You joined them in their gaze
Still holding my hand
You never let it go
Now I lay in the same place
Scattered fragments of a life lived
Surrounded by the same loving faces
About to take my last agonizing breath
You take my hand, lean in close, and whisper
The words are familiar
Comfort once again dispelled the agony
My child, I am death
I will never leave you
I will walk with you from your first breath
And carry you when you take your last
I love you.

Norah read it twice. The idea of death knowing her, loving her... *What a mind screw*, she thought as she studied the ornate leather cover embossed with an etching of a dove. It was a small book with few pages. Too much to think about, she placed it back on the shelf.

She returned to the bedroom, stripped naked, and wrapped herself in the infinity thread count sheets. A few minutes later, she walked outside and stood at the edge of the indigo river.

She had been avoiding the water, unsure what effect it might have on her body. But now she dipped her foot in the stream. It tingled. Like an effervescent peppermint pedicure, tiny bubbles enveloped her entire foot. She slowly inched into the water until she was waist-deep, her body vibrating from the intense energy. Nervous, about to turn back, the reality of nothingness stunted her.

What the hell? she thought. She popped a few Percocets and washed them down with the indigo water. The crisp minty freshness slid down her throat.

She wanted to take the entire bottle but couldn't bear the thought of Theo returning to find her lifeless naked body. She floated in the river until the welcome euphoric heroin lifted her onto a cloud, and then she crawled onto the beach and passed out, cycling in and out of sleep, the edge dulled by the beautiful pills. In a medicated trance, she drank the indigo water, downed pills, and stared aimlessly at the vast nothingness that had consumed everyone she ever loved.

* * *

Have months passed? Weeks? She stood in front of the empty encyclopedia cabinet and tipped the last pill into the palm of her hand and dropped the empty bottle on the floor. This was it. Not one tear had been shed since she found the holy grail of pharma, but now tears poured down her cheeks as she welcomed her final escape. She knew what was to come. That her body would soon revolt from the sudden end to her oblivion. That feelings and fear would soon assault her again. Her eyes closed. She waved into her last dreamless sleep.

She awoke to silence, drenched in sweat, her hands shaking as she pulled herself off the couch. Naked, her body now frail and thin, she walked slowly to the river and lay in the cool water. It relieved her throbbing body, which was getting worse by the second. She screamed under the water and begged the weak current to take her away. When that failed to work, she tried to stay under long enough to drown herself but didn't have the will. She crawled onto the beach, held her stomach in her hands, and wailed.

Eventually she convinced herself to leave the mansion to search for more painkillers. She willed herself to her feet and pulled on a black velvet Versace jogging suit, then stumbled towards the front door. When she grabbed the door handle, she started shaking uncontrollably, fell to the ground, and dry heaved. She let the pain have her.

*   *   *

Her eyes opened. The smell of puke and sweat permeated the room. She wiped her mouth and brushed the vomit from where her head lay. Unsure how many days had passed, how long the pain would last, she prayed for death and regretted not taking her life when she had the chance.

The silence screamed, tormenting her. In lucid moments, the same clip played on repeat: her sitting with Theo on the bench, snips of the conversation, them hugging. Him asking her to play Monopoly, her giving him the *Just one minute* excuse. The *Just one minute* that before the Shade, as she called what happened, added to a lifetime and that now ironically was the last thing Theo had heard from her. Sweating profusely, she keeled over in an endless pounding migraine, the pain worse than labour contractions. She was in a depression lower than even she thought possible. She hated herself, God, and anything else that dared enter her mind.

*   *   *

Lucid. Awake. No physical pain. No sweating. No chills. She sat up and looked around the room. She could hear her heartbeat. *How long has it been?* Her thoughts sounded audible. *A week? A month?* She wiggled her toes and stood. Feelings rushed her body and rose into something physical. A Tsar Bomba of emotions. She grabbed a picture and smashed it against the wall, picked up a piece of wood and catapulted it at the mirror, sent antiques and art flying across the room. Nothing was off-limits except the meticulously set up Monopoly game. It felt good to unleash a hell of that proportion—everything she brought, everything she lost, and everything new oozed into an uncontainable rage. A leather-bound Bible on the mantle caught her eye and she opened it, ripped out a few pages, and threw them at the brick fireplace. Then she slumped on the couch, screamed at God, and passed out.

When she woke, she dressed and packed a bag. Once again, her hand gripped the door handle and her body shook. She released the door and put the bag down. Anxiety and fear had built a fortress around her without permission. She picked up her journal and Bible and walked to the backyard. After she had piled wood and paper onto the massive firepit, she lit them and watched the flames. She ripped page after page out of the Bible and tossed them in the fire.

Her mind flashed to life before. To her obsessive excavation of the workings of her mind. To her relentless search for a deeper understanding of her human condition.

Briefly, in her twenties, she had been a born-again who had zealously followed the good word. It had heaved her out of a dark, drug-infested time and served its purpose well. She had slowly dwindled and secretly wondered if she was one of the seeds that had failed to sprout, or whatever the line in the Bible was. Following the Jesus years, she had blanked, frozen with fear of believing anything for the impending hellfire she might incur on herself and her loved ones. The Bible possessed many things, sheer terror being one.

Eventually, she had circled back to God on her terms and deep-dived into a quest for healing. She had tried everything apart from drinking the blood of a rabid goat: visiting energy workers, tarot readers, healing retreats, meditations, psychics, mediums, shamans—an exhaustive list, which at times had resulted in comedic experiences, other times blissful albeit temporary miraculous shifts.

The unsettling truth of it was that after a week or so, she had returned to her baseline: unsettled, anxious, and irritable. It left her feeling guilty for never getting it right. As if it was her fault for not being able to hang on, think positive, visualize enough, grasp the shift necessary to live happily. This cycle had gone on for years. The endless search for answers outside herself became an exercise in futility. One truth she knew for certain was that no one possessed answers, and those claiming to were nothing more than Godlomaniacs.

Now, the holy books that once controlled the masses lay powerless, nothing without the human hands that held them. For Norah, praying cultivated a breathless sorrow, a *cement pylon on your chest* type of grief. Nothing made sense. In reality, nothing had made sense before the madness either.

∗ ∗ ∗

Prepared for a disaster, the home was stocked with enough food to last an eternity. A pantry in the basement was lined with shelves filled with pop, granola bars, chips, canned goods, expensive organic grains, and soups. Norah continued to wash in the river and drink the indigo water with no adverse effects. Rather, her skin looked radiant. Her body acclimated to the lack of sunlight.

Bound by the house with much time on her hands, she explored it from top to bottom. She flipped through photo albums, their memories. The family had three children and the pictures all exuded happiness—a family you would see on a show, taking exotic vacations, smiling, and having fun. The classic *Pretend you're not posing* pictures that had drenched the internet before it ceased to exist. The wedding photos mimicked those from a fancy bridal magazine.

She scoured the house and unearthed every square inch, determined to find the hidden lies fragmented inside the walls. It became a near obsession to shatter the thin glass that held the house together. A welcome distraction from the severe agony of her grief and madness.

Most of her time was spent outside. She slept under the moonlight with the fire burning in the custom-built brick firepit. The stockpile of wood piled beside the house lasted a long time. When it ran out, she burned the high-end furniture.

A few outbuildings were scattered about the grounds. There was an old outhouse that she used when needed, as well as a small gardening shed with an electronic lock. She tried everything to open it but nothing worked. The windows were thick plastic, not the break-easily kind. Curious, she wondered if secrets hid buried beneath a floorboard in there, like an old mystery novel.

During one of her searches in the garage, she stumbled on a pointy metal tool. She smiled, knowing it was used to shatter glass under pressure. Her mom had given them for stocking stuffers one year with a long story about how they could save lives; for some reason, everyone had found it comical. She ventured outside, tapped the metal on the window, and voilà: it shattered. She poked her head through the window.

A massive black bird appeared from the darkness and flew towards her, its wing skimming her ear as it flew out. Terrified, she ran inside the house and tried to catch her breath. Her mind raced. *How the hell did a bird survive in that tiny shed? Did Satan's feather brush me? Is he sending a message that now the real hell is coming?* Her mind wandered to the movie *The Birds*. As funny as it sounded, it wasn't. She didn't sleep for days afterward, her mind replaying the psycho bird on a loop while she waited for a million more to swoop in and peck her to death. Time passed with not a single glimpse of Satan or his bird. Still, she was held hostage by the mysterious shed. Every time she walked by the window, a shiver ran down her spine. She missed the fire and moon but couldn't bring herself to go outside.

The day arrived when she woke with clarity. She looked around the trashed house and bubbled with rage. Exhausted from her fear, she was fucking furious at it. She went outside and crawled through the shed's window. Barefoot in the dusty shed, she yelled at the top of her lungs, "Fuck you, shed. Fuck you, shade. Fuck you, fucking fucked-up bird!" She slumped on the dusty wood floor and bawled herself into a migraine. Everything had been taken from her; everything except her life. Sitting in terror brutalized by the Shade was no longer an option.

She rummaged around, through old toolboxes and small closets. *Nothing worth locking up,* she thought, *mostly junk.* Behind some hanging rakes and shovels, she noticed an antique doctor's bag. It didn't fit in with the other things. She lifted it down and opened the clasp. It held an old heart monitor, a stethoscope, random first aid supplies, and a small wooden box with a tiny padlock. She hit the padlock with a hammer and broke the lock. Inside was a gorgeous white-gold ring with encrusted diamonds, woven into an intricate Celtic design, the most captivating piece of jewellery Norah had ever laid eyes on. She slipped it on her finger and it fit as if it was forged for her. Below the ring lay a precisely folded letter inscribed with the name *Gavin.* She sat on the floor and unfolded the paper.

Gavin, to call you my love would rob you of what you are—my soul, my everything. It is you. It has always been you and will always be you. In your fear of ordinary life, you left me to search the ends of the earth to find more. I waited for you for twenty agonizing years, and then I was forty-five. I believed you would never return, and I made a choice to live. I married Michael. We both wanted children, and time was of the essence. One year later, you came back and reached out to me. When I saw your message, my knees buckled. Had I only waited one more year. Just maybe.

I never told you I was married. I knew I was giving you one weekend of my marriage and no more. I would not leave Michael, as gut-wrenching as it was to see you and be with you again. It was a magical, heartbreaking weekend. You believed we would carry on where we left off, and I allowed it. I remember saying goodbye to you at the cottage. I knew it was the end and allowed you to think it was the beginning. This was the most excruciating moment of my life. I returned home, and nine months later, I gave birth to our beautiful son, Kane. I couldn't bear to tell you and open up the pain it would have brought into our life. He is you in every way and I have been blessed to carry a piece of you with me. I am sorry I kept our son from you. I have had news lately—there is not much time left. My body is sick; I will die soon.

My love, I am sorry from the depth of my being that I made our son a secret. In the end, I abandoned you. I desperately want to send you this letter, but courage has never come easy for me. I love you, Gavin, and I love our son. I pray after I'm gone, someone will dig up this letter and they will have the courage to find you. Please forgive me. It is my dying wish.

Tears rolled down Norah's cheeks. It had been so long since she had been touched by anything besides her own grief. Reminded of the complexity of humanity, she knew she had surrendered to her pain and imprisoned herself in isolation. Her cynical efforts to find the missing link had led her here, but the discovery was not one of boastful glory; rather, it was a depth that sparked a tiny flame of healing.

Something struck her in the letter: *I made a choice to live.* Alive for whatever reason, her heart still beat, and her body, although weak, functioned. It was time for her to make a choice, and she did.

She would live.

She was terrified to leave the house—not for what waited beyond but for what remained inside. The last place she had seen Theo. All she had were her memories of him, only what lived in her spirit. Losing him recalibrated every cell in her being. A permanent sadness settled into her bones. But no longer could she live in solitude and wait for her end to arrive. She went inside and wrote two letters.

My sweet son, Theo,

You were my heart beating outside of my skin. I can still feel it beating but know you have left this world. The connection I have with you is incomprehensible. I carried you in my flesh and brought you to life through complete and utter beautiful agony. And now you are gone. I wish we could have left this world together, that I knew where you were. I wish I could take back all of the moments I had other things to do. I was too busy, so imperfect.

I love you with every inch of my soul and there will not come one day where the edge of my breath doesn't die. I miss your hand in mine, your cute toothy smile, your hugs and kisses, all of the sweetness I took for granted. My brilliant, funny, and kind son. I will never leave you.

Mom

Seamus,

You left me alone in this world. I have completely lost myself and am unsure if I will ever be anything more than this shell I have become. I am comforted our sweet son is with you because you were the best dad. In all of our pain with each other, you loved him more than anything and would have given up your life for him if you could have. It wasn't your fault. I love you and am sorry for hurting you. I forgive you for hurting me. We tried hard to keep going, to keep fighting. I wish I could have told you what happened to me, I just couldn't bear the pain for both of us. Thank you for loving me and never giving up. You have our son now.

Take care of him.

Norah.

She returned to the shed and tucked the tear-soaked letters in the box. Her hands refused to release the wood box that sheltered her goodbye. She slowly peeled them off. "I'm sorry, Theo," she whispered and crawled out the window.

She packed her journals, water, and clothes, then pulled on the Balmain jeans, which now fit over her thighs. Her outfit added up to thousands of dollars and clung just right on her frail body. She stared at her reflection, at her wavy long dark hair, midnight-blue eyes, and full lips. Her mind was quiet, free from any self-hatred chatter because the woman staring back at her was now a stranger.

She rifled through the bathroom and put her toothbrush and toothpaste in the backpack's side pocket. A box of tampons fell on the floor. About to add it to her things, she hesitated. Her period hadn't visited since the earth changed. She decided to bring them just in case.

With a final sweep of the house, her eyes stopped at the untouched Monopoly game. She walked over to it and placed the metal shoe player's token in her palm. *Theo's favourite.* The pack weighed down her shoulders.

She made her way to the door and clutched its handle. The same handle her hand had rested on countless times since she arrived. She pulled away, lifting the pack off her shoulder and setting it down. "No," she said out loud. "You're going." She lifted the pack back onto her shoulders, pulled open the door, and looked out. She rubbed the sides of her backpack and inhaled a deep breath.

Her legs refused to move. stifled inside the agony of leaving. A scream bellowed from her chest. Notes of grief and fear echoed back. With another deep breath, her foot took its first step; the other followed. The concrete lions bid her farewell as she walked towards her new chapter.

No plan, just knowing it was time.

CHAPTER 4

EVERY BAREFOOT STEP ON THE STRANGE, CRACKLING ground pulsed into her legs. She thought about Seamus and smiled. Months before the earth shifted, they had binge-watched *The Walking Dead*. She had joked that if the zombie apocalypse did happen, she would be Michonne. He had cut back, saying she wouldn't last a day.

Under this moon, there were no zombies, no Rick or Daryl. Life moved slow, the air quiet.

She approached the emergency unit. Flashbacks of her initial arrival assaulted her memory. Something felt different now, untouchable, the intrusive thoughts now inaudible murmurs. She peered through the window and entered the unit. The halls were dark and sterile. Freaked out from the silence and darkness, she exited out a back door and headed down a small path. Around the bend sat the senior's home, a beautiful historic heritage hotel with around thirty rooms. She opened the building's heavy wood door and walked down the hall on the tattered hardwood floors, her hand trailing across the concrete brick walls, past couches, and cubbies with draped fabric. It was quiet.

A familiar scent drew her into a beautifully decorated room where books lined the shelves, eccentric ornaments and candles were dispersed on small tables and in nooks, fake plants brightened corners, and saris were used as curtains around a bed tucked in a nook. Smoke billowed out of an abalone shell sitting on a flat stone in the corner. *Sage.* She leaned over and drew the smoke to her face and heart. Serenity filled her spirit. It had been an eternity since she connected to ceremony. She sat in the small nook, placed a pillow behind her head, and pulled out her journal.

Grateful. I forgot. Feel like I've forgotten everything. Everyone. I feel lost, but it's nothing new. I was born feeling lost. Born with a predisposition to neurosis, overthinking, and worry. For the last year, it's been inside, my grief swallowed me whole, and I'm not sure how it spit me out, who I am or ever was. Before the Shade, I lived in compartments, separate identities— mother, sister, daughter, partner—but never really knew who I was. When I was alone, I panicked, stayed busy and distracted, focused on healing, deter-mined to shift the hatred I felt for myself. It always lingered. Is it still there? Something so catastrophic and unthinkable left me with myself. I stopped. My breath continued, in and out—apart from that, I died. Numbed, I gave up on the incessant unearthing of the recessed fear of my thoughts, body, and spirit. I let it take me, I didn't fight, couldn't resist, and the fear ran riot on me, my worst, my darkest, and yet here I sit, my breath still in and out. Alive.

"Are you lost?" spoke a voice gently.

Norah's heart palpitated. She looked up at a petite woman with thick long grey hair held up with a wool tie, linen pants, and a flowing antique lace slip shirt with a black knitted sweater. A crystal pendant hung from her neck and thick-rimmed black glasses sat low on the bridge of her nose. "Oh, you startled me," she said, hand to her chest. "Sorry, I shouldn't be in here?"

"Don't apologize. No time for that. I'm Ida; this is my room." She smiled.

"Hi, Ida. I'm sorry… ugh, sorry. It's been a long time since I've seen anyone. I've been living on Raven's Ridge. I'm…" Tears drowned out the words, caught as she was in a moment of utter disbelief for her life.

Ida sat beside her and put her arm around her. Surprised by how fast the emotion had bubbled, Norah rested her head on Ida's shoulder and cried; it had been so long since she felt the comfort of a fellow human. Moments passed. Norah lifted her head, about to apologize again, but stopped. "How long have you been here?" she asked.

"We've been here since the sun left, and the sky cried."

"There's more of you?"

"Originally, twelve." She paused. "Now, there are seven of—"

A young man with a dark complexion and curly brown hair entered and sat on the chair across from the bed. He didn't say a word.

"Tayo, what's going on?" Ida said. "This is Norah, she just arrived here." She glanced at Norah.

"Hey." His eyes were hidden under his ball cap while he stared at the ground. "I need another one." He took his hand out of his pocket.

"Another one?" Her tone was not angry but worried. "I already gave you three today. It's too much, Tayo."

"Please. I won't ask for extra tomorrow. I promise."

Ida stepped away for a minute and returned with a few pills in her hand. Norah knew these pills, her old friends. He grabbed the tablets and shuffled out of the room.

"Oh, Tayo." Ida sighed. "He's been here since the beginning. He's around twenty, only nineteen when everything happened. He was at the hospital with his parents and twin sister—she'd had her tonsils removed. The twins were left alone, then she vanished too. He got into the pills. We've been trying to help him ever since."

"It's been a year since the sun left?" Norah asked.

"Give or take, yes."

Norah grew silent. *A year*, she thought. *I was in that house for almost a year.* The reality sank in. She'd had no idea of the timeframe but didn't think it was that long.

"Shall we take a walk, meet the others? They will be thrilled to have someone new around." Ida smiled.

"Would it be okay if we walked alone for a while?" Norah said, overwhelmed at the thought of introductions. Grateful to have met Ida first, she felt exhausted from the few interactions she'd had.

Ida put her arm around Norah. "Yes, let's walk."

Ida toured her around the outside of the hotel. The walk was quiet with comfortable silence. She was surprised when they ended up at a charming, newly built gazebo. Eclectic old chairs surrounded a massive chimenea, and a fire was crackling inside the cast iron frame. Ida threw some more logs on the fire. Norah sat on a comfy chair and wrapped a small blanket over her lap.

"Would you like tea?" Ida asked.

"I would love one."

Ida left and returned moments later with a tea tray full of expensive teas and cookies and two ornate teacups, one decorated with daisies, the other sunflowers. She handed Norah the sunflower cup. Norah dangled one bag of peppermint and one green inside. Ida picked up the tea kettle and carefully filled Norah's cup.

Norah smiled. "Thank you, it feels so strange to be here." She picked up a cookie.

"You are more than welcome; it's wonderful to see a new face, especially one belonging to a kindred spirit." Ida sipped her tea.

Norah felt an instant connection to Ida, as if they were old friends. "If you don't mind me asking, why did you all stay here and not move somewhere else?"

Ida gazed at the moon. "We all have our reasons."

Norah nodded and felt a pang at having pried too soon.

"What about you," Ida asked, "why the Ridge for so long?"

Norah stared into her teacup, unsure how to answer. She looked at Ida, and then they laughed, caught in the what-the-fuckness of it all.

"So, what about the others?" Norah asked. "I'd love to hear about them."

"The others…" She smiled. "You already met Tayo—such a sweet soul, just young and lost. I wish I knew more about him, but it's hard to get close. I worry about him; he overdosed around a year ago. We scoured the hospital for pills and locked them away, tried to keep them from him, but he lost it. He's struggled to get sober." She sighed. "I think the problem is we were the only ones trying. I know addiction, the jargon, but it's just what we do—try to help. The pill supply is running out at the hospital, and we won't be looting pharmacies on his behalf." She sighed again. "Everyone's tired. He's promised he'd quit so many times. I'm charged with dispensing his pills, and I hate being his dealer, but he trusts me. Between you and me, I can't wait until the supply runs out."

Norah nodded. "Tough situation. Addiction wreaks havoc."

Ida nodded. "On a more upbeat note"—she smiled—"there's Eldon. He's thirty, a carpenter from Australia. He was raised the majority of his life in North America. He's a charmer, a chronic dater who never settled down." Ida lowered her glasses. "He's piping hot."

Norah laughed.

Ida continued, "Eldon didn't lose anyone close. He lived in Australia until six, when his parents passed away, then was shipped off to live with his auntie here. According to him, she embodied a stone-cold bitch. When the shit hit the fan, he wasn't left with a lot of pain."

"He sounds lucky not to have lost anyone," Norah said. "I imagine the Shade would be more bearable without loss."

"I think life, in general, would be easier without loss. It's the foundation of most pain." Ida paused. "The shade?"

"True. One way or another, it all goes back to loss. The Shade is what I call what happened. It seemed fitting." Norah shrugged.

"The Shade… yeah, it does fit." She smiled. "Back to Eldon—I'm getting to the gold of the story, the irony of how he ended up at the hospital. He was on a date with Brittany, a ditsy twenty-year-old Barbie look-alike trust fund baby studying fashion at an Ivy League university." Ida paused. "Now, keep this story to yourself. I'm the only one Eldon told."

Norah smiled. "I know how to be quiet."

"I'm no better than an old gossiping marm, but I just can't help myself." She smiled again and sipped her tea. "Eldon and Brittany were about to get together at his place when he got up off the couch and stepped on one of her heels—it lodged deep into his foot. He refused to let Brittany pull it out, so she frantically called 9-1-1. He insisted he go alone, but under no circumstance would she allow it, plus she had an extended healthcare plan he used to get into the new private hospital. They were only seeing each other casually for a few months—as in Eldon would text for a booty call when he was tipsy." She shook her head. "Eldon felt obligated to stay with her, and now they're in a relationship." Ida was struck with the giggles, and Norah couldn't help joining. "God, I shouldn't laugh. Poor Brittany, she follows Eldon around like a puppy dog. He even built a cabin by the river where no one, including Brittany, is allowed." They continued laughing. Norah found it refreshing to have a giggle with what reminded her of an old friend. "Are you tired, Norah? Did you want to get some rest?"

"I don't feel tired, I've been running on fumes for a while now. I'd like to hear about the others if you're not too tired."

"No, it's been a long time since I chatted like this. I love my family here, but it's different." Ida filled the teacups with more hot water. "Maggie and Murph—a married couple in their late sixties—the Shade brought them unbearable loss: four adult children and six grandchildren. Neither talks about it much, just enough for me to put the pieces together. They were at emergency with their daughter and granddaughter, who vanished. Maggie froze and refused to leave. Murph wanted to look for the rest of his family, but Maggie wouldn't budge. She didn't talk for a month, barely ate." Tears filled Ida's eyes. "An absolute mess, how do you even attempt to console someone? You don't. Can't even call it a loss, it's a quiet massacre." She paused. "Murph never showed his pain, at least to me. Within a week, he aged considerably. Funny, I'm telling you about these people as I know them in this insane reality. These people, including me, are strangers to themselves." Ida wiped her tears with the sleeve of her sweater and stared at the mountains. "Eventually, we settled into this bizarre existence. Tragedy visits and wreaks havoc on everything, except personalities." Ida smiled. "Murph is old school, rough around the edges, a retired tradesman. Let's just say he holds some pretty wild views." She lowered her glasses and glanced at Norah. "A fair warning: steer clear of any conversations about politics. I've gone down that road and now bypass anything beyond small talk."

"It seems funny that those conversations even happen anymore," Norah said, "but I guess old habits die hard. I mean before you would find common ground by talking about your family, or this and that."

"The common ground is our existence. I would have never spent time with these people in my old circle, and now they're all I have. Murph is rough, but how couldn't he be? I imagine he had rough edges before all this insanity, and with his loss, the roughness turned jagged. But I'll tell you one thing: that man is a workhorse. He never stops. At his age, he even gives Eldon a run for his money. Eldon can actually get Murph laughing, which is rare. Really, Eldon has a way of lightening things up for everyone." Ida smiled, crossed her legs, and put a pillow on her lap.

"How is Maggie now?" Norah asked.

Ida sighed. "Maggie was a devout Christian for years, but after all the shit went down, she leaned in with a focused intensity, convinced she was left behind to bring salvation to all of us… She may have bitten off more than she can chew." She laughed. "It's at the point where any conversation is contorted into her agenda—she even began a weekly church service which only her and Murph attend. Every Sunday, in the old dining hall, you can hear her singing old hymns. Murph sits tight and grumbles the songs, his eyes half-closed. I'm sure he'd rather be hiding in his room like the rest of us, but it's his cross to bear."

She paused before continuing. "One night, Tayo woke up to Maggie's hands hovering over him in prayer. He was so freaked out he slept in my room on the floor. She's been relentless in her pursuit of Brittany and Eldon marrying, even went as far as making wedding invitations. Brittany loved the idea, but Eldon had a near stroke. He took the invitations and made sure Maggie saw them burning in the fire. She quieted about the topic after that," she said with a smile. "So much funny shit, but if she can find a sliver of solace in her Bible, it's a beautiful thing."

"You know there isn't much in this world that comforts that kind of pain," Norah said, then paused. "Faith, regardless of truth, has a way of digging in and reaching untouchable grief."

"Did you have faith before all of this, Norah?"

"I've always had faith, kinda like my twin flame—even when I try to ignore it, it's there. I used to seek and pray, but now I don't. Just like everything in life, it changes, especially since all this." Norah sighed. "What about you?"

"I have a sordid past with faith. Had it as a child, was raised Catholic and, unlike most kids, I loved going into the big cathedral and listening to mass—something enchanting about it, I sensed it was bigger than me. Long story short, I was a good Catholic girl until my sexuality demanded the truth. I came out to my parents and church when I was fifteen, and let's just say it wasn't a smooth transition. I turned my back on all faith, couldn't see past the hurt. Even talking about it, I feel the judgment. It's one thing to have an opinion about someone's lifestyle but another to tell them they're an abomination who will burn in hell. There's something so jarring about hearing those words. A statement you don't forget." Ida teared up and sighed. "Obviously, still an open wound. I wasn't expecting to get emotional."

"I can't imagine the hurt, having your life connections cut you off at the knees. How could you not carry the weight of those words somewhere in your psyche? Being told your waking life is an abomination and your afterlife will be spent in a fiery hell. I mean, that's a tough pill for anyone to swallow." Norah sighed.

Ida burst into laughter, and although Norah intended to be serious, the laughter was contagious. They fell into hysterics.

"Norah, you really have a way with words." She giggled. "Enough about my oppression. I haven't told you about Ollie. He's twelve. An adorable kid, he lived in the foster system since three. His Dad was in and out of prison and his mom, an alcoholic who scoured the bars for her prince, eventually settled down with not-so-royal Ed, an even worse drunk who took to beating the hell out of Ollie, the poor kid." Ida's face looked sad. "He was in the same foster home for two years with a decent enough family, but his days as a nomad inside the children's services system took its toll. His foster parents brought him in for an asthma attack, not realizing it was a private hospital. They caused a big stink, so the hospital agreed to keep him overnight, but he was set for transfer the next day. He was on the same unit as Tayo's sister and stuck with them until they found us." She smiled. "I love that kid like my own son. Eldon is like his brother. Ollie adores him and hangs on his every word. Eldon taught him guitar and spends a lot of time building and kicking the soccer ball with him. Ollie is obsessed with photography and spends countless hours in the makeshift darkroom I helped him set up. I think for him, the Shade, as you call it, provided a sense of family and purpose he'd never had—freedom from his life of drifting inside the false protection of the system. I've always said the government makes terrible parents."

When Norah heard about Ollie, she felt a pain in her stomach—sorrow—and it made her afraid to even set eyes on him.

Ida gave Norah a compassionate glance. "How about we introduce you later? You've listened to enough of my endless bantering."

Norah nodded and sipped her tea. She knew Ida sensed her sadness, and they sat in silence for a few minutes. "Thank you for your kindness, Ida," Norah said quietly.

"Let me show you your room. I used to share it with my wife Myra, but she disappeared with the second horn a year ago. I couldn't bear to stay so I moved, but it's yours now. I knew I left it for a reason."

"The second horn?" Norah said, bewildered.

"Yes, different than the first one—louder but not as high-pitched and it lasted longer, around four minutes. It's what happened with the others. They vanished. Tayo's nineteen-year-old sister, Veronika, disappeared too."

Norah took a deep breath and revisited the beginning days at the Ridge. "I never heard it." She paused, unable to comprehend.

"Come on," Ida said, "let's go." She led Norah to a small outdoor bathroom consisting of three stalls with high-end compostable toilets.

"Who built these?" Norah asked.

"Eldon and Murph. They dragged them down from Home Depot. We have, like, twenty of them in storage,"

"You really are set up here," Norah said, impressed.

Ida showed her to the room. Norah loved the space. A closet was tucked in the corner beside a large bathroom with a clawfoot tub, and there was a charming nook by a large bay window overlooking the majestic river. The indigo water flowed with rhythmic fury as if it had never known any different. Decorated similarly to Ida's room, it made sense Myra and Ida had been partners, kindred spirits who loved life.

"How is this for now?" Ida asked.

"Oh, it's perfect." Norah paused. "I'm sorry for your loss, Ida," she said quietly.

"Thank you, Norah. She was my life, it's been hard to find my footing without her."

Norah nodded, put her hand on Ida's, and shared a tender moment. Ida left her alone to rest. The room felt safe, so she lit a candle and curled on the bed.

∗　∗　∗

Norah woke to the sound of faint knocking, disoriented and confused. *The hotel*, she reminded herself.

A gentle voice spoke from outside the door. "Norah, are you okay?"

Norah shuffled out of bed and opened the door. "Ida, I'm sorry, have I been out for long?"

"Well, yes, probably sixteen hours. I thought I'd better check on you. I brought an electrolyte drink, you're probably dehydrated."

"Thank you." Norah opened the cap and guzzled the entire bottle.

"I'll be by the fireplace in the dining hall, come find me when you're ready." Ida smiled.

Norah gazed out the window, watching the river crash over the moon-bathed rocks. The mystery of creation hypnotized her—the curiosity of why she was alive, if she had any purpose in this life. It was a familiar sensation—the vast uncertainty around the depth of the universe and the secrets it carried, the miracles that birthed the magnificent, brutal, and raw honesty of Mother Nature. An impossible conquest of the mind. The questions of creation and life seemed more complicated now. Maybe existence in itself was the ultimate answer.

She lit another candle and stepped into the bath. The cast iron chilled her skin, and she imagined hot water pouring into the tub. She caught a glimpse of her reflection—still unrecognizable, scars of grief etched deep into her once-unburdened skin, a sorrowed depth beneath the surface. She had often wondered if grief would be the catalyst for change, and it most certainly was.

She dressed in her designer clothes, slipped on her ring, and tied her long hair in a messy bun. She stepped out of her cozy haven and heard a faint noise muffled in the distance. *An acoustic guitar.* The sound led her to the dining hall, its door slightly open. Anxiety rushed over her. Her feet turned to leave. *You've been through too much to turn back now*, she scolded. With a deep inhale, she gripped the door's cold steel handle and pulled it open.

She scanned the room. Blue tile covered the floor, and at its centre was an incredible circular piece of abstract art made of different tiles, like a mosaic. A massive freestanding fireplace of brick and cement was circled by oversized leather couches and Papasan chairs, and the furniture was anchored by animal skin rugs. A ceiling-height bookshelf and floor-to-ceiling windows towered over her. On the far side of the room was a stainless-steel kitchen like she had never seen. A handcrafted wood dining table was surrounded by carved oak chairs with cushions of different colours. One wall was covered with hanging musical instruments.

Four people, including Ida, sat around the fireplace. Ida was sewing what looked to be a patchwork quilt. An older woman was reading a Bible. A man strummed a guitar and sang quietly; she recognized the lyrics and immersed herself in the sound of his rasped, swampy voice. Then she noticed a woman who looked like a Barbie doll was hanging on his arm.

Eldon and Brittany.

The reality of the situation slammed her. She grew self-conscious and wished an invisibility cloak were draped around her.

"You must be Norah!" The Barbie bounced off the couch and bombarded her with an overpowering hug. She reminded Norah of a cheerleader, one of those perfect-gene girls who practiced hot yoga in the womb. "I'm Brittany. I'm so happy, I haven't stopped talking about it since you got here. Right, babe?" She motioned to Eldon.

He glanced at Norah and gave her a crooked, slightly offside smile. "Hi, Norah, I'm Eldon." He was about to stand when Brittany cut him off.

"Where did you get those jeans? Oh my god, Balmain! I'm so excited to have someone with fashion sense around here. Oh my god, your ring! Whoa, is that your wedding band?"

"Hi, Brittany," Norah said quietly and sat on the couch by the fire. She was about to say *"Nice to meet you"* but the words stuck in her throat. "I have no clue about these jeans, they weren't mine." Norah didn't acknowledge the question about the ring. She wanted to say something to Eldon but felt awkward since his introduction had been cut short.

Ida smirked and shook her head. "Trial by fire, I guess." She gestured to the older woman. "This is Maggie, she and her husband Murph also live here."

Maggie was petite and round with rosy cheeks. She didn't skip a beat before initiating the Spanish inquisition. "Ida said you were stunning, and she wasn't lying. How did you get here? Where have you been?"

"Um, well, I was in a house at Raven's Ridge."

Maggie continued firing questions. "By yourself? What were you doing there?"

Brittany clapped her hands to her cheeks. "You were staying over there! I've been begging Eldon to move there. I heard Brad and Angelina had a house there." She sighed. "I hate this place, right, babe?" She motioned to Eldon again, but this time, he didn't raise his head, just strummed his guitar. "Anyways, he won't go, everyone is stuck here. Maggot won't leave because she thinks she's the second coming of Christ. Ida won't leave because she won't leave Tayo, who refuses to leave his sister." Under her breath, she whispered, "Who's dead by the way." She shrugged her shoulders. "I don't know why Eldon won't leave. I mean, we'd have each other." She scurried over to him and wrapped her arms around his neck.

It was a lot for Norah to take in after her solitary confinement. And she was surprised by Brittany, not expecting that level of brattiness.

"We go to the Ridge all the time," Brittany continued. "I swear we've probably looted through every single house. Which one were you staying in? I'm surprised we didn't see you."

"Uh, in the massive brick one with the cement lions at the front. I—"

"That one! Oh my god, you were staying there! I begged him to go in there, but he refused. He said it had bad juju. Tell her, Eldon!" She laughed and left the room.

Norah was silent, horrified at the thought of them finding her mentally mangled in the mansion.

Eldon lifted off his ball cap and stroked back his hair. "Man, that house had something about it. Not sure what, just felt off."

Norah nodded and half smiled. "You could say that." She remembered Ida's description of Eldon as piping hot and struggled to find evidence otherwise. She had expected a cheesy Guido-type of attractive, but no, he was tall with a muscular body, an olive complexion painted over his soft skin, dusky stubble, and dishevelled wavy curls around his emerald eyes that flirted unintentionally. Tattoos covered his arms and a mysterious symbol was on the side of his neck, where a white-gold ring hung off a silver chain. No denying that his imperfect crooked smile was adorable, but Norah was unaffected and didn't register a single swooning thought. There was a sweetness about him that one could mistake for innocence. But she knew better. He could charm the leaves off a tree.

Tayo shuffled into the room, his eyes still hidden in the shadow of his plain black ball cap. He picked up a guitar and strummed with Eldon.

A loud cough bellowed from the hallway. An older man stood in the doorway. He looked hardened, born with no ability to pretend.

"I'm Murph, you must be Norah," he grumbled in a deep voice.

"Hi, how are you?" Norah felt a pang of stupidity for asking such a dumb question.

"Oh, I'm fabulous, love this bullshit being stuck in this wasteland with hipster liberal lesbians."

Norah stared at him, stunned.

"Murph," Maggie interjected sternly, "enough."

Ida locked eyes with Norah and connected with a look that said *Holy Shit*. "Oh, Murph, stop. If you're worried about me trying to steal Maggie, she's not my type." Ida laughed.

Norah smiled, impressed with Ida's quick wit and unaffectedness.

"Muh, whatever, *grr*," Murph grumbled and left the room.

Maggie stood, straightened her white knitted sweater, and scuttled after him in a high-faluting fluster.

Drawn close by the music, Norah curled into a soft Papasan, pulled out the book she borrowed from Ida and pretended to read. Murph reminded her of her father, and she felt for him, born from a different world. His generation was often shamed for their ignorant beliefs, lacking the pretentious polish of academia. The world blinked and demanded they adopt new ideas and language. It required depth to unravel the complexities of where they came from: the head-down gritty work that built our comforts, upbringings with harsh beatings as discipline, beliefs cemented in church and tradition. Her views probably not aligning with most of his, Norah had the luxury of openness, something she was sure Murph was never afforded.

Ida brought a tea over to Norah. "When you're ready, I'll show you the makeshift shower outside that does the trick."

"Thanks, Ida, I'll probably just go to the river to wash up," Norah said.

"You go in the water?" Tayo asked.

"I do. Don't you?"

"The water's okay?" he said. "We spend hours boiling the shit out of it before we use it for anything."

Norah nodded. "I've been using it for a long time. Drinking it too."

"Drinking it! Holy shit, weren't you scared it would kill you?"

She smirked. "Not scared, hopeful."

He shook his head in wonder. "Ida, you hear that?"

"I'm up for less work, what do the others think?"

"I've been saying this since the beginning," Eldon shook his head. "I jump in the river all the time."

Ida laughed. "Sorry, Eldon, should've listened to you."

"It's settled, then, no more boiling water," he said.

Just as he finished his sentence, a massive pig strutted in as if he owned the place. A real farm pig, probably around six hundred pounds. He snorted, grumphed, and waddled over to Eldon.

Norah melted. Love at first sight. "Oh my god." She kneeled down and scratched his back while he rooted into her leg. Tears welled.

Brittany strutted in, also like she owned the place. Even her stride was oblivious. The pig waddled over and pushed her leg with his nose.

"Get away from me, Fatty. Ugh, god, why don't we just eat that putrid pig?"

Norah sat on the floor and kissed his nose. "Don't worry, honey, she doesn't deserve you." She said it loud enough for Brittany to hear.

A young boy plopped beside Norah and hugged the pig. "This is Fatty, he's mine." He smiled proudly.

Norah stared at him, her throat tightening. Theo's face shadowed over his. She swallowed. "Well, he's the sweetest pig I've ever seen. You're really lucky." She paused. "I'm Norah."

"I'm Ollie, I'm happy you're here." His cheeks scrunched into his sparkling blue eyes as he smiled. He had an innocent sweetness and certainly didn't wear the shit he had gone through.

She smiled back at him. "Thank you. I'm happy you're here too."

They sat together for a long time and giggled at Fatty's goofy mannerisms.

"Have you seen any other animals?" Norah asked.

"Not a single one," Ida said. "We found Fatty a year ago at a house we passed, just sitting in the backyard. We were nervous about approaching him, but he's a big softy. Our forty-five-minute walk turned into three hours—he's not the swiftest of creatures." She laughed. "But we all love him—well, except for Brittany. Even Murph gives him a little scratch here and there."

"Have you seen any?" Ollie asked.

"I saw a giant black bird, like a raven or a crow. It flew out of this shed at the Ridge. Scared the hell out of me. Never saw it again, though."

"I miss steak," Tayo said.

"I don't." Ida said. "The meat industry was vile."

Tayo rolled his eyes. "You a vegetarian, Norah?"

"Why do you ask?" Norah said.

He shrugged. "Don't know, kinda look the type."

She rolled her eyes and thought about the plant-based movement, a charged topic that had challenged long-standing societal values. Norah had never committed to any particular eating religion but could see the hypocrisy. The Facebook riots over a single tortured dog, comments furiously written by people while scarfing down a bacon cheeseburger. It was bizarre how people emotionally fell apart for the suffering of domestic animals but not for the ones on their plates.

Eldon changed the subject. "Were you alone in that house the whole time?"

She nodded, grateful for the interruption. "Pretty much."

Eldon looked down at his guitar and strummed. "So, you were in that lion's den a year by yourself? Did you see anyone else?"

"No, I was alone. It was pretty fucked up." She remembered Ollie's young ears were there. "Ah, sorry, Ollie."

"It's okay. Eldon swears like a gangster." He smirked.

"Come on now, what you know about gangsters?" Eldon smiled.

"I know more than you, frat boy." Ollie laughed.

"You're gonna learn the hard way." Eldon put him in a headlock.

"Let me go!" Ollie giggled and tried to fight him off.

Eldon released him and returned to questioning Norah. "Why didn't you leave sooner?"

"Well, I was stuck writing my memoir, crashing into the cuckoo's nest," she said in a deadpan tone without looking up.

He stared awkwardly for a moment. "Can I read it?"

She smirked slightly and lifted her eyebrows. "Can you read?"

His eyes widened. "Ohhh, I think we got a tough one here, guys."

She got up off the floor. "That's right, babe."

She returned to her room and pulled her journal out of her bag. The pen rested on the blank page but refused to move. Her words were frozen.

A faint knock at the door. Norah opened it to Ida holding two cups of tea. "Come in," she said, welcoming the interruption. "I hope I didn't leave too soon. I needed a breath."

They sat on the chairs around a small coffee table and sipped tea.

"I get it—Maggie was giving you the grills, and Brittany is something."

"Intense. I'm sure I'll get used to it."

"No, you won't," Ida said with a laugh.

"Eldon seems patient with her."

"He tolerates her. When I first saw him, I pinned him for a shallow Romeo, but he's kind and has depth. Funny too."

"How did you end up here?" Norah asked.

"I was a social worker on a contract with a pilot project at the eating disorder clinic. On-call overnights for crisis management. I woke up and the hospital was deserted. The patients gone. I wandered around in shock and searched for Myra—she was an emergency room doctor. I ran into a group of people in the dining hall. Brittany was in hysterics. I asked Eldon what happened, he said everyone suddenly vanished and they were waiting for a doctor to bring Brittany some valium. That's when Myra came through the doors. You have no idea the relief I felt. We tried to figure out what happened but we couldn't. Eldon's foot was in bad shape; luckily, Myra tended to it, though he did limp for months. For whatever reason, we didn't leave—probably in shock—and then after the second horn, we just got stuck."

"The same thing happened to me except I was alone," Norah said. "It's hard to believe this is our reality. Myra must've been run off her feet. I wish I would've known. My husband was in bad shape too."

"She was busy. A couple of stragglers came in the first little while. They were an absolute mess. She tried to help them but they both died. I shouldn't say this, but I was relieved. I got a terrible feeling from them."

Norah's heart pounded. The teacup shook as she placed it back on the table. "What was wrong with them?"

"It was pretty gruesome. Looked like someone mashed one of their faces with a fork or something. The other guy was equally horrific."

Norah fought a panic attack. "I did that to them." Her voice shook.

Ida put her hand on Norah's back. "I'm sorry, I'm an idiot for telling you."

"No. Thank you. I thought they survived. It tormented me. I'll sleep better now."

"You and me both, Norah." She paused. "If you ever need to talk…"

"Thanks," Norah said quietly.

"I should probably leave you to rest."

"No, please stay. I don't want them to be the last thing I think of before I try to sleep."

"I'll get more hot water." Ida returned a few moments later with the kettle and topped up the tea. "Here," she said, passing Norah a tiny pill.

"What's this?"

"Ativan. Thought it might help."

Norah lifted the pill to her lips, then placed it back on the table. "Thank you, but I had a hard time with pills at the Ridge; think I'll stay away."

"Of course," Ida said, putting the pill in her pocket.

"Do any other people come here?"

"We have the odd person come through. Most carry on, some stop and chat or stay for supper. It's nice to hear from others, get an idea of what's going on. One guy, Nathan, stops every six months or so. He's a nomad. Determined to find answers. I'm always happy to see him."

"Has he found any answers?"

"No, the city is empty. He rarely sees a soul. His plan was to sail to other parts of the country to see if it's the same. It's kinda hard to sail without wind, and rowing would take a lifetime." She paused. "If anyone can figure it out, Nathan can. He knew how to live on the land before all this happened—he's Apache. The only survivor from his tribe. His entire community vanished. I wish he would stay with us, but it's not his style. I really hope you meet him. He's a gentle soul." She smiled.

"When's the last time you saw him?" Norah asked.

"Around four months ago."

"I hope you don't mind if I ask, but how long were you with Myra?"

"I was married to my wife, Stella, for eighteen years. We had a son, Mike." She gazed down. "I carried the pregnancy with the help of a donor. We'd asked every male friend to donate but none would. As a last result, we asked Trip. God, I haven't said that name in ages." She shook her head. "A grocery clerk. I'm pretty sure he was a pothead who lived in his parents' basement. But we were desperate and he seemed decent enough." She paused. "Stella was extremely controlling. She didn't let me have any money and used Mike as a weapon. It took a toll. He started using at thirteen; by seventeen, he was mainlining heroin." Ida stared into her teacup.

Norah hoped she wasn't right about where this conversation was heading. "Ida, you don't need to finish."

"No, it's been too long." She took a deep breath. "I left Stella when Mike turned fifteen, but the damage was done—the guilt I carried for staying too long, not doing enough. Stella froze me out of the accounts. I had no fight left. I was in over my head with Mike. I started from scratch and worked as a receptionist. Made barely a liveable wage. Decided to go back to school to get my social work degree. I tried everything to help Mike— he's how I met Myra. He overdosed, and I brought him to emergency. I fell in love with her instantly. A week later, I visited emergency with a made-up symptom. She knew I was lying." Ida laughed. "What a fool I was. We got married and were together for six years. Mike died from an overdose two years into our marriage. Myra stood by me through the dark, ugly shit I crawled through. At some point, I stopped crawling and got stuck. You never recover from losing your child."

Norah squeezed Ida's hand. "I'm sorry you lost your son. They aren't supposed to go before us."

The air stilled. Quiet tears fell while the moon showered its light.

CHAPTER 5

IN THE FOLLOWING WEEKS, NORAH SPENT TIME WRITING, hanging out with Fatty, exploring the landscape, and getting familiar with the flow of life. The initial awkwardness around the others eased and she felt comfortable around them. Ollie stuck to her like a barnacle. She figured he responded to everyone that way, but Ida assured her it wasn't typical. Norah felt connected to him but struggled with the guilt.

Ida and Maggie prepared the meals. They seemed to find a balance of good conversation and appreciation for one another. There was zero supply of perishable food—no meat, fresh veggies, or fruit. They had tried to plant a garden and create a fresh food supply, but nothing would grow in the soil. And no livestock or animals existed to farm. The massive Costco, as well as other small grocery chains, were stocked full of enough non-perishable food to last a lifetime for the few of them.

Everyone contributed. Eldon and Tayo fetched wood, Murph kept the fire going, Ollie washed dishes, Brittany critiqued the food, and Norah helped out wherever she could. A half-decent cook, she enjoyed it, but her love-hate relationship with food caused a barrier. The more she cooked, the more she ate. Even now she paid close attention to her body and refused to grow out of her designer jeans. They ate together as a family. Norah enjoyed the meals and conversations.

"Pass that green stuff," Eldon said, motioning to Ida. "What is it?"

"It's mushy peas. Irish, I think."

"On the other hand, keep it over there. I don't think even Fatty would eat that." He smiled.

She giggled. "Well, I grabbed it on our supply run last week, thought it might be something different."

"Settle down, Chef Ramsay, let's not get too carried away." Eldon had a dry, witty sense of humour.

"You better stop, or those mushy peas will be in your runners," Ida teased. "I'm sure it would put a little bounce in your step."

"Well, I'm going running tomorrow either way," Brittany declared, unable to pick up on subtle humour… nor obvious humour either.

Ida whispered under her breath, "Maybe you should just keep going."

"Are you coming with us to explore next time?" Ollie asked Norah.

"Sure, where do you guys usually go? Do you ever see other people?"

"We have, but not often," Murph answered. "Calden is close, up the path on the east."

"Calden?" Norah felt confused. She thought the closest city was Trumlin.

"It's a small city, close enough to bike," Eldon answered. "But highway access is far from Trumlin. When they built this hospital on forest land, they cut into and destroyed tons of pathways for hikers and campers. They allowed the remaining paths to stay open for Calden residents. It was part of the agreement—the residents would pass the bill to build the hospital and stop delaying it if every single resident was given access to the hospital, regardless of health plans. It was pretty hush-hush."

"Is that where you all lived?"

"Most of us, except for Maggie and Murph. They lived in a small hamlet on an acreage."

"Eldon," Murph interjected and smiled, "remember the couple by the river?"

Eldon smirked. "How could I forget?"

"What happened?" Norah asked.

"Well, shortly after things changed, Murph and I went hiking down the river and camped along the way, seeing if we could find someone, find answers. We were gone for seven days and hadn't seen a soul. We decided to come back another way and found some old stables. We searched the whole thing, it was empty. We were about to leave when Murph opened a small closet to find two people fucking like rabbits—a bare white ass right in his face. He fell back and nearly had a heart attack. They jumped out and ran across the field, buck naked." Eldon killed himself laughing.

"Banging like they were saving the world," Murph said. "Watching those naked idiots running down the field was the best damn thing I'd ever seen." Murph laughed while Maggie gave him a death glare.

"Those sinners are no laughing matter, Murph!" she said, her face a deep shade of red. "I can't believe you would share that story, and in front of a young boy."

"Ah, Maggie, calm down. I remember visiting a few closets with you back in the day." He laughed hysterically.

Maggie stormed out of the room. "You're all going to hell!"

"Can't be much worse than this." Tayo smirked.

Norah had never seen Murph laugh. It was refreshing and contagious. The entire room ended up in stitches—even Brittany giggled.

"Too long, friends." A husky man stood in the doorway. He reminded Norah of a character from the movie *Revenant*. He was dressed in dirty Carhartts and worn hiking boots, two large leather packs were slung around his shoulders, and he carried a crossbow.

"Nathan!" Ida hugged him.

Everyone was thrilled to see him.

Ida ushered him to the table. "Come sit down, eat."

He lifted off his packs, sat down, and nodded. "Someone new, I see."

"This is Norah." Ida smiled. "She's staying with us."

He smiled gently and nodded. His eyes were kind.

"I hoped to meet you," Norah said with a smile.

"What's going on with you hillbillies?" He laughed.

"Same old," Eldon said. "Anything exciting happen on your adventures?"

"No. It's getting quieter. Haven't seen animals, plants, or people. Nada. I plan on heading north. Won't return for a long time, but I'll stay here for a few days before I go." He filled his plate with food.

"Have you guys come up with theories?" Norah asked.

"None that made sense," Ida said. "You?"

"The only one we came up with was having blood type AB negative."

"Who's 'we'?" Eldon asked.

"My husband, son, and I."

"You were married?"

"Common-law. Hated calling him my boyfriend, I'm not fifteen."

"No, you're not." Eldon smiled.

Norah rolled her eyes at him.

"Where are they now?" Brittany asked.

"They disappeared with the second horn," she said a matter-of-factly. The first time she said it out loud.

Eldon shook his head. "That's horrible."

"It is. I miss my son, Theo. He was eleven. You would've loved him, Ollie."

"You don't miss your husband?" Eldon lifted his eyebrows.

"Sometimes." Norah stared at her food and changed the subject. "So, what about the blood-type theory?"

"I'm AB negative," Ida said.

"Me and Mags are too," Murph said.

"Me too," Brittany said.

Eldon nodded. "Me too."

"I am too," Tayo said.

Nathan shrugged. "No clue."

"I don't know what it means." Norah paused. "Guess we're all waiting for the next horn."

"I wonder if Fatty is AB negative?" Brittany piped in.

Norah tried to hold back, but laughter spewed out and pulled everyone into another round of hysteria.

"What?" Brittany asked. Everyone was laughing too hard to answer. "Whatever, I'm over this." She got up and left in a tizzy.

Norah felt happy while falling asleep that night, grateful for the laughter and for meeting Nathan. It was a strange existence: the anguish close, but now a small opening for joy. A messy abstract painting that never made sense, sharp lines of guilt bordered her experiences' shapes and colours. The end goal was no longer to heal her broken parts and mold her struggles into disorders. There was no end goal. At this point, there was nothing she didn't accept about her life—not due to some miraculous shift but from crawling out of a literal hell.

Norah was excited to explore the vacant city, curious what it would be like.

"Norah, I have bikes outside, want to pick one?" Eldon asked.

They used bikes to get around, and Norah looked forward to riding one but worried she'd have to stop every two minutes to catch her breath like Fatty had and end up turning a fifteen-minute ride to the closest mall into an hour-long one.

"It's been a while since I rode," she said with hesitation.

"Ah, you'll be okay, come on."

They headed to the storage trailer. She hadn't spent time alone with Eldon. It was a rarity to see him without Brittany.

"How are you finding it here?" he asked.

"I'm grateful people are decent, and it wasn't a cannibal situation."

"Maggie might be a cannibal. I swear I saw a Hannibal Lecter mask in her closet."

Norah smiled. "Why were you in her closet?

He paused. "I like trying on her clothes."

"I could see that." She rolled her eyes.

Eldon laughed and opened the trailer doors; around fifty bikes stood in a row.

"Did you collect all of these?"

"Yup. Go ahead, grab one."

Norah found an old purple cruiser with a basket and flowers painted down the side. "I'll take this one, it's cute."

"Are you sure? There's lighter ones, easier to ride."

"It'll be okay. Thanks."

They sauntered on the way back.

"What is the ring on your chain?" she asked.

"My mom's wedding ring. She passed years ago."

"I'm sorry, how old were you?"

"Six."

"So young, must have been hard."

"It was a long time ago." He paused. "Do you miss your husband?"

"I got used to not missing him when we were together. It reached a point where I was indifferent. He was critical." She sighed. "Saw me in a negative light. I could've painted the Sistine Chapel and he would've walked in and pointed out a mistake."

"Sounds rough." He shook his head.

"What about you? How long have you and Brittany been together?"

"Things didn't get serious until shit went down." He sighed before he opened the door of the hotel.

Brittany jumped off the couch and ran to him. "Where have you been? I've been worried sick about you, babe."

"Why were you worried? I was only gone half an hour." He looked away, noticeably frustrated.

"I thought you might've disappeared. I've been pacing the entire time."

"I told you where I was going, why all the drama?"

"Drama? Are you serious? Well, excuse me for caring about you!" Brittany ran out of the room, crying.

Eldon sighed, rolled his eyes, and followed.

Twenty minutes later, Brittany returned, her eyes puffy and red. The crisis appeared to have been averted. Norah followed Eldon, Brittany, Tayo, Nathan, and Ollie outside to grab bikes. Eldon, Nathan, and Tayo attached trailers to theirs.

The cool, minty air blew through Norah's hair while she peddled along the path. As it started to incline, she realized Eldon's warning made sense. The heavy bike had only one gear. Within minutes she was huffing and puffing along the hilly terrain. Every push of the pedal shanked the side of her stomach. Her legs burned. Her face felt so hot she knew it was as red as a tomato. *Jesus fucking Mona this is brutal. I can't ask to stop, we've only been riding for three minutes. Shit, I am Fatty.* She stood up and pushed down on the pedals, trying to build momentum. To no avail. She spotted a rickety small church off the path.

"I wouldn't mind checking out the church," she yelled and veered toward the building, trying to hide her exhaustion.

"Why?" Tayo hollered.

"I like old churches."

The others followed. The white paint of the church was distressed, and it had large oak doors. At the altar, a creepy skinny Jesus stared down from his cross. She picked up a hymnal and flipped through the pages.

"What's your favourite scripture?" Eldon asked, his voice startling her.

"Amazing Grace," she said, out of breath.

He laughed. "I'm sure it is. I like the one about the stubborn liar who didn't heed advice and suffered humiliation."

She burst into laughter. "Okay, I can barely push the pedals."

He smiled and rolled his eyes. "I'll trade with you."

"Thank you, Jesus." She closed the hymnal and put her hands up in prayer.

He laughed. "Why are you giving Jesus credit? He's not the one who has to suffer on that stupid bike."

Norah laughed and walked outside.

"All done praying, Norah?" Nathan asked.

"Yes, my prayers were answered." She blushed.

Eldon hitched the trailer to the cruiser. Norah giggled as she watched him ride down the path like Mary Poppins. Her new ride felt effortless. She was relieved her body wasn't as out of shape as she'd thought.

Empty cars scattered the mall parking lot. The visual of the vacant mall created a stifling sense of aloneness she found unsettling. She followed the others to the large entrance doors, her aloneness now edged with eeriness. Darkness lurked. They switched on the wind-up flashlights they brought with them.

"Aren't you nervous about bumping into a lunatic?" Norah whispered.

"At first, but we rarely see anyone," Eldon answered. "I don't think many people come here—if there's even people left."

Norah's anxiety eased slightly. They stuck together. Brittany insisted on going to Urban Outfitters, and Norah joined even though she hated shopping for clothes. Brittany helped her pick an outfit, showing she had an eye for fashion—not the most relevant skill, but something.

"Do you still get your period?" Norah asked from inside the change room, staring at her new outfit in the mirror.

"Not once since it happened. You?"

"Never. I'm not complaining, it's awesome being hormone-free, just weird. I wonder what happened to our bodies?" She pulled a sweater over her head.

"No clue. I wouldn't wanna deal with tampons in this mess, yuck."

"Amen," Norah said, then came out of the change room in her new jeans and sweater.

"That looks awesome!" Brittany gushed.

"Come on, you guys," Ollie yelled from the entrance. Norah and Brittany found the others waiting on a bench.

"Look, Norah!" Ollie held up a brand-new deck of Uno.

She smiled and followed him into a bookstore and over to a wall lined with journals. She pulled out an oversized one, its cover etched with daisies and stuffed it in her backpack. It felt strange to be surrounded by all the stuff she had once mentally covered in *Don't spend too much* caution tape, now all free for the taking.

Out of habit, she found herself in the self-help section and flipped through a couple books. *What bullshit.* She shook her head and thought about the self-improvement movement. A gazillion-dollar industry that sucked on the veins of disconnection. Something plentiful before the Shade.

Norah flashed back to Lightened Arc, a healing retreat she'd attended in her twenties. It was the closest she had come to a cult. The guru guy had been dressed in white linen pants, a button-up shirt, and a necklace with a strange symbol. The retreat was on land outside of the city, and it mostly consisted of yoga and breathing techniques. It was innocent enough until the last night when the guru had pulled out his fucked-up manifesto and proceeded to read aloud to the crowd. Norah remembered looking around, wondering what the hell was happening. Her friend was passed out cold on the yoga mat to her left. She tapped her leg but she wouldn't wake up. The guy started ripping small strips of paper from his book, and one by one, people kneeled before him and took the paper like communion on their tongues. She kicked her friend and she finally woke. They ambled out of the circle and killed themselves laughing while they packed up their things.

Norah laughed out loud thinking about it.

She quieted and thought about the many communions of bull-shit she had swallowed, then put the book back on the shelf and noticed another title, something about enlightenment. *Barf,* she thought. The word had never sat right with her. It seemed a frenzied notion. The millions of self-proclaimed gurus who paid homage to themselves while lost followers bowed in reverence. She wasn't immune to any of it, had floated in the clouds with the best of them, but the word *enlightenment* made her cringe. Especially those who claimed it. The worst breed of egomaniacs.

"Come on." Ollie pulled her sleeve and startled her out of her thoughts.

She smiled. "Where are we going?"

"You need to see the cool stuff over here." He led Norah to the kids' section, a separate store attached to the original. "I love it here."

She stared at the wall of stuffies, her eyes drawn to a fluffy llama peeking through. She pulled it out, hugged it to her chest, and cried. The small details had faded. She wanted to return to the shed, rip the letter to bits, and take back her goodbye.

Ollie came over, put his arm around her waist, and leaned his head on her arm. They stood together in silence. She put the llama down, hugged Ollie, and left.

"What's wrong?" Brittany asked.

"Nothing," she said. She found her bike and rode back to the hotel, then went straight to her room and fell asleep, exhausted by the unexpected visit from grief. She woke hours later, clutched her old journal, and headed to the dining hall. Eldon was playing his guitar. She curled in a Papasan and closed her eyes.

"What was that?" she asked Eldon when the song had finished.

"A song I wrote, you like it?"

"It's beautiful." She absorbed the music for hours and sank into a familiar but heavier abyss. Eventually, she flipped opened her journal to writings from five years earlier.

October 12: Here, I stand stuck with petrified shit around my ankles, unable to move. A massive depressive flake who lives inside a migraine. I try to be a good mom, but, in the end, I know I'll screw him up. I have surface friends, but no one ever sees me. I'm invisible. Mute. Unable to articulate a single intelligent word. When called on to speak, I respond with something wholly meaningless. I'm an empty vessel floating aimlessly through this life. Desperate to crawl out of the shit I'm stuck in. At times I pull my feet out of the thick, shit mud and run towards the light, get some momentum, certain the mud has permanently dried.

Slam. I'm jerked violently, stuck again, left in more profound despair. I wish I would sink into the mud and disappear... No one would ever notice. I'm tired of these migraines. I am not alive but have no choice but to live. Purgatory. Self-hatred consumes me today. I am mummified in shame and worthlessness. I want to die now and never see this earth again because it is all rejection. I am never going to arrive at bliss. I am a tortured soul. I have spent my life fighting off this darkness, unbearable.

November 19: I wonder if it's painful when a snake sheds its skin. If it compares to crawling out of my skin. The shame-hardened shell cringes when the earthly air touches it. My nerves are frayed from exposure to these elements. The atmosphere of this world is polluted, not with emissions or smoke but with pain, and regardless of which way it blows, I am left writhing. Is it a transformation or just the way it is? Am I trying to find solutions to something with no answers? I feel lost, wandering, disconnected, purposeless. What the hell am I doing? My nails are raw. What is the point of this life? It all seems meaningless.

It was a dark reminder that her struggles preceded the Shade. Her mind had a fascinating capacity to forget the discomfort. Depression was an aggressive visitor, not quiet and sad but angry and disappointed. It knocked on the door, waited for it to open, and biffed her square in the nose. No matter how many times the door opened, she was shocked to be hit again, believing every visit was the last. With time, she learned to accept the returning guest. Sometimes she'd let it in, others she'd yell *"Fuck you"* from the other side. When it did open, she rode the wave. It always passed with time.

CHAPTER 6

BURIED ALIVE IN HER GRIEF, NORAH STRUGGLED TO BREATHE or get out of bed. Surrounded by darkness, consumed with the guilt of moving on and the pain of missing Theo, her mind revisited her choice to live and considered an alternative. She kept to herself and ate supper in her room. Alone.

A hand rested on her back. "It's time to get up, you can't lie here any-more," Eldon said.

"Just leave me alone," she mumbled from under the covers.

"You were alone for too long in that lion's den. It's not the first time this ghost has haunted these halls."

She pulled the covers from her face. Candles had been lit and the curtains drawn open. Moonlight filled the space. Eldon sat on the edge of her bed. He lifted his hand off her back and closed the journal resting on the nightstand.

Anguish flooded. "I don't know how to do this, why are we left to live with this? I don't want to breathe this fucked-up air anymore, I miss my son, my family, my friends. I can't move." She held the blanket over her face and cried, intermittently losing her breath.

Eldon put his hand on her head and let her cry. When the tears stopped, he spoke. "I don't know why we were left, but we are here. We've all suffered. Norah, you're not alone."

"You haven't suffered," she snapped.

"You don't know that," he answered quietly.

She sniffled. "I'm sorry."

"Sometimes, if the storm refuses to stop, you need to get out of your own way. Force your legs out of bed and get dressed." He paused. "I wanna show you something."

"How to tie a noose?" she asked.

He smiled. "Not today."

Having him step into her darkness, even if uninvited, shone a fragment of light, a small force of energy. She pulled herself out of bed and dressed, barely able to lift her legs, and found him waiting in the hall. She followed him towards the river down a barely visible narrow path through dense trees. They reached a clearing where a charming small cabin sat. Beside it was a massive firepit encircled by a thick metal ring with star cutouts, and antique couches and chairs surrounded it.

"You built this?" she asked.

"I've been working on it since the beginning. I catch my breath here. Come check it out."

Inside, the quaint room was made homey with antiques, eclectic art pieces, sculptures, paintings, candles, fly-fishing gear, a blue braided rug, a brick fireplace with a wood-burning stove, a luxurious bed, and a small desk topped with a journal and books.

"Did you bring all this furniture down from the Ridge?"

He smiled. "Slowly, from different places. All of the building supplies came from the unfinished wing on the north side of the hospital. It's been a project."

"I would say so. You write?" She gestured towards the journal on the desk.

"Music, sometimes poems."

"I would love to read some. Any haikus?" She smiled.

He laughed. "I'll write you a haiku if you stop feeling sorry for yourself."

"Nice." She smiled again. "You fly-fish? Seamus was obsessed with fly-fishing. He was teaching Theo."

"Well, he must've been a decent guy to have that passion. It requires rare patience and appreciation for nature."

"Never thought of it that way. He was decent and kind." She paused. "Are there fish in the river?"

"Some big salmons. I've caught some but put them back; don't know if they're safe to eat."

"Strange how there are still fish but no other animals, except Fatty," she said.

He grew serious. "I want you to come here whenever you need. Don't lie in your bed—it shuts everything down, and your pain needs to flow. You and I know it will return because it's part of you, part of all of us, but it doesn't have to own you. Come down and light a fire, watch the river crash into the rocks, write, put your bare feet on the earth, scream at the moon. Do whatever you need to do."

She was silent for a long time as she thought about what he said. "Why are you offering this to me?"

"Because you get it." He nodded.

She wondered what he meant by *get it*. "Something doesn't match up with you. Are you sure you were a playboy carpenter?"

He smiled. She caught a glimpse into his eyes. They mirrored her pain and she realized he, too, carried the scars of loss. They sat by the fire and talked for hours. She told him things she had never shared with anyone: the attack, the mansion, her relationship with Seamus and earlier partners, Theo, her family, and her upbringing.

Things she hadn't thought about for ages surfaced. Like her attraction to the darker side of life. She'd always appreciated the honesty that lived within gritty struggle and was drawn to people's angst. Drugs and alcohol pulled her in early; by seventeen, she was shooting heroin and living in a tattered crack house with disgusting men dripping off the walls. Something appealed to her about reaching the lowest low. If nothing else, she possessed determination.

A lifer by no means, she swallowed some pretty rank pills and circumstances and found herself broken on the verge of death. But she pulled herself out and lived decently from that point, leaving a trail of vomit-worthy men in her wake.

She told Eldon about her first love—or rather obsession—Silas. He majored in gas-lighting with a minor in narcissism. A hard guy to shake. For years she had yearned for a life with him and would fly on his magic carpet propelled by delusions of grandeur, only to get shoved off without a parachute and land bruised and bloody, then scramble to pick up the pieces of her life. Young and naïve, she believed he would become the man she needed, but it never materialized. His delusions of grandeur were spun through the reality cycle of life, leaving him with only tiny crumbs of unmet potential, barely visible to the human eye.

Eldon opened up about his early years in Australia with his mom, an artist, and his dad, a musician. It had been a perfect life with his carefree and loving parents. They'd lived as nomads and made their money at farmers' markets by selling pottery and art. In the last few years, they lived in a camper van and travelled like gypsies. One night, driving back from a jamming session, a semi hit the van. Both of his parents died on impact. He was the sole survivor.

With no other family in Australia, he went to live with the only kin left: his mom's older sister, Trudy, a woman he had never met. It turned out she made a living hustling, trying to make her fortune by blackmailing married wealthy men and whatever other side hustles she conjured. She was gorgeous with a hint of trashy and knew how to get a man under her spell. She fit Eldon into her life and escapades and used him whatever way she saw fit.

He was alone for most of his childhood and learned how to care for himself from a young age. Trudy caught wind of his gift for music and took him to every agent in the city in an attempt to get him discovered. It usually resulted in her banging the guy on his desk while Eldon sat in the waiting room. Those were prosperous years. A new list of ripe men filled her roster. Eldon was fifteen when she blackmailed the wrong guy, and others came forward. Trudy was sentenced to ten years in prison. He never saw her again. He talked the social worker into letting him stay at the apartment, dropped out of school, took a carpentry job, and made just enough to pay the bills. He talked about his many girlfriends and Brittany. About how he had never loved anyone.

The conversation flowed effortlessly with no awkward silence, although Norah did sense he was holding something back. She didn't want the unexpected magical night to end but dozed off in her chair.

"Thank you," she said when she woke. She leaned in and hugged him. Felt a twinge. Now possibly registering multiple swooning thoughts. She wondered if he felt the same. The idea of a man hadn't entered her mind in ages. No urge for intimacy or connection. Too much to process. She returned to the hotel.

Eldon followed moments later and was met with an interrogation by Brittany.

"Where have you been? You were gone for, like, eight hours."

He didn't respond, just sat down and strummed his guitar.

"I'm serious," she said, her face red with anger. "Where did you go?"

"I went for a walk with Norah," he said matter-of-factly.

"Where?" she snapped.

"Jesus, Brittany," he said, raising his voice, "just leave it alone."

"You know what, Eldon? Go to hell!" She ran out of the room.

He didn't follow, just continued strumming his guitar.

Ollie ran over and gave Norah a big hug. "I have something for you!" He raced out of the room, returned moments later, and handed her a gift bag.

"What's this, Ollie? Did you do this yourself?"

Ida smiled. "We don't even know what it is."

Norah pulled out the blue tissue paper and discovered a stuffed llama at the bottom of the bag. She reached in and lifted him out. "Ollie, thank you."

"We have to keep the sad things close to us, you know." He smiled from ear to ear." I missed you when you were in your room."

"You're so wise, Ollie." Norah squeezed the llama to her chest.

"Do you wanna play Uno?"

"Sure." She smiled. "Where's Nathan?"

"He left a few days ago," Ollie answered.

Norah felt terrible that she'd been too wrapped up in her own bullshit to say goodbye. She hoped to see him again.

Ida interrupted the Uno game a few minutes later. "Let's go for a walk," she said to Norah.

They walked down the path to the river. Norah told Ida everything—the cabin, the twinge, and the darkness.

Ida listened intently. "Were you surprised at the 'twinge' as you call it?"

"It was unexpected. I was pretty messed up. My signals were probably shorting out."

Ida rolled her eyes. "You think?"

"What do you mean?"

"I don't want to say anything. It certainly isn't any of my business."

"Ida, spit it out."

She smiled. "Well, it obvious he's enamoured. He has been since you got here."

"What!" Norah said, flabbergasted.

"You can't see it?" Ida asked, genuinely surprised.

"No, what the hell? I'm older—the opposite of a Barbie like Brittany. The last time he saw me, I was an absolute snivelling mess. How could he be enamoured?" Her heart beat out of her chest.

"Do you really think he showed you his getaway because you *get it*?" Ida sighed.

"Yeah?"

"I guess your signals really are shorting out." Ida giggled and shook her head.

An instant pang reverberated in her stomach. Norah revisited the hug, never one to pick up on signals. Her unworthiness skewed her reflection and wouldn't allow her to believe Eldon was enamoured with her. The thought terrified her, so she avoided him over the next few weeks. She did feel guilty, but every time he was close, her throat closed like she was having an allergic reaction.

✳   ✳   ✳

Norah had joined Murph for a few easy hikes. He was quiet and Norah's attempts at conversation fell flat, so they usually hiked in silence, with small natterings about the terrain. This time they planned on an overnight campout. Ollie joined too. An hour into the hike, Ollie asked for a rest. They sat on some old logs.

"You know, my daughter, Amanda, dealt with that stuff." Murph blurted out, the words coming out of nowhere.

Norah looked at him, curious. He rarely opened up about his life. "What stuff is that?"

"The mental stuff. Mags and I brought her to quack after quack trying to get answers. If you ask me, they're a bunch of schoolyard dope dealers."

"I've thought that, too. I've never taken any drugs for my shit, but I know people who it's helped. Always two sides to a fence, I guess."

"Amanda tried drug after drug," He glanced back at Ollie, who was trailing behind them, and continued, "I think it made it worse. Mags thought prayer would bring her out, but you know how that goes." He rolled his eyes. "Then there were the family counsellors, digging up all the shit we ever did wrong. I'm not the most open guy—I mean, the counsellor looked like a teenager. Did you deal with that your whole life?"

"Well, I don't remember being depressed as a baby." She paused. "Who am I kidding? I probably was." She shook her head.

He smirked. "For Amanda, it started in grade five. She got depressed and didn't want to go to school. I thought it might be my fault. I'm kinda rough."

"You are?" Norah asked. Murph looked like he was about to answer so she continued. "I'm kidding. Murph, it's not your fault. Most people who struggle with mental illness are sensitive, born with a thin veil of protection from the harsh world. Was Amanda sensitive?"

He smiled. "Jesus, that kid would cry if the wind blew the wrong way. And looking back, you know, there was something special about her. I don't believe in mumbo-jumbo, but it's like she sensed things. Can't explain it."

"I am too. Well, not special, but sensitive. Not in the sense that I cry all the time or about what people say. It's like my energy is a sponge for emotional pain—mine and anyone else's in a hundred-mile radius."

"*Energy* sounds like fluffy bullshit," Murph said.

"Fluffy but true." She smiled. "Anyway, it's not about fault. Raising a sensitive child is difficult, the world does a number on them. Parents are only human. We do the best we can with what we're given. Did Amanda get stronger as she got older?"

"She did, something settled. She married her husband and had kids, but she still struggled."

"Sounds like she figured out how to manage it."

"You're a good kid, Norah. Not uptight."

"Thanks, Murph. Not much left to be uptight about now." She laughed.

"Ain't that the truth." He started walking. "Ollie, your break is over. Get a move on, kid."

Norah appreciated the opening with Murph and pushed her luck with more conversation. "Do you ever struggle mentally?" she asked.

He looked at her seriously. "What do you think, Norah?"

Norah's heart beat fast, worried she had offended him. "Um, well, I would say no—or you hide it really well?"

Murph burst into laughter. "You're funny, Norah. You always seem scared, like a kid about to get in trouble."

She smiled. "I've never seen myself that way."

"Well, to answer your question, I don't know. I worked so bloody hard my whole life, didn't have time to think, I just kept going, couldn't afford to baby my feelings. They listened to me, and that was it. Even when my parents died, a couple tears fell on the grave and no more. I came from something different." He paused. "I will admit, this nightmare has brought me to dark times—the quiet. I don't think that's a mental struggle, though. It's the aftermath of something unspeakable."

Norah quieted and thought about his answer. She was surprised at his candour.

Ollie piped in, "I had a foster mom who said she was depressed. She ate fifteen boxes of Twinkies a day and never got outta bed. Worst home I was in. She gave me cash every morning to go to the store to buy Twinkies. I always said, 'I'll just buy fifteen right now,' and she'd yell at me she only needed seven, like she was on a diet or somethin'. Eight o'clock would roll around, and she'd yell at me to run back to the store for another seven boxes. I hated going to the store at night cuz bad guys hung around. They never hurt me or anything, just called me *twink* and offered me drugs. I hated her."

Norah and Murph made eye contact and tried not to laugh at the specs of comedy in the story.

"Sounds like a hard place to live," Norah said. "Do you still hate her, Ollie?"

Ollie looked at the ground. "What's the point of that?"

"No point at all, kid," Murph said. People will be people, not your problem if they're idiots."

Ollie nodded knowingly. "Yup."

The last two hours of the hike were silent. Murph led them to a run-down old hunting cabin. It was dusty, but the beds had blankets. A fireplace was situated in the middle, and crisscrossed snowshoes hung on the wall. Rustic and homey.

"This is cool, Murph, when did you find this?" Norah asked.

"I've been coming here since the first few weeks. I like the quiet." He bent down and picked up some logs from the pile, then built a fire.

"Does Maggie come with you sometimes?" she asked.

He stopped for a second. "Once. She fussed the entire time about the dust, said it affected her lungs. You know, at one time Mags was the life of the party. God, I could tell you stories." He smiled with a twinkle in his eye.

"Really?" Ollie asked.

"Best two-stepper in the county."

"What happened?" Ollie asked.

"Religion happened," he said, his voice stern. "Crept in slow at the beginning. I thought it was innocent, but it got away on me. Probably couldn't have stopped it anyway… All these years, her talking about being filled with spirit, if you ask me, all it did was drain her spirit. But I took my vows, and those mean something to me. Not like your generation, Norah, getting divorced 'cause of a bad haircut."

Norah laughed. "Didn't take much, that's for sure."

"People divorced cuz of haircuts?" Ollie asked.

"No, Ollie, he's exaggerating," Norah said, tickled by his random innocence. Sometimes he seemed so mature for his age; others, a regular kid.

"My parents never got married," Ollie said.

"No?" Norah asked.

"Kinda hard to get married in prison." He shuffled around in his backpack for a granola bar.

"Do you miss your parents?" Norah asked.

He opened his granola bar and took a bite. "Miss my mom."

"What was she like?"

"Pretty. Always had long nails and done-up hair—not like you, Norah, fancier. I didn't see her much. She said I was handsome like Dad, that I had good bones."

"She was right about that, Ollie." Norah smiled and fell asleep to the crackling fire.

*   *   *

Norah walked into the gazebo.

Ida was sitting in the Papasan and reading her book. She looked up at Norah. "How was it out there?"

"Nice," Norah said. "We stayed in a cute little cabin. Hope to go again." She grabbed a tea.

"How was Murph? Any rants?" Ida asked.

"No. I like spending time with him. He's quiet, kinda reminds me of my dad." Norah smiled.

"Really? My dad was the furthest from Murph. Intellectual, religious, and proper. You know, thinking about it, I prefer Murph." She laughed and changed the subject. "Have you noticed Brittany and Eldon haven't been spending time together? He's been down at the cabin for a week now?"

"I thought about that the other day. She's not hanging off him, no 'Babe this' or 'Babe that.' I've been avoiding him ever since the fiasco. Anyway, Brittany does seem withdrawn, not her usual bubbly self."

"Is that what you're calling it? 'The fiasco'?" Ida smirked. "Should we check on her? She is annoying, but she's also really young."

"She has a lot of growing to do. I think back to my twenties, and I was a fool. I'll go with you."

They knocked on her door.

"We brought some tea," Ida said. "Are you okay, Brittany?"

She opened the door and sat on her bed. "I broke up with him?" she blurted.

Norah felt uncomfortable and questioned why she'd agreed to come with Ida.

"When?" Ida asked.

"A couple weeks ago."

Ida sat beside Brittany. "What happened?"

"I'm done begging. He never loved me and never will. He stayed with me out of pity, and now I'm alone with a bunch of people who hate my guts. I might leave, go to the Ridge and live alone." Brittany stared at the floor, tears in her eyes.

"Brittany," Ida said, "we don't hate your guts. You're family—we don't have to like everything about everyone, but we accept you as you are. Sure, we make jokes, but it's not malicious."

"I'm sorry, Brittany. I'm here if you need to talk," Norah said uncomfortably.

Brittany's eyes shot daggers at her. "Why the hell would I talk to you? It's obvious—ever since you came here, he's been different. Before, I knew he didn't love me, and I pretended. Just take the asshole."

Norah fumbled to find a response. "You said a lot about Eldon not loving you, but do you love Eldon?"

Brittany stared out the window. Tears poured down her face. "No. I wanted someone to love me. I've never had anyone."

"You didn't?" Norah asked.

"No, I was an only child. My parents lived in Sweden. I was raised by nannies and went to boarding school when I was eight. It was like I didn't exist. I made stupid friends with stupid people and immersed myself in stupidity. I know it. I'm not stupid."

Norah was surprised by her honesty. "It does sound lonely, Brittany. I'm sorry you felt invisible. Believe me. I get it."

"You do?" she asked.

"I've felt invisible my entire life, like people see right through me. I have a feeling people generally feel that way. And loneliness—I could be in a room full of people and feel completely alone."

Brittany sniffled. "It seems like you're together and calm."

"I'm a hot mess, we all are. Anything you feel, I feel. There's nothing new."

"I guess," Brittany said with a shrug.

"We need to stick together," Ida said. "There's only eight of us, and we need each other."

Norah felt for Brittany, but the conversation's topic gut-punched her. *Eldon and Brittany broke up.* Concrete butterflies flew wild in her stomach, bringing her near vomiting.

She and Brittany returned to the dining hall to help with supper. Brittany walked over to Eldon and whispered to him, but Norah couldn't make out what she said. They shuffled out of the room and returned an hour later, looking lighter, as if they had hashed it out and landed in a better place.

Brittany made an announcement during supper. "Eldon and I aren't dating anymore, but we're still friends. For the record, I dumped his ass." She half smiled.

An awkward silence filled the room.

Eldon raised his glass. "To getting dumped on my ass."

Everyone laughed, but with an uncomfortable edge. Norah and Eldon glanced at each other and then averted their eyes.

After supper, the others dispersed. Ida and Norah stayed in the dining hall and chatted by the fire. Fatty waddled over to Norah and pushed his nose onto her leg. She scratched his back and noticed a note hanging around his neck.

Norah,

Why are you avoiding me?
Meet me at the church. We need to talk.
Eldon.

CHAPTER 7

NORAH PANICKED. "IDA, I CAN'T GO THERE."

She smiled. "You can't just leave him waiting."

"I can't breathe." Norah keeled over and held her stomach.

"Norah, just get your shit together and go see the man, for god's sake."

"What?" She laughed. "You pick now to pull out harsh?"

Ida laughed too. "Thought it might snap you out of it."

Norah returned to her room and slipped on her black summer dress, then stared in the mirror. She pulled her thick brown hair back and shook her head. Her throat tightened. Her nerves were frayed. She walked outside and found a note tied on the handlebars of the purple cruiser: *Your chariot awaits*. She smiled, studied the cruiser, and decided to walk. Lace beige lanterns hung on the dead trees surrounding the church and massive candles burned around the grand doors made of stained glass and oak. Her hand shook as she gripped the handle and turned it. The door creaked open.

Candlelight danced around the space. Eldon was nowhere in sight. Nerves raced inside her stomach as she took a seat on the cold wood of the front pew. She braced herself and inhaled a deep breath.

"You're here." Eldon's hand touched her shoulder and brushed her neck as he walked around to sit beside her.

"I didn't want to let Fatty down. He went to all the effort to deliver the note." She swallowed. The concrete butterflies were dancing.

He smiled, a sweet and innocent expression in his eyes.

Panic struck. *Shit… shit… shit…*

"Why here?" Her voice cracked, and she swallowed again.

"I like reading hymnals," he teased.

She giggled awkwardly.

"So?" He stared through her.

She averted her eyes. "So what?"

"Why are you avoiding me?"

"I'm not." She played dumb and begged her face not to be awkward.

"Lying again," he teased. "Have you always been a liar?"

She smiled gently and looked down. "I'm not."

"So why are you avoiding me? I shouldn't have to tie a message around a pig's neck to get your attention."

Her nerves unravelled. "I'm sorry. I don't know." She bit the side of her lip. *Stop acting like a freakin' buffoon.*

"Another lie. You know." He brushed her hair from her face. "We both do." He stood and held out his hand.

"What?" She shook, riddled with anxiety.

He smiled. "Take my hand, idiot."

"I can't," she stammered, flushed and shaky.

He lifted her hand and pulled her close, swaying her back and forth as he hummed quietly in her ear. He nuzzled his face into her neck, kissed behind her ear, and then, moving slowly, pressed his lips against hers.

Her legs trembled into a rush of unfamiliar feelings. She worried she might pass out.

He led her to the altar, and his gentleness turned rougher. He pulled her close, bit her bottom lip, and made his way down to her neck. He unzipped her dress and stared. He lifted his mouth to her ear and whispered, "I see you."

The words xanaxed her body. She knew he meant it. He pressed into her. Their bodies intertwined ravenously while skinny Jesus listened to her moans. When they finished, Eldon leaned over and kissed her forehead. She fell asleep breathing in his heartbeat.

Norah woke to goosebumps up her back.

"I want to show you something," Eldon whispered.

She slipped on her dress and followed him down the path and around a small bend to a clear pool of indigo water tucked in between two large rock faces. A giant lifeless tree stood in the centre of a shimmering crystal sand beach, beside a firepit and chairs. An intense humming echoed against the rocks. Her body was instantly covered in goosebumps. Never had she seen something so majestic.

He kissed her and let her dress fall, then released her and jumped in the water. She followed. The minty sensation she was accustomed to feeling in water intensified with electricity and vibration, a deeper intensity than the river. Eldon pushed her against the rocks and surged into her, the electric water pulsating her body. She gasped as she entered the summit of another dimension.

He led her around a small bend and stepped up a few stones onto a ledge. Billows of steam enveloped her body. She immersed herself in the hot electric water and nearly perished from joy. Hours passed at the inlet as they made love, talked, and laughed until they realized their bodies were starved. They returned to the hotel. It was impossible to dim their glow.

Norah worried about Brittany. She knew it was soon and didn't want to hurt her but was in over her head. Head over heels. It needed to be addressed.

Norah peeked her head inside Brittany's room. "Can we chat?"

Brittany didn't look up from her magazine. "I know," she said, her tone cold and bitter. "I didn't expect you to jump each other literally five minutes after we announced our breakup." Brittany flipped through the pages of *Cosmopolitan*, looked up, and shot daggers. "Look, we aren't friends. I barely know you. I don't love him and really don't give a shit what he does. I'm over it."

"I don't want to hurt you," Norah said.

"Hurt me? *You* hurt *me*?" She shot another piercing look at Norah. "How old are you, like a hundred? Seriously, just go. I'm done with both you losers."

Norah realized the relationship was beyond repair. She also realized she had jumped the gun on believing no drama would ensue. She went to Ida's room and flopped down on her bed.

"What the hell happened?" Ida said from her place at the desk.

"God, Ida." Norah shook her head. "I've opened a can of worms. Shit."

"Brittany's hurt, but she'll be okay."

"Maybe, but at what cost? If I hadn't come here, there would be no drama. I can't see this blowing over. This thing with Eldon…" Norah blushed.

Ida smiled. "Norah, focus on that. You've been through hell. We all have. If by some miracle you've been given a chance at love, take it."

Norah thought about what Ida said. She had been through hell. The majority of her life had been spent thinking about everyone else, toning it down to appease others' feelings, fearing judgment, and walking a tightrope of responsibility. Brittany was hurt, plain and simple, and Norah knew hurt people hurt people. The anger dissolved. She found clarity. "Thanks, Ida, I need to find Eldon."

She made her way to the kitchen and found him standing at the kitchen counter, eating a snack. "We need to talk." She brushed his hand.

"What is it?" He kissed her.

Her knees buckled. "Things blew up with Brittany."

"That's it?" Eldon shrugged. "When don't things blow up with Brit?"

"I never wanted to cause drama."

"I don't want to hurt Brittany, either, but sometimes drama is necessary for change." He pulled her close. "It'll take time—something we have in spades. We're in a bubble, we need to deal with it as it comes."

She leaned into him. Her body warmed, and her worries dissolved.

That night, Brittany walked into the dining room wearing a backpack on her shoulders so massive that Norah wondered how she wasn't toppling over from the weight. Brittany's face was pale and serious. She whispered something to Ida and left.

Ida looked at Norah. "She's gone."

"Where?"

"Not sure, said she needed space and not to follow. What do you think?"

Norah thought about it and remembered her time alone at the Ridge. The long, suffocating, and necessary time. "Ida, I think we need to let her be. It's her choice, and if that's what she needs, then so be it." Guilt waved over her, partially for being the cause of Brittany's departure, partially from being relieved.

Ida nodded as if she had known the answer but needed permission to let her go.

*   *   *

The next few weeks passed blissfully in hushed tones. Norah's veins pumped full of new love, her heart rushing with the euphoric drug. She spent time by the river, barefoot in the effervescent water. It seemed impossible to get grounded. She barely slept or ate, encompassed by him. She didn't want to lose herself to him, but the energy was too strong to fight. Other men had small fragments of her, but a vacancy swirled inside the connection—an emptiness she had accepted as truth, not believing in the possibility of anything else… until Eldon.

Without Brittany's spritely energy, a void hollowed in the group. Suppers were quiet, weighted with the curiosity of why Brittany left. Everyone knew she and Eldon had broken up, but no more.

Ollie smiled at Norah from across from the supper table. "Where were you guys this afternoon?" he asked.

Norah stammered, "Walking by the river, why?"

"Coulda fooled me, I saw you two." He giggled and blushed.

A hush came over the room. Norah's face heated, a ball grew in her throat. Eldon smiled at Norah and looked down. She flashed back to their time at the river, horrified. Her eyes begged Ollie not to continue.

"Is that what's going on?" Maggie's voice shook.

"Let's just finish eating," Ida said, staring at her plate.

"Lord, have mercy on you two," Maggie said. "It was enough with you and Brittany, Eldon. Are you just going to move around to every woman here?" She stared unblinkingly at him.

"Not my plan, no." Eldon stared at his dinner plate and tried not to laugh.

"Maggie, calm down," Murph said. "It's none of our business."

"None of our business? I'm happy to see you're comfortable dining with fornicators. And what about Brittany? It's her fault she left." Maggie shot daggers at Norah.

"Maggie," Murph said, voice raised, "nothing is black and white, and no one is to blame. Settle down, we were together five years before we got married."

"That was before we found the Lord!"

"You mean before *you* found the Lord!" Murph pounded his fists on the table. "It's enough, Maggie. If the Lord is our shepherd, he ain't a good one. He's lost our children and grandchildren and left us in this barren wasteland. And you're concerned about two people fucking. Jesus Christ, let 'em fuck their brains out, get some pleasure in this hell we're living in!"

Maggie stood up, straightened her sweater, and scuttled out. Everyone quietly finished eating and dispersed for the evening.

"Norah?" Ollie said, peeking his head in her room.

She stopped writing. "Come in, what's up?"

"I'm sorry," he said, his eyes glassy.

"Ollie, you have nothing to be sorry for."

"I hate fighting. My mom and dad used to fight cuz of me all the time."

"Ollie. This was not your fault. It's adult stuff. I'm sorry you saw us today."

"It's okay, I've seen people doing it before."

Norah's face turned red hot and she didn't know how to answer. She smiled at him. "You're a great kid. People would've found out sooner or later, you probably did us a favour."

He grinned. "Maggie really lost it, hey?"

"I'd say she wasn't too happy."

"She's nuts." He shook his head.

Norah let out a small laugh. "She's just hurting. We're all just doing the best we can."

"I'm happy you and Eldon are in love."

She pulled him in and gave him a hug. "Better go help Ida, you don't want to be in real trouble."

* * *

Six months later, Brittany was still heavy on everyone's minds. A night didn't pass without her showing up in Norah's dreams. Brittany was always in the mansion, standing between the lions or sitting by the river, but the dreams became increasingly more specific. Initially, Norah ignored them—until they reached a point where she couldn't.

"I have to go," Norah said to Eldon one morning at the cabin. She laid her head on his chest.

"Okay, bring me back a coffee," he murmured, half-asleep.

"No, not to the hotel. I'm going to look for Brittany, I know where she might be."

He sat up on his elbows. "What do you mean? You're not going alone, I'm coming with you."

"No, Eldon, you're not. I'm not fragile."

"I know that, I'm just worried about you. Where are you even going?"

"I'll be back in a few days, I promise."

He pulled her in and pressed into her body. Breathless, Norah got up from the bed, dressed, and filled a small backpack. She leaned over, kissed him on the forehead, and left.

She never planned to return to the mansion, unsure if her dreams were even real. Her instincts guided her. The walk brought her back. A gentle shower of emotions lingered inside every step. Barefoot, she let the magnetic earth pulse into her body. It was rare for her to wear shoes now; the energy was addictive. A beautiful eeriness surrounded her: trees that once breathed oxygen now stood dark and leafless. Somehow, she still sensed their spirit.

As she walked, she saw flashbacks of her time on the path, of the course her life had taken since the Shade. She noticed a small clearing and veered off the path. She came upon a small wooden bridge with a tiny creek flowing below it. Her senses heightened. The air tingled. She pulled out her journal.

Why now this inner knowing? This deep sense of gratitude for a life lived, lost, and lived again. Why now, on this bridge, do I find myself, do I know myself, and will I lose myself when I stand up? The years in the mansion, the years in the machine, imprisoned by my loss, my pain, my sorrow. Confined, unable to see a foot in front of me, and this, so close, this beauty surrounds me, but I couldn't see it. Is it a choice to be blind? To coil in these human experiences, writhe in my own suffering? I used to ask God these questions, now I don't know who I'm asking, maybe I'm asking my own inner knowing—isn't that God anyway? The Shade has given me many things, one of them the certainty that a cruel god yelling from the clouds does not exist. God is here now, on this bridge. My sorrow, my love, my life, my heartbeat. There is no separation. I have hated the God in the clouds, blamed him, cursed him, and felt guilty for it all. I don't feel the same about the here and now.

The lions were now visible, faithfully guarding their posts. She took deep breaths, slowing her pounding heartbeat, as she stood at the end of the driveway and took in the mansion. She never really saw it before. Her hand lifted and slammed down the heavy metal doorknocker. With no expectation of an answer, she waited a few minutes and then entered.

It was organized and clean, all the debris and broken glass gone as if her time had been erased. She called out Brittany's name. No answer. Upstairs every room was organized, immaculate. Immeasurable hours would have been required to get it to that state. She was shocked.

She returned downstairs. A three-wick candle sat in the middle of the kitchen table on a crocheted tablecloth. The Monopoly game had vanished. The mangled mess of the library was no longer a mess, all the fallen books neatly back in place. She curled into the oversize leather brown chair where she had spent countless hours writing. On the coffee table three books were piled beside a candle, a pen, and a canvas with paints strewn around. A small, vaguely familiar notebook caught her attention. She opened it. Her words were scribbled on the page. She was confused, certain she had burned all her writing.

Where am I where am I where am I where am I why, why did you. Who's there, where are you, answer me. I hear knocking, fighting, yelling, am I asleep or awake? Is this a nightmare or real. I can't feel anything real. Please kill me. Please kill me. Please kill me. How could you do this to me. I hate you. Hate myself. Why am I so weak? Where are they? Where are they? Where are they? Where am I. where am I? Where am I? Where am I? I hear knocking, fighting, yelling. I hear pain, I hear anguish. I listen to it all because it's coming from Me. You killed me. You did this to me. Why why why why why why why why why why. STOP YELLING AT ME. STOP FIGHTING. STOPPPP. I WANT TO DIE. I WANT TO DIE.

She flipped through the entire notebook—a mess of jumbled writing, complete mental fuckery. Unable to believe they were her words, she tucked the notebook in her bag. It belonged to her. She caught sight of another familiar book, *Love Letters to Death*. A mind screw, she hadn't looked at this book since the day she had found the pills. The poem from long ago jumped out. It felt different, comforting. She flipped to the next page.

My Child,

I never meant for you to fear me. It hurts to know you are terrified at the mere mention of my name, that you hold me with little regard. Why have you avoided me and taken extraordinary measures to pretend I don't exist? You only think of me when you're forced. While I think about you often and am always close.

You honour birth as a queen and life a king and give me no honour at all. I know your heart. I never leave your side. Without me, birth and life could not exist. I desperately want you to see me, acknowledge me.

I am not your enemy. We walk together.

Love, Death

She closed the book. *How did this book get here? Of all the books, why this one?* she wondered. *Whoever thought about death as love, and who was this author, Torsy Smeegendon?* She opened the book again to a random page.

Dear Life,

We have walked together for so long. Without you, I would cease to exist. You balance me. I admire your spirit but have never fully understood you. You have a beginning and an end, something tangible. But my spirit is eternal. Even within that, we come together, time and time again. Your spirit carries on but eventually dissipates, even when something powerful echoes in its wake.

I hold you in high regard. You are who I am here for, there is no union stronger than ours. Just as you disappear with time, I, on the other hand, never dissipate. I am there for the first and last breath, where my journey begins.

You release the final heartbeat, and I carry souls into something they yearn to know but never will while their heart beats. Many have surmised, reasoned, and claimed to know my spirit, what I possess, but they lie.

Humans possess supernatural powers in creating experience, stories, and feelings but never actually see me or feel me, except for very few. They've built confusion around me—guilt, ideas, religion, beliefs. None are me.

They only feel my aftermath, the lessons left behind. In my aftermath, they've come up with theories and rationalizations. I don't blame them, it's hard to reconcile, especially those who, in their eyes, I've visited much too early or in an unfair way. The intensity of emotion is incomparable to anything. I know this.

I soar through life and touch everyone and everything on a small and grand scale. An unavoidable reality that I will see them one day, I beg them not to avoid me in terror, but they don't listen. Instead, they hold on to you as if they have you forever. I do not choose. I do not punish. I am not emotion.

As we both know, there is something of great confusion: the act of dying. Dying is in your hands; I am not responsible for how one dies, that is your domain. If a heart is still beating, it's yours. I come in after the last breath when you are gone. I am not responsible for those left behind, they are for you to sort out. I know it bends humans to a breaking point.

If only they knew, they are not breakable. Your spirit, the spirit of life, is resilient, revolving, evolving, and strong. It can carry an immensely heavy load of emotional pain and tragedy, which I so often leave behind.

My closest companion, I respect you and love you.

Yours always, Death

∞

Dear Death,

What does it mean to lose someone? Are they really lost, misplaced? Like a gold chain that ripped off your neck swimming in a tide. Have they misplaced their map or taken a wrong turn? Are they floating aimlessly in the universe? So many meanings for the word loss, *but is it the right word?*

With love, Life

∞

Dearest Life,

I do not deal with loss. Loss is for the living. It's something humans have coined, something they cling to. I assure you. Your loved ones are not lost.

Your job is to live and celebrate what you have been given. Celebrate the life of those who now walk with me, and if there is nothing to celebrate, you rip open the scars they left and set yourself free.

I am a miraculous healing force that touches lives in a way nothing else does. I carry the most potent mirror. When held up, it reflects back the smallest detail of who you are, what you need to do, what no longer serves you, and how you wish to meet me when we walk together. I bring out unique and intensely raw emotion, but you were born with a spirit who knows me. A spirit who can handle my visit.

I beg you to not fear me. Lean into me, I am never far.
Love, Death

The beautiful and cryptic words resonated through Norah's spirit. She flipped to the last page, the author's message.

Friends, family, kindred souls, lovers, haters, all who have guided me throughout my life…

Only thirty, and I lay waiting for death to take my hand. One year ago, I lay down in what you called my deathbed, I succumbed to my fate, and pain ran through me like wild horses running for freedom. I felt my spirit shut down, quiet inside me, and prepare for death's visit.

My experience, although short, has been enough. I leave this world with no regret and much love. I know that death will take care of me. I feared death, as you all do. You see, my body declines, my energy dwindles. It hurts you more than it hurts me.

Soon you will be left to live in the absence of me, the absence of my spirit breathing on this earth, and this is for you to reconcile because I will be home.

Embrace life fully, feel life. As death said, you are magnificently brilliant. I assure you that death does not take the love that one has for their clan. You know who you are.

Love, Torsy

She thought of Theo and Seamus, her family, herself.

An arm squeezed her shoulder. Norah lifted her head. Brittany. They embraced and cried together.

"I'm sorry, really sorry," Norah said, surprised by the emotional encounter and how much it affected her.

"It's not your fault. I'm sorry too." Brittany sniffled.

Norah lifted the book in her lap. "How did you find this?"

"I didn't. It literally fell off the shelf when I was grabbing *Twilight*." She smiled.

Norah laughed. "When I was here, that same book just fell out. I read a bit, then shelved it. I was so mangled… as you probably gathered."

"Really?" Brittany asked. "Well, not about being mangled"—she smiled—"but about the book. How random. I could probably recite it from memory at this point—something about the words."

Norah nodded. "Have you been here the entire time?"

"Yeah. Not sure why I came here. I remembered you saying it's where you stayed, and felt safer for some reason."

"You sure cleaned it up. When I left, it was a disaster. I can't even remember, to be honest."

"It helped me, being here. I worked through a lot of stuff. I read your old notebook. Sorry," she said sheepishly.

"I have nothing to hide. My time here was brutal."

Brittany teared up. "I know. I'm sorry. I never thought of other people—what they lost. I couldn't see past myself. It's been hard being alone. I wanted to go back to the hotel but couldn't leave."

"I get it. This mansion held me hostage too. You'll know when it's time."

"Would you stay awhile?"

Norah nodded. "Of course."

Brittany lit a fire, went to the kitchen, and returned with a plate of cookies and tea.

Norah bit into a cookie. "Did you bake these over the fire?"

"Yes." Brittany laughed. "After many attempts."

"They're delicious."

"Thanks." Brittany paused. "So, are you and Eldon…?"

"Yes." Norah felt sick answering.

Brittany smiled. "I had to learn to be alone—like, really alone. It sucked. I don't know how many nights I didn't sleep, freaked out and terrified. Eventually I realized I never needed him." She stared out the window, the same window Norah had stared out for countless hours.

"You know, Brittany, I didn't know how to be alone either. I was always with my son, or husband, family; if not, I was distracting myself with anything I could find. Food, TV, my phone—anything to avoid silence. My mind chatter was uncomfortable. When I was in this house, I felt the same fear of aloneness. After a while, I didn't. Being alone doesn't terrorize me now."

"I want you to know I am okay with everything. Not that you need my blessing, but you can move forward without angst from me. I mean that."

"Thank you. I really don't know what to say other than that. We all miss you at the hotel. It's quiet without you."

"Really? I didn't think anyone cared." She looked down.

"Brittany, why do you think I'm here? I haven't stopped thinking about you since you left. I've dreamt about you every night—my dreams led me here. Murph's been searching for you, too, but always returned empty-handed. I thought he searched here. Everyone, including Eldon, misses you."

Her face lightened into a glow. "I had no idea."

"Well, it's true. Not many people shine like you." She smiled.

Brittany showed off her art projects to Norah, especially proud of the outfits she had sown out of old fabric and clothes. They laughed and talked well into the night, then nodded off by the fire.

*　*　*

Norah woke, startled to be in the mansion. Out the window, her eyes fixed on the shed. A sense of calm washed over her.

She went inside the shed, opened the box, and read the letters. She glanced at her hand, at the beautiful ring from so long ago. The ring that had carried her and given her strength. She slipped it off her finger and placed it back in the box. "Thank you," she whispered. No tears, just gratitude.

"What are you doing here?" Brittany said, peeking her head through the window.

"I left something behind."

Brittany smiled. "I'll leave you alone. I made tea, come when you're ready."

"Brittany, thank you for everything, but it's time for me to get back. I hope you come home soon."

"Thanks for coming. I don't know if I'm ready." She looked down at her hands.

"We'll be there when you are." Norah grabbed her backpack, gave Brittany a hug, and headed home. She stopped at the bridge, lit a small fire, and burned her old journal. As the flames released the madness, she rested her head on the backpack and her eyes grew heavy...

She awoke to a rustle. Fear pulsed through her. She grabbed a rock.

Brittany walked into the clearing.

Norah dropped the rock. "Oh my god, I could've killed you!" she gasped.

Brittany was in stitches while Norah tried to settle her adrenaline rush.

"I decided I was ready," she said, still laughing.

"God, I haven't been that scared in ages." Norah shook her head and laughed. "But I'm happy you're coming home."

When they arrived back at the hotel, Eldon wrapped Brittany in a big bear hug, making it evident to Norah he cared more than he had let on.

Brittany cried when he put her down. "I love you, like a brother."

"I love you, too, squirt. Don't ever scare us like that again." He smiled.

Murph gave her a hug. "I searched for you, where were you?"

"In the lion's den where Norah stayed," she said. "Thanks for looking, Murph, I had no idea you all cared."

"Are you kidding, Brittany?" Ida gave her a hug.

Murph looked perplexed. "I looked through every house at the Ridge, I can't believe I missed that one."

"Don't worry, Murph," Norah said, "there's something about that house." She winked at Brittany.

Ollie ran up and gave Brittany a big hug. "I missed you, and so did Fatty."

"I'm not sure Fatty missed me," she said with a laugh, "but I missed you, too, Ollie."

Tayo walked up and gave her a wordless hug.

"Thank you, Jesus," Maggie exclaimed. "I've been praying for you, sweetheart."

They gathered around the table for supper like old times, and everyone was at ease. It was obvious that Brittany had experienced a radical shift. Her affect was natural and calm, while still bubbly and spritely. Just not manic.

CHAPTER 8

CLARITY, AS IF THE SKY HAD PARTED AFTER A SIX-MONTH storm. The atmosphere lightened. Norah and Eldon sat around the fire at the cabin; she wrote, he strummed his guitar.

Tayo joined them and sat on the big cushy chair. His demeanour was pale and sick, but that was not far out of the ordinary. Norah knew little about Tayo. He was closed and high most of the time, but like many pill addicts he was high in a functioning way, a vacancy resting in his eyes. Tayo often sat around the fire, but this time was different. Mist glazed his eyes and rolled into tears. He put his head in his hands.

"I can't do this anymore, man." His voice trembled.

Eldon put his hand on Tayo's back. "You're done when you say you're done."

"I either die now or stop." He sounded angry.

Eldon nodded. "Then you stop. Because losing you is losing too much."

Tears flowed freely down Tayo's face. "I miss her, miss them."

"We all miss someone, lost someone. You're not alone, Tayo. If you're ready, I'm here, we'll all help you dry out and get on your feet. Just say the word."

"Sorry to be a bitch." He wiped his eyes with his shirt. "You would do that? I'm sure you'd rather be spending time with Norah."

"Tayo, you're my brother."

A long silence ensued.

"I'm ready."

Eldon put his arm around Tayo's shoulders. "Then we are too. Let's go back to the hotel, Ida will help."

Eldon talked to Ida, and they decided to take shifts while Tayo detoxed, but they would need supplies. Ida gave Norah and Eldon a list.

"How do you know so much about this?" Eldon asked Ida. Norah wished she could have warned him that it was a loaded question.

"I knew someone who suffered addiction," Ida said bluntly. "Helped him detox many times."

"Someone close?"

"My twenty-three-year-old son, Mike." Ida looked away.

"I'm sorry."

"Thanks, Eldon. I lost him. He was kind and complicated. You remind me of him sometimes."

As Eldon and Norah walked to the utility trailer, Eldon asked, "Did you know Ida had a son?"

"Yeah." Norah shook her head. "Sometimes I forget about other people's losses. I'm so wrapped up in my own."

"It's hard not to be consumed by it."

They hopped on their bikes and rode down the path to the department store. Eldon pulled the crumpled list out of his pocket.

Orange juice (7 big bottles)

Chocolate bars (as many as you can get)

Candies (as many as you can get)

Advil (A lot)

Cans of pop

Gravol

Towelettes

"Why the hell does she need so much candy?" Eldon asked.

Norah shrugged, and they began to collect the items on the list. The produce at the grocery store was clumped into a dusty, powdered mold. "What was it like in here at the beginning?" she asked.

"Terrible. At least there weren't any bugs or animals, but the stench made our eyes water. We wore gas masks."

"God, the meat and dairy. Just horrible."

They pushed the cart out and loaded the stuff onto the bike trailer. Norah watched Eldon lift the heavy boxes, his arms ripped and strong. She had never been with a man as physically beautiful as he. It was disarming and unusual. She walked over and kissed the tattoo on his neck.

"Why won't you tell me about it?" She stared at him.

He touched his neck and kissed her cheek. "Another time, maybe," he said, sadness on the fringe of his voice.

She didn't press further, just kissed his cheek and continued to load supplies.

* * *

As Tayo crawled through the hell of withdrawal, Norah remembered her detox. She had cluelessly suffered through it alone. It became clear why Ida had requested the sugar. Once Tayo came to, he turned into a sugar fiend, eating six chocolate bars in one sitting and guzzling orange juice as if he had been stranded on a desert island for the last year. His spirit slowly re-entered his body, his eyes brighter, his skin no longer grey.

He contributed and socialized, sharing things about himself no one knew. He'd grown up cooking with his dad, a famous Iron Chef, and had won many junior competitions. His ability to whip a gourmet meal with only dry goods was nothing short of a miracle. He soon became the resident chef. Ida was happy to pass the torch; she had grown tired of conjuring meals from thin air, with no fresh produce or meat.

Tayo talked about his twin sister, Veronika. He was born last and had died right after birth. The nurse was about to take him out of the room, but his mom screamed for her to bring him back. She lay him beside Veronika on her bare chest. Within moments, his heart started beating. The twins became inseparable. He said they could read each other's minds. After she disappeared, dreams robbed his sleep. Hence the pills.

Now sober, the dreams returned, but he learned to deal with them. Ida told him to write every detail in a journal, and he did. The dream was usually the same: Veronika lifeless, surrounded by water under the bright sun.

In recovery herself, Maggie found Tayo a Big Book and helped him work the steps. He found it helpful. Like everything under the Shade, recovery looked different with no meetings or community support, but Norah overheard Maggie drilling the concepts—*Just for today* and *Keep It Simple*.

* * *

Norah and Eldon moved to the cabin. She loved breathing the crisp, minty air and pressing her bare feet onto the electric soil. The concrete butterflies she felt around Eldon were still heavy. Every time he looked at her or touched her, she was met with a pulling deep in her belly.

Eldon kissed her neck. She opened her eyes, and he handed her a piece of folded paper. "What's this?" she asked and rubbed her eyes, blurry from fresh sleep. "Maggie made wedding invitations for us? It says it's tomorrow."

"I asked her to." He brushed the hair away from her eyes.

She stared at him, speechless. He took off his necklace, removed his mother's wedding ring, and slipped it on her finger. It fit perfectly above the one she had found in the shed. "I want you to be my wife," he whispered and handed her a small box. Inside was a thin white-gold chain with a metal Monopoly shoe token clasped to the end.

"I thought I lost this!" she gasped.

He put it around her neck and held her hand.

"Yes," she whispered. She pulled him close and pressed into him. They dressed and headed to the hotel.

Ida hugged her. "I'm going to officiate. Is that okay? I'm not a real minister, but I'm already writing my sermon."

Norah scrunched her eyes at Eldon. "You were pretty certain I'd say yes?"

"How couldn't you?" He winked.

Norah turned back to Ida. "Of course, Ida... It could never be anyone else."

"It's coming together—Tayo's playing guitar, Ollie's taking pictures, and Brittany is desperate to do your hair and makeup."

"This is overwhelming. I don't want anything fancy."

"Oh, Norah, there are few opportunities to celebrate. We are taking it. It's not about you." She smiled.

"Sounds like my dream wedding. I hate being the centre of attention."

"Good, it's settled."

Norah stopped for a moment and took it in. Ida was right; it wasn't about her. A stir of excitement brewed into the usual quietness.

"Are you okay to do it at the church tomorrow?" Ida asked.

"Yes." Norah thought about skinny Jesus and blushed. She looked around and realized Eldon had left. "I'll be back, I'm going to find Eldon."

She found him fishing by the river. "Hey, you disappeared," she said.

He put his fishing rod down, pulled her close, and laid her down on the rocks.

She pushed him away. "I don't want to marry you, knowing there's a piece of you you're keeping from me."

He grew quiet and turned away. "I had a son, Nash." He paused. "I was seventeen. His mom, Megan, was sixteen. We tried to raise him together, but she got into drugs and took off when he was a month. I raised him myself, my partner in crime. He was five when he was kidnapped. He went to the park across the street with a ten-year-old neighbour kid, Cole. I watched them from the window and looked away for a few seconds to hear Cole screaming. Nash was grabbed and put into a car." He inhaled a deep breath. "His body was found three weeks later in a forest on the edge of the city." His eyes grew misty. "My neck tattoo is the Chinese symbol for a tiger. Nash was obsessed with tigers. Tiger pictures plastered all over his room, striped pajamas… sometimes, he'd wear a full tiger costume for the entire day." He smiled. "We were at the library that morning and found a book about the Chinese zodiac. He nearly levitated when we realized he was the year of the tiger. The entire walk back, he was roaring and jumping around, summoning his powers. When we got home, he begged me to draw a tattoo of the symbol on him. I said no 'cause I thought permanent marker was bad for his skin, but he was relentless. I asked him where he wanted it, and he pointed to his neck. I laughed and called him a little cholo, but he was serious about his tat." He sniffled. "I drew it on him. He ran to the mirror and jumped up with his arms in the air, so stoked, he ran outside to show Cole. The tattoo was still on his neck when they put him to rest." Eldon fell apart, weeping with his head in his hands.

Norah leaned into him, and he put his arms around her. They tangled into each other and allowed the grief to swirl between their flesh.

* * *

Norah's eyes opened to quiet. A note with her name on it was folded on the side table.

My love, I won't see you till our wedding. Go find Brittany.

She sipped yesterday's cold coffee and carried her journal outside, planted her feet on the earth, and inhaled deep breaths.

> *I've never known love. I've never loved myself. How can I feel this now? Seamus breathed an honesty that hurt, but his intention was never to harm me. He tried to love me. But couldn't. He didn't see me. Or hold me. I never wanted the life I had. The conventional marriage. I didn't know what I wanted. So how could I ask for it? Now, without asking, I have been given something. Do I deserve this? Can I keep it or will my pain destroy it?*

"Are you getting cold feet?" Murph stood behind Norah.

"My feet are always cold." She laughed and walked to the hotel with him. Brittany immediately whisked Norah into a room. A cream Celtic wedding dress hung in front of the window. She loved the soft lace sleeves flowing over its shoulders and the A-line waist with magical satin material strewn down the front.

Norah's eyes filled with tears. "How did you do this? It's the most stunning dress I've ever seen."

"I found one at the mall and tailored it. I was in fashion school, remember?"

"Brittany." Norah grasped her by the shoulders. "Thank you."

"Okay, okay, just sit down here." Brittany beamed.

Two hours later, Norah looked like a stunning medieval princess. Brittany had woven small braids into her long flowing hair and tucked tiny flowers throughout. She stepped out of the room to see Murph in a tuxedo. He reached out his arm, and she slipped her arm inside his elbow. Her heart hurt. Murph reminded her of her dad, who'd never had an opportunity to walk her down any aisle.

Candles led to the door of the church. When she reached the entrance, she locked eyes with Eldon, who was standing at the altar, a classic tuxedo and bow tie accentuating his toned body. He was gorgeous. Her knees buckled.

Ida stood at the front in an elegant silver dress. Ollie stood beside Eldon, dapper in a tux and bow tie. Fatty lay on the altar, a bow tie around his neck.

As Tayo strummed "Over The Rainbow," Norah walked towards Eldon. No jitters or nerves. He pulled her close and whispered in her ear. She blushed.

Ida began to speak. "We're gathered to share your love. Norah, thank you for coming into our lives, for becoming part of our family." She paused. "Eldon, my adopted son. We love you both." She smiled. "Now the vows."

Fatty grunted. Everyone giggled.

Norah froze and squeezed Eldon's hands.

"Eldon, you saw my pain and moved closer,

You saw beauty in my brokenness,

Your music is my medicine,

Your love has changed my breath."

Not a dry eye in the room. Eldon kissed Norah's cheek.

"Norah.

I see you.

I will always see you.

I will always choose you."

"I have no power vested in me," Ida said, "but with all of my heart and soul, I pronounce you husband and wife." She motioned to Eldon. "Now, give your wife a kiss!"

Eldon picked up Norah, gave her a squeeze, and kissed her. Fatty waddled to them mid-embrace, rooted his nose through Norah's dress, and left a slimy wet spot.

Norah leaned over, scratched Fatty's head, and gave him a big kiss. "Don't worry, Fatty. You'll always be my true love."

Ida called Ollie. Proud to take the pulpit, he cleared his throat.

"Eldon and Norah

You are the best

Two little birdies in love in their nest

I like you both the way you are

I make a wish on a little star

That you stay happy and try to be nice

Cuz marriage is just a roll of the dice."

"Ollie, did you actually write that?" Norah asked.

"Yup, I took a 'Learn to write poems' book from the store."

They hugged him. "Ollie, it's the best poem ever."

Ida asked Maggie to share what she had prepared.

"I am blessed to be here and share in this splendid occasion," Maggie said. "This is the scripture I found while praying for your marriage. Proverbs 30:18-19: *'There are three things that amaze me—no, four things that I don't understand: how an eagle glides through the sky, how a snake slithers on a rock, how a ship navigates the ocean, how a man loves a woman.'* Witnessing your love for one another has opened my heart. I see it and have no concern about the pure intention of your union." She returned to the pew.

Murph lifted her hand and kissed it. A rare tender moment.

Norah appreciated the scripture and remembered the magnificence of the Bible, how religion weighed it down with human lies. Like skinny Jesus, the poor guy resembled the crypt keeper when, really, he was a beautiful, spirit-filled man who loved on everyone with no exception. His heart was pure and he would be the first to stand and fight injustice against all of mistreated humanity.

Norah and Eldon hugged Maggie.

"Let's go outside. Tayo prepared a feast," Ida announced.

The area outside the church had transformed into a magical fairy woodland. Lanterns were spread over the leafless trees, and a picnic table was covered in colourful tapestries and burning candles. Ollie strummed the guitar. Eldon and Norah danced. Maggie and Murph joined. Tayo danced with Brittany. Ida and Ollie swayed back and forth. Fatty grunted and snuffed and tried to get some crackers off the table.

Eldon raised his glass. "To our lost loves: our sweet sons Nash and Theo, Seamus, Murph and Maggie's precious family, Ida's Myra, Tayo's Veronika, Ollie's parents. To all the pieces of our hearts. Never forgotten."

Everyone weepily raised their glasses. They drank wine and danced for hours and eventually passed out, strewn around like wounded soldiers.

* * *

Norah pried open her crusted eyes to a blur of images. Her wedding dress was tangled around her body, and her hair was dishevelled. She was slumped over Eldon, his tux half off. Although her head pounded and stomach churned, it had been a blissfully fun night. She hadn't touched alcohol in over eight years.

Her vision cleared to see Fatty asleep, his face covered in cracker crumbs. Brittany was passed out in the bushes. Ollie and Ida were out on the church pews.

"Eldon, wake up." She shook him.

He smacked his lips together, his mouth so dry he could barely get a word out. "So rough," he murmured and held his head.

"Get up, let's go to the inlet," she whispered.

He nodded and they stumbled to the inlet, still partially drunk. They undressed and crawled into the water, and within minutes of swimming and drinking the water, their hangovers vanished. They realized they were at full capacity and ravenously consummated their marriage.

Ida smiled when she saw Eldon and Norah return. "You two on your honeymoon?" Her eyes were sunken; she looked rough.

Eldon laughed. "Something like that. Whoa, rough night?"

"God, Eldon, I haven't drunk like that in years. Have you seen Tayo?"

"No, wasn't he here last night?" Norah asked.

"Yeah, but not this morning," Ida said. We shouldn't have let him drink, maybe he was triggered." She looked down and shook her head. "I should've known better."

Norah could see her guilt and felt it herself. The wedding had over-shadowed everything. His being supported had fallen to the wayside.

"Quite the crowd, can't handle your liquor or what?" Murph said as he and Maggie walked over.

"Did Tayo go back to the hotel with you guys last night?" Eldon asked.

"No, I tried to talk to you, Eldon," Maggie said. "Tell you to take the bottle away from him."

Eldon shook his head. "I don't remember."

"Well, I was the only one with my wits about me," she droned on, "and he wouldn't listen. Piss-poor behaviour if you ask my opinion."

"Maggie, nobody asked you."

Norah cut him off. "Let's go look for him." She pulled him towards the hotel.

"She's too much," Eldon said to her. "I've never had to force myself to not flip out on someone as much as her."

"I know, she's irritating," Norah said, challenged to find any other words.

"I feel bad I wasn't there for Tayo, but her talking condescending to me like that—frig, sometimes I wanna throat punch her voice box right out the other side."

"Jesus, Eldon." Norah shook her head.

"Enough about the relentless dodo bird, we need to find Tayo."

They found him laid out on the couch at the cabin, an empty pill bottle resting in his open palm, pills scattered on the ground below. Eldon shook him awake.

"Sorry, man, did I ruin your wedding?" he mumbled. Even the moonlight seemed too bright for his pupils. He smacked his lips, mouth dry as paper.

"No, man. I'm sorry, I wasn't thinking about you," Eldon said.

"No, no. I hate being like this." He held his head in his hands. "My head is pounding. I'm gonna go to the hotel." The pill bottle dropped and hit the rock below. He leaned down and picked it up, then began to stumble off.

"Tayo, give me those, you don't need them."

"No man, I got it." He kept walking.

Eldon raised his voice. "You've been sober for a month. Don't throw it away over one night."

"I got this man, just leave it." Tayo waved his hand at him.

"I'm not messing around, Tayo."

Eldon grabbed his shoulder. Tayo pushed him hard.

"Eldon, stop," Norah shouted.

Tayo turned around and disappeared into the hotel.

"He's really messed up." Eldon paced around the fire. "We can't just leave him be, I've never seen him like that."

"What can we do? He can't be watched every second. We can't imprison him."

"I don't know, but it doesn't feel right. I'm going to check on him."

Norah followed him to the hotel. They knocked on Tayo's door. No answer. Knocked again. Nothing. Eldon wiggled the door handle. It was locked.

"Tayo," Eldon shouted.

Norah's stomach dropped.

Eldon backed up and kicked the door down. Tayo lay sprawled out on the bed, vomit down the side of his mouth. Eldon panicked and shook him. Norah put her hand on his cold and clammy forehead.

"He's not breathing." Eldon's voice shook. He tipped the boy's head up and started chest compressions. "Thirty-two four. Thirty-four two. What the hell is it?"

Norah couldn't remember.

"Just do twenty and three, count it out loud." Her head pounded and hands shook. Her breathing shallowed. *Narcan kit!* She remembered seeing one in the kitchen. She bolted and rifled through the cabinets. *Where the hell is it?... Shit, the sink.* She opened the cabinet under the sink and grabbed it, then rushed back to the bed. "Have you used one of these?" She slammed it on the bed and zipped it open.

"No." Eldon continued counting.

"Fuck." She spread out the kit, two vials, and two syringes. Filled one. "Where?" Her hands shook as she looked at Eldon for direction. He shrugged. *Shit.* She plunged the needle into Tayo's arm and pushed in the liquid, then stood back and waited. "How long does this take to work?"

"Norah, I don't know," Eldon snapped.

A minute passed… Nothing. Another… Nothing.

"Should I do the other one?"

Eldon didn't answer, just continued pressing on Tayo's chest.

"Fuck it." She filled the second syringe and blasted it into his other arm. "Come on. Come on."

Another minute passed… Tayo plunged back to life, his eyes opening as he gasped for air. Norah fell back on the bed and tried to catch her breath. Eldon slumped beside her. No one said a word.

Norah broke the silence. "I'll go get some water."

When she passed a bottle to Tayo, his hand shook too hard to hold it, so she held it to his mouth. After he took a sip, he grabbed her hand and started to weep. She sat beside him on the bed and rubbed his head.

"I'm sorry," he stammered between sobs.

* * *

Tayo's overdose shook him to his core. He was done. For real done. Over the next few months, an insatiable hunger for knowledge had him reading book after book about addiction, neuroscience, and the brain, and he talked openly about his struggles. He meditated and wrote daily and ate as healthily as he could, and he started doing yoga and running with Brittany every morning.

One day, Norah came out of the cabin to find Brittany sitting by the fire, her face pale, serious. "Hey, is everything okay?"

"Are you alone?" she whispered.

"No, Eldon's inside. Wanna walk?"

They set off towards the river. Brittany danced around whatever bothered her, making small talk with long pauses in between.

Norah stopped and faced her. "What is it? I know you didn't come down here to talk about the weather. It hasn't changed in years."

Brittany burst into tears. She sat on the ground. Norah joined and put her arm around her. "I'm… I'm pregnant."

"What? You and Tayo?" Norah asked.

Brittany nodded and smiled.

"How far along?"

She shrugged. "Hard to tell with no periods. I've been bloated and gaining weight. I took a test today."

"How do you feel about it?"

"Terrified. I've been with Tayo for, like, two months." She paused. "How am I going to raise a baby in this world? I love him, Norah. I've never felt like this about anyone, but what if it's not real? What if he relapses, and I need to raise a baby alone in this nightmare?" She tried to catch her breath. "And I don't want to get fat." Moments passed, her crying eventually turning to sniffles and her breathing calming.

"Brittany, it's normal to be a wreck. Your hormones are all over the place. Focus on what you can control. Right now, you are in a relationship with someone you love and I'm sure loves you. It's a beautiful thing."

She nodded. "I'm more spastic than usual. I've been yelling at him all week about nothing, making him sleep in the dining hall. He's so patient with me."

"Obviously he's nuts about you, of course he's patient. Be gentle with yourself and Tayo." She smiled. "Plus, your baby will probably get your perfect genes."

"A lot of good those did me." She giggled.

They headed back to the cabin and joined Eldon.

"Hey, squirt, what's going on?" Eldon smiled.

"Nothing," Brittany said.

"Come on, I know you better."

"I'm just a hormonal mess." She sniffled.

"Worse than usual?"

"Shut up." She rolled her eyes. "I'm pregnant."

The expression on Eldon's face made it clear he was struggling to take in the information. Brittany shook her head, buried it inside her hoodie, and cried.

Tayo walked up the path. He looked vibrant and handsome. He was a gentle, sensitive soul, with a disarming sense of humour. He sat beside Brittany and put his arm around her.

"You okay, doll?" he whispered.

Brittany curled on his lap. "I am now, I'm sorry."

"No, never, I'm happy to sleep in the dining hall and share the napkin-sized blanket with Fatty." He kissed her forehead.

"Well, you'll be sleeping with another fatty soon." She sighed.

He smiled. "Oh, hush."

"Brit," Eldon said, "sorry about my reaction. I didn't even know you two were together. I'm so happy for you both." Eldon put them in a bear hug.

"Thanks, Eldon." Brittany hugged him back. "Do you remember having your son, Norah?"

"Of course." Norah lifted her eyebrows. "Are you wondering about giving birth?"

"I guess." She shrugged her shoulders. "Is it as bad as people say?"

"No… it's a million times worse."

"Ugh," Brittany sighed.

"I'm kidding. It's intense but short-lived and immediately overshadowed by your sweet new bundle." Norah paused. "My pregnancy was high risk though. I wasn't supposed to have children. After I had Theo, they had to do an emergency hysterectomy. So, I think my story is a bit different."

"Sounds brutal. Did you get an epidural?"

"No, just laughing gas. Sadly, it won't be an option for you anyway." Norah sighed.

"I'm scared. What if I pop a vein on my face? My body's going to be a mess."

"Brit, you'll bounce back, you're in great shape. Even if you didn't, who cares."

Tayo smiled. "Yeah, you're beautiful no matter what."

* * *

The following week, Norah and Eldon got up early and left for the small honeymoon they had planned months before, up the mountain to the west of the hotel. During one of their earlier walks, they had stumbled on a narrow path on the rock face beside the inlet. Surprised they hadn't discovered it earlier, around a slight bend their eyes weren't naturally drawn to, they wanted to explore it. The rock path around the inlet narrow was just wide enough for their feet. Norah felt withdrawn as she sauntered down the path.

"Do you want to go first?" Eldon asked.

She shrugged. "No, why?"

He stopped. "What is going on with you? You've been off since we woke up this morning."

"I don't know." She looked down, hating her insides. She felt his arm around her, his lips on her cheek.

"Let's take a break," he said.

"We've only been walking for five minutes, Eldon."

"So what?" He sat on the path, his back against the rock wall.

She joined him and leaned her head on his shoulder. "I'm sorry. I'm off… I've dreamt about Theo the last three nights. I'm trapped in his room, yelling, and he opens the door. I'm so happy to see him, and when I look, his eyes have black blood pouring out. I wake up terrified."

"Terrible dream." Eldon shook his head.

"It's getting to me. I've grown to accept this strange reality we live in, but sometimes it hits me—the not knowing, us being alone on this massive planet with no idea what happened." She looked out over the inlet. "Why us? I want to know where he is, where they all are. Maybe they didn't die? No bodies. Where did they go? Is he safe or being tortured somewhere?" She put her head down and cried.

"Knowing isn't always better," he said quietly.

"I'd rather know, even if it was terrible." She paused. "I'm sorry."

"Knowing, not knowing—either way, it leaves you with a broken-ness. I'm just saying, the pain is the same. I wonder too. Believe me, every possible theory crosses my mind… Maybe we're in a human experiment or an alternate reality. It's bizarre, us left here. There's an easiness about it that feels wrong—enough food and water, supplies to last more than a lifetime—as if this city was just left for the six of us and whatever few stragglers still wander."

"I know, I'm feeling it heavy right now." She sighed.

"Love, let's go back. It isn't the right time. We'll leave in a few days, once your nightmares settle."

"I'm sorry."

"Norah, you have nothing to be sorry about. We have the luxury of time, leaving in a few days makes no difference." He kissed her forehead and they headed back to the cabin.

For the next few days, Norah battled her familiar demons and remembered what Eldon said about pain needing to flow. She planted her bare feet on the soil, watched the dancing flames in the firepit, and filled her journal with ramblings.

God, I don't know you, I never have. This deep unsettling in my bones has carried me my entire life, questions asked are no longer questions burned from an ordinary place, answers sought out by billions are now answers sought out by few. I am one of those few. Why me? Left behind without my son. Many days, I hated life before you took the sun away, and now another love burns inside me. How can I reconcile what I have and what I lost? There is no between. How can I love what I lost and what I have without betraying a part of it all? It was a mess before, and it's a quieter mess now. I was impatient before, irritated and angry about so many things.

The malfunctioning machine caused a rage inside me. Most of my time was spent feeling guilty about my imperfections, and now I live with the whys and hows of who I was and who I am now. I tried to be better, settle my mind, and only live in love. Impossible. This demon holds the cloak of darkness and waits for me to grow weary so he can lay it over my spirit. I have begged for death, and it never came. I can't admit life on the planet is better now because it implies I don't miss the ones I lost. For now, I rest in the gift of the love I do have.

*   *   *

Waking to the sound of music, Norah went to Eldon, took his guitar out of his arms, and curled in his lap. He lifted her face to his and pressed his lips against hers, then picked her up, carried her inside, and made love to her.

That night the terrors settled. Her mind eased back into acceptance. Gratitude returned. She thought about what Eldon had said about the easiness, about how the life they now lived had strands of idealism. A strange and beautiful utopia.

*   *   *

No longer weighed down with the cloak of darkness, Norah and Eldon set off on their adventure the next morning. Norah walked barefoot down the path, her feet now able to withstand the rough terrain. The earth's vibration grounded her. She gripped the slate rock as she scaled the mountainside. With every step, the humming intensified. Eldon, an arm's length in front of her, didn't lean on anything and unintentionally showed off his perfect balance.

Barely ten minutes into the hike, with the inlet no longer visible, Norah stopped for a drink. She leaned on the slate wall, then suddenly crashed inside the mountain and landed on soft ground. Eldon pulled her out. Speechless, they gazed inside the opening at a massive meadow blanketed with light-indigo clover and tiny dark-indigo flowers, which sprawled up the sides of the surrounding rock walls. Norah inhaled a deep breath. The fragrant air reminded her of honeysuckle and freesia. At the far side of the field laid an unearthed tree the size of a metropolis billboard, its roots exposed in an entangled, intricate labyrinth. Indigo crystal geodes of all sizes shot up from the ground and down from the ceiling in every direction, some as tall as giant sequoia trees. A geode crystal forest. The geodes glowed dimly enough for them to see their surroundings.

A faint harp-like humming, a sound Norah's human ears had never registered, beckoned into her body.

"Should we go in?" They said in unison.

"What if our feet melt?" Norah said.

"What do we have to lose?"

She put her hand in his and ducked inside the opening. Her feet squished into the soft clover and slightly sank with each step. The energetic intensity from the field, a highly magnified version of the inlet, shot through her feet and waved through every cell of her body. Sheer ecstasy. The intensity made her dizzy. She lay down, let the earth pulsate through her body, and breathed in the sweet air.

Eldon pulled his boots off and lay beside her. They lay frozen in the gravitational pull of the meadow. Hours later, Eldon stood, stripped naked, and lay back down. Norah followed. The magic coursed through their veins. Eldon put his hand over hers. The electricity shocked their bodies. They made love, devouring each other in ravenous madness. To say they were insatiable before was finite compared to the magnitude of their passion within the rock walls.

They rose to their feet slowly and headed toward the labyrinth, unsteady from the energy. Norah brushed the geode structures as she passed. A buzzing shock waved through her body. Her legs strained as if pushing through a strong current. What should have been a ten-minute walk took an hour.

She stood before the labyrinth, in awe of its magnificence. A warm breeze blew through her body as if it were a hollow shell.

Eldon reached out and touched a root with the tip of his finger. Explosively thrust back at least twelve feet, his body slammed against a geode.

Norah screamed, fought the current, and kneeled beside him. She lifted his head in her arms, and blood gushed profusely while the life drained from his body. He was gone. Void of breath and pulse. She pierced the air with an inhuman shriek, then slumped over and shook him furiously.

She crawled to the unearthed tree and grabbed a root. Nothing happened. She pounded her fists over the roots until her knuckles were bloody and raw, then she keeled over and vomited. "Take me! Just fucking take me!" She screamed at the labyrinth until she fell into a pile of skin at the bottom of the roots and wept like an abandoned newborn.

"Norah."

A hand shook her shoulder. She gasped and shuddered back into reality, opening her eyes to see Eldon. Her hand trembled as she brushed it down the back of his head. No blood, no wound.

"You're covered in blood, Norah, what happened?"

She held her hands in front of her face. Her knuckles had healed.

"Norah, what the hell happened? Talk to me."

"You died."

"What?"

"You died. Touched that root and died." Her voice shook. As she pulled her bloody clothes off, her mind raced. *Why can I touch those roots? Why isn't he dead?*

"Do you remember what happened?" she asked.

"No?" he said. "I can't remember a single thing. I woke up and found you under the tree."

"This field, the humming, the geodes, and the inlet… Eldon, you came back from the dead. We need to tell the others."

"We will." His expression turned into one of curiosity. "Do you see those?"

"What?"

"The tiny slants of light between the rock wall and edge of the tree, barely shining through."

"I see it now. Looks like tiny splints of sunlight." They walked to the edge of the labyrinth. She placed her finger on a slant of light. She felt it being vacuumed in place by powerful air pressure. She tried to release her finger. It wouldn't budge. Eldon gripped her hand with both of his and pulled. They fell backward. A small red burn was etched into her fingertip. She pressed it against a nearby geode and the wound vanished.

She studied the entire edge of the root system and searched for a larger slant. All were paper-thin. She pressed her ear close and listened. She heard an excruciating frequency, similar to the first horn but higher pitched. "I think it's sunlight on the other side. I'm guessing it's where the horn came from."

"Why can you touch it?"

"Better yet," she said, "where is the other side of this tree?"

From the outside, they could only see a flat mountain wall and exposed roots.

They stayed in the cave for days. The air had an oxygenated floral crispness, not minty but misty indigo clover. She wanted to stay forever, never leave, but knew they had to return to their family. She nestled into the labyrinth one last time and bawled her eyes out.

"Norah, it's okay," Eldon said from a distance.

"I can't leave," she sobbed.

"Norah, we'll be back, it's only ten minutes from the hotel."

"It doesn't feel right. Something isn't right." She forced herself to crawl out of the labyrinth.

"Love, it's going to be okay, we'll come back soon."

She burst into tears again, lifted her backpack, and headed towards the opening. When her feet touched the ground on the other side, minty air tickled her lungs. As soon as they reached the cabin, Ollie ran to Norah and fell in her arms.

She held him tightly. "What is it?"

"We thought you were both dead?" Ollie squeezed her.

Eldon and Norah looked at each other, confused. "We were only gone a few days?"

Everyone made their way to meet them.

"Norah." Brittany pointed at her huge round stomach.

"How is that possible?" Norah asked. "How long were we gone?"

"Four months," Tayo said.

Fatty grunted towards Norah and knocked her to the ground. She laughed and rubbed his bristled tummy.

They shared their experience in the cave. The others sat around them and listened like children at library storytime, all at a complete loss for words.

"I wanna go there," Brittany said, breaking the silence.

"There's no way in hell, Tayo said. "You're seven months along, what's going to happen to her when you lose time like they did?"

"Her?" Brittany smiled and touched her stomach.

He winked. "I just have a feeling."

"Awe." She smiled at him. "Anyways, yeah, you're right, babe."

"Well," Norah said, "you can come to the inlet. You don't lose time there."

"Okay." Brittany bounced to her feet.

They collected their swimsuits and headed down the path.

Ollie kicked the dirt and stared at the ground. "I'm pissed at you guys, you know."

"I'm sorry, Ollie, can you forgive us?" Norah said.

"I guess." He shrugged his shoulders and ran ahead.

Ida's face looked older, sad. "Norah, I missed you. The last months were endless without you both."

"Ida, I'm sorry. I would never leave like that. The cave... I don't know."

"It's not your fault, another mind fuck. Should be used to them by now. I'm just relieved you're back. Don't go into the cave again." She put her arm around Norah.

"I promise." Norah leaned her head on Ida's shoulder and fought back the tears. It made sense now—the emotions, the pull to stay. Merely ten minutes away, like Eldon said. A visit to the cave now weighed with the dreadful consequence of lost time.

They jumped in the magnetic water and agreed that in the future, they would tie a red ribbon around the giant dead oak at the start of the path to indicate when the inlet was occupied. Norah watched her family and felt grateful. Eldon put his arms around her, and she burrowed into his neck. She yearned for the labyrinth but didn't want to miss Brittany's birth or leave the others.

They discussed it endlessly: *What if we just went back for an hour and left quickly? What if everyone moved there?* The variables were far too many to consider. She found herself again bound by duty, firmly planted in connections. A return was inevitable, but she grounded herself back into her familiar reality.

CHAPTER 9

"COME QUICK, NORAH," OLLIE SCREAMED FRANTICALLY, "THE baby's coming!"

He woke Norah from a dead sleep. She looked over at Eldon's side of the bed and remembered he was gone camping, and then they hustled to the hotel. Screams echoed the halls. Brittany was bent over in the throes of a contraction.

Tayo was bracing himself on the bed frame and looked as though he might faint.

"Not looking so good, Tayo," Norah said and smiled. "Brit, you're doing great." She grabbed the mother-to-be's hand.

"No, I'm not," Brittany screamed into another contraction.

"How long has she been going?" Norah asked Ida. "How many minutes apart?"

"Contractions for a few hours. She's really close."

Over the past months, Ida had been ingesting book after book on childbirth. At this point, she carried the title of uncertified midwife. Maggie brought her own qualifications from experience. She had been present at all her grandchildren's births, not to mention having a brood of her own.

Within an hour, Brittany had pushed out a precious baby girl. Ida laid the chubby baby on Brittany's bare chest with the umbilical cord still attached. Brittany and Tayo wept as their little bundle latched onto her breast. It had been a seamless birth. Everyone gathered, overjoyed with the beautiful baby.

"Sweet little Tilly," Brittany whispered. "Norah, I did it." She smiled.

Norah smiled back. *An hour*, she thought. *An hour-long birth.* She shook her head and headed to the kitchen to get Brittany a ginger ale. Halfway down the hall, a shrill cry blared from the birthing room. She ran back to find Brittany screaming in a fit of panic, her face covered in snot and tears.

Tilly's face was blue. Her body limp.

"No, no, no, do something," Brittany shrieked. Her arms shook as she held her lifeless baby.

As Norah surveyed the chaos, her senses heightened and everyone in the room moved in slow motion. Her mind flashed to Eldon in the cave. She reached over, cut the umbilical cord, pried the baby out of Brittany's arms, and wrapped her inside her sweater.

She looked at Tayo. "Take care of Brittany." She ran towards the cave, her breathing shallow, her heart slow and heavy.

She stopped in front of the slate opening and glanced down at the lifeless baby, then entered. She fought hard against the current, reached the labyrinth, and laid Tilly on the indigo clover. Kissing her cold, pale forehead, Norah clasped her tiny limp hand in her palm and grabbed the root. Electricity surged through her body.

* * *

Norah's eyes opened to the sound of gurgling. She saw tiny legs and hands kicking in the air. Unsure how long she had been out, she cradled Tilly against her chest and wept. She didn't waste any more time and headed back.

Brittany ran towards Norah to find Tilly asleep in her arms. She lifted the baby out of her arms, rocked her back and forth, and fell apart.

Tayo ran to them, broke down, and embraced Norah. "Thank you," he whispered.

Norah fell to the ground and put her head in her hands. She was emotionally spent. "Where's Eldon?" Nobody answered. She wiped her nose on her sleeve and looked around at everyone. "What?"

Ida sat on the ground and wrapped her arm around Norah's shoulder. "He followed you into the cave when he came back from camping."

"No. I would have seen him." Norah panicked. "How long was I gone?"

Ida looked away. "Three weeks."

Devastated and exhausted, Norah returned to the cabin and curled into bed. She wanted to follow him but knew the risks.

*　*　*

Four months passed with no sight of Eldon. Norah plummeted into a dark depression. Fatty stayed by her side, and Brittany brought Tilly for visits, which sprinkled joy into Norah's dark space. Tilly was plump with dark mocha-indigo skin, brown-indigo eyes, and a platinum afro with indigo tips. Norah had never seen a child like Tilly and found it hard not to become mesmerized by her unique spirit.

She spent hours at the church, reading, writing, and painting. Ida joined and distracted Norah with the buzz of the family. She raved about Brittany and Tayo as parents and laughed about Murph and Maggie's multiple visits to the inlet. Norah knew precisely what she meant and enjoyed the stories.

"Norah, I know you miss him. But we miss you at supper. Why don't you come tonight?" Ida dabbed her brush in a blue dollop of paint and slopped it onto the canvas.

"I'm stuck in dark misery; it's like I can't breathe... Not only that, I've been sick since he left—puking and nauseous." Norah closed her book and looked at Ida.

"You didn't tell me that, Norah? You're puking?" She looked at Norah intently for a moment. "Could you be pregnant?"

"God, no. I wasn't even supposed to have children in the first place, and giving birth nearly killed me. After Theo was born, they did surgery. It's impossible, Ida."

"Oh, I didn't know." She lowered her gaze.

"I was happy with Theo." She paused. "Thank you for being there for me, Ida, you're my anchor."

Ida smiled. "Please come for supper tonight, we need you just as much as you need us."

"Okay."

Norah left Ida at the church, went to the inlet, tied a red ribbon around the oak, and jumped in the water. The energy washed over her but didn't take away her exhaustion or melancholy.

When she got back to the hotel, Tayo was preparing pasta with alfredo sauce and baking bread on the fire. Brittany was curled in the Papasan with Tilly gurgling in her arms.

Norah noticed *Love Letters to Death* was clasped in her hand. "You still have that book?"

"I read it to Tilly. Is that weird?" Brittany asked.

"No." Norah smiled. "Weird doesn't exist anymore." She wrapped her sweater tighter around herself and pulled a blanket over her legs. "Read me a page?"

"Now that's weird." Brittany laughed at her own joke, and Norah laughed in appreciation of Brittany. "But, sure. I never read out loud, though." She flipped to a random page.

Today, I am with you today. I am with you every day. You can't see me, but you feel me. Often, when you do, you push me away, fight, as if acknowledging me will bring me close.

No end exists, my child, and I am close. Avoiding me will not keep me at bay; opening your heart to me softens you into humility.

Whether you hide from me or embrace me, my presence remains the same. I show up in quiet moments, your foot stepping on a dried leaf, the changing seasons, cycles of life.

Those left behind in the sorrowed aftermath of grief long for another moment. I ask you, how many moments would have been enough? The answer—infinity—would not suffice. The insatiable hunger for more time goes against the grain of life.

I never came intending to make sense. I fit in perfectly with the mystery of life. Life needs me to exist. For now, I will let you be. Rest easy and be not afraid of my visit.

Love, Death.

She put the book down, Tilly sound asleep. Norah remained quiet, thought about the writing, and pulled out her journal.

I hate this, hate the cave, love it at the same time, feel soured with Eldon being gone. Why did he follow me, what was he thinking, idiot. What if he doesn't come back. Fuck, my mind, just incessant. Can I live without him here? Really, can I? Of course I can, fuck, I'm such a baby. I know it. I can't snap out of it. Maybe I should just go back to the cave, follow him. If I go, I won't come back, I know this. I feel alone, surviving this quiet

nothingness without him, unable to find joy in what I still have.
Ugh. I'm sick of my victimized musings.

"Come play Uno with me, Norah!" Ollie said, breaking her attention.

She lifted her head, ripped the page from her journal, and threw it in the fire.

"Deal 'em up," she said, sitting across from him.

They had played a couple rounds when Ollie jumped up. "You gotta hear this, I've been practicing." He grabbed a guitar and strummed the song Eldon had taught him, "Oats in the Water." Norah closed her eyes. Her ears pulled toward a voice, a recognizable swampy rasp. She opened her eyes to see Eldon, his arms stretched towards her.

"Take my hand, idiot." He lifted her and nestled his face into her neck. She sobbed. "What's wrong?" he asked.

"You've been gone for four months, Eldon." She sniffled.

"I was only gone a few hours," he said, confused.

"No, Eldon." She pointed at Brittany and Tilly.

His eyes widened. "She's alive?" he whispered.

Brittany grinned. "Norah saved her. What happened in there?"

"Nothing. Looked for Norah, laid down, fell asleep for a few hours, and came back." He looked at Tilly and then arched a brow at Brittany. "May I?" She placed Tilly in his arms. His eyes moistened as he stared down at the baby. "She's magical, I've never seen a baby like this."

"She's an angel," Brittany said with a smile.

Everyone was ecstatic to see Eldon. Norah wanted him to herself. Strange times to process, from him thinking he had returned from a short nap to Norah worried sick about him for months. Her heart filled at having him back, the risks and miracles of the cave more apparent than ever—four hours into four months. Nothing made sense.

She guided him to the inlet and they made love with an intensity rivalling their time in the cave. Afterward, he lit a fire on the beach and she cuddled into him, her heart pounding with raw emotion laced with intense gratitude.

"Something feels different about you," he said, "curvy." He tickled her back and squeezed her close.

"What?"

"I don't know. Have you been eating more? You look… fuller."

"Fuller?" She lifted her eyebrows. "Tread lightly, my friend."

He laughed and bit her ear. "Love, you just look filled out."

She thought about it. "I've barely eaten since you left, can't see how it's possible. I mean, I haven't worn jeans either—lived in my sweatpants." She paused. "You scared me."

"Never again, I promise." He kissed her, webbed his hands between hers, and pressed inside. The cave's energy filled her body. She lost time with him. They passed out on the beach wrapped in blankets until the fire dwindled into embers.

They returned to the cabin. She pulled out her sweet Balmain jeans and attempted to pry them on. They wouldn't even pass her hips.

"I've definitely gained at least twenty pounds," she said, irritated.

He put his guitar down. "Are you pregnant?"

"Eldon. You know I can't have kids. I told you already that when I had Theo, it was slightly impossible, but now it's actually impossible—they literally removed the necessary parts."

"Norah, there is no impossible in this world anymore, you should know that better than anyone."

"I don't have the parts to make a baby," she said with voice raised, then cried herself to sleep.

* * *

Her eyes opened. She jumped out of bed. Barely out of the cabin, she keeled over and puked.

Eldon rubbed her back. "Puking in the morning?" he said.

"What?" She wiped her mouth.

"Norah, you're pregnant. The cave brought Tilly and me back to life. I'm sure it can put one in your belly."

"Fuck." She burst into tears.

"We're going to have a baby." He rested his head on her shoulder.

She put her hand over his. "Anything life throws at you, you accept."

He sighed. "Norah, you know that isn't true. I've been through hell and can't afford to step into despair, and even if I could, this wouldn't be something that propelled me there. Our child…" He smiled. "A beautiful thing."

"I'm scared… I don't know who's growing inside my broken womb. What if it isn't even human?"

"We created whoever is inside you." He lifted her chin and gazed into her eyes. "Us." He kissed her forehead. "I'm scared, too, of loving another child. Nash is right there—a hundred years could pass, and he will always be right there." He paused. "This isn't what we planned. I don't throw the word *miracle* around, but…"

*   *   *

Norah visited the inlet daily and wrote with fervour. With so many unanswered questions looming, it was an emotional pregnancy. She was depressed and withdrawn. Hatred attacked her growing body, and guilt ensued. A miraculous pregnancy, with the man she loved, and she could not get her shit together. She worried about letting Eldon down, worried he would decide he'd had enough of her. Neurosis buzzed in her brain. Sound sleep gave way to insomnia, which added another layer of insanity. The one difference: she didn't take it out on Eldon the way she had with other partners. She internalized it.

The last few weeks before the birth, she shifted. Acceptance and love overshadowed the fear and moodiness. Unsure why it transpired, she was grateful nonetheless.

Her stomach expanded until she couldn't stand for even a few seconds. Ida insisted she move into the hotel and go on bedrest. The baby tossed and turned in her stomach relentlessly. Eldon never left her side. He rubbed her stomach and back, played guitar, and served her meals.

"You hungry, Fatty?" he said as he walked into the room.

She rolled her eyes. "Shut up."

"I was talking to the pig." He smirked.

"You're holding my lunch." A smile forced itself out.

"You're gorgeous. I would take you right now." He leaned over and kissed her head.

"That's not gonna happen." She sighed. "I'm so bored. I wish I could binge-watch something. I haven't missed TV until now."

He casually flipped through a fishing magazine. "There was definitely a time and place for it."

"Well, it was all the time back then—pretty gross." She stared out the window.

"Why don't I get a book and read it to you?" He looked proud of his suggestion.

"*The Notebook*," she said, feeling excited.

He shrugged. "I don't know that book, but I'll do my best."

"You don't know *The Notebook*?" She scrunched her face in disbelief.

He returned an hour later, the novel in his hand. Her heart dropped at the sight of him when he walked into the room. *Funny how it still happens*, she thought. She loved everything about him—his wavy hair, his muscly frame. She glanced down at her body and felt disgusted. The pregnancy had brought out the old ugly cancerous cruelty. *How is he even with me?...* Her inner voice attempted to yell reason inside the cruelty of her loud and persistent notions. *Stop, Norah, just stop.* She prayed for remission once she felt a smidge of her normal body, but even this enraged her. What had happened to her unconditional love for herself?

Eldon started reading. It initially felt awkward, but within a few pages, they eased into it. A little over four hours later, he read the last line. Norah sniffled and wiped her tears with the bedsheet. She thought about her pre-Shade cynicism around romance and fairy tales, about the angst in relationships and suffering families, including her own.

"I'm scared the baby will change us." She lay back against her pillows. "We live easy, what if the stress causes us to drift?"

Eldon sighed, took his hat off, and slid his hand over his hair. She could tell he was worn down from her incessant nonsense. "Norah, I know this pregnancy has been hard for you. But you need to reign in your mind. It's racing around looking for things to ruminate on. I see you. No matter what. Why don't you trust that?"

She started to cry. "I don't know. Fuck. I'm sorry. You're getting a glimpse of the old me."

"I love every Norah—Neurotic Norah, Fatty Norah, Sweet Norah, Silly Norah—I love every single bit of you."

"What about—" She gripped the sides of the bed and shrieked into a sudden contraction. She was instantly drenched in sweat, no easing into the pain.

Eldon shouted down the hall.

Ida and Maggie ran into the room. "Did her water break?" Ida asked, a slightly detectable frenzy in her voice.

"I don't know." Eldon's face turned white.

"It didn't break," Norah blurted, lying on her side, profusely sweating.

"We have to break it," Ida said. "Get Brittany," she shouted at Maggie. "We need help."

"Fuck, fuck, no, no…" Norah squeezed Eldon's hand and screamed.

"Breath in," Eldon said.

Norah tightened her grip on his hand. "You try to fucking breath."

From that point, Eldon's lips didn't dare utter advice.

Ida pinned the sac, and water gushed into a puddle. She put dry towels under Norah and checked dilation.

"How many?" Norah gasped.

"Not even close," Ida answered.

"Not close?" Norah bawled her eyes out at the thought of suffering another second. Eldon rubbed her forehead with a warm towel. She noticed the lost look on his face but had no time or sympathy for his confusion. She cried harder.

After eight hours of intense non-stop contractions, Norah entered a trance of exhaustion and pain while she intermittently sucked on laughing gas. She dozed off for a few seconds, then woke to stabbing knives inside her stomach and inaudible frantic murmurings.

"C-section."

"No," she gasped. "Not a c-section."

Ida touched her arm. "I don't know what choice we have?"

"No. No. The baby will die, you don't know—" Norah screamed and dozed off for a second, woke to murmurs.

"You can't cut her open. You have no clue what you're fucking doing!" Eldon shouted.

"I know, Eldon!" Ida yelled back, her voice shaky. "We're gonna lose them both. She's barely dilated, contractions are too close—something's wrong."

Norah hunched over in excruciating pain. She could feel her life force slipping from her grasp. Wretched body. She knew the ending. The woman who died in childbirth before modern medicine and the irony of now being at a state-of-the-art hospital without the knowledge or skill to get her through. Her eyes blurrily surveyed the room: chaos, panic, and fear. She pulled Eldon down, stared into his eyes, and accepted. He could do nothing.

A split second of clarity crept inside the terror. Her lungs filled with air and exhaled resolve. She got to her feet, paced the room, and cupped her belly. She took deep breaths and closed her eyes. The room disappeared, and the pain recessed. "If you go, I go, if you go, I go," she repeated to herself. She pushed hard on her belly, moving her hands down and around the sides to the bottom, again, again. The baby twisted and turned with every burning push, the resolve of their mother. Fight or die. Twenty minutes passed. She felt a low pulling in her pelvis. An urgency to push. She lay on the floor and pushed with every ounce of her spirit and being. Again, and again.

Ida, incoherent through her tears, said, "One more push, Norah, one more push."

Norah pushed, red-faced, veins near exploding, drenched in sweat and blood.

Ida plopped a sweet baby girl on her bare skin. Norah wept relief. Eldon pulled his shirt off and nestled beside them. His tears fell on her chest and rolled onto the baby's arm.

Norah screamed and nearly dropped the baby, overtaken by another fierce urge to push.

"There's another one!" Ida yelled.

Eldon lifted their daughter and held her on his chest while Norah gave birth to their son. Emotion filled the room as Eldon and Norah lay with their babies. Ida sat in the middle of the room and cried. Brittany shouted for the others. Ollie, oblivious to the alternate ending he could have walked into, went over and kissed both babies.

Murph put his hand on Norah's head. He didn't say a word, just fought back tears. Norah looked at him and fell apart into a mess of tears. For a moment, she saw her father. She wiped her eyes and gazed down at her son and daughter. She thought about Theo, his sweet little face. It all meshed together. Tears of joy and grief intertwined as they flooded her face. She touched each forehead.

"Freya and Kitchi, welcome to the world."

CHAPTER 10

SIX YEARS LATER

(TWINS, SIX; TILLY, SEVEN)

"MAMA, COME ON." FREYA TUGGED ON NORAH'S DRESS AND tried to lead her to the swimming hole.

Norah's daughter wanted to spend every second at the inlet. Her swimming abilities were far beyond her six years. With her thick, curly auburn hair flowing past her waist, intense emerald-green eyes with flecks of indigo, and fair opaque skin with tiny brown-indigo freckles splattered over her cheeks, she looked nothing like her parents.

None of the kids resembled their parents—something to do with the indigo water and geode forest. Their blood was reddish-purple and their wounds healed quickly. Their skin tingled with the same magnetic pulse as the earth. Norah could see an indigo aura around them. Since the cave, her sensitivity to energy had heightened. She had been empathic before the Shade; now she could sense Tayo and Brittany fighting from a mile away or Murph's sadness. Eldon's feelings were no longer his own. She felt every frequency of his emotions.

"Freya, we're going swimming soon, I'm helping Kitchi with his painting right now."

Freya jumped on Norah's lap and stroked her face. "I love you, Mama."

"I love you, too, baby." She squeezed her shoulder.

Kitchi jumped off his chair and joined Freya on Norah's lap. He touched her face with his paint-covered hands. He was tall for his age, with black-purple freckles, an olive complexion with a deep indigo hue, blackish-purple eyes, and bone-straight indigo-tinted black hair that was as thick as a horse.

"Kitchi, you're silly." She tickled him.

Freya jumped off Norah's lap and tickled her. Eldon grabbed Kitchi.

"Are you being rough with Mom?" He spun the boy in the air and held him like a potato sack. "That's it, you're going in the river."

Kitchi giggled hysterically. "No, Daddy."

Eldon put him down, and Kitchi karate chopped his leg. Eldon tried to grab him, but he ran outside. "You better run, turkey." He picked up Freya. "How's my little chicken?" She squeezed his nose and kissed him. He put her down and walked over to Norah. "How's my little piggy puff?" He nestled into her neck.

"God, how is that my pet name?" She laughed.

"Because it is." He bit her neck.

Freya tugged on Norah's shirt and continued to beg to go to the swimming hole.

"Can't we just lock them in the cabin and go to the swimming hole alone?" Eldon whispered.

Norah laughed and pushed him away. "Maybe Ollie will watch them later."

He reached down to pick up Freya. "Mama and I want to make more of you."

"Can I help, Daddy?"

"No, we got it, sweetheart."

He winked at Norah, then threw Freya on the bed and tickled her neck. Kitchi and Tilly ran inside in full attack mode and jumped on Eldon's back. They tried to overpower him. Norah pressed his tickle spot. He laughed and tried to free himself from the army. He pinched Norah's inner thigh.

"That's offside." She laughed and pushed him away.

Fatty grumphed and jumped on the bed to join in the fun. The bed-frame busted—again. Fatty often grew tired of sleeping on the floor and tried to jump onto the bed, repeatedly cracking the frame. They tried to make him sleep outside, but he relentlessly scratched the door.

"Fuck sakes, Fatty, not again." Eldon pushed him away.

"Eldon, don't swear in front of the kids."

"Freakin' pig! We might as well put the mattress on the floor."

Norah quieted, knowing it would pass. The pig wore him down, but Eldon loved Fatty. He had even created a small saddle and stirrups so the kids could ride him, and they did, all over the place. Initially, she'd worried he might trample them but realized he would never hurt them. Fatty was an intelligent and easily trained pig if he felt like learning. He adored the kids and grew ferociously protective, even nipped Murph once when he leaned over to pick up Freya. Needless to say, not even the odd scratch was doled out to Fatty by Murph anymore.

Norah shuffled everyone, including Fatty, outside. She could hear Eldon swearing and hammering and couldn't help but giggle at Fatty's oblivious indifference.

"Fatty broke the bed again?" Ollie asked, his voice deep and raspy. Around twenty, he resembled a guy from *The Outsiders*: tall and muscular with a pompadour hairstyle, he wore blue jeans, a black T-shirt with smokes tucked in the sleeve, and a black leather jacket with the collar flipped up. Norah couldn't believe what a handsome man he had grown into. She felt for him the many rites of passage he never experienced. He appeared content, but Norah knew a well-hidden disappointment rested within. The kids idolized him and hung on his every word.

"Yup," Norah said, shaking her head and smiling.

Kitchi and Ollie picked up guitars. Ollie was now a talented musician, and he and Eldon had taught the kids to play once they could grip one steadily. Freya took the small hand drum she had painted and curled up with Norah, the stuffed llama cuddled on her lap. Tilly sat beside Freya and brushed Llama's hair with her hand.

Eldon sat beside Norah and gave her a peck on the cheek. "Sorry." He motioned to Fatty. "You're walking a fine line, pig. I'm slathering oil onto your rock so you'll slide into the river."

Norah laughed. "Eldon!"

"Hey, Ollie, what's up?" he asked.

"Oh, you know, hot date tonight." Ollie smiled.

"Man, I wish it were true for you."

"Daddy, sing a funny!" Kitchi shouted.

"Okay, okay, settle down, fans." Eldon picked up his guitar and strummed the music of "Puff the Magic Dragon" but changing the lyrics.

"Fatty, you little bastard

You broke the bed once more

You think you are a guinea pig

But you almost break the floor

You eat us out of house and home

Not leaving us a crumb

You grunt and squeal and get your way

And you look just like Mom."

"Eldon, for god's sake!" Norah said.

Eldon put his arm around her and bit her ear playfully. She pushed him away and laughed.

Tilly got up to walk back to the hotel, tripped, and fell on a rock. Kitchi jumped up, put his arm around her, kissed her knee, and wiped her tears with his shirt. She lifted her head and smiled. "Thanks, Kitch," she whispered.

Norah's heart melted. Kitchi adored Tilly.

Norah and Eldon often revisited the idea of returning to the cave but always came to the same conclusion: too risky. They wanted to share it with the kids and were pretty sure they would stay together, but "pretty sure" wasn't enough.

Ida had taken up resin projects, resining anything she could get her hands on—coffee tables, pictures, sculptures. She'd also stepped in as resident teacher and held studies in the dining hall, teaching the kids reading and math; the others pitched in too.

Eldon and Murph were helping Tayo build a cottage by the river, an ongoing project. Brittany despised the hotel, especially with Tilly. They had come close to moving to the Ridge but decided against it. She wanted to keep the kids close. Maggie had distanced herself since the twins were born. She still contributed to meals but disappeared soon after. A strain grew in the air.

"Freya, eat your peas, honey," Norah said at dinner that night.

Freya ignored her and flicked the peas in Kitchi's direction. Eldon picked one up, threw it in the air, and caught it in his mouth. Freya tried and missed; luckily, the mess these games created disappeared quickly with Fatty's help.

Kitchi jumped off his chair, walked over to the sink, and passed Maggie his plate.

"Get away, cretin," she murmured under her breath.

But Norah heard it. And she knew why Maggie said it. She had known for years—five-and-a-half years exactly—but kept it to herself, the inevitability of it unravelling lingering. She flashed back to the moment she realized.

Maggie had left her Bible on the table by the fire. Norah had accidentally knocked it to the floor, and when she picked it up, a paper fell out. Her eye caught Kitchi's name.

Kitchi Lucifer in the flesh, Lord. I know. Lord, you confirmed it with a vision. You came to me, prophesized the return of the dark prince in the form of a child, I see his eyes, evil, pure evil, Lord protect me. (For we do not wrestle against flesh and blood, but against the rulers, against authorities, against the cosmic powers over this present darkness, against the spiritual forces of evil in the heavenly places).

Norah looked up. Eldon was standing by Maggie.

"Go see Mom." He sent Kitchi in Norah's direction. "What is it, Maggie?" He looked amped, his face red.

"Nothing," Maggie responded in her shrill, irritating tone.

"You're shooing my kid away. What exactly is your damage?"

"Just leave it, Eldon. We're all entitled to our opinion." Maggie rinsed a dish, unperturbed by the interaction.

Eldon slammed his hand on the table. "Opinion? What the hell does that mean?"

"*Hell*—exactly, that's where he came from," Maggie said, her voice raised.

"Who!" Eldon fumed, but she didn't answer. "Who!" He slammed his fist on the table again.

Norah asked Brittany to take the kids to the cabin, then went over to Eldon. "You need to go. Now."

He clenched his fist and tightened his body. He looked Maggie in the eye. "Stay away from my family, you psychopath." He walked out of the room.

Norah stayed behind. Maggie continued rinsing the dishes, ignoring the depth of the situation.

"Maggie," Norah said sternly. Maggie didn't respond. "Maggie, look at me." Norah reached into the sink and placed her hand over Maggie's. She finally made eye contact. "I have walked a wide circle around you and your beliefs because I know what you have lost, but you crossed a line. My children live here, my son. I will not have him around someone who believes he's the devil." She paused. "You don't love Jesus, you're addicted to fear. Something needs to change. You leave or we leave."

Murph walked through the door. Norah locked eyes with him. A pang of sadness and guilt flipped inside her stomach. Since the twins were born, his relationship with Maggie had been hanging by a thread. He slept in another room and was the only one Norah had told about the Bible incident. He admitted Maggie had gone off the deep end and could do nothing but apologize profusely. Norah didn't blame him; she felt sad for him. His ruggedness softened after Maggie turned unreachable. He held his cards close to his chest. The years left him depressed.

"I'm sorry, Murph. I love you, but this just can't go on."

Maggie dried her hands on a towel, righteously pick up her Bible, and headed out of the room with an air of zero responsibility or humility.

Norah filled with rage. She wanted to slam her against the wall and shake her senseless, but instead she yelled, "Maggie, you're a fucking bitch!"

Maggie stopped, straightened her sweater, lifted her head, and continued to walk. Norah lunged at her.

Murph grabbed her arm and dragged her into the hallway. "Norah! This isn't you. Get back to the cabin!"

Norah tripped into reality. She stared at Murph, shocked at her own reaction. She turned away and headed to the inlet, then plunged into the water and screamed below the surface. Her body calmed. She returned to the cabin, where everyone was gathered around the fire. The children played in the distance with Ollie. She leaned her head on Eldon's shoulder, ashamed at her loss of control.

"It's been going on for too long," Ida said, continuing the conversation.

"Murph won't let Maggie go by herself," Tayo said. "I know they haven't been great for years, but he's loyal—and anyway, Maggie isn't well, it's not right to cast her aside."

Norah sighed. "I know she's not well, but how do we move forward? Her delusions worry me. What if she hears Jesus tell her to do something terrible? It's not that far-fetched, is it? Or have I lost my bearings?"

Brittany nodded. "I feel the same, Norah."

"It was a heated exchange, maybe it can blow over," Eldon said. "We need to revisit tomorrow, after we sleep. Get Maggie and Murph at the table, like a family, and give everyone a chance to share."

"You're right. We all need to talk." Norah paused. "I hate religion. Look at us, only ten left, such bullshit." She paused again. "I've known this for years, but I only ever told Murph. I'm sorry I didn't tell any of you."

Ida raised her eyebrows. "Norah, we knew something was up."

"This is ridiculous," Eldon said. "Me, the father of Lucifer's son, what does that make me? Satan himself?... We'll regroup tomorrow. Ida, maybe you could check on Maggie?"

"I will when I get back to the hotel. I'm sure they both know what's at stake. Come to the dining hall in the morning. Hopefully, we can move past this."

* * *

Norah crawled out of bed. She squeezed her upper arm, bruised and sore from Murph's grip. An unwelcome reminder of yesterday. She headed to the river to meditate and reminded herself how long she had known Maggie, who was present for her wedding and the children's birth. She was part of the family, and Norah needed to show her compassion. What Tayo had said about Maggie being unwell stuck with her. Norah had never considered that her religious fanaticism could be a mental health issue. In reality, she had never considered Maggie. Except for the odd eye-roll.

She dipped her feet in the river, closed her eyes, and focused on Maggie. A pang of irritation hit her stomach. Since the beginning, Norah had tolerated it but couldn't stand her. The way she walked, talked, dressed—everything about her.

Eldon's voice interrupted her solitude. "Norah, come on."

She opened her eyes. *Lotta good that did*, she thought. "Morning." She kissed Eldon. "I was trying to meditate before our meeting today."

"Did it help?" He added a log to the fire.

"No." She sighed. "Not looking forward to this."

"Me either, but it has to happen. Come on, they're probably waiting for us."

Everyone but Ollie, who had volunteered to stay outside with the kids, gathered around the table, waiting for Maggie and Murph.

"Where are they?" Norah pulled a heavy oak chair out from the table and took a seat.

Brittany shrugged. "Haven't seen them yet."

As Norah poured a cup of tea for herself and Eldon, Maggie and Murph shuffled into the dining hall. Murph's face was pale and serious. Maggie held her head high, her Bible clasped in one hand, a cup of water in the other.

Murph nodded. "Morning." His voice sounded weary.

"Morning, Murph." Norah smiled gently. He slightly smiled in response. "Morning, Maggie," Norah said. Maggie didn't utter a word. She set her Bible on the table and clasped her hands on top. Tension rose up inside Norah. *Deep breath, not going there today*, she thought. No one seemed prepared to lead the discussion. It turned into a game of chicken, waiting for someone to break the silence.

Finally, Ida clapped her hands. "Okay," she said, "we need to do this, air it out. I used to run groups." She held up a pen. "We'll go in a circle and use this pen as a talking stick. No one but the person who holds it can talk, no exceptions. I'll start." She paused. "I'm sad to be sitting here. Sad about the conflict. I love all of you and worry about us separating." She paused again. "It's all I have, for now. A start." She passed the pen to Tayo.

"Feels weird," he said. "I mean, we all talk, but not like this. I don't know what to say. I don't want this conflict. Maggie, you've supported me in my recovery and I want to be there for you. I hope we can move forward." He passed the pen to Brittany.

"Don't know what to say." She passed the pen to Eldon.

He was silent for a minute, then sighed. "Yesterday hurt. I haven't felt that angry in… I don't even know when." He stared across the table. "Maggie, for you to think our child is evil is… I don't know how to move forward with this, with you." He sighed and passed the pen to Norah.

"Yesterday was brutal," she said. "I was hurt. I want to apologize for yelling at you and calling you names." She teared up. "Murph, I'm so sorry." She looked at Maggie. "I love my children more than anything, and to hear you say my son is evil… I also don't know how to move forward."

Norah passed the pen to Murph. He immediately handed it to Maggie as if it burned his hands.

She held the pen, took a sip of water, put down the cup, and pulled a piece of paper from her Bible. "I am sorry to hurt any of you," she said, her voice shrill, "but I will not apologize for what the Lord has shown me. I am a vessel, a messenger, what God shows me is not for me to decide. No matter how unfavourable." She unfolded the paper. "For the Lord has—"

"Shut up, Maggie," Murph said, his face red, furious. "Just shut up." He tore the paper out of her hand and ripped it to pieces. "You don't know how to stop. Do you remember our children! What if someone told you one of our children was evil?"

"Murph, our children were not evil, and if the Lord himself told me they were, then how could I argue?" she said righteously.

Murph picked up her Bible and threw it against the wall. He stared at everyone around the table and then walked out quietly.

Silence. A cemented reality of hopelessness. Nowhere to go. Tayo nodded and walked out of the room; one by one, they disappeared, until Norah and Maggie were left alone at the table. Norah tried to find words—something—but couldn't. Emotionless, Maggie rose from her chair and collected her Bible. She poured herself another glass of water and walked out of the room.

Norah caught up with Eldon. "Maybe you should check on Murph," she said. "I've never seen him like that."

"I think he needs to cool down. I'll check after a dip. I need to stop thinking about this." He continued to walk down the path.

"Where are the kids? I didn't see them playing?"

"Ollie took them for a walk."

"Just stop." She grabbed the back of his shirt and hugged him. He rubbed the back of her hair.

"We're gonna be okay," he said quietly.

They walked to the inlet, floated in the water, and voraciously meshed bodies. Norah stopped midway.

"Something's wrong." She rushed out of the water.

"What? Come on, one more minute, you can't leave me like this," Eldon said, trying to lure her back.

Without answering, she put her clothes on and rushed toward the hotel.

"I'm still hard, for god's sake," Eldon said as he caught up to her.

"Eldon, something's wrong. What the hell were we doing anyway?"

Tayo met them at the end of the path. His dark skin was ashen green.

"What is it?" Eldon asked.

Tayo steadied himself on a nearby tree. He kneeled, struggling to take in air. Norah's entire body flooded with a ringing silence. Her hand gripped Eldon's and her feet stepped robotically in slow motion down the path. Brittany was on the ground outside of the hotel, her arms wrapped tightly around her stomach, puking and wailing. Screams were bellowing from inside the hotel.

Norah put her hand on Brittany's back. "What is it?"

"It's—" She gagged. "Murph," she wailed.

"Where is he? Where are the kids?" Eldon asked.

Tayo crouched down and held Brittany. "With Ollie."

Inside, the wailing led them to the storage room. Norah took in the scene. Her eyes fought the truth. Knees crashed to the floor.

Murph's stocky, lifeless body hung by an old extension cord. Maggie, her face was wet with snot and spit, was clutching his feet, screaming. Ida, shell-shocked, was trying to lift the body down. Maggie wouldn't let go. Eldon fell down and leaned his head on Norah's back.

Tayo tried to pull Maggie away from Murph's body. "Get the fuck away from me," she shrieked, turning her rage on him as she hit him over and over until she fell limp in his arms. A second later, she pushed him and stumbled away.

Eldon and Tayo lifted Murph's body while Norah and Ida stood on a stepstool and pulled the cord from around his neck.

They laid his body on the cold tile floor. Norah lifted his head in her arms and wailed. She kissed his forehead and placed her sweater under his head. Tayo laid a blanket over his body. Norah left the storage room.

Ollie walked into the hotel, oblivious, and the kids ran towards Norah.

"Stop!" she yelled. The kids stopped in their tracks.

Ollie looked past Norah and caught a glimpse of Murph's feet. He started to back up. "Come on, you guys." He bumped into a table and turned around to shuffle them outside.

"Mama, what happened?" Freya yelled.

"Just go with Ollie."

Norah helped wrap the body in a blanket. Eldon wheeled it outside on a stretcher, away from the kids. Ida placed a bucket of water and bleach outside the door of the storage room. She passed Norah a pair of rubber gloves and pulled some on herself. They didn't say a word. As Norah pulled on the gloves and grabbed a mop, she flashed back to her attack. She plunged the mop into the water and began cleaning the fluids and potent stench of death. With every push of the mop, she gagged. She glanced up at the storage room ceiling, then fell to her knees and fought for air. Ida squeezed her arm, right on the bruise Murph left. Norah let out a shriek of unbearable pain. Sweat poured down her face. She braced herself with the mop handle and stood, stared down at the floor, and continued to mop.

*　*　*

Norah wiped her brow. An overpowering stench of bleach now masked the tragedy. She squeezed Ida's hand as they robotically stared into the vacant storage room. They headed outside to find the kids, instead finding Ollie alone by the fire. His eyes were clouded with despair.

She struggled to find words. "Where are the kids?" she finally asked.

"At the inlet with Eldon." His voice sounded numb.

"Let's go." Norah reached out her hand.

Ollie grabbed it and started to get up, then sat back down. "Why?" He stared at Norah, his eyes lost.

Norah put her arm around him. "I don't know."

When they reached the inlet, the kids were swimming while everyone else sat around the fire, sniffling, eyes red and swollen, swirling inside tragedy. Norah plopped down beside Eldon and nestled into him.

Tayo broke the silence. "The body can't stay there long. It needs to be buried."

"Tayo!" Brittany scolded.

Eldon nodded. "He's right. There's no refrigeration."

"Do the kids know?" Norah asked.

Eldon let out a sigh. "I tried."

"Guess I'll deal with that too," Norah snapped.

Eldon pulled away so he could see her face. "What?"

"I spent the last two hours cleaning death, and you *tried*?"

"Sorry." He squeezed her shoulder.

Norah put her head in her lap and bawled, "I can't fucking believe this."

"You told me to check on him. I should've checked on him," Eldon said, shaky.

"Listen to me, all of you," Ida said. "It's nobody's fault. We can't turn on each other." She whimpered.

The kids ran out of the water. Kitchi cuddled into Norah's lap, Freya into Eldon's.

"Mama, why is everyone sad?" Kitchi asked.

Norah took a breath, "Kitch—"

Eldon interrupted her. "Kitchi, something sad happened today. Our friend Murph died." He choked back tears.

"Will he come back?" Kitchi asked.

"No, sweetheart," Norah whispered. "He's gone."

Freya furrowed her brows. "Where did he go?"

Nora took her daughter's hands in hers. "Freya, when someone dies, we don't know where they go. It's a mystery. I believe they go somewhere beautiful."

"Beautiful like our swimming hole?" Tilly asked.

"Yes, Til," Brittany said.

Kitchi used his toe to draw circles in the sand. "If it's beautiful, why are you sad?"

"We're sad because we won't see Murph anymore, visit with him, play games," Tayo said.

"Not ever?" Tilly asked.

He squeezed her shoulder. "No, Til, not ever again."

"I miss Murph," Freya whispered.

"All of us do," Ollie said. "Maybe he'll visit us in our dreams."

Kitchi's expression brightened. "Really?"

"Maybe." Ollie looked down and played with the sand.

CHAPTER 11

A SOBER STATE OF SHOCK AND SADNESS WEIGHED NORAH down. She couldn't focus on anything. Murph's suicide had brought her the closest she had been to visceral death since she had lost Theo. Eldon and Tayo built a coffin—*"Not fancy,"* Eldon said, but good enough. Norah couldn't help but laugh at the coffin. Eldon was a talented builder but wasn't joking when he said it wasn't fancy. It reminded her of something sixth-graders would build in shop class. The children decorated: hearts, stars, glitter, animals, and paint splatters, with *Murph* scribbled on the top.

"We're going to the church to dig a burial hole," Eldon said. "We'll come back when it's done. We can pull the body in the coffin on the bike trailers and all go together. Norah, you should check on Maggie. She should be a part of this."

She knew he was right. She and Ida knocked on Maggie's door. It was open a crack. Norah pushed it open. Maggie was sitting on the floor in the middle of the room in one of Murph's shirts, her body gently rocking back and forth.

"Maggie," Norah said quietly. She didn't answer or acknowledge them. "Maggie," Norah said again. No response. She walked up slowly and touched Maggie's shoulder.

Maggie flipped around and pushed Norah, who slipped and fell against the door.

"Maggie, stop!" Ida yelled, then helped Norah to her feet.

Maggie plunged towards them, landed on the floor, and screamed. She crawled towards Norah's feet and tried to grab her. They shuffled out of the room and closed the door. The sound of Maggie's sobs echoed.

"What do we do?" Norah asked, her legs shaking from the altercation.

"I don't think there is a lot we can do," Ida said. "We can't make this any easier for her."

Norah and Ida found Brittany sitting in the gazebo, her legs slung over the oversized leather chair. A cigarette dangled from the side of her mouth. "Here," she said, passing Norah a smoke.

Norah put it between her lips and puffed into the flame of the lighter Brittany held. She inhaled a deep drag and sat down.

"I've never seen you smoke?" Norah said.

"I used to for a year or so. Found these in Murph's room on the side table. Didn't even know he smoked." She puffed lightly on her cigarette.

"I did." Norah smiled. "Used to sneak away with him all the time."

Brittany flicked her cigarette into the fire and stared at Norah. "How do we get through this?"

"We won't. But we will learn to live with it. Eventually."

"Give me one of those," Ida said, reaching for the cigarettes. She lit her smoke and rested her head on Norah's shoulder.

Brittany lit another smoke. They sat together in heartbroken silence. The dinner gong bellowed.

Eldon and Tayo looked exhausted. The coffin holding Murph's body was loaded onto the bike trailer. The others, except Maggie, walked in a procession down the path to the church. They carried the coffin to the edge of the burial hole. Beside it stood a large white boulder.

Eldon wiped the sweat off his forehead. "We placed him with his hammer, hiking boots, a picture of Maggie, and his favourite flannel shirt."

"You etched Murph's name into the bench. Beautiful," Ida said as she studied the antique wrought-iron bench beside the gravesite.

Time blurred while they shared memories of their dear friend. Norah read the poem from *Love Letters from Death*. Brittany stared vacantly for most of the service. Eldon shared the "fucking in the closet" story, and Tayo strummed his guitar.

"Murph," Ida said. "Maggie's love. Father of five. Grandfather of eight. Friend to many. You will be missed. Fly free now, my friend." She sniffled.

They stood in silence, staring at the coffin in disbelief.

Each of them grabbed the coffin and lifted. It wouldn't budge. Eldon went inside the church and returned moments later with curtains. They worked together to shimmy the fabric underneath and created handles on each side.

They managed to lift the coffin slightly enough to move. Norah physically shook from the weight. They suspended the coffin over the hole, and halfway down, unsure of who lost their grip first, the coffin slammed into the hole. Murph's dishevelled body ended up sideways, mangled underneath the painted coffin. They stared down at the carnage, unable to comprehend the insanity of what had transpired.

"Well, shit," Eldon said as if he'd just bought the wrong kind of lettuce.

Norah manically tried to stuff a giggle down, to the point where her body hurt. She lost the fight and burst into uncontrollable laughter. Like dominoes, one by one, they all ended up in stitches. Every time someone tried to speak, they ended up in another bout of hysteria.

"That's all, Murph," Eldon said with a nod as the laughter dwindled. "He would've fucking loved that." He grabbed a shovel, lifted some dirt, and dropped it in the hole. Norah started singing "Amazing Grace." She hadn't thought of that song in ages. Everyone joined in and cried as they took turns scattering dirt over their friend.

* * *

Maggie's Bible sat on the table, untouched, like an abandoned orphan. She had taken to the drink days after Murph died. Empty vodka bottles scattered the hotel. Everyone struggled to give her words of comfort because none existed. Norah and Ida were hesitant to reach out, especially after the last attempt, but decided to try.

Norah knocked on her door. No answer. They went inside. Maggie was passed out on her bed. A rotten stench permeated the room. Bottles were heaped into piles in the open closet. Ida cracked the window.

"What do you want?" Maggie grumbled, squinting her eyes.

"We're worried about you, Maggie—the drinking. You haven't picked up your Bible in weeks," Ida said.

"Worried? You sounded worried when you were kicking us out on our asses," she slurred.

"Maggie, we wanted to work it out," Norah said.

"Burn in hell."

Norah and Ida looked at each other, at a loss for words.

"We're here if you need us," Norah said, lightly brushing Maggie's shoulder.

"Just get out, you filthy harlots!" She threw a bottle at the wall.

* * *

Norah woke drenched in sweat. The night terrors had quieted over the past couple of months but still visited on occasion. She knew sleep wouldn't return, so she stretched her sweater over her head and went outside. As she walked up the path to the church, she noticed a light in the hotel. *Maybe Ida's up*, she thought and quietly went to the dining hall. Maggie was sitting on the floor by the fire. She ripped out a page from her Bible and tossed it in the flames.

"Maggie, what are you doing?" Norah asked.

Maggie didn't acknowledge her. "I killed him, I killed my Murph." She rocked back and forth. "It was me. I blame everyone, and it was me. I killed him." She ripped out another page and tossed it in the fire. "He was right about the Lord. He ain't no shepherd. I killed him. I killed my Murph." She gasped for air. "I killed him. I killed my Murph."

Norah sat on the floor beside her, certain she had landed in the nucleus of a psychotic break. She sat with her for two hours and didn't say a word. Finally, Maggie stood up. She threw her Bible in the fire and walked out. Norah returned to the cabin, curled up with Eldon, and closed her eyes.

Freya jumped in the bed and snuggled between them. "Daddy, I love you." She kissed him.

Kitchi jumped in a second later. Norah was hypnotized by his black-indigo eyes. He and Freya were inseparable, their hands never apart. Norah called them her shooting stars born into the flesh.

*   *   *

"Morning, Ida," the kids said as they ran over to Ida, who was cooking breakfast.

Ida looked up at Norah. "Norah, you look rough. Didn't you sleep?" Norah told her about the night. "You should've woken me."

"It's okay. Eldon's taking the kids to the inlet later. I'll take a nap."

The others trickled in for breakfast. The kids ran around and played hide and seek while Eldon and Tayo strummed their guitars. It was a peaceful morning.

Maggie strutted in adorned in her Sunday best. She lifted the charred Bible out of the fireplace and walked outside. They watched out the window as she headed down the path.

As she dried dishes an hour later, Norah looked at Eldon and said, "Someone should check on Maggie, it's been over an hour."

"And by 'someone' you mean me?" Eldon shrugged his shoulders.

Norah smiled playfully. "By 'someone,' I mean start walking to the church."

"You're bossy," he said with a smirk.

"I'll come with you, okay?" She dried the last dish and placed it in the cupboard. "Ida, can you watch the kids?"

*   *   *

They found Maggie sitting on the bench beside Murph's grave. Norah noticed the charred Bible perched on the rock.

"You did a nice job with his stone," Maggie said quietly, her voice clear.

"Eldon did it." Norah joined her on the bench.

"Murph was a good guy," Eldon said.

"He was." Maggie paused. "I burned my Bible."

"Why?" he asked.

"It's complicated." She stared at the gravesite. "You know, I used to be a mess. I trolled bars and men well into my early thirties."

"I didn't know," Norah said, surprised at how little she actually knew about Maggie.

"I was a wreck in red lipstick and painted jeans." She shook her head. "I saw Murph at my nightly stomping ground—he wasn't a regular. I tried everything to seduce him, but he wasn't having it. He brought me home and tucked me into bed. It was the only time I didn't wake up next to some drunken fool." She smiled. "I felt rejected and was determined to make up for it with some idiot the next night… A few nights later, he came back, and I tried again. Same thing—I woke up classy tucked in my bed. Went on for six months. One morning, I woke up to him sitting on my couch, reading the newspaper. I wasn't used to seeing a sober man in the morning. I felt embarrassed. He looked at me and said, 'When are you going to stop this and be my wife?' I said, "Be your wife?' and laughed. He left. I was in a tizzy, thinking, 'Who does he think he is coming here and talking like that?'" She wiped her tears. "He was at the bar every night after. Sometimes, I would go home for a romp with another man, sometimes with him to get tucked in. Went on for a year." She paused and smiled. "One morning, he said, 'I love you, Maggie, but I'm leaving. This is the last time you'll see me.' I realized I loved him too. The first time I laid with a man sober. I quit drinking that day. We were inseparable and had our family. Five years later, I picked up the bottle and put my family through hell. Went to AA and got sober. Grew close to Carla, a born-again Christian, and insisted Murph marry me. The rest is history."

Eldon shook his head. "What a story."

"He tolerated me after I found the Lord. I knew he wasn't thrilled, but he put up with it." She looked at them. "It wasn't God who saved me. It was Murph." She burst into tears. "And now I don't know who I am without either of them."

"You don't have to leave God." Norah passed her a Kleenex.

Maggie sniffled and dabbed her eyes with the tissue. "No, I guess I don't." She looked at them again. "I'm sorry." Her voice was sincere and kind.

"Water under the bridge." Eldon put his hand on her shoulder.

"The kids… They're different. It scares me."

"Life has always been scary," Norah said. "Before the Shade, kids were spoiled. Now they're a little mauve."

Maggie laughed. "I'm going to sit for a while, alone, if you don't mind."

They nodded. Eldon started to walk in the wrong direction, towards the city.

"Where are you going?" Norah asked.

"I'm going to get Maggie a new Bible from the bookstore."

Norah grabbed his hand and joined him, touched by his thoughtfulness and capacity to forgive.

When they returned, Maggie hadn't moved. Eldon placed the gift bag on the bench. Her hand shook as she lifted the bag and pulled out a classic leather-bound Bible. Unable to fight tears, she whispered, "Thank you."

As she and Eldon made their way home, Norah glanced back. Maggie was flipping through her new Bible. Norah never thought she would feel such relief to see her holding the holy book.

*　*　*

Kitchi sat at the dining hall table with a scattered pile of pencil crayons spread around his sketchbook.

Norah's eye caught a glimpse of his drawing, and she gasped. "Eldon, did you tell him?"

Eldon leaned over Kitchi's shoulder and studied his drawing. He shook his head. "No."

"Kitchi, what is this?" Her voice shook.

"It's our place." He continued drawing.

"Have you been there?" Eldon asked.

"We play there in our sleep."

"Yeah, in the flowers." Freya bounced onto Norah's lap.

Goosebumps covered Norah's arms. "What is this?" She pointed at the scribbled drawing of the labyrinth.

"Where we play hide and seek."

Norah and Eldon stared at each other.

Norah flipped through the sketchbook; the pictures exploded with detail. She put her arm around Kitchi and set the sketchbook down on the table. "Come on, sweetheart, let's go to the inlet."

The children bolted out the door and down the path.

"What the hell was that?" Norah asked Eldon when they reached the beach.

Eldon shrugged. "We'll probably never know." He kneeled and picked up a football lying on the sand. "Head's up," he yelled at Tayo on the other side of the beach.

Norah plopped herself down on the sand. "Hey, Brit, you guys been here all day?"

"Pretty much. Tilly is obsessed with the rope swing Eldon put up."

Norah watched the kids play. Tilly and Freya were on the swing and Kitchi was wearing his goggles, searching for treasures.

"You'll never guess what just happened," Norah said.

"What?"

"Kitchi's—"

"Mommy, look!" Tilly yelled, her hands and legs wrapped around the swing as she readied to let go.

"Lookin' good!" Brittany yelled back. "I swear to god, this is the twentieth time I said that today." She laughed. "What were you about to say? Oh yeah, how was Maggie?"

"Genuine. It was a real conversation. I think she's going to be okay."

"I hope so. She's been through hell."

"I know. It's been so hard since Murph." She paused. "I looked through Kitchi's sketchbook, it—"

"Mom!" Freya shrieked.

Tilly was hanging off the rope swing by her hair.

Brittany and Tayo charged over and untangled her hair from the rope. Tilly squealed in pain.

"She slammed on the rock," Freya said.

Brittany laid Tilly on the beach and frantically scanned her body for injuries. Only a tiny scrape was visible on her shoulder. "Til, talk to me," Brittany said, rubbing her forehead.

"I'm okay, Mommy," she whimpered.

Freya tugged on Norah's dress.

Norah shuffled her away. "Just a sec."

Freya pulled harder. "Mama!" she cried out.

"What is it?" Norah snapped, looking over at her daughter.

Freya pointed at Kitchi, who was halfway up the path towards the cave.

"Kitchi, come back here now!" Norah screamed.

He walked faster. Eldon, Norah, and Ollie bolted after him. Freya lagged behind.

"Get back, Freya!" Norah yelled.

Freya ignored her.

Kitchi stood at the cave opening, his foot about to enter.

Eldon pulled the back of his shirt. It slipped out of his hand and Kitchi tumbled inside.

"Kitchi!" Norah screamed.

Eldon grabbed her. She grabbed Ollie. He grabbed Freya. They all tumbled inside and rolled onto the indigo clover. Kitchi was far ahead, racing toward the labyrinth. Freya let go of Ollie's hand and chased after him. Norah felt drunk from the dense energy, her eyes blurry and body dizzy. The kids looked to be unaffected. Freya caught up to Kitchi, and they ran through the current with no struggle. Norah yelled as they plummeted towards the roots. It was no use. She grabbed Eldon's hand. Electricity surged through her body as she pushed her way through the current.

Kitchi's hand was an inch away from the root.

"No!" Norah begged him to stop and continued to fight the current.

Kitchi touched the root. He didn't explode or get thrust back. He gripped the root, climbed up, and held out his hand to help Freya. Norah reached the unearthed tree and leaned on the root. Kitchi stretched his hand towards her and smiled. She gripped it, pulled herself onto the root, and put her arms around them, her stomach sick from what could have been.

Freya wiped away Norah's tear. "See, Mommy, we're safe."

"Come on," Norah whispered, "Daddy wants to hug you. You scared us."

"Can we stay, Mommy?" Kitchi asked.

"Yes. But not forever. Our family will miss us," Norah assured him.

The kids jumped off the root and ran over to Eldon. He squeezed and kissed them.

Ollie gave them big hugs. "So, this is the cave?"

"You finally get to see it," Norah said.

The adults lay on the ground and let the indigo clover tickle their skin while the children played hide and seek around the glowing geodes.

Eldon kissed Norah's cheek and glanced at Ollie. "Will you keep an eye on them?"

"Sure," Ollie said.

"Don't touch those roots," Eldon warned.

"Eldon, what about the kids?" Norah asked.

"Norah, we can't protect them. If anything, they'll protect us." He tugged on her arm. "Come on."

It had been long since they had lain in the flowers together. Norah followed Eldon to a private spot surrounded by geodes on the far side of the cave and let the energy envelop their bodies.

Afterward, Norah laid her head on his chest and caught her breath. "Thank you."

Eldon played with her hair. "For what?" he whispered.

"For seeing me. Loving me."

"I don't know who I was without you. I remember hearing that you needed to find yourself to find real love. Well, I found myself inside our love. Thank you." He kissed her gently and twisted into her body again.

"We need to get back to the kids." Norah kissed him and slipped on her dress.

∗   ∗   ∗

"We wanna show you."

Kitchi and Freya pulled Norah, Eldon, and Ollie towards the minuscule slants of light. Kitchi reached out his hand to touch one.

Norah remembered the pressure and burning from years ago. "Kitchi, no." She slapped his hand away.

"Mama, it's okay." He placed his hand over the slant.

The slant widened. They shielded their eyes from the intense light.

Norah peeked through her fingers slightly. "Kitchi! How did you do that?" she asked.

Freya placed her hand on the same slant. It closed. The twins turned it into a game, narrowing and widening the slants of light.

"Freya, enough—"

"Hi, guys." Tilly ran past Norah towards the kids.

Norah looked back to see Brittany and Tayo fighting the current. Her heart filled at the sight of them. "I can't believe you followed." She hugged Brittany.

"I know." Brittany smiled.

"We haven't been in here for months, have we?" Eldon asked her.

"Not that we know of. We followed you right after. It took us a while to adjust to the energy." Tears welled up in Brittany's eyes while she watched Tilly place her hand on a slant and open it. "What the hell is that?" Brittany covered her eyes.

"No clue," Eldon said.

"Those roots, were they the ones that killed Eldon?" Tayo asked, his hood pulled over his eyes.

"Don't touch them," Eldon said seriously.

"Close it," Norah shouted at the kids.

Tilly placed her hand on the slant and laughed as it closed. Norah stared as the children, in unison, placed their hands on the same slant. It widened into a door-sized opening. Sunlight beamed into the cave.

CHAPTER 12

GOLDEN AND TEAL MOSS MELTED BETWEEN NORAH'S TOES. She was not in a cave but under an open blue sky with thick cotton clouds and a massive bright sun. She lay on the moss and basked in the warm light. Her body had forgotten the warmth. She realized it was silent. Her ears had grown accustomed to the faint humming of the moon. She studied the flat and solid wall they had passed through from the cave. No visible slants or openings.

Three deer leaped in the distance. The kids charged towards them. The deer didn't move or get startled.

Norah heard howling. "Did you hear that?" she asked.

"Maybe a coyote," Eldon said.

A fallen tree, double the size of Rockefeller and equally as wide, connected to the labyrinth of roots on the other side of the cave. Golden, indigo, and teal leaves dotted the intertwined branches that protruded in every direction. The barkless trunk was blanketed in indigo moss and tiny icicle-like geodes. A thick indigo geode glowed inside the centre and shot through the branches.

Norah kneeled and plucked some indigo moss. The moment it touched her hand it turned into a soft talcum powder. "We need to find a way to get back. We have no food or water." She blew the powder out of her hand and clapped her hands together.

"You're right, the kids haven't eaten in a while."

"Mommy, come on," bellowed Tilly's voice from the corner of a massive branch.

Behind the branch, the kids stood at the edge of an endless shimmering golden lake. An enormous teal geode glowed on the shoreline, with branches protruding out like a tree with dangling golden leaves. The untouched beach was blanketed with sparkling indigo pebbles and teal and golden sand the texture of talcum powder.

Goosebumps covered Norah's body. "What do you—" A wasp buzzed in her face. "Shit. I hate them." She swatted manically around her face.

"Should we go in?" Tayo asked.

"I'm not—"

Without warning, Eldon whipped by in his underwear and catapulted himself into the lake.

"Eldon!" Norah yelled.

He splashed around, laughing. Suddenly he was pulled under. His arms flailed as he fought for air. The water turned still.

Tayo jumped in after him.

"Jesus, Tayo!" Brittany yelled.

Tayo was pulled under. The water stilled.

Norah's face flushed. Her body shook. The kids screamed at the shoreline. Brittany started hyperventilating.

"I'm going in," Ollie said, running towards the lake. Norah tripped him face-first onto the sand.

Like dolphins, Eldon and Tayo jumped up from the water, hysterically laughing.

"Are you kidding me?" Anger flushed Norah's face.

Tayo splashed around. "Come in, the waters nice."

"Go to hell," Brittany said furiously. "I can't believe you."

"I'm sorry." Eldon smiled.

"You're sorry?" Norah snapped. "It's idiots like you who always die first. And you traumatized the kids."

"You're both absolute morons." Brittany shook her head at Norah.

"Come on, don't stay mad," Tayo begged.

Eldon began slow dancing with Tayo. "I guess it's you and me."

Norah stared at Brittany. "I can't believe we're with these fools."

Eldon ran out of the water and charged at her. She screamed and tried to run away. He potato-sacked her over his shoulder and tossed her in the lake. The water was softer and colder than the water in the inlet. A subtle translucent residue shimmered on her skin. The kids jumped in, playful laughter echoing across the water as they tried to push the guys under.

"Do you think we should drink it?" Ollie asked.

Norah filled her mouth with water and swallowed—not minty, but a touch of floral sweetness. They all quenched their thirst with the golden water.

Given their lack of exposure to the sun's rays for so many years, Norah was surprised their skin wasn't starting to burn. Before the Shade, Brittany's fair skin would have turned the colour of a cooked lobster within ten minutes.

"We need to go back," Norah said, trying to be the voice of reason. "We have no clue about the time warp. Ida and Maggie could be old women by the time we return."

"How do we even get back?" Ollie asked.

Norah turned to Kitchi. "Can you open another slant?"

"Don't know." He shrugged and stared at his sand sculpture.

They returned to the tree and spent hours walking around its edge. No slants anywhere. Defeated and hungry, they sat on the tree trunk to regroup.

Norah noticed Freya eating small clumps of moss. "Freya, don't eat that. It could be poison."

"It's sugar, Mama."

"How much have you eaten?"

Freya didn't answer.

Norah plucked a tiny clump and put it on her tongue. The texture and taste of floral icing sugar, it melted on her tongue. She collapsed. Faces melted and contorted into putty. Voices warped as if they were being played on a broken record player. Her body floated towards the sun and she could see herself below, lying on the ground, everyone gathered around her in a frenzy. Floating higher and higher, she stopped at the halo of the sun. A door opened. Now inside the moon, she exited through another door and landed at the inlet. Her feet floated above the ground beside the hotel. She looked through a window and saw Maggie and Ida playing cards as Fatty rested by the fire. Norah slammed her hands against the glass. Maggie robotically walked over to the window and stared out, blood pouring out of her eyes while she slammed her Bible into the glass over and over until the glass shattered.

Norah stumbled backward and fell. She landed inside the mansion at the Ridge and was sitting at the table with Theo. He held the Monopoly dice in his hands and laughed maniacally. Seamus put his hands on her shoulders and kissed the top of her head. His face melted into her skull and pushed her down. She sank deeper and deeper into the ground. Theo screamed and tried to pull her up.

Unable to breathe, she spun inside a vortex and landed outside the shed, which was raging on fire. She fell to her knees, crawled to the window, and tried to climb inside. Her hands melted and fused with the windowsill. The black bird flew out and pecked her eyes. She fell over and landed in the cave. Geodes exploded into shrapnel and indigo volcanoes erupted from the ground.

She lifted herself into the labyrinth. The roots turned into snakes and strangled her. She woke up underwater, struggling for air. She fought her way to the shore of a river she had never seen. It was surrounded by fruit trees. She picked an indigo peach with fuzzy skin. Her teeth bit down.

Her body sunk deeper into the earth until she landed in a pitch-black room. A hand grabbed her ankle and yanked. She closed her eyes and screamed until she landed on a cold table made of rock. A foreign tribe, dressed in gold, surrounded her. Seamus and Theo joined a young boy and a stunning woman. They both had cinnamon skin and long horse-like golden hair with brown highlights, and raised golden scars covered their bodies. The woman lifted a sharp weapon and stabbed it into Norah's chest. Norah gagged on her own blood and rolled off the table. She landed on a pile of branches.

Her eyes were drawn to a slight slant of light. She reached out and touched it and woke inside the teal geode in the middle of the lake. A young girl with indigo freckles waited on the other side with her hands outstretched. A door opened. The girl laid her hand on Norah's arm. A golden light swirled around the wound and it disappeared. The geode led to a tunnel with flowering vines hanging from the ceiling and an opening at the end. She stepped through the opening.

Her feet landed on a flat rock surrounded by water. The sun blazed down. Dark figures ran towards her. A red shadow demon with bloody golden eyes and bat-like teeth swooped in and bit Norah's cheek. She slipped off the rock, fell into the water, and drowned.

* * *

Norah's eyes opened. She gasped for air and screamed. She trembled on Eldon's lap while he stroked her hair.

"How long was I gone?" she asked.

"Ten minutes." He kissed her forehead. His face was pale.

"Am I bleeding?" She touched her face.

"You were. It's slowed down. Jesus, Norah, what happened?"

She shook. "Is there a bite mark on my cheek?"

"How do you know?"

"I know where the slant is," she said.

"How?"

"I saw it. I might know where some food is too."

"I know what you saw, Mama," Kitchi said.

"Kitchi, *I* don't even know what I saw."

"You saw the other place, it's in my dreams."

"I think we're in an in-between," Norah said. "A crossover to another place, like the cave to the moon. I saw it, there's an opening inside a geode." She leaned on Eldon. "Come on, let's go find food."

She guided everyone to the river. The fruit trees were exactly as she had envisioned. The fruit was delicious and fresh. They rested and then she led them to the wall at the base of the tree. The slant was precisely where it had appeared in her vision.

No more frolicking. The kids opened the slant and everyone pushed their way through the current. Tayo and Tilly were the last to leave. Tayo picked up Tilly and plopped her outside of the cave. Brittany took her hand and waited for Tayo. Several seconds passed, but Tayo never appeared.

"He's in there, he's still in there!" Brittany screamed into the empty opening.

"I'm going back," Eldon said.

Norah shot daggers at him. "We promised, Eldon. You know you won't find him. We need to go to the hotel and wait."

"We found you in there," Brittany pleaded.

"Brit, it's a one-off. Every other time, it's been a time warp. It's not going to help Tayo if he returns and you're gone, not to mention the kids."

* * *

"How long, Ida?" Norah said, startling Ida in the dining hall.

"Norah!" She hugged her. "A year—it's been devastatingly quiet." She surveyed the group of returnees. "Where's Tayo?"

Tilly wrapped herself around Brittany like a koala bear. Eldon lowered his head.

"No…" The colour drained from Ida's face.

"No, no…" Maggie whimpered.

"He didn't come out of the cave," Norah stammered in shock. "He was right behind us."

"Hope he'll be back soon, Mama," Kitchi said.

Brittany sat at the table and nestled into Tilly. Ida pulled up a chair beside them and put her arms around them. Kitchi and Freya joined.

Brittany lifted her head. She looked pale and sick. "I need to go lay down."

"Do you want me to come with you?" Norah ached for them.

"I need to be alone." She looked at Ida. "Can Tilly stay with you?"

Ida forced a smile. "I'd love to spend time with Tilly."

Brittany let Tilly go and stumbled off, her hand cupped over her stomach.

Norah went to the cabin and wrote down everything she remembered from her vision. Still high from the hallucination, her body felt like it was floating on a cloud.

* * *

Norah jerked up from a dead sleep, gasping for air and clutching her neck. The red shadow demon had been choking her while she was paralyzed in sleep. The moonlight reminded her she was safe. She wiped her sweat-drenched face with a sheet, then ran her fingers down her cheek and touched the fresh bite mark.

She planted her feet on the uneven hardwood floor, then slipped into a sweater and jogging pants. As she made her way from the cabin to the hotel, her bare feet pressed into the magnetic earth.

Norah walked into the dining hall and plopped beside Fatty, who was sprawled out on his cushion. "What's on your face, sweetheart?" She scratched his double chin.

"It's peanut butter." Ida smiled. "His emotional eating got pretty out of control when you were gone."

"Oh, Fatty, I understand—believe me." She leaned her cheek on his belly.

"Hey." Brittany sat on the couch and pulled a blanket over her feet. Her face was pale and makeup-free, not even lip gloss.

"Brit, I'd ask you how you are, but…"

"I can't fall apart. I have Tilly." Her voice trembled. She lifted her water bottle to her lips. Her hands noticeably shook.

"What's going on?" Norah asked.

Brittany put the water bottle down. Her face turned white and became drenched in sweat. She gasped for air.

Norah plunged beside her and put her hand on her back. "Breathe, Brittany. Breathe." She smoothed her hair.

Ida passed her a cool cloth.

"I'm—" She gasped again and put her head between her legs. "I'm pregnant," she blurted.

Norah stared at Ida. Both women's eyes widened in shock.

Brittany lifted her head and wiped her face with the cloth. She looked terrified. "In the sun, we snuck away. I said to him after, 'We're having another baby.' He laughed. I told him I was serious. I could feel it. It was so bizarre."

"Are you sure, Brit? We've only been back for a few days?"

"I'm sure." She put her head back down between her legs.

* * *

Brittany was pregnant, and her pregnancy was nothing like her first. Her insides burned constantly and her stomach was hot to the touch. She was drenched in sweat every second of every day and had many sleepless nights. The only relief she found was by floating in the inlet. After a full-term pregnancy, her labour was a merciless sixteen hours. She prayed for death out loud and with a vengeance. A few times she promised to kill Tayo if he ever returned.

Despite the struggle, beautiful baby Sunny was born. She weighed only five pounds and was gorgeous. She had light mocha skin, golden eyes flecked with indigo, and fine, bone-straight dark-brown hair with golden zigzag streaks.

Norah knew the instant she laid eyes on her. Sunny was the child from her vision.

CHAPTER 13

FIVE YEARS LATER

(SUNNY, FIVE; TWINS, ELEVEN; TILLY, TWELVE)

THE YEARS FORCED BRITTANY TO ACCEPT HER FATE AS A widow, years of sleepless nights, tearful chats around the fire, torturous unknowing, and unsettled loneliness. Loss had a way of bringing hearts closer. The family leaned on each other heavily and kept moving. Even in loss, life moved forward. The old adage, *Give it time*, had always seemed flippant to Norah—a good snip to say to someone amid a struggle—but she appreciated it now. Even the most horrific events dulled with time. One of the more tangible gifts life bestowed upon humanity.

* * *

"What's wrong?" Norah asked Brittany.

The question was all it took for Brittany to spill. "I don't know if I'm coming or going anymore."

"Why?" Norah asked even though she knew what it was about.

"It's Ollie. He has feelings for me, and sometimes I'm confused. He's like my brother. Tayo would kill us."

Norah took a moment before she answered. "Brit, it's a slippery slope. Ollie's never been in love, never been with a woman. It could lead to a painful situation for both of you and the kids."

Brittany sighed. "I'm lonely, crave affection and love… He kissed me last night."

"Oh?"

"I pushed him away. Will you talk to him? He listens to you."

"It's you who has to set it straight."

"Tayo isn't coming back. Am I doomed to a life of celibacy?"

"I don't know, Brit. I really don't."

She sighed. "Me either."

Norah returned to the cabin, lay beside Eldon, and told him everything.

"Poor Ollie," Eldon said," I don't blame him. It's a tough one—he's never had anyone, and Brit's been alone for five years."

"What if Tayo returns? He'll lose it. Maybe you should talk to Ollie. He might appreciate some support."

"Are we really going to butt into this Norah? As hard as it is to admit, I don't think Tayo is coming back." Eldon put his head down. "Why can't they find happiness with each other or figure it out on their own?"

"You're right. I'm scared of things unravelling. Even today, life without Murph and Tayo feels different. Having them gone changed everything… God, the advice I gave Brittany today—terrible. What the hell was I thinking?"

"Norah, we live in a bubble, of course lines get blurred. All we can do is be there for them, regardless of what they do. And don't beat yourself up, you always give terrible advice." He smirked.

She smiled and rolled her eyes. "I need to find Brittany."

She walked to the cottage and found Brittany outside with Tilly and Sunny, drawing a picture. "Hey, can we talk?"

She and Brittany walked to their usual spot and sat on the big rock.

"What's up?" Brittany asked.

Norah sighed. "I need to apologize. Our conversation today—I gave you bad advice. I get you guys would be pulled towards each other, and you're right, Tayo might not return. Just ignore what I said, do whatever your heart feels."

Brittany laughed. "Norah, you're funny, don't even worry about it. It's not like I don't think for myself, I'll figure it out." She looked up at the moon. "Wanna have a full-moon ceremony tonight?"

Norah laughed. Years ago, she had blurted out, *We should have a full-moon ceremony tonight,* and everyone had gone into stitches at the stupidity. The joke stuck.

Norah returned to the cabin and sat in front of the easel she kept set up by the fire. She lifted her paintbrush to the canvas—the same canvas she had worked on for months. She had no intention of finishing the piece but found it relaxing.

Ollie tapped her shoulder.

Startled, she dropped her brush. "Jesus," she gasped.

"Sorry, Norah." He laughed. "Wasn't trying to scare you."

She smiled. "I didn't even hear you come up."

He walked past her and sat with Eldon by the fire. They didn't say a word.

Ollie lit a smoke and broke the silence. "I kissed Brittany."

"Oh," Eldon said.

"I think I love her, but I don't wanna mess things up."

"When you say you 'think,' what do you mean?"

"I don't know. I want to be around her and the kids all the time."

"Maybe you want a family more than you want her?"

Ollie inhaled a drag of his smoke. "Maybe?"

"Because if you did, you wouldn't say 'I think'—it's something you know."

"I'm twenty-five, never been with a woman, probably never will. What's the point of sitting watching you guys raise your families?"

"What are you saying?"

"Needs to be more for me than this." He shrugged and walked back to the hotel.

Norah painted for a while but, distracted with worry, went to talk to Ollie.

His door was slightly open.

"Can I come in?" she asked gently.

"Sure."

He was sitting at his desk, doodling. Norah leaned against the wall beside his desk. Posters from *The Outsiders* movie, photographs, and drawings hung around his room. She noticed a black-and-white picture of Murph in his old flannel plaid shirt, his head slightly tilted, a hint of a smile on his face. She smiled and glanced at Ollie, remembering why she was visiting.

"I'm worried about you." she said.

"When aren't you worried, Norah?" He half smiled.

Norah thought how handsome he was, how kind and gentle. A perfect catch. "I know, it's a condition." She sighed and smiled. "Seriously, though, are you okay?"

"It's just getting to me—day after day with no hope for anything different."

"You're not thinking of offing yourself?" she asked matter-of-factly.

"God, Norah." He kind of smirked. "No. I'm thinking of leaving, going to the cave, and trying to get to the other side."

She wanted to discourage him but had no argument. His life consisted of watching other people live their lives, not having any of his own experiences. "You can't open the slant; what's your plan?"

"Don't know, thought we could all go back."

Norah shook her head. "It's too risky."

"I'm just desperate." He sighed. "I've been dreaming about my mom lately, thinking about my life, how fucked up it really was." He paused. "I wish I could see her again; after all these years, it's right there." He began drawing again. "She lost words, went silent, and sat for some time." Ollie stood and handed Norah the paper he'd been sketching. "This was her."

Norah studied the portrait of a woman. "She was beautiful, Ollie."

"I know." He took the drawing and tacked it on his wall. "I'm going to talk to Brittany."

That night, Norah lay sleepless, dwelling on her conversation with Ollie. She wanted to help him, but the outcomes were terrifying. She tucked away the idea and fought her eyes shut.

*   *   *

"Come on," Eldon said, gently shaking her out of her slumber. "Ida's watching the kids."

"Where?" she said, her eyes barely open.

"I found something I wanna show you. Pack clothes for overnight."

She dressed and drank a quick coffee, excited for the surprise.

The path was unfamiliar, covered in dense brush.

"When did you walk here?" she asked.

"The other day, running—got bored of the same terrain."

An hour had passed when Norah stumbled on a small hut in the middle of the trees. "A sweat lodge!" she gasped.

"Cool, hey?" Eldon smiled, proud of his discovery. "I know you talked about them before, I thought we could go?"

Norah smiled. "You are the sweetest—albeit ignorant—man, but I am not going in there."

"Why?" he asked, puzzled.

"Because it isn't ours. You have no idea who or what was in there."

"Isn't it like a sauna?"

"God, no. It's a ceremony. Sacred."

"Isn't it for everyone?"

"Sometimes—depends. But it's not ours. I mean, anyone could visit a synagogue, but you're not going to put on a yarmulke and call yourself a rabbi."

"Never thought about it like that. They did them all the time at the yoga retreat by my house."

"I was blessed to attend a ceremony with an Elder, not some flake wearing Lululemon."

He laughed. "Well, that blew up in my face."

She laughed too. "No, you're adorable."

He laughed again. "Let's keep walking, find a place to camp."

They hiked for a couple hours and stumbled upon a steep hill with orphaned toboggans—no snow but a sheen of flattened dead grass.

Eldon's face held the expression of an excited child. "What's the worst that could happen?"

"I can think of multiple things," she said, her voice flat.

He ran, hopped on one, and blazed down the hill like a kamikaze, the smooth dead grass more slippery than snow. He tumbled off at the bottom, rolled into the dirt, brushed it off, and yelled, "That was fucking awesome!" He bolted back up the hill and told Norah to hop on behind him.

Norah felt nervous, not having let loose in ages, but tucked in behind him, and he pushed down. They tumbled off midway and rolled into a fit of laughter, so weak they could barely stumble to the top again. Norah went down alone this time, gaining so much momentum she blazed between two trees and screamed bloody murder, fearing her end had arrived.

Eldon frantically chased after and found her lying in a slump in front of a tree. He flipped her over, and they killed themselves laughing, hysterical for a full twenty minutes. "I don't know how I breathed without you." He brushed dead grass from her hair and kissed her, peeled off her dirt-covered clothes, and twisted into her body. Then he got up, buck naked, and ran towards the toboggan. "Come on!" he shouted.

"You're crazy!" She laughed.

"I'm serious!" he shouted again.

Him buck naked on that toboggan was the funniest picture she'd seen in ages, so she didn't have the heart to leave him hanging and joined him. She immediately regretted her decision and tried to get up. "This is so stupid, I'm getting off."

He pushed her shoulders down, laughing hysterically. They whipped down and tumbled off at the bottom, their bodies covered in dirt and foliage. Hours passed as they acted like kids, playful and silly.

They decided to camp by the hill and lit a fire, then fell asleep early, exhausted from the day. Morning came, and they headed home, reeling from the fun.

* * *

Later, Ida and Norah sat around the fire outside. "Do you notice we aren't aging?" Norah said. "I'm forty-five, don't look it?"

"Of course I noticed you aren't aging. Me, on the other hand, I definitely see a few more greys."

"Ida, you were almost fully grey when the Shade happened." She laughed.

Ida smirked. "I can feel it. Life is too slow anyway. I want to age. Maggie's aged, too. Maybe it's because we don't visit the inlet as often."

"Maybe..." Norah thought about it. "The kids are growing, though. Ollie's still young. Hard to tell if he stopped. Brittany's a robot, either way. Anyway, I'm not complaining. I'll take eternal youth." Norah smiled.

She was unable to tell if Fatty was aging, he looked as dapper as ever. The average lifespan of a pig was around twenty. Norah had no clue how old he had been when they found him. He swam more than anyone at the inlet. Norah hoped that had bought him time; the thought of losing him was heartbreaking.

"Well, Eldon's still piping," Ida said.

Eldon walked in. "What are you ninnies up to?"

"Ida was just saying how piping hot you are." Norah smiled.

"Oh, Ida." He grinned and hugged her from behind.

"Oh stop, you couldn't handle me." She squirmed away.

"Now that I believe." He laughed, grabbed his guitar, and sat beside Norah. She still buckled at the knees when he sang—when he did anything, really.

"Supper's ready!" Kitchi yelled.

Ollie, Brittany, and the kids sat around the feast Maggie had prepared. Norah tried to get a sense of the situation but couldn't get a read. Maggie said a prayer; after picking up her Bible years ago, she had calmed down with the brimstone and hellfire and asked if she could say grace before meals. Her words—now focused on love, not fear—were appreciated, and she even taught the kids a few scriptures. Kitchi, who was insightful for his age, found the Bible interesting and listened intently. Maggie grew to love him more than any of the kids.

They held an annual memorial for Murph. Without fail, Eldon retold the "banging in the closet" story, putting everyone in stitches, even Maggie. She shared funny stories about their marriage and her party years, some hilarious material lived within the tales of her rendezvous.

"Mama, a man is coming," Sunny shouted from the hall.

It had been years since they had seen Nathan or anyone else. Initially, besides Nathan, a small group of people or loners would stumble on the hotel a few times a year. Most harmlessly passed through. The family would invite them to eat, even offer to let them stay, but none accepted, usually on their own mission to find out what happened. The story was the same with each of them: no one had a clue. Norah asked them their blood type, and the answer was always the same, if they knew—still the only thing they had in common. Some visitors lived like nomads, journeying for years on foot, from one city to the next. They reported the same thing everywhere: few survivors, desolate and vacant.

Norah watched out the window as the figure grew closer. Her jaw dropped. Eldon and Ollie embraced the man. She glanced back at Brittany.

"What?" Brittany asked. Norah stared at her, speechless. Brittany's face went pale. "What is it, Norah?" Her voice shook.

Norah pulled her close and whispered, "It's Tayo."

"No, no…" Brittany trembled and braced herself on the wall. She took Norah's hand and walked outside.

"Why did you guys run ahead?" Tayo asked. Brittany stood in the door frame, in shock.

Eldon put his hand on his friend's shoulder. "Tayo, you were gone for five years."

"You guys are idiots." He laughed and shook his head.

Brittany ran to him and fell in his arms.

Tilly joined in the hug. "Daddy, you're home."

He looked at the gorgeous girl, her wild platinum-blonde afro with indigo tips tied in pigtails with bright pink bows, and clearly did not realize she was his daughter.

"Tayo, it's Tilly." Brittany stared at him intensely, as if willing him to comprehend.

He scrunched his face in disbelief and turned pale. He kneeled and clasped Tilly's face in his hands, then looked at Brittany again, unable to grasp the truth.

"I missed you," Tilly whispered.

He opened his mouth, but no words came out. He squeezed her and Brittany tightly to him. Sunny joined and put her arms around them all. He loosened his embrace and stared down in confusion at this child he had never seen.

Brittany smiled and inhaled an audible breath. "Tayo, this is Sunny... your daughter."

"My daughter?" He gasped and gently squeezed her shoulders.

She held his face in her hands. "I'm Sunny." She smiled.

He sat on the ground, put his hand on his chest, and struggled to take in air.

Norah nudged Eldon—a hint to give them time to catch their breath—and they headed into the hotel. She glanced at Ollie. He stood dumbfounded and stared at the reunited family. Her heart broke for him. He locked eyes with Norah and walked away sombrely. She wanted to follow but knew he had to feel it.

She sat around the fire with the others, no one uttering a word. Eldon strummed his guitar, the kids sang and coloured. At this point, questions like *What happened?* or statements like *I can't believe it* didn't cross their minds. Events such as these were shocking, yes; unbelievable, no.

An hour later, Brittany, Tayo, and the kids walked into the dining hall, supper now cold on the table.

"Let's eat, you guys. I want to wait before we go to the cottage." Brittany smiled from ear to ear and hung off Tayo's arm.

Norah knocked on Ollie's door. "We're about to sit down and eat. Are you coming?"

"No, I'm okay," Ollie said quietly. "I ate enough."

Norah stood outside his door, about to knock again, then changed her mind and returned to supper. Brittany lifted her eyebrows, subtly asking Norah if he was coming. Norah shook her head.

"Where's Ollie?" Sunny asked.

"Uh, he's not hungry, sweetie," Brittany answered.

"He's always at supper, Mom. Can I go get him?"

"No, Sunny, just leave him alone."

Sunny let it go and started eating her cold peas.

Tayo glanced at Sunny, then Brittany; it was obvious he was trying to read in between the lines.

Maggie smiled at him gently. "I'm happy you're back, Tayo."

"Thanks, Maggie, can't even begin on this one." He scarfed down his food. Norah remembered how hungry she had been after that journey.

"Let's go to the cottage," Sunny said, pulling on Tayo's sleeve.

"Want to show me how much work I have left?" Tayo laughed, oblivious of the time passed.

"Come on." She pulled again, impatient.

"Let's go." Brittany stood, and they all headed to the cottage.

Tayo stopped dead in his tracks and put his hand over his mouth when it came into view. It was only a few wood pieces when he left days before. "You guys." Tears fell without permission.

"Eldon and Ollie did it for us." Brittany smiled and took his hand.

"You built my family a home." He sniffled and looked around. "Where's Ollie?"

Brittany looked down. "He'll come by soon, I'm sure."

Everyone dispersed and left them alone. With the shock fresh, settling in was far from close.

*   *   *

Over the next few weeks, Tayo regained his balance and immersed himself in his family. He and Brittany were like teenagers in the throes of passion. He adored his daughters and spent every spare second getting to know them. When he saw Tilly last, she had been into colouring books and My Little Pony; now, she was interested in *Twilight*, photography, and sketching.

Ollie distanced himself from the family, spending most of his time alone and leaving for days at a time on excursions.

Norah dozed off curled inside the comfy chair Eldon had helped haul to the church. Over the years, Norah had spent endless hours basking in the beauty of the chapel. It was her sanctuary to be alone and write.

She was startled awake by someone shaking her gently.

"Norah," whispered a voice.

She opened her eyes and gathered her bearings. Candlelight bounced off the reflection of the moon. Brittany was standing over her. "Brit, what are you doing here?"

"Need to talk, thought I'd find you here." She sat cross-legged on a cushion beside the chair.

Norah yawned. "Is everything okay? We haven't talked much since Tayo returned." She still had no clue what had happened between her and Ollie. If anything.

"I'm sorry, been so wrapped up in him."

"God, don't apologize, I'd be the same."

Brittany was silent for a few minutes before she spoke. "Tayo questioned me about Ollie, he could tell something was up."

"Hard to hide anything in this small family. What happened?"

"What happened with Ollie and me or Tayo?"

"Both."

"Well, Ollie and I ended up talking while you and Eldon were away. We both decided it would be better to stay friends." She paused and sighed. "But then… when he was about to leave, we shared an innocent hug, and it led to something." She put her head in her hands.

"What?" Norah asked.

"We… we kissed, then made out heavy. It was intense, he's such a good kisser." She blushed. "It took all my strength to stop, but we came close… I decided to be with him. I was gonna tell him the next day, after supper, ask him to come back to the cottage." She stared at the ground and flicked dust around. "Then… Tayo." She grimaced at the awkwardness.

"Oh, Brit,"

"When I saw Tayo, I fell apart. I love him more than anything. It was so long since I saw him, it dulled, but the minute I felt his arms around me, I melted. It wasn't a choice." Brittany sniffled. "And there Ollie was, watching it unfold. I felt fucking horrible."

Norah sighed. "What about Tayo? You said he asked you."

"He knew something was up, I had to tell him, what choice did I have?" Her face looked sick with worry.

"What did he say?"

"He flipped out, broke the picture of us beside the bed. I begged him not to confront Ollie—he's been through enough. Like, what the fuck, he was gone for five years. We got into a brutal fight, the worst one I've been in with anyone. What did he expect me to do?" She sobbed. "Ollie helped build the cottage. Tayo's being a total prick."

Norah felt the heaviness of the situation. "Where is he now?"

"He stormed off. I came here. What if he hurts Ollie?" Brittany fought for breath.

Norah crawled out of the chair and joined her on the floor. "Take a deep breath, Brit, you can't control what Tayo does. Anyway, Ollie isn't even there, he's gone, won't be back for a few days. Let's go find Eldon, maybe he can talk to Tayo."

Brittany inhaled a deep breath and exhaled. "He's gone?" she asked.

"He went to the old cabin where we went years ago."

Brittany sighed relief. "Thank god."

Norah made her way home and shook Eldon awake. "Get up," she said. He pulled her onto the bed and groped her. "Eldon, not now. Brittany's out by the fire. We need to talk."

"Okay, okay." Eldon let her go and joined the women outside a few minutes later. "What's going on?"

"It's Tayo," Norah said. "He knows about Brittany and Ollie; we're worried he might hurt him."

"What?" He looked half asleep and confused.

"Eldon!" Norah snapped, thinking how daft he was.

He looked at Brittany. "What happened with you and Ollie?"

"We made out." She shrugged.

"And you told Tayo?"

"What should I have done, lied?" Brittany sounded frustrated.

"Maybe." Eldon yawned.

Norah shot him a *What the hell?* look. "Not helpful, Eldon."

"Okay, okay. I'll find Tayo." He walked away.

Norah rolled her eyes at Brittany. "Jesus Christ."

They laughed at the ridiculous conversation. Their laughter dwindled as the weight of the situation returned. They went inside the hotel and found Ida and Sunny in the dining hall. Sunny was busy with her play food and kitchen, and the other kids were out exploring the river, oblivious of the drama.

"Brittany, are you okay?" Ida asked.

"Things got a little nuts," she said. "Did Tayo come over here a while ago?"

"Haven't seen him." Ida seemed concerned. "I did see Ollie, though. He came back from the old cabin early, said he forgot to pack his sleeping bag."

Norah's stomach dropped.

"I need to find—"

Brittany was cut off by shouting outside. They all ran out and found Ollie on top of Tayo, about to punch his face.

"No, Ollie!" Norah yelled.

The kids screamed, watching it unfold.

"Ollie, stop!" Sunny begged, tears rolling down over her indigo freckles.

Her voice seemed to trip Ollie out of his rage. He looked over at her, then down at Tayo. Shame and sadness covered his face. He grabbed Tayo's shirt, lifted him at his chest, and screamed in his face. Spit and blood splattered from his mouth. He slammed Tayo back to the ground, scurried to his feet, and stumbled off.

Eldon ran out from the cabin and looked at Norah. She could tell he felt terrible. Tayo inched himself off the ground, spit out a bloody tooth, covered his face with his hoodie, and limped towards his cottage.

Brittany kneeled and hugged Sunny. "Everything's going to be okay, sweetheart." She released her and looked at Maggie. "Can you take Sunny inside?"

Maggie shuffled the girl into the hotel. Eldon followed Ollie. Brittany followed Tayo. Ida and Norah sat in the gazebo.

"What the fuck?" Ida asked, clearly reeling from the insanity.

"It escalated fast. Tayo found out about Ollie and Brittany."

"What about them?" Ida's asked, her brow furrowed.

"Long story short, they made out—came close to being a couple before Tayo returned."

Ida shook her head. "Am I so far out of the loop?"

"No, this all happened within a week—well, not them growing close, but Brittany never talked about that till recently." Norah stared at the bloodied dirt. "Ollie, that rage—he was obviously holding it in all these years."

"How couldn't he? His life before, it doesn't just go away." Tears welled in her eyes.

"I guess I know that. It was just so long ago, I forget people's lives before all of this—sometimes even my own."

Ida dried her eyes with her sweater. "Ollie probably went through things neither of us will ever know. I hope Eldon finds him; he needs to know he's loved no matter what."

"You don't think he knows that?"

She shrugged. "Who knows."

Shouting bellowed from the cottage.

"Norah glanced at Ida and lifted her eyebrows. "When it rains, it fucking pours, I guess." The look on Ida's face—a combination of disgust and *What the fuck?*—struck Norah as funny, and she burst into laughter.

Ida shook her head.

Brittany came into the gazebo and slumped onto the couch, then bawled for fifteen minutes.

"Where do we go from here?" She sniffled and rubbed her eyes.

"It'll pass, Brittany, things get heated," Norah said, trying to comfort her.

"You call that heated? Ollie almost killed Tayo." Brittany burst into tears again. "Sunny saw it, it's not okay, friggen assholes."

"No," Norah said. "It's not okay, but it happens, Sunny got an unfortunate glimpse of violence, but she's resilient."

Brittany inhaled an audible breath and sighed. "Tayo left, he's out of control. Can't see his wrong, his overreaction. I told him not to come back, he's not right in the head. The lost years messed with him, and this shit with Ollie tipped him over the edge. What if he doesn't come back or uses?"

"Brit, I didn't realize he was struggling," Ida said. "He seemed happy to be getting back into the business of life."

"Just little stuff, a shorter fuse." Brittany sniffled.

"He needs to sort it out, and he will," Norah said with resolve. "For now, you need to take care of your kids. Don't let this swallow you whole. We've both been there."

Brittany nodded and wiped her eyes. "You're right, my kids have been through enough."

Eldon stood outside the gazebo, looking downtrodden. "I couldn't find him."

"He probably headed to the old cabin. Did you go that way?" Norah asked.

"Yeah." He shrugged. "I don't know where he went."

"Hopefully, they'll both get air and come back," Ida said. "We all need rest. Go get the kids, and go home. We'll regroup tomorrow." She hugged Brittany and went inside.

They listened to what she said—nothing left to do with the situation. They spent the evening with the kids, swimming at the inlet, then turned in early for bed.

Norah dozed on Eldon's chest.

"I feel terrible," he said.

"Maybe you could have stopped it, maybe not. Maybe it had to happen."

"I can't stop thinking about Ollie. I know Tayo will be okay, he's proven he can come through a lot. But Ollie, he's sensitive."

"Ollie is stronger than we give him credit for—also younger. We need to let the chips fall, like you always tell me. It's out of our control."

They dozed off. Norah woke to rustling outside the cabin. She crawled out of bed. Eldon didn't budge from his slumber.

Outside, Ollie was stumbling around the fire. "Ama, gimme ama." His breath reeked of whiskey and cigarettes. He toppled over and landed ass down on a rock.

Norah helped him onto the couch. "What are you looking for?" she asked, sure he hadn't touched alcohol before.

"Ama, Llllama." He spit out the words.

"Llama?"

"Mm-hmm." He burped.

Norah couldn't help laughing. She went inside, lifted Llama off the shelf, and brought it to him.

He hugged it like a child and stared at Norah with the saddest puppy dog eyes. "Fanks." He struggled to stand and stumbled off.

She smiled and remembered when Ollie gave her Llama, his sweet gift. She noticed the Pall Malls on the ground. Years since she'd had a smoke, she pulled one out, lit it, and inhaled. Dizzy, she sat on the couch and took another drag. Ecstasy. She lifted her journal and began writing.

Fuck I love smoking. Not sure why I gave it up. Not aging anyway,
might as well just enjoy. Seeing Ollie drunk reminded me of Silas,

long since I thought about him or his drinking. Not sure why he popped into my head. He was such a tornado. Destructive. Life before the Shade seems so far away. Broken fragments. I was a different person. I see my body now, don't hate it, don't love it either. It's always there, the tiny voice. Sometimes I lay with Eldon and lose my breath, feel like an imposter, a woman who doesn't belong in his bed. Fear one day, he'll wake up, open his eyes, and realize he's with the wrong person. Not that there's much choice for him anyway. I had a dream about Sarah and Brie last week, it was like they were there. I tried to remember what they said when I woke up, but it vanished, just like they did. I miss them. Miss Mom and Dad. So much meaning lost. My kids will never know their grandparents, this other life we came from, and how do we explain it? Sounds as far-fetched as our life now would sound to someone then. Some things need to exist to survive, the necessity of gratitude for what remains.

She slipped back into bed and tossed and turned for the rest of the night. She woke exhausted the next morning and went to the hotel. Everyone was buzzing around the kitchen.

Ida glanced up from her breakfast. "Any sign?"

"I saw Ollie last night, he was drunk," Norah said. "Any sign of Tayo?"

"No, neither. I checked Ollie's room, he's not there."

"Maybe he passed out by the river. Eldon will go look for him." Norah filled a mug with coffee.

"Ollie was drunk?" Brittany asked.

"Yeah, he wanted Llama." Norah smiled.

"Awe." Ida looked down at her lap.

* * *

There was no sign of Ollie or Tayo for three days.

On the fourth morning, Norah opened the doors to the church and was startled to see Tayo sprawled on the couch, remnants of the brawl on his face.

"Tayo, what are you doing?" she asked.

"I don't know." He sat up. "I've been wandering, figuring out what the hell happened." He stared at the hardwood floor.

"Where did you go?"

"The mall"—he rubbed his forehead—"of all places." He smiled slightly.

Norah laughed. "You do know your wife, right?"

"I don't know what I was thinking, pushing Ollie." He paused. "I've been angry since I got back. I should be happy. I'm fucking angry at the cave. The lost time with Brittany and the kids."

"I get that, Tayo, but you know better than anyone where it leads. You need to figure out how to deal, and not with your fists."

He pulled a bottle of pills from his pocket and handed it to her. "Here."

"Did you take any?"

"No, I put two in my mouth but spit them out." He sighed. "It's like before, when Veronika showed up in my dreams, except now it's Sunny's voice screaming for Ollie to stop." He teared up. "I can't do this to my kids."

Norah nodded. "And you won't."

"Did that guy ever help you?" Tayo motioned to skinny Jesus.

"Sometimes I think he did," Norah said thoughtfully.

Tayo smiled, nodded, and left the church. Norah returned to find him and Brittany cuddling in the gazebo. She sighed with relief, grateful to have one piece put back together.

Another seven days later, there was still no sign of Ollie. Norah decided to hike to the cabin. She hadn't been back since Murph but hoped she remembered the path. Eldon insisted on joining her, but she wanted to go alone and brought Fatty instead. The trail seemed darker; she felt jumpy in the dusky eeriness of the moon. She stumbled onto the old cabin, more rustic than she remembered. A light burned inside.

"Ollie?" She tapped on the door and creaked it open.

He looked over at her. "Forgot you knew where this was."

She struggled to make sense of his expression as she walked in and sat on the bed. "One of the funnest trips, with you and Murph." She noticed Llama on the mantle.

"Seemed innocent back then," he said.

"Kinda what growing up is about: unavoidably losing your innocence."

He shrugged. "Thanks for the good tidings."

"Always… Are you okay?"

"Keep thinking about the fight. It wasn't even Tayo's face I saw. It was my dad's." He sighed. "Does that mean I was fighting myself?"

"Ollie, you're not your dad."

"I am half monster." He put his head in his hands. "Him beating the shit out of my mom while I hid, peeking out of the closet like a little pussy. He was locked up most of the time, but when he was free, she always welcomed him back… until she met fucking Ed."

"Don't think that makes you a pussy, Ollie, you were a kid." Norah shook her head. Her heart beat fast and her stomach ached. Hearing him talk about his life made her want to burst into tears, but she refused to make it about her.

"I didn't protect her." His eyes begged Norah for forgiveness, as if she were his mom.

Norah fought tears. "You couldn't protect her, Ollie, there's a difference."

"Tried once. He had her on the floor. I jumped out of the closet with a wire hanger and pounced on him." He laughed. "A fucking wire hanger—lotta good that woulda done."

"How old were you?"

"Round five, same age as Sunny." He teared up. "She saw me, just like I saw my dad. She'll never get that image out of her head."

"She will."

"No, Norah, you can say a lot of things, but she won't forget."

She knew he was right. They sat in silence for a while.

"How's Tayo?" Ollie asked.

"A little rough. He came back, though."

"Good." He paused. "I don't even hate him. I love him like a brother. Doubt he'll forgive me."

"Ollie, that is something I can speak to—he will."

Ollie lowered his chin to his chest. "I don't deserve his forgiveness."

"I think what's more important is forgiving yourself."

"How? Sunny was terrified."

"Ollie, you may be right, she might not forget, but all the beautiful moments you've had and continue to have will overshadow one event."

"Did you hurt Theo?" he asked.

Norah, taken back by the question, didn't know how to answer.

"Sorry." He looked down at his hands.

"I did hurt him. I struggled with anger, a short fuse. I got mad at him a lot more than I should have." She cringed.

"Did he forgive you?"

"Always. I lost him so young, who knows what damage I did." She paused. "Do you forgive your mom?"

"Yeah." He shrugged. "I'm sure you were a great mom, better than mine."

"Your mom did the best she could. If you knew her history, you might realize she was hurt too. Pain recycles down generations."

"I don't know if I can come back." He sighed and picked Llama off the mantle. "Take him home. I need some more time. I promise I'll come back, won't off myself like Murph."

Norah gave him a surprised look. Murph would have appreciated his candour. "I know you won't, Ollie, just come home soon." She hugged him and left.

"Thank you," Ollie yelled.

She turned and smiled, hugged Llama to her chest, then continued on. She felt heavy as she walked through the forest, thinking about what Ollie said, the shit he went through as a child.

*   *   *

Norah found Eldon at the inlet, playing with the kids.

"Did you find him?" Eldon asked as she walked towards him.

"Yeah. I think he'll be home soon." Norah sat beside him and put her head on his shoulder, tired from the hike.

Kitchi and Freya ran out of the water when they saw her. Kitchi lay on her legs; Freya hugged Eldon.

"Did you see Ollie?" Freya asked.

"I did, he said he misses you." Norah played with Kitchi's thick hair and watched Brittany and Tayo in the water with Sunny. They looked happy, normal.

The next day, Ollie walked by Norah in the dining hall while she was cleaning. She followed him. "Ollie, you're back." She smiled with relief.

"I've decided I'm going to move to the old cabin, just grabbing my stuff." He sounded determined.

Norah watched him stuff his belongings into a large backpack. She realized how few possessions he had—his camera, drawings, clothes, and other odds and ends. "Are you sure, Ollie?"

He stopped. "Yes, Norah. I thought about things after you left. I've leaned on you all since I was a boy. I need to sort shit out in my head, be alone. I know you worry..." He smiled. "I'll be okay. I can take care of myself."

She took a deep breath. "I know, Ollie, I just miss you when you're gone."

"I miss you, too, but it's something I need to do."

Norah grabbed a pile of books and helped him pack. When they were finished, she hugged him. "I love you, you know."

He smiled and secured the pack on his back. Norah watched him walk out of the room.

He popped his head back in. "I love you, too, you know."

Her heart melted.

She watched from the window as he carried on to a new chapter, a lifetime of belongings on his back. He didn't stop to say goodbye to anyone. When he was out of sight, she turned away from the window and noticed a pile of envelopes on his desk: one for everyone. She opened hers, and a picture of him, Norah, and Llama fell out. Ida had taken the photo years before when he gave it to her. She had never seen it, had almost no pictures of herself. She looked at Ollie's sweet face, smiled, and tucked the picture back in the envelope. She walked to the cottage and handed the envelopes to Brittany.

"What are these?" Brittany asked.

"Ollie left them for you. He decided to leave, stay at the remote cabin."

Sadness darkened her face. "Will he come back? I wanted to talk to him."

"I'm sure he'll come back soon."

Brittany passed Tayo and Sunny their envelopes. They looked at the pictures: Ollie and Brittany laughing by the fire; Tayo and Ollie fishing by the river; and the last, Ollie and Sunny reading a book together. An extra picture fell out of Brittany's envelope. They stared at a black-and-white photo of the entire family, happy and together. Norah lifted it off the ground and smiled. Her heart had faith in the strength of their connections.

CHAPTER 14

SEVEN YEARS LATER

(SUNNY, TWELVE; TWINS, EIGHTEEN; TILLY, NINETEEN)

KITCHI WAS NOW A SIX-FOOT-FIVE BEAST WITH SOLID PIPES and a twenty pack. He wore his thick indigo-hued black hair in dreads, and his gorgeous, chiselled olive complexion and deep-purple freckles were hidden under a face full of stubble. His black-indigo eyes were disarming, but his demeanour was funny, playful, and carefree. Like his Dad. But Eldon looked like a little girl when they arm-wrestled. He joked about Kitchi kicking his ass for real one day in an epic father-son battle, but lucky for Eldon, no real angst existed.

Freya was equally stunning with her green-indigo eyes, fair opaque skin, and brown-indigo freckles splattered across her cheeks. A perfect gene girl. Her auburn-indigo curls now flowed past her waist, which she usually tied into a thick braid. Freya was gentle, kind, and inquisitive. Her voice never rose in anger. She could read Kitchi's thoughts, and he, hers.

Tilly shone uniquely with her platinum-blonde, indigo-tipped afro and dark mocha-indigo skin. She was robust and intuitive. She, Freya, and Kitchi were inseparable. They spent every spare second together, going on their own supply runs and exploring freely.

Sunny followed them everywhere, a spitfire who was able to climb any tree or building. Wiry and agile, her hair grew at sonic speed and needed to be trimmed daily. Her wild spirit buzzed wild.

The parents weren't too concerned about their adventures—not many could rally against Kitchi and stand. Fatty joined them on most adventures; even though he slowed them down, they loved his company. Kitchi and Tilly had been enamoured with each other since they were small. For some reason, they never told each other—maybe they feared ruining the trio. The confession loomed as an inevitable certainty. Brittany and Norah chatted about it often and wondered when they would get together.

Kitchi, Freya, and Tilly returned to the cave and the sun often. Initially, the adults tried to stop them, but they rebelled when the teen years arrived, and over time, the adults realized it didn't affect them the same way—they never lost time. Now mature, they were able to fully open the slants with the force of one hand. Norah called them Slanters and attributed their abilities to being born on the new Earth.

The sun summoned Sunny and she begged to join them when they went to the cave, but Brittany and Tayo adamantly opposed, and the trio respected their wishes. Norah knew Sunny was the only one able to open the geode to the other side. She dreamt about her every night: Sunny would be standing inside the geode under the sun. Norah didn't understand it but knew she was different from the others—the only one conceived under the sun. Norah called her Sparrow because she remembered an Elder sharing a story about sparrows being dimension travellers; it seemed fitting.

Kitchi wanted to bring Fatty to the other side, to let him feel the sun on his back and explore a new world, but the poor pig barely fit on the narrow path. Determined, Kitchi built a stretcher on wheels and planned to strap Fatty on and pull him up the trail. Norah vehemently opposed, unsure of the impact on animals in the cave of the sun. Then Kitchi found a small mouse-like creature under the sun and carried it through the slant into the cave, but it died during the crossover. He laid it down in the flowers, and within moments, it dissolved into ash. He realized animals couldn't handle the crossover and gave up on the idea of bringing Fatty with them.

It grew more apparent that none were aging except for Maggie and Ida. They wanted to live out their days in human years and meet their natural end. Not having partners, the days passed quietly, and neither wanted to mess with natural law. Norah never really intended to mess with natural law, either, but the inlet was part of her life and her time in the cave had happened by chance. Regardless, she celebrated not aging, and who could blame her.

The cabins outgrew the families, so they built two more. Kitchi and Ollie lived in one, Tilly and Freya in the other. Ollie had stayed at the remote cabin for four years. The family didn't see much of him the first year; he'd show up randomly. Time was needed to heal the relationships after the drama, but slowly, it settled, and the closeness returned.

Tayo, Brittany, and Sunny hiked up to see him a month after he left. Brittany told Norah how strained and awkward the visit had been, especially for her. But Tayo continued to visit every week, and the strain eventually dissolved. Sometimes Norah would join, other times Eldon, but everyone joined at least once. Tayo had persistence about him, a resolve Norah hadn't seen in many people—a quiet, thoughtful-leader quality. Norah noticed a shift in Ollie throughout his time at the cabin; he learned to accept his life—what he had and didn't have, his past. He realized his love for Brittany was more a love for a sister.

* * *

A familiar unknown sense startled Norah awake, her arms covered in goosebumps, the hairs on the back of her neck standing straight. She went outside to breathe in some air, and the moment she opened the door, a gentle breeze blew around her. She gasped and ran back inside.

"Get up." She shook Eldon.

He turned his back to her and snored into his pillow.

"Eldon, get up!" She shook him harder.

"What is it?" he murmured and struggled to open his eyes.

"Something's off."

He propped himself up on one elbow, raked a hand through his hair, and yawned. "What's going on?"

"I woke up sweating. I can feel it, something's wrong. I went outside… I felt a breeze." Her hands shook as she sat on the edge of the bed.

"A breeze?"

"Eldon! There hasn't been wind since the Shade."

He stared, confused. "Norah, I don't have your spidey senses, I don't know what to say." He rubbed her back. "Just come back to bed."

She sighed, unsure what to do. She glanced at her journal; not compelled to write, she slipped back into bed. Her mind raced and exhausted itself into sleep.

She woke up an hour later. "It's still there," she murmured. Eldon stood by the fireplace, making coffee. Her feet scrambled to the floor as she shuffled out of bed. She poured a cup and stepped outside. Her arms broke out in goosebumps again and her heart slowed—a familiar sense, the same eerie feeling from the campsite. She walked over to the gazebo and piled some paper and wood in the firepit. Her hand shook as she tried to light a match; one after another, each lit and then blew out. Her brain struggled to focus. She felt disoriented and threw the box of matches into the fire.

Arms wrapped around her from behind and Eldon whispered, "It's okay, just sit down."

She turned around and burrowed her face in his sweater. She released him and curled up on the couch. Eldon lit the fire, an expression of concern on his face. She stared at the moon. Terrified of what she didn't know.

She looked over at Fatty's rock. It was bare. He always lay on his rock in the morning. He didn't come when she called his name. She walked around the cabin and found him lying in a dirt hole, his entire body trembling. It was unusual behaviour.

"What are you doing, Fatty?" She kneeled and brushed the dirt off his back. "Eldon! Something's wrong with him," she shouted.

Eldon came over and scratched Fatty's bristly back. Norah walked to the massive gong outside of the hotel and hit it three times—a calling system they had created years before. The family trickled into the gazebo and sat around the fire.

"Mom, why did you hit the gong?" Kitchi bellowed in his deep voice.

"Something is really off," Norah said.

"Isn't the bell for emergencies, not weird feelings?" Freya smiled.

"Thanks, Frey." Norah smiled and rolled her eyes. "Does anyone else feel off?" she asked. "I had a long, restless night. Woke up and went outside. Swear I felt a breeze." She tried to hide her shakiness.

"I was up last night, too," Tilly said. "Didn't go outside, though."

Kitchi looked at her. "You never said anything."

"Yeah, woke from a dead sleep in a panic."

"Something isn't right," Norah said. "Let's stay close today. No adventuring."

Everyone agreed and returned to their day. The uneasy feeling dwindled. Fatty settled on his rock. Norah buried herself in a book. In the early evening, everyone headed to the inlet, except Eldon, who stayed behind to work on the firewood shed, and Maggie and Ida, who remained in the kitchen to prepare supper.

Norah floated in the water while the others jumped and splashed around. Suddenly the earth below the water trembled, and the mountain wall shook. Boulders smashed into the water. The middle of the bay turned into the spin cycle of a washing machine and pulled Sunny under. Kitchi fought the current, dove into the swirl, and dragged her to shore. She was shaken but okay. They braced themselves on the beach, collectively terrified. The trembling ceased and left behind an eerie stillness. Norah's senses had been right. They rushed to the hotel.

Maggie ran frantically towards them. "Did you hear it?"

"Hear what?" Tillie asked.

"The horn, another horn!" Ida trembled.

"No," Kitchi said. "There was an earthquake at the inlet."

"Where's Eldon?" Norah noticed he wasn't working on the shed.

"We haven't seen him," Ida said.

A search ensued, but he was nowhere to be found. An hour passed, then another, then another. Norah went to the cabin, lay on the bed, and screamed into her pillow.

"What's wrong?" Eldon stood in the doorway.

"Jesus, Eldon, where the hell were you?"

"Fishing at a tiny inlet I found the other day," he said, an oblivious expression on his face.

"I thought you were building the shed. We were searching for you."

"I got bored. What the hell is going on?"

"God, Eldon, I said to stay close, and you ignore my instincts?!"

It was rare for Norah to get angry at him.

"I'm sorry." He scrunched his face. "What is actually going on?"

"Did you hear the horn?" she snapped.

"No?" He stared at her.

"Or feel the earthquake?"

"No, nothing. Is everyone okay?"

"Yes. I thought you disappeared. We need to tell everyone you're okay."

He put his arms around her. "I'm sorry, Love. I do trust your instincts."

"I don't forgive you, you're a real dipshit sometimes." She smirked.

"There it is. You can't stay mad at me." He leaned over to kiss her. She blocked his mouth with her hand. He pushed it away, held her arms, and bit her neck.

"Stop it!" She tried to push him off and laughed angrily. "I'm serious, we need to tell the kids you're okay."

He let her go. She shook her head and walked to the dining hall.

"Look who I found," she announced with an eye roll.

They rehashed the event: a third horn, but no one had vanished. What did it mean? Why did the earth shake? With no answers, they put the day to rest.

Norah had another sleepless night, her mind racing for hours. Her thoughts were interrupted by a faint tap on the door. She tiptoed out of bed and opened the door. Ida stood outside, her face pale, filled with uncertainty or fear—Norah couldn't quite tell. She grabbed a sweater and joined her by the fire. The small red embers still glowed from hours before.

Norah broke the silence. "What is it, Ida?"

Ida inhaled a deep, audible breath. "There are…"

"What?" Norah had never seen Ida this frazzled.

"People in the hotel," Ida spit out.

"What do you mean? Is everyone okay?"

"Yes." She looked down at her feet and entered another long silence.

Norah's heart pounded. "Ida, I'm getting freaked out."

Ida took Norah's hand as if bracing her for something. "A… a man and young boy are at the hotel." Her hand shook. "Their names are Seamus and Theo."

Norah's heart dropped to the ground. She stared at Ida. "No, no, no…" Her entire body dizzied with uncertainty. She leaned forward and dry heaved, her breath shallow. It felt as if the emotions were cocooning her from the outside, suffocating her into blackness.

Her eyes opened to Ida and Eldon kneeling over her. Eldon helped her back into her chair. Her head pounded, time stood still, her breath started constricting. She felt Eldon's hand on her back, and her airways opened just enough to prevent her from passing out again.

"What the hell is going on?" Eldon asked.

Nobody answered.

"Are they the same age?" Norah held her stomach.

"Who?" Eldon said, looking from Norah to Ida and back again. "Someone needs to tell me what's going on."

Ida took a deep breath before answering. "It's Seamus and Theo, they're at the hotel… Norah, Theo looks to be about twelve."

"They haven't aged?" Any remaining colour drained from Norah's face. "No…" She leaned over and gasped for air. "Do they know they've been gone?"

"No." Ida paused. "They came from the mansion, they're looking for you."

Norah put her head in her lap and nearly passed out again. "Where's Kitchi and Freya?"

"They're in the dining hall with them."

Norah tried not to throw up. "I'll come."

"I'll go with you," Eldon said.

"No, Eldon, I need to go alone. It's too soon." She lowered her chin to her chest and sobbed.

Eldon nodded, kissed her forehead, and went ahead with Ida.

Norah sat on the edge of the bed, crying with joy. She inhaled a few full breaths, dressed, and headed to the dining hall. Her legs were heavy, as if walking through cement. Her hand trembled on the door handle as she flashed back to her initial arrival. Now standing on the other side, her sweet son. With another deep breath, she slinked inside, crouched behind the bookshelf, and peeked out through a tiny crack. The dining hall buzzed, unfamiliar faces mixed with faces she knew.

"Myra!" Eldon shouted.

Norah gasped. Ida's Myra had returned.

"Hey, man, I'm Seamus. This is my son Theo." Norah slid down the back of the bookshelf and sank to the floor, held her head in her hands, and fought for air. An eternity since she'd heard Seamus's voice.

"Oh, hey, I'm Eldon." His voice shaky.

"I'm Theo. Have you seen my mom? Her name is Norah."

Norah covered her mouth and bawled quietly.

"I think you'll see her soon," Eldon said.

"I have no idea why she's here," Seamus said. "We were just at this mansion, I came in from the garage, and she was gone."

"We were waiting to play Monopoly, and she ditched us," Theo said.

Norah smiled, hearing his sweet voice.

"Oh, you're—" Freya began.

Eldon cut her off. "No, Frey."

"You sure look like Norah," Eldon said to Theo.

Norah stood and peeked through the crack, about to show herself, when Fatty waddled over and rooted in Theo's leg.

"Dad, look!" He sat on the floor and scratched Fatty's belly.

"That's a massive pig," Seamus said and laughed.

Eldon smirked. "His name is Fatty."

"How long have you been here?" Seamus asked Eldon.

"Around twenty-one years."

Seamus looked confused but didn't question further. "Is Norah actually here? I'm starting to wonder if this is some weird cannibal party."

Eldon's face paled. "She's here, she'll be here soon, I'm sure."

Ida walked over. "Sorry, Eldon, I got caught up." She grinned. "Myra."

"I know." He pulled her in for a hug.

Norah slinked out the door and stood outside for a moment, then nodded and entered.

"Mom!" Theo jumped up off the couch.

The ball in her throat hardened into pain; it hurt, trying to stuff the emotion down, pretend it hadn't been twenty years since she's seen him. She failed and wept. She held his face in her hands and pulled him close, not saying a word.

"Mom, what's wrong?"

"I love you." She wept.

He pulled away. "Why did you come down here without us?"

"Theo, I would never leave you. Things are… not as they seem." She caressed his face.

"What are you talking about?" He noticed her necklace. "My Monopoly shoe?"

She touched the token-slash-pendant and smiled. "My friend made it for me."

He looked confused.

Seamus hugged Norah. "What's going on? You're looking at us like we're ghosts."

She stared at him, speechless.

"Norah, seriously, what is going on?" he asked again. "Why are you here?"

Norah turned to Brittany. "Can you take Theo to the inlet?"

Brittany didn't skip a beat and enthusiastically introduced herself to Theo. He didn't put up a fuss and followed, over-the-top excited to swim.

Norah gave Eldon a slight smile and walked outside with Seamus.

He planted himself beside her at the picnic table. "Why would you leave without us and come down here?" he asked.

She noticed his eyes were different, laced with a golden hue. "Seamus, what I'm about to tell you is…" She paused, unable to find the right words. "You're going to be confused."

"Why?"

"You know the Earth changed. We aren't dealing with life as it was when the sun shone." She inhaled a deep breath. "You've been gone for twenty-one years. Another horn blared when we arrived at the mansion, and you both disappeared."

Seamus rubbed his forehead, his face showing that he was struggling to compute her words.

"I stayed in the mansion for a year and then came here," she continued, "where I found some of the people you just met."

Seamus studied the wood of the picnic table as if it had answers. "It's impossible… I went to the garage and when I came back, Theo was ready to play Monopoly."

Norah sighed and put her hand on his back. "Seamus, you disappeared. It's been twenty-one years."

He stared at her, no anger in his face, just disbelief. "No, it's impossible; you don't look twenty-one years older."

"Well… yes. That's another story." Norah frowned. She didn't know how to talk about this, how to explain. All these years, all the suffering and the healing and the pain and the love…

He interrupted her thoughts. "You've been with these people for all these years, living here?" He shook his head.

She looked him in the eye. "Yes."

He leaned forward and balanced his chin on his hand. "I don't… I don't understand."

She didn't either. How could she tell the man she once loved how much things had changed? How much she had changed? Then, suddenly, he leaned towards her. Dear God, he was going to kiss her. Norah turned away.

"What is that?" He was staring at the rings on her finger.

"It's—"

"Mom," Theo said, "can I go back to pet the pig?" Norah was grateful for the interruption. She slipped her hand under her thigh.

Brittany stood behind him. "Sorry, he didn't want to go without you."

"It's okay." She ruffled Theo's hair. "Yes, honey, go ahead." She glanced at Seamus and looked away. "Let's just go inside, we can talk more later."

The dining hall was charged with a bustle it hadn't seen in ages. Eldon was sitting on the couch with Kitchi and Freya. Norah locked eyes with him and sighed.

"Mom, did you see the pig?" Theo smiled and put his head on Fatty's belly.

"Fatty, yes, he's my old friend." She sat with him and scratched Fatty's back.

Seamus sat beside her and put his hand on her leg.

Jesus Christ, she thought, *he was never affectionate, barely even noticed me. Ever.*

"I love you," he whispered and smiled sweetly.

His hand felt like a hundred-pound weight on her thigh. She swallowed, could feel Eldon's eyes staring at them. Her stomach sank. She put her hand on Seamus's hand, squeezed it, and smiled back at him. His eyes filled with fear and confusion. He was loyal to her, and she was all he had. The heaviness of the situation gut-punched her. She had to break his heart. She stuffed it aside, got up, and filled a cup with water. Unable to look at Eldon, she returned and sat on Theo's other side, away from Seamus.

"I love him," Theo said.

"That's my pig," Ollie announced. "You must be Theo." He joined them on the floor.

"Hi." Theo smiled at him.

Seamus reached out his hand to Ollie. "I'm Seamus."

Ida came over, holding hands with a petite, curvy woman with wavy blonde hair and bright-blue eyes.

"Myra, I'm so happy to meet you." Norah stood and hugged her, grateful for the distraction.

"You too, Norah, I've heard a lot about you." She was soft-spoken and gentle.

Norah smiled, then caught a glimpse of Seamus's face; he was grimacing with confusion.

Tayo came over, beaming from ear to ear. "This is my sister, Veronika."

"Hi," she said with a wave. She was cute and petite, with long braids, flawless mocha skin, deep brown eyes, a nose ring, and a denim jumpsuit. "This is a lot to take in."

"I'll say," Seamus said. "Do you remember anything?"

"No. It's like I never left. And yet I come back from a walk to find my twin brother married to the whitest girl I've ever seen and with kids who look like they're from a comic book."

Brittany smirked. "I'm not that white."

Tayo shook his head and laughed.

"Does anyone remember how we got here or where we were?" Myra piped in. None of the others had any recollection of the last two decades.

Kitchi handed Norah a pop. "Here you go, Mom."

Norah's eyes widened.

"Why did he call you 'Mom'?" Theo asked, confused.

"Shit," Kitchi said, realizing his mistake.

Seamus glanced around the room, the colour siphoned from his face. "Is he your son, Norah?"

"He is. Theo, this is your brother, Kitchi… and Freya, your sister." She gestured toward Freya, then stared at Seamus, her throat tight with emotion.

"If these are your kids, then…" Seamus paused and put his hand on his head. "Eldon… that guy is their dad." His face turned another shade of white as he glanced at Eldon and then at Norah. Anger took over his tone. "There it is." He stood and stormed out of the room.

Norah followed him. "Seamus. Stop."

"It's too much." He held the brick wall to brace himself.

"I'm sorry you have to deal with this." She put her arm on his shoulder.

"How long?" His face turned red.

"What?"

"How long, Norah!" He punched the brick wall.

"Around a year and a half." The words hurt coming out. She knew they were daggers in his heart.

"So much for you preaching about being alone. Didn't take you long to give it up." He stared down at his bloody knuckles.

"Fuck you, Seamus. You and your self-righteous, pompous bullshit. There is no high horse here!" Her voice shook. "I came close to death in that fucking mansion, mentally mangled. You never saw me, you complained and belittled me. You couldn't even protect me when I was getting raped!" Norah screamed and punched his chest. "I love our son, but this was done long before the sun vanished." In a second, she had been transported back to the place of wanting to rip the flesh off his face. She never felt like this with Eldon, not once in twenty years had she been triggered to a depth of such rage.

Ida put her hand on Norah's back. "Seamus, it's been a long and exhausting day. Let me show you to a room."

"Theo's staying with me in the cabin," Norah said. She slid her back down the wall, rested her head on her knees, and bawled.

Brittany sank down beside her. "Norah, it'll be okay," she whispered.

Norah lifted her head, stretched her neck back, wiped her face with her shirt, and headed into the dining hall.

"Mom, what's wrong?" Theo asked.

"Sweetheart, let's go to the cabin, we need to talk." She put her arm around him and glanced at Eldon, who was on the couch with Kitchi and Freya. "Eldon, can you sleep at Kitchi's tonight?"

He smiled and nodded. "Yes, Love, anything." He got up and was about to approach her, but she shook her head and turned away.

Norah and Theo held hands as they walked back to the cabin. They talked for hours around the fire. With nothing easy about any of the circumstances, Norah led with honesty, which at that point was the only thing she possessed. She knew she couldn't protect him from the absurdity but could still be a steady force in his life, a life she was grateful to have back.

All the tears, grieving, and horror she had gone through, and there he was, his heart beating next to her.

Theo understood more than she'd expected. He worried about Seamus but said he felt relieved to be around other people. Not as scared as when alone. He was also excited to have a brother and sister—especially a brother like Kitchi, who resembled a character from a Marvel comic.

After Theo fell asleep, Norah tossed and turned. She worried about Seamus, left alone, reeling from the insanity of his day. She felt terrible about flipping out and was surprised at how fast it had bubbled. His condescending tone was like a snake charmer to her rage. Now that she was no longer required to put up with it, she had to find some grace and compassion.

A faint knock pattered on the door. When she opened it, Eldon wrapped his arms around her.

"I needed to see you," he said. "Are you okay?"

"I'm exhausted." She kissed his hand.

They lit a fire and cuddled on the couch.

"Theo," he said, his eyes glassy, "he's the sweetest kid."

She fought back her own tears. "I know." She sniffled. "I feel terrible about Seamus."

He wiped her tears. "Don't beat yourself up."

"How do I move forward with all of this?"

"Love, let whatever you can't control go."

She nodded and nestled into him. They made love by the fire, not allowing the craziness of the day to drive a wedge between them. She wanted him every day, under any circumstance, under the sun or the moon. Always.

* * *

"Get up, Mom," Theo whispered, shaking her gently.

It felt like a dream. She squeezed him. "I love you so much."

"Mom! I looked for him everywhere!" He lifted Llama off the shelf.

Sunny barged into the room. "Rise and shine. Norah, can I show Theo around?" she asked, clearly excited to have someone her age to hang out with.

Theo's face turned a deep shade of rose. He'd never seen anyone like Sunny before, and he was mesmerized. He'd had little crushes appropriate for his age, but this had intensity. A soul connection. Sunny grabbed his hand, and they ran outside.

Norah sat by the fire and planted her bare feet on the earth. She closed her eyes and breathed deeply, her body tingling from the minty air she now so often took for granted. She blew the dust off her journal, long since she'd felt the urge to write in it.

I woke to Theo, touched his face, held his hand in mine. Never did I think. I rarely pray, knowing deep in my being a nothingness fills the air. But today, I'm making an exception. God, love, spirit—whomever or whatever you are. Thank you. Thank you for bringing him home. Too many wires crossed, all worth it. Worth having him back. I ask you to bring this family together, heal the wounds, pull us closer, not further away. Give me the grace to deal with it. I lose myself in my emotions, and I know Seamus needs me. Give him strength and purpose. This will be it for now, probably a long time, but I would be remiss to not stand in awe of the miracle.

She ripped the page out and laid it over the embers. *Ashes to ashes and dust to dust* popped into her mind. She didn't know why, had never felt attached to those words.

Ida sat with Myra at the table, eating breakfast. Norah had never seen her glow with joy; it warmed her heart.

"Ida, have you seen Seamus?"

"How are you holding up?" She sounded concerned.

Norah smiled. "I woke up with my beautiful son this morning."

Ida brushed her thumb over Myra's hand and nodded. "I put Seamus in my old room, haven't seen him yet."

Norah knocked on the door. She could hear him inside, but he didn't answer. "Seamus, it's Norah." No answer. She walked in. Fatty followed. Seamus was sitting in front of the window and staring out, a blank expression on his face.

"Here," she said, handing him a Gatorade.

He tried to twist the cap off, but his hand was still bloody and sore from punching the wall. She took it from him and opened it, then handed it back. "Thanks," he whispered, then guzzled the entire bottle. He looked at Fatty. "God, that pig, of all the animals to survive." He shook his head.

"I know, he's something… Seamus, I'm sorry. I didn't expect to get so angry yesterday."

"Nothing new, is it?" He shrugged.

"New to me. It's been twenty years since I felt that way," she said quietly.

Silence filled the space.

"You said something yesterday," he said.

"What?"

"You were raped." He had an awkward expression on his face.

Her heart jumped. She'd forgotten she had said it. "It was a long time ago, Seamus, I shouldn't have said anything."

"Tell me," he pleaded.

She sighed and sat beside him. "It was at the hospital. You were unconscious. Men"—her voice shook—"attacked me."

"Men?" His voice shook as well.

"Two." She cringed.

"I was lying a room away?" He looked horrified.

She nodded. He punched the desk with his good hand, over and over—now both hands were bloody and raw.

"Stop, Seamus," she pleaded as her tears poured onto her lap.

Emotions barged out uninvited. "I'm sorry I didn't protect you." He held his face in his sore hands. "I'm sorry for everything."

They sat in silence for a long time.

"I need some air." He wiped his eyes with his sleeve.

She nodded and led him to the inlet. A fire burned on the small beach.

"It's amazing," he said quietly.

She smiled gently. "I know, it's magic."

Seamus had spent a lifetime holding in his tears but the dam cracked under pressure. Tears flooded. "I love you, Norah. I know I didn't show it. I couldn't."

"I know you do, Seamus." She touched his face. "I love you, too. That will never change. You're family." She rested her head on his shoulder.

"I don't know how to do this." He sniffled. "Yesterday you were mine—as messed up as we were—and now... You're my best friend, my only friend."

"Seamus, I never felt like your best friend. Our relationship was strained survival. We fought constantly and lived in a state of anger, irritability, and anxiety." She paused, not intending to be cruel but wanting to be honest. "I guess most relationships were about survival when the sun reigned—probably the fear and dripping ego that saturated the planet."

"Oh, Norah." He sighed.

"Sorry," she said, realizing she had gone on a tangent. "You don't have to go through this alone, Seamus. I'm here... there's an entire family here."

"Who, you're husband?" His voice was shrill.

It was her turn to sigh. "Everyone, Seamus, including our son. Can you step outside yourself for a second and think of me? Do you have any idea of the heartbreak I went through when you disappeared?"

"Dad," Theo interrupted, "this is Sunny."

"Hi, Sunny," Seamus said, noticeably taken back by her mysterious looks.

Sunny placed her hands over his bloody knuckles, and the wounds healed. She leaned over and kissed his cheek. "I'm happy you're here." Her face filled with joy.

He stared at her, dumbfounded.

"Come on, Theo!" She ran and jumped in the water.

"Can I, Mom?"

"Go ahead. Just so you know, it might feel a little weird," Norah cautioned.

"Weird?" Seamus asked.

"Hard to explain. We think it's one of the reasons none of us are aging."

"I'm going in too." He stripped down to his underwear and turned toward the water.

Norah gasped and touched his back.

"You're not making this easy." He turned around and grabbed her waist.

She felt pulled to him for a split second and stumbled backward.

He leaned towards her again. "No, Seamus. Stop." She took another step back. "It will never happen."

He turned away.

"I touched your back," she stammered, "because it's covered in strange golden scars. The wounds look like brutally thick gashes."

He touched the raised skin and stared at Norah. Her stomach sunk into his heartbreak. He turned and ran into the water.

She felt sick.

She went to the hotel and knocked on Ida's door.

Myra opened it, smiling warmly. "Come in. I was just heading out for a walk." She excused herself.

Norah sat on the bed and burst into tears.

Ida put her hand on Norah's arm. "What's wrong?"

She sniffled. "I had a moment with Seamus at the inlet."

"A moment?"

"Like I was attracted to him." Norah dropped her chin to her chest.

"Did you act on it?"

"Never. I would never do that to Eldon." She breathed in. "It just surprised me."

"You were together for a long time. I'd say the reaction is pretty normal."

Norah winced. "I'm sure Eldon won't think it's normal."

"Do you think he needs to know?"

She bounced the question back. "Do you?"

Ida shook her head. "You need to decide that."

Norah nodded, walked to the church, lit some candles, and opened her journal.

This is mine. No lines were crossed. I trust Eldon. But reactions aren't about trust. Reactions are a surprise bag, you never really know what you'll get. Everyone becomes a stranger when confronted with something new. And this is new. Really it isn't only about reaction but a necessity. Before, I left the book open for everyone to read with zero discernment. Now, I choose to allow discernment, free of guilt, or some desperate need for absolution.

This is mine. I don't need to share it. There's too much shit going on to process more.

She went back to the cabin and fell onto her pillow, zapped from the emotional upheaval. Eldon crawled in beside her. Relieved to feel his arms around her, she kissed him. He undressed her and pressed her body into a needed release.

He brushed her hair out of her eyes. "I saw you walking to the inlet earlier." She didn't say anything. "Should I be worried, Norah?" His voice slightly broke.

She stared into his eyes. "No, Eldon, you have nothing to worry about." She bit his lip, made love to him again, and fell asleep.

"Mom, wake up." Theo was knocking on the cabin door. Eldon snored beside her.

"Be out in a sec." She tried to gather herself.

"Can we go for a walk?" he muttered through the door.

"Where's Dad?"

"He went to nap."

"Okay, just wait by the fire for me."

She and Eldon joined Theo by the fire a few moments later.

Theo looked up at Eldon. "Are you coming too?" he asked, seemingly oblivious of any awkwardness.

"Am I invited?"

Theo shrugged. "Yeah."

They set off down the path. Theo chatted up a storm about Sunny and the places they had explored.

Kitchi and Freya caught up to them. "Can we join?"

"Of course." Norah twisted her arm around Kitchi's elbow.

"We've heard so much about you, Theo," Freya said with a smile.

"Did Mom tell you I was this handsome?"

"No, she described you more like a hairy troll," Kitchi quipped. Theo punched his arm. Kitchi picked him up and tossed him over his shoulder.

At the inlet, Seamus was sitting by the fire. Awkwardness laced the minty air as they approached him. Norah knew it was impossible to move through it fast; it would take time to process, to find their footing.

Theo sat beside Seamus. "Thought you were napping. Are you having a moment?"

"You could say that." Seamus appeared blanketed in discomfort.

Ollie walked towards them, geared up for fishing. "Anyone up for a cast?"

Seamus's eyes brightened. "Do you have any extra waders and rods?"

Ollie smiled. "I'll hook you up."

"I'm coming too," Tayo said.

Usually, Eldon would have joined, but he stayed back out of respect.

Norah watched them walk away, relieved for Seamus and herself.

CHAPTER 15

THREE MONTHS PASSED IN FRAGMENTS, RIDDLED WITH AWK-
ward moments, emotions, and silences. Norah knew it couldn't be avoided
and walked through it gently.

Seamus and Ollie grew close and fished together every day. They
were all capable fishermen, but they relied on flies from the fishing store,
and supply was running low. Seamus, who knew how to tie flies, showed
up right in time and was in his glory. He figured out the salmon habits
and tied elaborate flies, enabling him to catch salmon way beyond an average weight, blowing everyone else out of the water. Obsessed with the fish
habitat, he explored every inch of the riverbanks. Someone usually tagged
along and soaked up his knowledge.

Norah leaned on a rock by the river, writing.

"Mom, guess what?"

She looked up and smiled. "What is it, Theo?"

"You'll never guess what me and Dad found!" Excitement beamed
off his face.

"What is it?" Norah laughed, waiting to hear the story.

"We went exploring and stumbled on a tiny channel off the river. Dad noticed something different about the current, and—"

"Theo, you sure ran fast." Seamus laughed and looked at Norah.

"I'm telling Mom what we found." He looked back at Norah. "Dad let out his line and couldn't get a bite. These little bugs bounced on the water, like cashid flies. Right, Dad?"

Seamus smiled. "Caddisflies."

"Yeah, cadishflies. Mom…" He paused to make sure she was paying attention. "They were glowing purply, like fireflies!" He almost levitated.

"What?" Norah looked at Seamus. "I haven't seen bugs since things changed."

"I know," Seamus said. "They were glowing purple. Nothing like I've ever seen. We're heading to that mall to gather materials for a fly. Come on, Theo." He motioned to him.

"Can I go find Sunny instead and help you later?"

"I'll come find you when I get back." Seamus headed towards the city.

Eldon was heading in the same direction at the same time for a supply run. Norah could see neither man wanted to obviously turn around, so they walked away together. Anxiety panged in her stomach. She breathed in, returned to her journal, struggled to write, and decided to return to the cabin. She fell asleep and awoke to Eldon shaking her.

"How long was I out?" she murmured.

"I was gone for two hours." He passed her the tea he'd made.

"Thanks." She took a sip—one bag of green, one mint. Her favourite. "I saw you leave with Seamus."

"Kinda weird at first but got easy. I like him."

She laughed. "Try dating him."

He shook his head. "Seriously, he's a good guy. I feel for him, can't be easy." Eldon sighed.

"I feel for him too. What did you guys talk about?"

"I don't know. Life before the Shade, how hard it was… Life now. His complete memory loss of where they were. Don't you ever think about that?" he asked.

"I think you forget who you're talking to." She sighed. "Of course I think about it, but just like everything, thinking doesn't help it make sense."

He nodded. "You won't believe this. Has he told you about his nightmares?"

"No?"

"Every night the same thing—there's a woman and young boy in a tribe with golden scars on their arms and faces, similar to the scars on his back. They're standing in some sort of circle surrounded by fire, and liquid gold is boiling in a cauldron. He screams in pain, wakes up."

Norah went silent.

"It's from your vision." Eldon looked like a kid who had just solved a mystery.

"Sounds like it." Norah felt confused but not surprised at the baffling connection. "I'm going to talk to him about it."

They walked to the hotel and bumped into Seamus and Theo in the hallway.

"Mom! Look at this fly Dad tied. We're going back. Eldon, you coming?"

Seamus motioned to Eldon. "Come on, man, grab your rod."

"Dad, I'm gonna get the others. Wait for us."

Theo ran off and left Norah, Seamus, and Eldon in the hall. Norah's stomach hurt, the awkwardness silencing her.

Seamus broke the silence with random conversation. "Is that a Bible that Maggie's reading all the time?"

"She's really into it," Eldon answered.

"Are you guys into it?" he asked.

"We're actually waiting for Ida to finish sewing your baptism gown," Norah answered. "Then Maggie will bring you to the inlet."

Seamus shook his head. "Tell Ida I don't need the gown. I'd prefer to be baptized naked," he said, his voice flat.

"Would you prefer Maggie be naked too?" Eldon answered, equally as flat.

Norah laughed. "Joking aside, it is just her. A lot of history with her and that Bible." She shook her head.

"An ocean under that bridge." Eldon sighed.

Theo ran into the hall. Ollie, Tayo, Kitchi, Freya, and Sunny tagged behind.

"Wow, Theo, you really rallied the troops." Norah giggled.

"You're coming, too, right?" Theo asked.

"Wouldn't miss it." Norah smiled and followed Seamus to the hidden channel. She felt closer to him than she had during their relationship. Without the resentment veiled over her eyes, she could appreciate him. "Eldon mentioned your dreams?"

"Oh?" Seamus responded.

"He knew I'd want to know."

"Why's that?"

"Long story short, we visited the sun side. You've heard the stories. I ate some moss, thinking it harmless, and ended up having a vision like I dropped ayahuasca. The woman and boy from your dreams were in my vision. You were standing with them, and she tries to kill me."

"That's nuts. I have them every single night. They're getting more vivid."

"Are you writing them down?"

"No."

"Well, you should. It obviously has something to do with where you guys were."

"Maybe." He shrugged.

"They could be your wife and son. Have you thought of that?"

"Not to give too much information, but in most of my dreams I'm making love to her."

"Oh, is that why you wake up all sweaty?" She smirked.

He shook his head. "No. Those ones are of me trying to save her off a rock table, like a sacrifice. She's about to get her head axed off."

Norah gasped. "That was in my vision, but it was me on the table, and she had a blade. She was stunning."

"An upgrade for sure."

"Shut up!" Norah walloped him.

He laughed, then paused a moment before he spoke. "Jesus, this is messed up. Look at us, Norah. Do you remember our house? Our life before?"

"How could I forget? I loved our house, we had a good life."

"We didn't see it. Wrapped up… God we always fought, and for—"

"Mom! Look!" Theo shouted, standing at the perimeter of the channel.

Norah sat on the edge and dangled her legs in the clear indigo water. Tiny glowing bugs jumped off the surface. The guys let out their lines.

"Jesus!" Seamus yelled a second later.

He was nearly pulled into the water as he fought his reel. Tayo dropped his line, grabbed Seamus from behind, and placed his hands over

Seamus's. Seamus started laughing while they thrust back and forth. The others followed, all ending in a line of grown men bear-hugging each other from behind, thrusting in unison, grunting and pulling with all their might.

Norah keeled over in uncontrollable hysterics as she watched the absurdity unfold. They succeeded in dragging the beast out of the river. It was not a salmon but an unknown species resembling a beta. A long mane wrapped its body with shimmering indigo scales. They stood in awe of the magical, mermaidesque creature with wisdom in its eyes.

Norah panicked, scared it would die, and opened her mouth to say something.

"Catch and release!" Seamus yelled.

No one moved, just stood around as the creature slapped its scales on the rock and fought for its life.

"Put her back in the water!" he yelled again.

They gathered around and gently lifted it back into the water. It floated, belly up. Norah started to cry when suddenly it splashed and disappeared into the mysterious deep. Everyone let out a communal sigh of relief. They sat on the rocks and caught their breath.

"Catch and release!" Tayo yelled, then fell into a bout of laughter.

Seamus keeled over and killed himself laughing too. Everyone held their stomachs in stitches. When a lull in the laughter came, they stared at the water.

"I've never had a man thrust me from behind like that," Seamus said deadpan, staring off into the distance as if trying to reconcile a trauma.

Everyone roared with laughter and keeled over again. They were unable to get their shit together for the rest of the day, randomly bursting into hysterical laughter. Tayo teased Seamus mercilessly about his catch-and-release command, an inside joke that never lost its edge. Not a day would go by where one of them didn't yell it randomly at inappropriate times—in the middle of saying grace or when Ida and Myra were caught in an embrace. Not to mention Seamus continually bugging Tayo about not putting his fishing pole away before helping him reel in the fish.

* * *

Norah walked to Freya's cabin. She missed her and felt as if they had become two ships passing in the night. Freya was introspective and quiet, not one to shoot the shit about nothing.

"How are you, honey?" Norah put her arm around her shoulder.

"I'm good, Mom. How are you?" Freya smiled, her auburn hair in a wild bun.

"I feel more settled. The last few months have been something." She shook her head.

"I know. We love Theo. He's so cute."

"He is. I'm happy he gets to know you and Kitch."

"Seamus is nice too."

Norah nodded. "He's a good guy." She paused. "What's happening with Kitchi and Tilly?"

Freya rolled her eyes. "Is that why you visited?"

"Freya, I miss you. I feel like my mind's been elsewhere. Sorry."

Freya laughed. "Mom, stop worrying. Why don't you ask Kitchi about his life?"

"I don't know. He doesn't talk to me as much… I've just noticed them closer than usual, if it's even possible."

"I'll tell you your instincts are right, but that's it." She smiled.

"Fine." Norah smiled too.

Kitchi and Eldon joined them.

"Hey, Kitch," Freya said, "Mom was just grilling me about you and Til." She laughed.

Norah blushed. "Freya!"

"Mom, you just can't help yourself, can you?" Kitchi smiled.

"No, I can't." She lifted her eyebrows. Eldon put his arm around her and kissed her cheek.

"I love her," Kitchi said.

"Awe, Kitchi." Norah felt like jumping up in celebration. "Did you tell her?"

"I did." He paused. "I asked her to marry me." It was his turn to blush. "She said yes." He beamed.

Norah teared up. "You and Tilly. The sweetest. I'm so happy for you both." Norah hugged him. "Have you been dating?"

"Since we were born." He smiled. "My heart wants to marry her first."

Norah looked at him and understood what he meant. She melted. They had never pushed any beliefs on him, not even a whisper of waiting for marriage.

"Kitchi, you are a sweet old soul, and you'll be a wonderful husband. Has she told Brittany?"

"Thanks, Mom, I learned from you and… Dad."

Norah choked up.

"Thanks for the honourable mention, son." Eldon smiled. "I'm proud of you. You guys are lucky to have each other."

"Thanks, Dad. She's telling Brittany tonight."

"When's the wedding?" Freya asked.

"A week." He shrugged.

"Wow, soon!" Norah laughed.

"Mom, I may be an old soul, but I need that honeymoon." He smiled and walked away.

Norah glanced at Eldon. "Can you believe it?"

"We just let them grow beside us, they did the rest," Eldon said quietly. He kissed her neck and led her into the cabin, where they tussled and fell asleep.

Norah woke unsure of the time and went to find Brittany She was curled in the blanket Maggie knitted years before.

"Our babies!" Norah stretched out her arms and hugged her.

"We did it." Brittany smiled. "We raised them in this strange world. Kitchi, what a gentleman, I couldn't believe what I heard." She paused. "I assumed they had already."

"Me too." Norah sighed.

"Guess we have a wedding to plan. I really want to do the hair and makeup," Norah teased.

Brittany's face went blank.

"I'm kidding!" She smiled.

"I love you, Norah. I don't know how I would've survived without you. I was a bratty kid when we met." Tears rolled down her cheeks.

"I love you, too, Brit. We've both grown."

* * *

Kitchi and Tilly wed at the inlet in an intimate and emotional ceremony. Ida officiated, and everyone joyfully pitched in. Brittany sewed Tilly a gorgeous mauve dress with gold accents, and Tilly wore her hair wild with golden and mauve flowers woven through it. Kitchi wore a slim-fitting golden tux with mauve accents. Both were barefoot and stunning. Ollie was best man and Freya, maid of honour. Tayo walked his daughter down the aisle and shared how grateful he was for Kitchi, a man he considered a son. A sober reception followed; over the years, the family naturally progressed to zero alcohol. Guitars played, and everyone danced.

Norah noticed Ollie and Veronika dancing close, whispering and laughing. She was flooded with emotions: sweet Ollie had finally embarked on his own adventure. They made a suave couple—Veronika, with her long braids and boho style, and Ollie with his greaser vibe.

Everyone released purple balloons and watched Kitchi carry Tilly up the narrow path towards the cave, where they would spend their honeymoon. It was a magical evening, sent off with the love and blessings of their family.

Kitchi and Tilly returned two weeks later, glowing, inseparable. Norah's body warmed when Tilly hugged her—she knew she carried a child. It took much restraint not to run and tell Brittany or Eldon, but it wasn't her news to share, so she kept their secret safe for a full month.

"We have an announcement," Kitchi said, on a rare occasion when everyone was gathered around the supper table.

"We're having a baby!" Tilly exclaimed.

Elated with the news of another little bundle, the family buzzed with joy.

"I have news too," Ollie piped in. "Sorry, I didn't want to overshadow the wedding, and now this amazing news. But… Veronika is moving into the cabin with me. We're an official couple." He beamed from ear to ear.

"A toast!" Eldon raised his glass. "To having babies and banging in closets!"

"What about banging in closets?" Seamus asked.

The room roared as Eldon told his favourite story, remembering their old friend Murph. Seamus bust a gut, hearing it for the first time.

* * *

Nadie was born eight months later. She had a pitch-black golden-tipped afro, alabaster skin, piercing green-indigo eyes, golden freckles, and three tiny golden scars on the nape of her neck. Kitchi and Tilly were doting parents. The family fell in love with Nadie, especially Sunny, who refused to leave her side. They were both children of the sun, Sparrows, able to open the geode to the other side. When Sunny held Nadie's hand, a golden aura glowed around their hands.

Kitchi and Tilly brought Nadie to the sun at three weeks old. Within hours, she became deathly ill. At the same time, Sunny turned deathly ill. No one realized the connection until Kitchi and Tilly returned and put them in the same room. Sunny reached out and held Nadie's hand. Both were instantly restored to health. They were unable to be apart for more than an hour without getting sick. Sunny rose in protest and insisted on joining them on their journeys to the sun. Brittany and Tayo were left with little choice. If they didn't let her go, they prevented Tilly and Kitchi from visiting the sun.

Theo was devastated whenever Sunny left and begged Norah and Seamus to let him go too—a request they adamantly refused. He wasn't like the others and could easily slip into a time warp. Norah's heels were dug in, terrified at the thought of losing him again. Whenever Sunny left, Theo plummeted into darkness. Norah struggled with seeing her own reflection and worried about him fighting the same demons. Theo's experience was different, though—not random nonsensical heaviness, but because his heart ripped out when Sunny left. Sunny felt the same way, but her connection to Nadie trumped everything.

CHAPTER 16

FIVE YEARS LATER

(SUNNY, SEVENTEEN; THEO, SIXTEEN; NADIE, FIVE)

THEO REFUSED TO BE CONTAINED INSIDE HIS PARENT'S FEAR. Norah hated seeing him suffer anyway and felt relieved to stop the fighting. Sunny promised she would hold Theo's hand when they went through the openings, and it seemed to work. In the past months, they had visited frequently. Theo was blown away by the magical realms.

The families were open about intimacy and sexuality, but their parents were concerned about the relationship between Sunny and Theo and the intense sexual energy the cave brewed. Not to mention the babies afterward. They had been in love since they were twelve, and it had been innocent enough the first couple of years, but when fourteen hit, they couldn't keep their hands off each other. Theo was now handsome and robust, with a stocky frame, curly brown hair, blue eyes, and a short beard hiding his dad's dimples. He dressed like a rapper. Seamus joked about him being a wangster, but Theo didn't care; he loved the style. Sunny was petite and wild, with her fine, straight Rapunzel hair that still needed trimming every day. She dressed like a hipster with big thick-rimmed glasses and high-waisted acid-wash jeans. It was funny to see their mismatched styles combined. Theo's energy was calm, and Sunny's buzzed wild.

Freya visited the cave and sun often, many times alone. She rarely spoke about herself, but of all the children, she was closest to Ida.

Seamus lived nomadically since Theo grew up and spent most of his time with Sunny. He loved his solo life, the freedom to do as he pleased. Gone for days at a time on expeditions, he explored every inch of the river and habitat. He even fixed a small boat and nearly died on multiple occasions from the rough waters. His dreams intensified, and he wrote them down as Norah had advised, but it didn't help to make sense of them.

Eldon and Norah were also enjoying a new sense of freedom. They planned a hiking trip to a hamlet marked on an old logging map, around three hours away. The path was rough terrain through dense dead foliage.

"How long have we been walking now?" she asked.

"A couple hours, I think. Shouldn't be much longer."

"I wonder how Theo's doing?"

"I'm sure he's better than ever." Eldon smirked.

"God, I hope he uses the condoms we gave him. They're so young." She grimaced.

"Are they, though? It seems young now, but I was younger."

"I know, I just don't know if I handled it right?"

"I don't see much choice. What are you going to do? Lock them in the church?"

"Parenting is hard," she said, defeated.

"You also worry too much, Norah."

"I guess." She shrugged.

"How old were you?" he asked.

"I don't know, twelve or thirteen." She played with a stick she found on the ground.

"That's ridiculously young," he said, surprised.

"Haven't we talked about this before?"

"I don't remember." He shrugged. "Why were you so young?"

"I was lost. No one talked to me about my feelings around sex. Only the physical stuff. My mom gave me a horrifying book full of chubby bodies and eighties pubes. I came up with my own ideas. Thought sex would make me older and more confident." She sighed. "It left me feeling disgusting and used. God, the guy, was nineteen." Norah hadn't thought about it in ages.

"Nineteen? Isn't that rape?" He shook his head.

"Never thought of it like that, but it was gross and horrible. Disgusting Tony with his perv stash and rusty old Ford truck." Norah stared down at the stick and sat with the fact that she was a victim then too. "What about you?

"I was fifteen. Her name was Sara. I liked her; we dated for six months before we had sex… It was awkward but sweet." He put his arm around her. "I'm sorry your first time was so awful."

Tears surfaced. "I can't believe I'm crying about this? It was a million years ago." She sniffled and remembered how empty and alone she had felt with no one to talk to. Her young body never acknowledged the hurt. She had so many scars from the *no big deal* incidents that occurred one too many times. The incidents society trained her to ignore and chalk up to nothing.

The remainder of the walk was quiet until they stumbled on the hamlet an hour later. Norah was surprised they even found it. About ten houses, a small church with red paint, and a massive garage made up the tiny village. Eldon was about to wander in when Norah pulled him down on the ground. In the distance, six men sat around a fire.

The movie *Deliverance* popped into her head. "The hills have eyes," she whispered as nerves rattled in her stomach. She was surprised people were living so close and was curious how they had survived the last two decades without being noticed. How had Murph never run into them? He went everywhere.

They decided to shelve their adventurous side, realizing they had grown too comfortable. They returned to share their discovery with the family and then carried on as usual, not giving the strange hamlet another thought.

*   *   *

Seamus returned from a fishing expedition a few days later and joined them around the fire.

"Something didn't feel right, walking back here," he announced.

"What do you mean?" Eldon asked.

"I felt like I was being followed. I kept switching paths but couldn't shake it."

Everyone went on high alert. Norah and Eldon told him about the hamlet.

"Do you think someone followed us?" Norah asked, worried.

"I can't see how," Eldon said.

"Maybe everyone should sleep in the hotel tonight," Seamus said.

A few guns were stored at the hotel, covered in dust, and they each grabbed one. The night passed slowly as they took shifts on guard. The uneventful night led to a string of nothings, and the fear slipped away.

*   *   *

A week after Seamus's eerie feeling, Eldon stared down at his plate.

"I never thought I would fall in love with powdered mashed potatoes."

Norah laughed. "And canned peas."

"Gross." Seamus laughed.

They were all startled by two men at the door. Norah recognized them from the hamlet, and they carried the same stench of her attackers. Tension filled the room, and the men hustled to their feet.

"Don't get up, sir, we're just stopping by." The man who spoke was greasy, with crooked teeth and sunken eyes. He wore dirty jeans and an old ball cap.

"Where are you coming from?" Eldon asked.

"Oh, you know, around," said the other guy, who resembled a squirrely meth addict. "How long have y'all been here?"

"Long enough," Tayo said.

They stared at Brittany, salivating.

"You guys should take off, we're in the middle of supper," Tayo said, ready to pounce.

"No hospitality, hey?" The guy resembling an addict sneered at his derelict friend, his teeth rotten and yellow.

"Okey-dokey. Well, take care, folks." He smiled at Brittany, lowered his ball cap, and walked out.

They all watched out the window as the men walked towards the church, certain it wasn't the last of them.

"Should we go after them?" Tayo looked at Eldon, revved to fight.

"And what, beat the shit out of them?" Eldon said.

Seamus nodded. "Yeah, sounds good to me."

"I'm not leaving our families," Eldon said. "We need to keep our heads on straight, there's more of them at the hamlet."

"Did you see the creep staring at me?" Brittany was shaking.

Tayo put his arm around her. "Don't worry, he won't touch you."

They grabbed their guns and took shifts again. Days passed with no sight of the men, but this time, they didn't relent. Holed up in the hotel, everyone grew antsy.

* * *

Norah and Brittany sat in the gazebo, reading. Seamus was with them, on his shift, his gun on his side. Norah saw the others walking towards the hotel, home from the cave. Brittany started walking towards them, but Seamus grabbed her arm and pulled her back.

"Just let 'em get over here first."

She didn't listen. She and Norah met them halfway.

"Where's Tilly and Nadie?" Brittany asked Kitchi.

"At the inlet for a swim, they'll be back soon."

Norah's stomach sank.

"What is it?" Kitchi asked, looking confused.

"Horrible men visited a few days ago," Norah said. "We've been on watch ever since—we don't think they left."

While Eldon, Ollie, and Seamus stayed behind to keep watch, Kitchi and Tayo booked it to the inlet. They returned minutes later, looking panicked. Nadie walked beside them, crying.

Brittany started shaking. "Where's Tilly?"

"She's gone," Tayo said, "we found Nadie at the beach alone." His voice shook.

"No," Brittany gasped.

Norah picked up Nadie. "Sweetheart, where's Mommy?"

Nadie didn't stop crying. "A man carried her away."

Brittany hugged Norah and Nadie, crying and shaking.

"Where is it?" Kitchi said, his voice filled with rage.

"I'll take you." Eldon grabbed his gun and handed one to Kitchi.

Tayo shot a look of daggers at Eldon. "We should've got them when they came!" He gripped his gun. "I'm coming. Seamus and Ollie, you stay with the others, and stay alert."

"I'm coming," Norah declared.

"No. You are not." Eldon commanded sternly.

"Eldon, I'm coming. Brittany will stay with Nadie. I've been on the path already. I'll be there for Tilly." Norah questioned herself, why she insisted on going. The thought of Tilly alone with those disgusting men…

Eldon shook his head, unimpressed. "Norah, you're so fucking stubborn. Just grab a goddamn gun."

They followed the dead foliage path to the hamlet, behind the men by minutes, but there was no sign of them. Kitchi blew through the woods at a super speed, but Norah didn't even struggle to keep up, running on adrenaline. The three-hour hike blazed by in an hour and a half. Norah felt like vomiting the entire way, thinking about Tilly, the mother of her grandchild; she loved her like her own daughter.

A fire burned at the hamlet. Norah gasped at the horrific scene, etched in her mind forever. Tilly was tied to a chair, her shirt ripped open. Five men stood around her, one groping her like an animal. He unzipped his pants and pushed her head down.

Like a raging bull, Kitchi barrelled towards them, shooting two men on the way. The other men fumbled to get their guns; one shot at him and barely grazed his arm, another ran at him from inside a house. Kitchi knocked him out cold. He reached the fire, grabbed one of the guys' guns, picked him up, and lobbed him onto the fire. Another wrapped his arms around Kitchi from behind. Kitchi backward head-butted him, turned, and pummelled his face into meat.

Norah's jaw dropped. She knew he was a machine, but not like this.

Tayo and Eldon slunk around the sides to make sure no others were hiding. Kitchi stood face to face with the cretin. He had positioned himself behind Tilly, with a knife to her neck, his hands down her dress. Norah watched Tayo creep up behind him with a crowbar, then wallop him over the head. He untied Tilly. She ran into Kitchi's arms, and he pulled his hoodie off and put it over her. Tayo let out a warrior scream and readied his gun, about to shoot the guy. Kitchi stopped him and hugged Tilly, then whispered something. Norah watched the ensuing tears of rage fall down his cheeks.

Norah walked to Tilly. Her face was bleeding, her hair matted, her eyes vacant. She fell into Norah's arms and sobbed. They sank to the ground, and Tilly put her head in Norah's lap and began to shake. Norah gently rubbed her head and cried.

Kitchi dragged the unconscious guy over to the chair and tied him up, his head slumped over. Norah didn't want to watch but couldn't stop, her eyes glued on her son and the creature. Eldon approached Kitchi, said something she couldn't hear, and walked away. Moments later, Norah heard gunshots, one after another. She knew. Her kind, gentle husband was on a killing spree.

Tilly cupped her ears and screamed.

The guy in the chair woke, realized he was now naked from the waist down, and began squirming and swearing. Kitchi squeezed his face with one hand and crushed his jaw. His teeth popped out like candies. Norah turned away, about to throw up, but looked back. The guy's mouth hung loose like a ventriloquist's puppet. Kitchi took the tip of a blade and held it in the fire until glowed red, then seared the guy's eyes shut. He shrieked. Kitchi grabbed a shovel, lifted a huge blazing rock out of the fire, and slammed it onto the guy's crotch, making sure his pants would never unzip again. He hissed and screamed through his broken face while the hot rock burned his lap. Norah nodded. As brutal as it was to watch, the fucker had it coming.

Eldon approached Kitchi. He glanced up the hill at Norah. Their eyes locked, shocked at their son's capacity for vengeance.

Kitchi climbed the hill to Norah and Tilly. Tears filled his eyes as he transferred Tilly's head onto his lap.

Norah grabbed his gun and walked down to Eldon. The guy's hissing and squealing was unbearable.

"What are you doing here?" Eldon whispered.

"Kitchi's with Tilly, he said there wasn't anyone left?" she whispered.

He shook his head, clearly irritated she'd come down to him. "We've searched through all the houses except for that one." He pointed at a run-down small blue house.

Norah followed Eldon and Tayo inside. She had never smelled a stench so rank. Like a dump, food rotted in the corners and whiskey bottles and cigarette butts lined the floor. There was no furniture except two broken lawn chairs in the middle of what might have once been a living room, every inch decrepit and decayed. They masked their mouths with their shirts and climbed the stairs. The bedroom upstairs was empty except for a small bed. The bare mattress was peppered with discoloration and stains, and rusty handcuffs hung from the frame.

Norah gasped and squeezed Eldon's hand.

The stairs squeaked as they made their way down to the kitchen. Norah tripped on a small handle protruding from the rotted lino floor.

"What is that?" she asked, her voice muffled by her shirt.

Tayo pulled up on it, opening the door to a cellar. Their nostrils whiffed an inhuman stench. Tayo vomited in his shirt. Norah let her shirt fall and puked, cupping her mouth with her arm.

Eldon winded his flashlight and shone it down, then jumped back and fell on the disgusting floor. "What the fuck?" He gasped for air.

"What?" Norah shook. "What is it!?" Her body was tremoring with fear and she was sweating profusely.

"Someone…" Eldon pointed at the cellar.

Tayo took the flashlight and slowly approached the door. He shone it down, and mortification clouded his eyes. "Norah, hold this." He handed her the flashlight and stepped down.

"Don't go down there!" Norah pulled him back. Her eyes watered. She tried to take a deep breath, but the stench wouldn't permit it. She shone the light down. "No!" she gasped, putting her other hand over her mouth.

A young girl, around eight, was curled in the corner. A filthy flannel nightgown drooped on her frail body and her hair looked like it had never met a comb. Beside her, a worn-out rotting mattress held a decaying woman's body. The small cellar was only big enough for the child and the bed. Surrounded in the stench of shit, piss, and death.

Tayo reached in and lifted the girl out. She bit him and ran to the corner of the kitchen, shaking and feral. They sat on the floor a distance away from her. Norah reached in her backpack and pulled out a water bottle, then slid it across the floor. The girl guzzled down the entire bottle.

"We won't hurt you," Eldon whispered.

She winced at his voice and stared, feral, like a wild animal caught by hunters.

Tayo approached her slowly and reached out his hand. "Come, you're safe, we aren't going to hurt you."

She scuttled away.

Norah, struggling to breathe in the stench, let her shirt fall from her nose and stretched out her arm. "Come on, love." She smiled. The girl didn't scuttle away this time, just stared at Norah, shaking. Norah inched closer. Within an arm's reach, she brushed her hand. The girl pulled it away. Norah touched it again. The girl blinked profusely, stared at Norah, and lifted her hand slowly. Norah nodded and gently clasped her boney fingers, fighting tears. She helped the girl to her feet, and she collapsed, unconscious. Norah wrapped her sweater around the child's frail body, and Eldon carried her out. The minute air touched Norah's face, she braced herself on Tayo and fell apart.

They returned to Tilly and Kitchi. Both were clearly struggling to make sense of what they were seeing.

Tilly touched the girl's head and screamed. "No!"

Tears poured down Eldon's cheeks and splashed onto the unconscious child cradled in his arms.

Sniffling people and crackling earth were the only noises heard on the trail home. Everyone was grappling with a reality none could face.

With the dense bush behind them, they approached the gazebo. Norah's eyes locked onto Ida's. She lowered her head and wept. Brittany and Nadie ran to Tilly and squeezed her into a hug, then let her go and stared at Eldon, struggling to register what their eyes were taking in.

Myra came out, the only one who didn't in some way fall apart as she zoned into doctor mode. "We need to get her to the hospital."

"I'll go with you," Norah said.

Ida nodded. "Me too."

Eldon looked at Tayo. "You need to come too... keep your gun."

Tayo looked puzzled. "Why?"

"That little guy wasn't there," Eldon said.

"What?" Tayo asked.

"One of the guys who stopped into the hotel, he wasn't there. I just realized it."

"Did you see the other one?" Tayo asked.

Eldon nodded and lowered his eyes. He laid the girl on a stretcher and rolled her to the emergency unit.

Myra stopped and studied the medication cabinet, knocking bottles over and reading the labels. "People must've looted the pain killers. Surprised they left the antibiotics."

Norah and Eldon shot Tayo a look. He shook his head and shrugged.

"Found something." She held up a syringe and filled it with liquid from a few different bottles.

Norah flashed back to herself standing in front of the cabinet, filling a syringe.

The girl began flailing and thrashing. Eldon and Tayo held her down, and Myra injected her with a needle. She passed out.

"I'll examine her while she's out," Myra said. "Ida, can you help?"

Ida nodded and inhaled an audible breath.

Eldon, Tayo, and Norah went to the waiting room, jumpy with every creak and noise.

Brittany was sitting on a metal waiting room chair, pale and red-eyed. "How is she?"

"Brittany, you shouldn't have come here alone," Tayo snapped. Then he walked over and hugged her. They fell apart together.

Norah put her head on Eldon's shoulder, exhausted.

"Where's Tilly and Nadie?" Tayo asked Brittany.

"With Kitchi, they went to lie down." She sniffled. "I want to ask what happened, but I can't." She stared at the floor.

No one said a word. They didn't talk about it because the words were razor blades in their mouths.

Norah nodded off on Eldon's shoulder. She woke to Ida's voice.

"The girl is still out." Ida braced the wall and sank to the floor. Myra sank down beside her and wept. Norah sat on Ida's other side and put her arm around her shoulder. "Monsters," Ida whimpered.

"Will she make it?" Eldon asked quietly.

Myra wiped her tears. "She's severely malnourished and dehydrated. Her body"—she lowered her head—"she's probably around twelve. We'll have to take shifts and slowly help her hydrate."

"She guzzled an entire water bottle when we found her," Eldon said.

"It probably shocked her body. We'll take it slow from now on." Myra took a deep breath. "I'll keep administering antibiotics; they're old but hopefully have some potency left."

Brittany handed Myra a set of Sunny's old pajamas. "These should fit."

"She needs to be washed first," Ida said.

Norah stood up. "I'll boil some water."

Eldon followed her out of the emergency room. She cupped Eldon's face in her hands and stared into his vacant eyes.

Back at the hotel, Maggie stood at the sink in the kitchen. Norah leaned over, grabbed the water jug, and filled the cast iron pan.

"The girl?" Maggie whispered, her voice shaky.

"She's alive. I'm boiling water to help clean her," Norah said flatly, emotions spent.

"I'm helping you." She put her hand on Norah's. "Who would do this?"

"I don't know, Maggie." She squeezed her hand.

They pulled the jugs of warm water to the hospital in a grocery cart. Ida and Myra were asleep on the floor in the hall, slumped over each other. Brittany and Tayo stared silently at nothing.

"Thanks, Norah," Brittany said. "Are you okay if we go check on Tilly and Nadie?"

"Go, I'll come down after," Norah replied, then pushed the water into the room.

Maggie gasped at the sight of the frail skeleton of the girl.

Norah put her hand on the older woman's back. "Maggie, if it's too much, it's okay."

"No, I'm here." She straightened her sweater in pure Maggie fashion.

Norah was grateful Maggie didn't leave her alone. She grabbed the scissors, cut the rags off the child's body, and tossed them in a garbage bin. Maggie hummed a Christian song. Norah surprised herself when she started to sing along; she knew it from her Bible days. They both sang quietly while they washed the girl and finally dressed her in the fresh pajamas.

Norah stopped singing and studied the matted mess of hair. "I think we have to cut it."

Maggie nodded, picked up the scissors, and cut the hair short. Norah shampooed out the dirt, dumped the water in the shower, and watched the filth drain down. The girl looked fairy-like, with her short straight dirty-blonde hair. Norah tucked her under some blankets with Llama and then wheeled the wagon outside.

Myra woke. "How long were we out?"

"Not long," Norah answered. "Maggie and I cleaned her as best we could."

"I'm going to check on her." Myra stood.

Ida sat up and shook her head. "Thought for a second it was just a nightmare."

"It *is* a nightmare." Norah sighed and went outside with Maggie. They threw the rags and towels in the fire. She embraced Maggie. "Thank you," she whispered.

Hours later, the frail girl woke, and she was calmer, not thrashing. Myra tried to talk to her, unable to determine if she was mute.

Over the next few days, while shifts of two people stayed at the hotel, the girl ate small pieces of bread and took sips of water. Sunny and Theo brought books and read them aloud to her, reporting that she even smiled at one point. They had an innocence about them, somewhat oblivious to the weight of the situation.

Norah hurt for Tilly. Flashbacks of her own attack surfaced, along with the visceral shame and rage.

"May I?" Norah sat with her at the fire. "How are you, Til?"

"Feel off. Don't want Kitchi to touch me. I've never felt like that before." She looked down at her lap.

"It will take time to get back on your feet," Norah said. Tilly shrugged. "I was attacked after the Shade," Norah continued. "It took me time to heal."

Tilly looked up at Norah. "I'm sorry, Norah. Where did men get the idea that we're theirs whenever they desire? I read about it in books—the old world, the horrors women suffered, not to mention my people's history. Why are humans so ugly?" she asked, looking for a genuine answer.

"I wish I had answers, Til."

"I don't know how to move forward." She stared blankly.

"Slowly. A wise man once told me not to hide away. To put my feet on the ground, scream, write, do whatever I needed to do to move through the pain."

"Yeah," she whispered. "Think I'll go lay down. Thanks, Norah." She forced a smile.

Norah returned to the cabin to find Kitchi sitting by the fire, holding his head in his hands. "Hey," she said.

"I don't know how to be there for her, Mom."

She put her arm around him; it barely stretched around his shoulders. "You just be there. At her pace. Be gentle and patient."

"All I can see is that guy groping her." He let out an angry growl. "I feel like killing someone."

"Kitchi, look at me." He looked up at her. "You did kill someone. It won't help." She paused. "Take your focus off them and put it on Tilly. Okay?" She nodded and waited for him to nod back.

"Okay." He nodded.

"Why don't you take her to the sun for a while?"

"I will." He paused and then changed the subject. "The girl, how?" His face furrowed in confusion and sadness.

"I have no answers for the evil in the world."

They stared silently at the fire.

Sunny burst into the room. "She's taking steps, come on!"

They headed to the hospital. The girl was bracing herself against the wall and taking teeny steps. Norah figured she must have gone outside at some point. The cellar was too narrow to move around. Fatty waddled up to the girl, and her eyes widened in shock; it was evident she hadn't seen an animal before. She smiled and scrunched her face awkwardly as if searching for an appropriate expression, then sat on the floor and laid her head on his side.

Norah laughed tears of relief and joy, watching Fatty work his magic. She walked up and sat down. "This is Fatty, he's a pig."

The girl stared at Norah, her face wrinkled and contorted. She put her hand on Norah's cheek and brushed her hair off her face. "Pretty," she whispered, barely audible.

Norah smiled. Tears welled again. She caressed the girl's cheek with the back of her hand. "You're pretty."

Sunny and Theo joined them. The girl started panicking. Norah helped her back to her room, tucked her in bed, and sung to her until she fell asleep.

Norah left Sunny and Theo at the hospital and went to the cabin.

"What are you doing?" she asked Eldon. He was sitting on a chair with his hands folded in his lap, staring at the wall.

"Nothing," he answered coldly.

She had never seen him like this. Broken.

"Why don't you come out, spend some time with Nadie?" She put her hand on his knee.

"I shot six men in the head." He continued to stare at the wall.

"You protected us." Her stomach sank at her feeble attempt to spin the narrative. Irritated with herself, she tried again. "Yes. You killed six men."

"I don't know... how to look at Nadie, how to look at you or anyone."

"I'll tell you how." She lifted his chin and forced eye contact. "You just look."

He screamed into his hands, "I can't fucking look, all I see is their faces! I took their heartbeats, I chose!"

"Eldon. You chose. Would you do it any differently now?"

"No," he said flatly.

"We can't afford to lose you. I can't afford it... What we've all seen, gone through. We're swimming in a soup of PTSD and shock. We don't have support groups and therapy." She sighed. "We have each other... and it's enough."

He kneeled and laid his head on her lap and bawled. His body shook, drenched in sweat. He lifted his head, pulled her into him, and released his pain inside her. "I'm going to the river," he said, a hint of relief on his sorrowed face.

When he was gone, she picked up her journal.

Falling into this madness, I need to keep my feet grounded, I will not crumble. I won't let them have me, have my family. Too much, too long, too far, my journey, not for nothing. Some are human, some are serpents, some are in between. The ones I breathe with now, human. This is my resolve, my reckoning. I will not give my attention to belly-crawling serpents.

"Gwama." Nadie walked around the corner, holding Eldon's hand.

"Nadie!" Norah kneeled and hugged her. Nadie handed her a folded paper, and Norah opened it. "Beautiful, did you draw this?

Nadie beamed. "It's our family."

"I love it." She tacked it onto the wall, along with the other collage of drawings collected over the years.

Eldon picked Nadie up and scrunched his face into her stomach, bringing her to a fit of giggles.

"Put me down, Gwampa," she begged. Norah looked at Eldon and smiled, relieved to see some life in him.

CHAPTER 17

THE WEEK MOVED SLOWLY, THE AIR THICK WITH GRIEF. Sunny and Theo prepared one of the hotel's empty rooms for the girl, who hadn't spoken since she'd said *pretty*. They painted the walls light yellow and decorated the room with flowered posters and stuffed animals. Norah and Maggie found a wheelchair and pushed the girl over to the hotel; she could take small steps daily but lacked the strength for anything substantial. When she arrived, the others gave her space, not wanting to overwhelm her. The minute she entered her room, she beamed. It was the first time Norah saw her smile. She rose from the wheelchair, did a small twirl, and plopped in the soft beanbag chair, exhausted. She curled up and hummed to herself.

"I hope you'll join us for supper." Norah smiled and touched her shoulder. She didn't move, just kept humming.

Half an hour later, Sunny walked into the dining hall, holding the girl's hand.

"Come sit." Norah motioned to a chair and smiled.

The girl sat and looked at the place setting in front of her. She lifted the fork and tapped it on the plate.

"I know we've asked you," Norah said, hoping she might speak, "but what is your name?" If she even knew.

The girl kept tapping the plate. "Peaches." Her voice trembled.

"What a beautiful name." Norah glanced at the others, who were shuffling in around the table.

"Mama named me," she whispered.

Norah glanced at Eldon, heartbroken. The body in the cellar.

"Did she teach you to talk and walk too?" Sunny asked.

"Mm-hmm… Papa let us outside to walk." She kept tapping her fork.

"Papa?" Theo asked.

"Papa lived on the outside with the others." She shook. "Before Mama." She looked down at her plate and stimmed back and forth, repeating *Mama* over and over. Maggie put her arm around her, and she stopped. "Papa stole Mama and made me in the cellar with the peaches… Papa didn't give enough food, so Mama gave me hers."

Kitchi smiled. "Peaches. We're happy you here with us now."

She started shaking and turned paper white, then cupped her ears and rocked back and forth. Ida helped her walk to her room, and Maggie followed with a plate of food.

Theo put his head down. "I should've known not to say anything."

They ate in silence and turned in early.

The next morning, Sunny and Theo wheeled Peaches to the inlet. It was her first time in the water, and she loved floating with her life jacket. Everyone joined them around the fire on the beach, and the guys brought the guitars. Peaches wrapped herself in a towel and sat in the sand beside Theo, leaning on him as she listened to the strumming. Out of nowhere, an angelic voice bellowed. Peaches, not giving it a second thought, was belting a beautiful song not fitting of her meek, unassuming nature. The guys continued playing, in awe of her mind-blowing voice. "Where did you learn how to sing like that?" Sunny asked when she stopped.

"Mama." She shrugged.

"You have an amazing voice," Theo said.

The ghost of a smile appeared before she ducked her head down and stared at Nadie. "Mama sang better, she was famish."

"Famish?" Sunny asked.

"People paid dollars to hear her sing."

"You mean famous?" Ida said.

Peaches nodded.

"What was her name?" Theo asked.

"Mama."

A famous family could have easily lived in an affluent area. They were baffled to think a celebrity could have an end so brutal. Strange how the Shade obliterated fame. Superstars could have roamed, lost; money was irrelevant.

Norah and Eldon returned to their cabin. They were not yet through the door when yelling bellowed from the hotel. They rushed over. The creepy straggler Eldon had been worrying about was behind Brittany, holding a knife to her neck.

"I don't want trouble, just Peaches," he sneered.

"How do you know Peaches?" Seamus asked.

"She's my girl. I'll trade this whore for her." He yanked Brittany's head back by the hair. "Peaches get out here now, it's Papa!" he yelled.

Brittany squirmed. "Don't give her to him!"

He pulled her hair again. "Shut up, slut." Clearly his screws were not just loose but had fallen out.

Tayo looked like he was ready to jump out of his skin, his back against a wall—not willing to send Peaches or lose Brittany. A literal standstill.

Peaches appeared, breathless. "I'm here, Papa,"

"Get over here, you little tramp," he spit, eyes wide and crazy.

She inched towards him, shaking.

He slammed Brittany to the ground and grabbed Peaches, the knife blade now pressing against her neck. He nestled into her ear. "I missed you, darling."

Brittany clamped her teeth down on his ankle and clenched. Norah heard the bone crunch. He kicked her face with his heel. She held on. Kitchi grabbed his arm, and the knife dropped. Peaches toppled down. Norah rushed to Brittany, who was coughing, clutching her throat, her mouth covered in blood. Kitchi lifted the guy and rag-dolled him onto a massive rock. His head cracked open, and blood gushed. Dead.

"No!" Sunny ran to Peaches, who had blood pooling around her head. "The knife nicked her jugular." She frantically tried to close the wound with her hands. Then she closed her eyes. Her arms illuminated, and a faint golden light swirled around Peach's neck. Sunny screamed a piercing shriek. Her hair turned pure gold, and her skin became covered in golden freckles. She passed out. Brittany slumped over her and screamed.

Norah rushed to Peaches. No more blood gushed, so she took her sweater and wiped the girl's neck. No wound.

Peaches coughed and gasped for air. She propped the upper half of her body up with her forearms, hyperventilating. Then she crawled to Sunny, who still lay limp on the ground, and rested her head on Sunny's forehead, weeping.

Theo ran out of the hotel, turned white as a ghost, and lifted Sunny.

"No, Theo?" Brittany said, holding on to her as if it were a tug of war.

"Brit, please," he said gently, "there isn't time."

Brittany released her and fell into a pile of tears. Theo ran towards the cave.

"Where's Tayo and Nadie?" Norah asked, fighting for breath.

"The church." Brittany barely pushed the words out between sobs.

The remaining men lifted the guy's body and walked towards the hospital with it. Norah never asked what they did with it; simply put, she didn't care where it lay.

Ida and Myra took Peaches to her room, and Norah helped Brittany to the gazebo, then left for a second and returned with a wet cloth and a few water bottles. While Brittany swished water in her mouth and spit it in the fire repeatedly, Norah wiped the blood off Brittany's face. Then she put her arm around her friend's shoulder and stared at the bloody aftermath: no tears, only a rage-laced numbness.

How much more can we carry? she thought.

Nadie ran into the gazebo. "Gwama, look!" She handed Brittany a picture.

Brittany pulled her onto her lap and squeezed her. Tayo stood at the gazebo's opening, the colour drained from his face. "What?" His voice shook.

Brittany stammered, "It's S-S-Sunny."

"What about me?" Sunny asked. She stood in the doorway, smiling. Theo held her hand, pale, still in shock.

Sunny sat beside Brittany and Nadie and put her arms around them. Norah put her arms around Theo.

"What happened?" she asked.

Theo put his hand on his forehead. "Halfway to the cave, she just… woke up… as if nothing happened."

Peaches, clean and in fresh clothes, walked past. She stood before the stone, still bloodied with remnants of skin and tissue, and rocked back and forth. Sunny went to her and put her hand on her back. Peaches looked over, touched Sunny's face, and smiled.

*　*　*

The violence left a permanent residue on each heart. Norah had never experienced this quiet—even after Murph, life moved. Now, silence engulfed unspoken words and the hollow stares of too much.

Sunny fell ill a few days after she let her light out to save Peaches. Weak, she barely ate or drank and her body plummeted into a decline. Myra ran what tests she could and reported Sunny's blood didn't even register a type. No medication touched her. Theo didn't leave her side, worried sick, and he barely ate either. Norah's and Seamus's dreams intensified.

Norah knocked on Sunny's door.

"Come in," Sunny whispered, her buzzing energy now subdued.

Norah's heart sank at the sight of her and Theo. Both broken and sick. She kissed Theo's head and put her hand on Sunny's arm… dry and scaley, covered in an eczema rash.

"I had another dream last night, under the sun." Sunny's breath rattled. "I need to leave the moon. Forever. I won't make it much longer." She coughed into her pillow.

"Sweetheart, you need to tell everyone." Norah fought tears and looked at Theo, feeling heavy with the inevitable separation.

Theo squeezed Sunny's hand and spoke to Norah. "Get everyone for supper tonight." Norah nodded as he cast his gaze to the floor.

Outside, she scanned the surroundings, her home. An eclectic mix of personalities could be seen in the bright colours and fabrics strewn around, the carved wood structures, giant sculptures, and quaint décor from their downtime over the years. As tragic as the Shade was, it birthed freedom by not needing to work and rely on money, having what they needed at their disposal. They were free from the pressure of manically harvesting the success of the old world: RRSPs, RESPs, and every other irritating acronym.

The days of bank massacres died with the sun. When the money of the people was stolen in plain sight, the banks were the criminals. The lie of lifelong mortgages. The false security that fed on the guilt of what we will leave the children. Norah had battled the sense of being an underachiever. Feeling she hadn't accomplished enough to be someone, she believed her light dimmed in comparison to the educated elite. A belief born out of academia's lie that education equalled intelligence.

Worth had been measured by degrees. But worth came at a cost. A hefty admission was required to enter the walls of academia prison, and if you couldn't afford it, you borrowed until it shone like success. A business. The businessmen. Modern-day gods. The shiny success turned into insurmountable debt on the backs of the winners.

*　*　*

Sunny sat in a wheelchair at the head of the table. "We need to talk about something." She coughed. "I'm getting sicker. Weaker. I don't have much time." She looked at Nadie and wept.

A density entered the room. Theo inhaled a deep breath. "I don't know how to do this." He paused. "We have to leave, and we won't come back."

"We know," Brittany cried. Tayo held her hand. "We're coming with you."

"Mom, you don't know if you can survive there."

"I won't survive here without you," she declared.

Norah looked at Seamus and cried. She knew Theo, Kitchi, Tilly, and Freya would follow. "We're going too," she said, squeezing Eldon's hand. Eldon nodded.

"Me too," Seamus said.

"Me too." Peaches whispered.

"Us too," Tilly said.

"Us too," Ollie and Veronika said in unison.

Ida cried during a long silence. "We're staying here."

Norah's heart was crushed. She couldn't even look at Ida.

"Me too," Maggie said, tears falling down her cheeks.

"We're leaving now." Theo inhaled another deep breath and looked at Norah. "We'll wait for everyone by the lake under the sun."

Norah nodded. The others planned to leave in one week. Everyone hugged them, emotional. Sunny was too sick to fall apart more.

"We'll see you soon," Brittany whispered to Sunny, then looked at Theo. "Take care of her."

"I'm not letting you go alone, brother," Kitchi said. He and Tilly stood from the table.

"We'll pack up and see you soon, okay?" Tilly smiled.

A weighted blanket of heaviness draped over the family. They never imagined something would tear them apart. Forever. It felt like a terminal diagnosis. Norah had already lost her mother, her world, and now Ida, her surrogate mother. Fatty rooted in Norah's leg. *No,* she thought as the realization settled into her bones, *he wouldn't make the trip.*

Eldon and Norah drew closer. One of the gifts of their relationship was that pain pulled them together, not apart. They spent hours at the inlet and hot pools, trying to move through the sadness. The hotel—what they knew, where they had fallen in love and gotten married and had their family—every moment was lived there, it held their life. The unknowns of the other side brewed anxiety, variables dangled in the air, psyches unsettled. The excruciating bittersweet pill of leaving the others. A tarnished lining, for everyone.

Norah visited the church for the last time. Over the years, it had transformed into a gypsy-like sanctuary, deconstructed with big comfy chairs and pews in random places, sheepskin rugs, and Ida's resin projects.

The altar was covered in the gems and crystals Norah and Ida had collected, some so massive Eldon had to pull them back with the trailer. Holy books from every religion and faith were scattered about, along with tarot cards, crosses, musical instruments, smudging shells, salt lamps, dripping candles, and graffiti murals where the kids had gone wild with art. Tapestries covered the walls, and Kitras glass balls and windchimes hung from every inch of the ceiling. The chapel was unrecognizable except for skinny Jesus.

Norah lay on the floor and sobbed. Her religion wasn't in seeking. Her faith lived in nature—the soil resting between her toes, the river crashing into the rocks, the love she made to Eldon, and her children's laughter. Her spirit lived through connection, the beating hearts that breathed love into her life. God never lived inside the walls of a church but in moments. In her breath. The spirit she sought resided within; she carried the holiest of the holiness in her veins. One of the few left with breath, Norah still had no understanding of what had transpired so long ago when the sun left the moon orphaned, alone to cast shadows every second of every day.

Sorrow-filled pixie dust swirled the space. She lifted *The Tibetan Book of the Dead* and flipped to a random page. Words danced off: *This world can seem marvellously convincing until death collapses the illusion and evicts us from our hiding place.* She was being evicted from her hiding place, the safety of her home. She fell at the altar and wept tears of an ending. She had lost her blood family many moons ago, and now she broke with the fragile farewell to her indigo tribe.

A hand brushed her back. Eldon—she hadn't heard him come in. He burrowed into her hair and absorbed the weight of the moment. She let him touch her, and they gave skinny Jesus his final moaning concerto. They dressed afterward and blew out the candles. She stood in the door, stared at the sanctuary, and bid farewell to skinny Jesus. They walked towards their own final supper, the air burdened with grief.

* * *

Eldon lifted his glass. "I can't find words to touch the way I feel—we feel. Our family is separating. The souls who carried our lives watched the births of our children and grandchildren. When I first looked around the hospital wondering what the hell had happened, I saw your faces and was terrified." Everyone laughed. "I thought, who are these people, and what the hell am I going to do?... You people became my everything. Somehow the world ended, and we stumbled into a family most of us never knew." He looked at Ida, tears falling. "Do you know how many times I've wanted to beg you to come with us, knowing if I made a strong enough argument, you might? I couldn't. All these years you've accepted us, listened to us cry and moan, cooked and cleaned for us. I can't imagine life without you." He smiled and looked at Maggie. "We've been through hell and back. You taught me to love, forgive, showed me the power of faith in overcoming pain, and I love you. Murph loved you more than anything." He put down his glass and wiped his tears.

The food was barely touched. They all prayed for time to stand still. Norah brought dishes to the sink.

Ida took her hand. "Come with me." She led Norah to her room, Fatty following on their heels.

Norah sat on the edge of her bed, the place she had spent countless hours crying and laughing. Ida went into the closet and came out with a gift wrapped in a colourful sari.

"Oh, Ida."

"Go on, open it." She smiled.

Norah unfolded the fabric to find a quilt with a giant moon in the centre circled by stars.

"How long have you worked on this?"

"A long time. Funny, I finished this last week. There's one star for each of us." She sniffled.

Norah hugged her, stomach aching. Ida poured her tea. They talked for hours, trying to keep morning at bay. Eventually, Norah left the room with Fatty by her side, walked to the river, and stared at the sky, soaking in her last night, immersed in the magic of the moon.

Eldon beckoned to her. "Norah, we're leaving soon, in a few hours."

She still sat by the river, not a wink of sleep. The cabins were empty, backpacks filled with what they could carry. The heaviness now hardened to concrete in Norah's stomach. She looked at Fatty, her sweet friend and brought him down to the inlet for a swim. She bawled her eyes out as she watched his funny little hooves running in the water, the curly tail she adored. They lay together on the beach. She tried to get up, but he kept grumphing and rooting in her lap. She had to return.

"Come on, Fatty, we gotta go back, sweetheart." Usually, he would have run behind her, but he refused to move. She pushed his bottom. He just lay in the sand, staring and whining. She walked away, and he finally got up and waddled behind her, rooting his nose into the back of her knee-caps every few seconds.

At the hotel, she fell into Eldon's arms, a blubbering mess. He lifted the backpack onto her shoulders, and they headed to the inlet, a silent procession, wishing each step was a year. They stood in a circle on the beach, arms wrapped around each other, Fatty in the middle. No words. Only sniffles.

"I love you, Ida," Norah said. "I wouldn't have made it without you." They held each other's shoulders, nodded their heads, and let go. Norah embraced the others. She sat down with Fatty and laid her head on his bristles. "Fatty," she sobbed, "I love you, sweetheart. You healed my heart. I'll miss you, my sweet love." She kissed his nose and bawled her eyes out. She forced herself to her feet. It reminded her of the shed; she had to move. Her feet now on the narrow path, one foot in front of the other, she repeated the motion.

Fatty squealed behind her, struggling up the hill, his fat body too wide for the narrow path and his hooves slipping on the rocks.

"Go back, Fatty, you're not coming this time," Norah yelled, but he kept fighting until he finally slipped and fell into the water. Norah watched him swim back to shore. "I can't do this, Eldon." She squeezed him, snotty and mangled.

"Norah"—he lifted her chin—"our children are leaving."

She nodded and pushed forward, hearing Fatty's squeals the entire way up the path.

They stood at the opening, exhausted, emotionally spent. Norah glanced back. Fatty's screams were now barely audible. She inhaled a deep breath and took a step forward, her feet melting into the indigo clover. She collapsed and let the energy wave over her, Fatty's cries etching her heart.

CHAPTER 18

THEY STAYED IN THE CAVE FOR A DAY SO THE OTHERS COULD acclimate to the energy before crossing over. Norah lay inside the labyrinth for hours, letting the mysterious energy encompass her body. Nadie ran wild, climbing the geodes and tangling inside the labyrinth. Peaches was mesmerized, randomly bursting into tears at going from being in the cellar her entire life to now walking barefoot in the clover. She exploded with joy, frolicking and twirling like a princess. Norah was grateful she had joined them. If anyone deserved light in their life, it was Peaches. Ollie and Veronika went off on their own, soaking the vibes of the cave. Norah liked Veronika; she was easygoing and quick-witted, like Tayo. Seamus slept for hours, basking in the energy and overwhelmed by the buzz of the cave.

Brittany and Norah went for a walk, one arm woven into the others. Norah pulled out the moon blanket from Ida.

"Wow," Brittany said.

"Ida made it for all of us; I forgot to show you."

"Stunning." She fingered the edge of the quilt. "I'm sorry, Norah. I know how much you love Fatty. I love him, too, you know. He didn't leave much choice."

Norah smiled. "No, he didn't."

"Do you think the others will be okay?"

"I do. Ida and Myra are content, and Maggie—well, she never really required much, just lived simply."

"I'm going to miss them." Brittany looked down at her feet.

Norah sighed. "I already do."

"I'm scared to go over. What if we don't make it, and Nadie?" Brittany said quietly.

"We're all scared. I worry about her, too, and Sunny."

Eldon and Tayo joined. Eldon casually played with Norah's toes.

"Look at our children," Tayo said. "To think where we were years ago."

Brittany and Eldon looked at each other and smiled. "It was long ago," Brittany said. "God, Eldon, I was so nutty with you." She laughed.

"No, babe. You were completely sane." Eldon rolled his eyes.

Everyone giggled.

"Oh my god," Brittany said, "I just remembered your foot going through my high heel."

He squinched. "Jesus, the most pain I ever had."

"Imagine if we wouldn't have been together. It all led to this, our families."

"I know, our silly date—did you leave the shoe on purpose?"

"I wasn't that desperate." She rolled her eyes. "I've never told you this, but I was going to dump you."

"Nooo," Eldon gasped.

"I knew you were a player. I was going to have another round and drop you... Sorry, Norah."

"He probably deserved it." Norah smirked.

"He did! Eldon, you were such a jerk," Brittany teased.

"I know, Squirt, I'm sorry."

"I don't care, I wasn't a gem myself. I can't believe I'm admitting this, but I'm the one who hacked your Insta and posted all the gay porn."

"Brittany! I had to delete my entire account." He shook his head. "Tayo, be grateful the internet's dead."

"What's so funny?" Freya asked, joining them.

"Should I tell her, Brit?" Eldon lifted his eyebrows. She shot him a death glare, and he smiled. "We were talking about funny relationship things."

"From when you dated Brittany?"

"Yup." He nodded.

"What was she like then?" Tilly asked.

Eldon looked like a deer caught in headlights and started to laugh. "Uh... crazy."

Brittany hit his arm. "Eldon!"

He killed himself laughing.

"Speaking of crazy..." Seamus piped in, deadpan. Norah looked at him and shook her head. "This one here." He motioned to Norah. "Remember the wasp-infested futon?" He rolled his eyes, and she smiled. "I think guests were coming or something, and we didn't have a spare bed. Norah found a used futon on Kijiji and assumed it would be good 'cause it was from a rich area. I pulled it up onto the porch and took the back off to clean it. A giant wasp nest was stuck inside. I had to put on a full ski suit and balaclava and put it back in the truck."

Norah laughed. "Could you imagine if we'd brought it inside? Our guests would've been riddled with stings." She paused. "Too much ridiculous shit went on in our life."

Seamus looked at her, straight-faced. "It sure did."

"Are you nervous about meeting the woman and boy from your dream?" Tayo asked him.

He shrugged. "I guess. Who knows if they even exist?"

"What if they're your wife and kid?" Freya asked.

"I don't know, guess I'll take it as it comes."

They spent hours sharing stories and laughing about life in the old world. Then it was time. Freya opened a slant, and sunlight blasted through. Norah and Brittany had remembered to bring a variety of high-end sunglasses for everyone, but even with them, it took time for their eyes to adjust. Within an hour, everyone could open their eyes without the glasses except for Peaches; every time she squinted her eyes open, she shrieked in pain. Norah grabbed a black buff from her backpack, folded it over Peaches's eyes, and guided her through the slant. The sun warmed her skin.

They found Sunny and Theo lying on a blanket at the beach and Kitchi swimming in the water.

Sunny walked towards them slowly, looking slightly better but still weak. "You made it." She smiled.

Brittany hugged her. "You have some colour in your face."

"Maybe." She shrugged. "Peaches, why do you have a blindfold on?"

"Her eyes couldn't adjust," Norah said.

Sunny lifted the buff off and laid her hands over the girl's eyes. Within moments, Peaches opened her eyes and gasped at the wonder of the sun. Sunny near toppled over. Tayo put his arm around her and helped her back to the blanket.

"Sunny, you let out more energy." Theo shook his head.

"She deserves to see the sunlight." Sunny coughed. "Just give me some time, we'll cross over soon." She lay down.

An unavoidable fear danced around the final crossover, around the unknown outcomes they'd soon face.

Norah let her feet sink into the talcum-powder beach and took in the lush greenery surrounding them. Bright teal and golden leaves hung down from the strange trees, their exposed roots covered with a thick layer of golden moss. Golden geode rock walls with jagged cliffs were covered in teal moss. A waterfall gushed into the lake from both sides. Giant boulder geodes scattered the beach. Deer with furry golden antlers grazed on teal grass. Norah approached one and held out her palm; it stared and licked her hand. Her body tingled as she pet the soft and delicate fur, like that of a rabbit.

"Norah, come on!" Seamus called.

The deer skitted off, and she returned to the lake. Eldon nodded. It was time.

Theo helped Sunny stand. She took Nadie's hand, and they placed their free hands on the glowing geode. Light burst from the top. Their bodies shimmered gold. An opening widened, and they passed out. Theo lifted Sunny while Tayo lifted Nadie, then they ran through.

Norah peered into the opening. It looked just like her vision: a golden geode tunnel with long-flowered vines hanging from the ceiling. The energy was wavy, hypnotizing. With a collective breath, everyone else stepped through.

*   *   *

Alone. She stood barefoot on a massive flat shimmering gold rock, a sea of endless golden water rippling at the edge exactly like in her vision. She stepped forward. Her body felt weak and she became dizzy, so she sat and put her head on her knees, allowing the gentle energy to wave through her body. She lifted her head and inhaled the warm air into her nose—a subtle hint of lavender—then she exhaled, and her lips cooled.

Dolphinesque creatures jumped out of the water—not blue but golden with teal eyes. Lush golden bushes and teal trees surrounded the glimmering flat-rock beach. Whimsical misty clouds wove through the indigo sky, laced inside gold and teal ribbons. Tiny indigo stars were splattered around the sun, a hundred times the size of stars in the old world but the light gentle—her eyes adjusted easily with no urge to squint. Giant shimmering metallic abalone shells sat in pockets in the rocks. Hundreds of small teal birds chirped around her, similar to hummingbirds with much longer feathers. At the edge of the rock, talcum-powder sand led into a dense bush. In the distance, she could see a rough path and a bridge leading to a small lagoon. With her body now stabilized, she rose to her feet and followed the rocky sea edge, praying for a sign of the others.

Terrified and exhausted, unsure how long she'd been walking, she curled inside an abalone shell and fell asleep. She woke to a distant voice calling her name. She shuffled onto the rock. *Eldon!* She screamed his name and walked towards his voice. It grew closer, and then she spotted him, the others close behind. Tears of relief and joy flooded her cheeks as she ran into his arms. She glanced over his shoulder. Sunny and Nadie bounced towards her, full of life. She gasped and embraced them and the others.

"Where's Ollie and Veronika?" she asked, looking around.

"We're still looking for them." Tayo looked worried.

"Did you all land together?"

"No. Just me and Tayo," Eldon said. "We had to find the others." He pulled her close and kissed her head.

"Let's keep looking." Tayo's voice was sombre.

Norah glanced at Brittany; she, too, looked worried.

An hour passed. Around a small bend, they found Ollie holding Veronika's lifeless body. Tayo lifted her head in his arms. Tears drenched the stone. Ollie lost the love he had found, and Tayo lost the sister who had returned. Everyone was emotionally shipwrecked, scattered gratitude inside grief-stricken desolation. The sun beat down on their weary hearts. Hours passed in silence.

"I remember," Seamus declared. "I remember everything." His face was a white sheet of paper. "My wife and son, Marama and Keme—he was five." He stared at the sea. "Glidumaras—our tribe—they've lived here since creation and had never met people from the other side. We were the first. I speak Glidu. The scars are from ceremony." He paused. "For the first two years, we lived in a small hut a mile from the village." He began speaking quickly, almost manically. "They took Myra, considered her a medicine woman. She helped us. They told us stories about the tree—it stood for eternity, a shaking in the earth's deepest core caused the tree to fall, leaving the labyrinth and opening to the moon. Only a few survived; they called us the ones with the indigo blood."

"How many are there?" Eldon asked.

"Twenty-five."

"Do you remember when you arrived?" Norah asked.

"I tried to get back, I knew you were alone. We were in the mansion, and the horn went off. We blinked, and we were on this side but not on this rock—I think on the other side of the island. Theo and I walked for days, trying to find someone. Eventually, we stumbled on Veronika and Myra in a tiny cave." He looked at Theo. "Do you remember?"

Pale with shock, Theo was holding Sunny's hand. "Keme, my little brother. Dad, I remember."

"Twimo," said a gentle voice.

Norah gasped—it was the woman from her vision. Cinnamon skin and a long half-gold, half-brown horse-like mane. Flawless skin and piercing golden eyes with a golden hue on her full lips. Elaborate tribal clothing ribboned with gold and indigo. Three men and a woman stood behind her.

Seamus lifted her off the ground and kissed her passionately. He wiped her tears. "Keme?" he asked.

"Dad, it's Keme," bellowed a deep voice. The man who spoke towered over the others, the same size as Kitchi. He was strikingly gorgeous with long brown-gold hair, cinnamon skin, and the same piercing golden eyes as his mother.

Seamus looked at his son: the small boy he left, now a grown man.

Theo walked to Keme. "It's your brother, Theo."

Keme hugged him and laughed. "My big brother, I miss you."

"Keme." Seamus touched his face, emotional.

Keme gathered his father and brother into a bear hug and lifted them off the ground.

The woman approached Norah and brushed her scar, her eyes kind. "Norah, I'm Marama."

"Marama, I'm happy to meet you. This is my husband, Eldon."

Marama touched Eldon's heart. "You are kind and strong."

It was the first time Norah ever saw Eldon blush.

Seamus introduced his family, then Marama introduced her brothers, Sawa and Supay, and her sister, Toma. They were magical and stunning people, a gene pool boiled in golden perfection. Marama and Keme spoke fluent English, thanks to Myra, Seamus, and Veronika. Marama was the daughter of Gwada, chief of Glidumaras, and he, too, spoke English.

Struck by Sunny and Nadie, Marama touched their cheeks and pulled her hand away, gasping as if she had seen a ghost. "Glints!"

"Glints?" Brittany asked.

She looked at Brittany. "The ones with the sun in their blood, light travellers." She walked to Brittany and stroked her blonde hair. "Cinderella."

Brittany giggled. "Cinderella... Where did you hear that?"

"Theo taught us the fairy tales. You are Cinderella."

Brittany smiled and touched Tayo's arm. "This is my husband, Prince Charming."

Tayo reached out his hand and smiled. "I'm Tayo, our daughters are Sunny and Tilly, our granddaughter is Nadie."

Marama walked to Veronika's body and placed her hands on Veronika's stomach and head. Her eyes rolled back and turned into pure gold and then returned to normal. She motioned to Sawa and Supay and commanded them in Glidu. They lifted the body.

"What are you doing?" Ollie asked, visibly upset.

"She needs to return to the village. Help them carry her," Marama ordered.

Tayo and Ollie helped lift the body and walked away with Sawa and Supay.

Keme stared at Freya, Kitchi, and Tilly. "Gwists," he said to Marama.

She touched their cheeks. "Yes, Keme."

"What are Gwists?" Kitchi asked.

"Auricle openers," Keme said. "Come now." He walked towards the bridge.

Norah called to Seamus. "Is this safe? Those scars on your back… Is that going to happen to us?"

"No, no. These were by choice, a rite performed during marriage and other ceremonies. You're safe here."

Norah whispered to Eldon, "Does *Twimo* mean Village Eunuch?"

Seamus turned around and shook his head. "You really are an idiot."

Large gold baskets hung from gargantuan trees spread with indigo and gold leaves. Soft beds nestled inside, some baskets closed with doors made of golden branches and others open. They hung in a circle around a half-buried massive golden geode boulder. A fire blazed in the centre, burning not wood but transparent golden crystalline rocks, the flames golden and light pink with indigo sparks. Golden talcum-powder sand covered the ground.

Animals not of their world roamed free—sheep with shimmery golden coats, snakes with intricate golden and indigo designs, a massive golden eagle, and giant bear-like dogs with exploding fluffy golden coats and round faces, whose eyeteeth protruded over an underbite and whose eyeballs darted in different directions, their feet pointed inwards. Norah couldn't help but wonder if they were boiled in a separate gene pool. Filled with the sorrow of missing Fatty, she wondered how many years it had been since they left. Some of the dogs were hairless; Norah assumed the tribe used the fur for clothing and bedding. One dog ran up and jumped on her, knocking her over and licking her face playfully. She laughed and played along until it licked her scar and whimpered, then ran off. She looked at Eldon with a *What the hell?* expression.

"Keme, what are those dogs?" Eldon asked.

"Gwugs. They are hunters, give us warmth, and protect us. Deadly creatures."

Norah and Eldon looked at each other wide-eyed, naïve in the new habitat. Norah's senses were overloaded. She wanted to take Eldon into one of the tree pods, curl up, and sleep forever, forgetting about the moon, the Shade, everything.

The men carried Veronika inside the half-buried boulder in the middle of the circle. Marama explained they were taking Veronika to see the chief. Norah and the others followed them down a staircase made of geodes into a dome-shaped room also made of geodes. In the centre lay a round slab of translucent teal rock. To the left, a man of mighty stature sat on an amethyst throne that had been built into the wall. He was a perfect specimen: glistening light-cinnamon skin and intense, teal-flecked golden eyes that were majestic and wise, beyond his years. He possessed a presence that naturally commanded respect.

Aghast, Norah and Brittany locked eyes; they'd never seen a man this gorgeous. Eldon and Seamus appeared to be small children in his presence. She glanced at Eldon; he shook his head, unimpressed. She stuffed her rising inappropriate laughter and struggled to acclimate to the man's beauty.

The man stood up slowly, as if he rushed for nothing, and those around him silenced and listened intently with a hint of fear. He hugged Marama, then placed his hand over Seamus's heart. "Twimo, my son, you returned." He gripped his shoulder.

"*Twimo* means First Sacred Son," Marama translated.

"Too long since I've seen your face, Gwada," Seamus said with sadness. "I've been gone for many years but didn't even remember this side, my family, until moments ago."

"Twimo, the sides are uncertain. Even I don't understand. You are back now." He studied Theo's face. "Swick, you're a man, strong." He squeezed his shoulders.

"*Swick* means Sacred Holder of Thoughts," Marama said.

Gwada motioned to the men who held Veronika's body and addressed them in Glidu. They placed her body on the slab. He shouted another command. Moments later, a man returned with a rock bowl, a stick, and a pile of golden moss that looked like cotton candy. Gwada placed a handful of the moss in the bowl and added drops of gold liquid, stirring it with the stick until it turned into a paste.

He opened Veronika's eyes and pressed the poultice inside. It held her eyes open. He put some in her ears and under her tongue and then liquefied the rest with water. He punctured her neck with a hollow glass stick and then poured the liquid inside, sealing the end of the hollow stick with moss. He charged someone with another order. The guy returned holding a golden wool quilt intricately woven with ink and fabric. Gwada laid it over Veronika and motioned for everyone to leave.

"Ten waves," Gwada said in English, and then he spoke to Seamus in Glidu.

Seamus translated. "He says ten days. They measure time with the rise and fall of the waves. Her body has to stay in the cave alone. He thinks her blood was too slow to metabolize the air. There's a chance she will recover."

"Recover?" Tayo said. "She's been dead for hours." He swallowed.

"This isn't the same earth," Seamus said, leading them over to the buckets seats made of rock geodes lined with fluffy wool cushions that circled the fire. The sun beat down as the fire burned; the flames didn't create heat but rather a cool breeze and mist, the crystalline sparks evaporating in the air.

Gwada addressed them in Glidu.

"He wants to see who you are," Seamus translated.

Gwada stood before each of them in turn, placing his fingers on their cheeks, closing his eyes, and focusing for a long time. When he spoke, Marama translated.

"Ollie is Sula, The Noble Prince of Joy.

"Freya is Glowa, Light Shifter.

"Kitchi is Sohan, Heart-Filled God Warrior.

"Tilly is Gwuha, The Moon Whisperer.

"Sunny is Hallah, The Giver of Life.

"Nadie is Twalo, The Wild Tree Spirit."

With his hand now on Eldon's cheek, Gwada laughed as if he had known him for a lifetime. "Minnaw, Sacred Wisdom Holder."

Tears poured out of Gwada's eyes when he placed his hand on Tayo, never having seen the horrors the world had birthed, created by the depravity of fear-consumed and power-hungry men. He pulled his hands away, laid his hands flat on the boulder, and screamed, allowing the rock to absorb the pain. He returned to Tayo. "You are Gwape, The Sacred Forgiver."

Tayo wept. It had been long since he reflected on the brutality and horror his people suffered.

Gwada touched Brittany and wept. "Your tribeless tribe caused much pain. Terrified of the gifts they didn't possess. Why?"

Brittany was shocked by his question. No one had ever asked her about her people. She shook with the weight of responsibility, with the dark history her ancestors birthed and the bloodline kept alive. "I don't know why." She squeezed Tayo's hand. Tears gushed.

Gwada placed his hand on her cheek and smiled. "Surah, Shining Star of Compassion."

As he stood before Peaches, his hand shook. He touched her cheek with the tip of one finger, and terror blanketed his face. He screamed out tears, kneeled at the boulder, and wailed for humanity. Norah could see that it hadn't registered with him that if the world had caught wind of the Glidumaras, they, too, would have become victims of cultural genocide—obliterated, raped, domesticated, colonized, deprogrammed into malfunctioning robots, robbed of their homes and land. These magical, stunning people would have met a much different history. He beat his hands on the boulder and wailed.

The tribe gathered, heartbroken at his words, devastated their fellow humans were so terribly lost.

Gwada returned to Peaches, touched her cheek, and smiled. "You are Whillah, Carrier of the Sacred Medicine Song."

She smiled, caressed his cheek.

He let out an unfiltered, jolly laugh, touched by the most resilient human spirit any of them had known.

CHAPTER 19

GWADA CUPPED NORAH'S CHEEKS AND STARED INTO HER eyes. His finger brushed her scar, and he pulled away as if he'd touched a hot stove. "Where did you get this?"

"I ate moss under the sun before the tunnel and had a vision. I was bitten by a red shadow-like demon. When I awoke, I was bleeding… it left this scar."

His eyes filled with fear. "Twill."

Marama gasped.

"What is Twill?" Norah's voice shook.

"Pure evil from the underbelly of the sun," Seamus said. "Released only when the earth shakes and the sky cries. No one has ever survived a bite. It pulls out your spirit and feeds off the pain." Seamus studied her for a moment. "Are you able to touch the roots of Suwin?"

She scrunched her eyes. "Suwin?"

"The labyrinth."

Norah nodded.

Gwada spoke to Seamus in Glidu, and Seamus translated for her. "Norah"—he lowered his eyes—"he needs to check the blood around your heart."

"What?" she asked. Seamus was staring at her, and she knew by his expression it wasn't good. Her heart beat out of her chest. "How bad?" she asked. He shook his head, his face pale. "Do I have a choice?" He shook his head again. Norah tried to calm her breath. "No. I'm not doing it."

"Norah"—Seamus held her hands and stared in her eyes—"he's going to do it one way or another. He's never studied the blood of someone who survived the Twill."

"Mom, I'll stop him." Kitchi puffed up slightly.

She glanced at Eldon, who also looked ready to fight.

Her thoughts raced. *Shit, shit, fuck...* "I'll fucking do it." She shot a piercing look at Seamus and inhaled a deep breath.

Eldon pulled her close and whispered in her ear. "We will stop him."

"No. Don't. No matter what," she whispered. "Promise me."

Eldon nodded, his face sick and pale.

She followed Gwada and Marama to the edge of the forest and entered an opening into a massive tree trunk. Inside, she saw the table from her vision.

Marama now held the same weapon from her vision: a tiny pointed blade on the end of a hollow, glowing geode staff. "Take your shirt off and lay on the table," she said gently.

Norah's body shook. "What do you do?"

"I can't explain in your language. Hold my hand."

Norah's throat felt like it was closing. She pulled off her shirt and climbed onto the rock. Her bare back chilled on the cold stone. She glanced down at her naked breasts and then looked at Gwada and Marama. *This is fucking absurd,* she thought. Gwada stuffed some moss inside her cheek, and she fell into a trance—faces melting, voices slowing—and her eyes closed. She felt pressure on her chest and grabbed the sides of the rock. A poke turned into a puncture. She writhed in pain and screamed, shrieks so horrifying the moon shook. The blade broke through her rib cage at the edge of her heart.

Her eyes opened. No pain in her body, just exhaustion. She lay soaking in a puddle of sweat.

Eldon squeezed her hand and sighed. "I thought I lost you." His face was pale and he was on the verge of tears.

Marama entered. "Not so bad, right?" She smiled.

Norah stared expressionless, not in the mood for banter.

Marama brushed the medicine off her wound and checked it. The skin was smooth, with no memory of the trauma. She nodded. "Come out when you're ready."

Eldon lay with her on the stone and kissed her neck. "I'm sorry, I tried to stop him."

"It's over, let's go, I can't lay in this puddle of sweat anymore."

They returned to the circle, and Gwada put his hand on her shoulder. "You are strong," he said, Seamus translating. She lowered her gaze. He lifted her chin. "No more looking down, you are strong, like your son."

She stared at him, speechless.

"You are a Gwail, it's why you can touch the roots. The blood by your heart is clear. You don't carry pain from your ancestors. Your cells are clean, perfect."

"Impossible." She squinched her face, trying to compute his words. "Why have I been riddled with depression and anxiety?"

"Norah, there is no depression or anxiety here." Seamus looked confused as he tried to translate. "He said it's not your pain. You were too clear to live in the harsh world. Everything you felt belonged to someone else—their pain and suffering released onto you. There's nothing you could've done because you carried the pain of millions. The Twill didn't kill you because your spirit is clean. Nothing for it to take."

She struggled to reconcile his words with what she had felt. "I had pain. It had a lot to pull out."

"Norah, you will never be free of the human condition. Loss is part of life; the Twill can't pull pain from loss. Loss doesn't break a spirit; it prepares us for our own death. Twill feed on the pain of your ancestors."

She tried to grasp his words but couldn't.

Gwada placed his hand on her cheek and smiled. "Norah, you are Mahara, The Clear-Blooded Queen." He bent over and kissed her scar.

She cried and thought about the million fallen tears of her lifetime.

"He wants to show you the homes they have prepared for you so you can rest before the celebration tonight," Seamus said, looking exhausted. "There will be a feast of freshly hunted Dwars, animals similar to deer."

"I have a question before we go," Norah said. "How old are you, Gwada?"

Gwada stared at her. "I don't know," he said in Glidu, and Seamus translated.

"Do the Glidumaras not die from age?" she asked.

"We die, but not."

"They barely age," Seamus explained. "A human year on normal earth would be equivalent to a thousand Glidu years. Gwada is probably around four thousand years old. They're ancient, but their tribe will eventually die off due to lack of procreation. Many have already died from the Twill. There used to be another tribe, the Danu, but the Twill annihilated them."

"How are the Glidumara still alive?"

"Gwada found medicine that keeps the Twill away, a powder from the Seento flower. The hanging lanterns on the poles around the village, they're full of Seento, also the satchels around their necks. The supply is overflowing right now but will run out in thousands of years." He paused. "Gwada said Norah will protect them when it runs out."

Norah peppered Seamus with questions. "How will I protect them? Will we age the same under the sun? Slowly?"

"He doesn't know, earth humans haven't lived here long enough. I lived here for five years, and neither Theo nor I aged." He paused. "You will protect them by being here—the Twill won't come within a twenty-mile radius of you. It won't be for ages, they have enough Seento to last thousands of years."

Norah's heart plunged. *Thousands of years,* she thought. It suffocated her. She didn't know her purpose or what she might do for an eternity on the strange new earth. She glanced at her family, a reminder of why she was there and nodded her head.

"Does that mean Nadie won't age? Tilly asked.

Gwada spoke to Seamus. "There is medicine to induce aging, to bring a child to maturity so they have a purpose in the village. She will drink it every day until she reaches eighteen."

"Is it safe?" Norah asked. "What about Theo and Sunny?"

"Yes, they will drink it too," Seamus said. "Everyone needs to reach the age of maturity."

"Why didn't I drink it before, Dad?" Theo asked.

"I don't know, it's the first I'm hearing about it."

"He knew you would leave," Marama said, "see your family again."

Norah turned to Gwada and touched her heart. "Thank you for the years with my son."

He smiled and motioned to the Glidumaras. Marama's sister, Toma, showed Norah and Eldon to their basket. She was tall with sharp features, and her curly hair was thick like yarn and hung down past her waist, tied with glowing gold ribbon. An intricate gold tattoo covered every inch of her skin, even her face. Sparkling geode spheres were pierced in a row up her ear. With a devilish grin and twinkle in her eye, she looked fearless. Norah sensed her good-humoured nature and liked her instantly. She was the kind of person you wanted to be around.

When they reached their basket, Norah and Eldon smiled and thanked her for the hospitality. The basket was filled with a soft mattress and a warm, feather-filled wool blanket. A small rock table held a candle made of unfamiliar materials, the flame glowing inside some sort of rock with no wick.

Norah pulled out the few belongings from her backpack and set them on the small woven ledge: her journal, the black-and-white picture of the family, a black-and-white photo of Fatty, the death book, and Llama. She stared at the pictures and smiled, then lay her head on Eldon's chest, her body grateful for rest. She pulled the blanket Ida made over them and nestled into him, in a deep slumber within seconds. Sleep felt different— more resonant, quieter without the humming of the moon.

They woke to loud shouting, drumming, and singing. Eldon kissed Norah's neck and then down her body. The basket swayed back and forth.

"Norah, my clear-blooded queen." He stared into her eyes, breathless.

"Eldon, my muddle-headed prince."

They kissed and swayed the basket one more time, then dressed and returned to the circle. Everyone was gathered, watching the Glidamarus shouting, singing, dancing wildly around the fire, and pounding the drums. Norah wondered how her small life had become magic. She smiled at Kitchi, and he lifted his eyebrows and laughed. Theo and Sunny were curled up in a chair. Freya sat beside Toma; Norah sensed something between them but thought she might be reading into things.

The drums stopped. Gwada stood by Peaches and drummed gently. "Twaho," he said.

"*Twaho* means to sing," Seamus said. He glanced at Norah. She flashed back to him lying on the couch in his mermaid pose. Now, he was the village translator… for eternity. Sure, he had his own *What the hell?* moments.

Peaches broke into a haunting tribal song. It resonated into the bones of those gathered and drew out their pain. Emotions rose and released as the drum beckoned their hearts. Sawa passed an ornate teal goblet filled with gold liquid and motioned for them to drink, even Nadie. Norah lifted the goblet to her lips and took in a small sip. She dizzied, and her body melted into the flames, in a trance.

She gazed around, unsure if her eyes were telling the truth. Nadie lay on the ground, laughing hysterically. Brittany and Tayo were enraptured in a hypnotizing dance. Sawo refilled the goblets all night. Norah basked in the vision of her family, before and after the Shade, dancing together around the fire.

She woke in the basket with Eldon with no recollection of sleep, her spirit energized. Eldon opened his eyes and pressed into her, their bodies warm, still buzzing from the liquid gold. Interrupted by a screaming commotion outside, they dressed and rushed to the fire.

Supay held Sunny's arm during a heated exchange with Seamus, Theo, and Tayo. Gwada and Marama stood close.

"Supay," Seamus said, "Sunny is Theo's partner, she's with him."

Supay responded with angry words in Glidu. Sunny looked terrified.

"Seamus," Tayo said, "he can't take her, we have to stop him!"

"What is going on, Seamus?" Norah asked, trying to figure out what the hell was happening.

Seamus waved his hand at her to be quiet. "Tayo, if we stop him, they'll kill you."

"We just let him take her? I'll kill him," Theo said.

But Theo was no match for Supay, so Seamus quieted him, his face showing that his mind was racing to figure something out. "Marama, she is our son's partner, Theo's girlfriend, we can't let Supay take her," he pleaded.

"Seamus, we—"

Gwada cut her off. "You know the law: any woman who dances with a free man chooses him."

"Gwada. It was a mistake." Her face reddened with anger. "Show mercy."

Gwada yelled, "Marama, you overstep! It is the law!" He hit his staff on the ground.

"Theo will never beat Supay," Seamus said. He locked eyes with Norah, his face sick with worry. "Give me some time to discuss with the others, Gwada."

Gwada nodded in agreement. Seamus gathered the others.

"What is going on?!" Norah said, voice raised.

"Sunny... she danced with Supay last night," Seamus said. "After drinking the liquid gold, she thought he was Theo."

"It was a mistake!" Norah shook her head.

"Norah, there isn't—"

Theo cut him off. "I'm fighting, it's settled."

"Theo, you dead isn't going to help anyone." Norah trembled, realizing the gravity of the situation.

"What kind of a man am I if I can't protect her?" Theo shouted.

Seamus squeezed Theo's shoulders. "Son, it's not protecting. It's a death wish. She will end up married to him, and you'll be dead. Supay is a beast—I've seen him kill a Gwahalan with his bare hands."

"It's me," Kitchi declared, "the final word."

Tilly held back tears and fell into his arms. "You come back to us. Do you hear me?"

He lifted her off the ground and kissed her. "I'm not dying," He lifted Nadie and kissed her forehead. "I love you, little bean."

"Love you, Dada." She stroked his face.

"Theo, you're my brother," Kitchi said, "and I'm fighting to keep our family together."

Norah gave a nod of acceptance, her stomach sick. She hugged him and ran back to the basket. Returning moments later with some indigo stones she picked up years before, she placed them in Kitchi's hand. "For strength."

Seamus and Kitchi approached Gwada. He honoured Kitchi's request for a battle and brought him to a nearby cave, where he would sleep alone for two days. Supay was put in a different cave. Sunny was led to her basket, where she wasn't allowed to see anyone or leave, except to use the bathroom.

Proper battle preparations ensued. With the tribe's customs foreign to the family, the fear of doing something wrong, like Sunny's naïve dance, lingered. Norah didn't sleep for the two nights, her mind fixated on Kitchi and Sunny and the future.

The tribe danced without stopping as they wore large satchels around their shoulders. Whenever Gwada hit the side of the rock with his staff, they would reach into their satchels and pull out a different colour of dust and release it into the massive gold cauldron hanging on top of the fire. Steam billowed from the top as inside a thick golden liquid boiled non-stop but never evaporated, a mystery even to Seamus.

Norah, Freya, and Tilly told Marama they refused to watch the fight. Her response: No. Everyone needed their eyes open, she said, because it honoured the warriors. If they refused, their loved one's death would be on them. Norah didn't know if she could watch her son die in front of her eyes, but what Marama said resonated. Her son faced the fight of his life. How could she cower from his pain? Her own pain. But Norah fought adamantly for Peaches to stay back, arguing there was no reason for her to take in new horrors. Marama agreed.

The drumming silenced. They followed Gwada in single file to Sunny's basket, where he repeatedly hit his drum, a five-second pause between each hit. Sunny stood outside her basket, adorned in tribal gold, her face painted, her hair woven with golden and teal threads. Gorgeous. Norah noticed her hand trembling; her heart sank. Marama motioned Sunny in front of her. Gwada led the procession to the first cave and summoned Kitchi, who covered his eyes when the sun hit him. As he walked behind Sunny, Norah saw him touch her hand. Gwada led them to the other cave and called out Supay; the light didn't affect him as he took his place in front of Sunny. He didn't look angry or pumped; Norah realized, for him, it was a ceremonial battle. Anger had no part of it. They walked uphill for an hour until they reached a field covered in talcum-powder sand and golden flowers, with a large stone circle in the centre. Gwada covered Kitchi's and Supay's cheeks with gold dust, placed his forehead on each, and spoke in Glidu, then released them and motioned to the circle.

Seamus translated Gwada's instructions to Kitchi. "You will go in the circle. When the drum beats three times, the battle begins. No rules." He paused. "Fight to the death." He looked into Kitchi's eyes and squeezed his shoulders, tears welling. He nodded. As Kitchi walked towards the circle, Seamus yelled, "No catch and release today." Kitchi looked back and nodded. No one else was permitted to address the warriors.

Tilly grabbed Norah's hand, both trembling. "Keep your eyes open," she whispered.

Norah squeezed Theo's hand, leaned her head on his shoulder, inhaled the lavender air, and stared at the circle.

Gwada walked around the circle, sprinkled powder onto each stone, and hit two small gold rocks together. The spark created a fire around the circle, surrounding Kitchi and Supay in iridescent indigo flames. Supay took Kitchi's shoulders, smiled at him, and spoke gently. Kitchi reached out his hand. Supay stared at him until Kitchi lifted Supay's arm and taught him to shake hands. Supay laughed.

The drum beat three times.

Supay clicked into beast mode, pushed Kitchi over, and hammered his face. Kitchi looked disoriented, his eye covered in blood. He reached up and clenched Supay's hair, slammed him into a rock, and kicked his back with repeated brutal blows. Kitchi glanced at Tilly for a split second and was met with a vicious blow to the back of his head. He fell over and shielded his head while Supay kicked him senseless, his head gushing blood. He summoned the strength to rise, head-butt Supay and kneed him in the groin, then gripped his hair and uppercut him until his chin split open. Supay caught Kitchi's knuckle in his teeth, bit down and ripped off the skin, and spit it out. He then squeezed Kitchi's neck and lifted him off the ground. Moments from passing out, Kitchi grabbed Supay's groin in an iron grip and twisted. Supay released his neck and both fell to the ground, exhausted, bloody, and raw.

Kitchi crawled over and was about to grab Supay when Supay kicked him in the face. Kitchi wiped the blood from his eyes and struggled to get up on his hands and knees, but a brutal kick to the stomach sent his body back. Kitchi tried to move but couldn't. Norah gasped—he had nothing left. Supay bent down, picked up some sand, and rubbed it in his hands.

A haunting song bellowed from the base of the hill. Norah looked back. Peaches. Her voice echoed into the circle.

Supay blew the sand off his hands and barrelled towards Kitchi. Kitchi rolled over just as he was about to deliver the final blow. Supay's eye met the side of a rock. Blood gushed.

Kitchi rose to his feet, Peaches still singing. He stumbled over to Supay, lifted his head, and pummelled it into the rock, then lifted his leg and slammed his foot down an inch away from his head. He reached out his hand to Supay. Supay tried to lift his arm, whispered something, and passed out. Kitchi toppled over and hit the earth with a loud thud.

"No!" Tilly screamed, running towards Kitchi.

Gwada scolded in Glidu and put his warriors in charge to stop Tilly. No one would enter the circle uninvited.

Norah walked to the edge of the warrior circle. Seamus was inside, talking to Gwada. He motioned to Norah to step back, and she flipped him the bird. He shook his head and motioned again to get back.

"Gwada!" she yelled. "I'm going to see my son!"

Gwada responded in Glidu. "He said we need to wait," Seamus translated.

"No!" She screamed at the top of her lungs. "No! My son did what you asked—fought and nearly killed your man while we watched." Her face felt red-hot. "You cried at the horrors of humanity, and this is what you do? A bloody and brutal fight?!"

Gwada stared at her.

"I am getting my son! Kill us if you want to!" She pushed her way through the warriors and ran to Kitchi. "Come help me!" she yelled to her family.

The Glidamarus watched, bewildered.

Angry tears poured out as her eyes locked with Marama's. "This is your brother! Come and help him!"

Marama glanced at her father and walked over to help carry Supay. The Glidamarus followed.

"And Seamus, grab a pair of fucking balls!" she yelled at him.

Eldon pinched her arm. "Enough, Norah."

She snapped out of her rage. Marama instructed which cave to bring the men's bodies to. Gwada followed and beat his drum. He and Marama went into the cave and doctored them with medicine. Sunny and Tilly didn't leave their sides.

They feared retaliation—no one rose up against Gwada—and even Marama was nervous. After Gwada had doctored Kitchi and Supay, he disappeared. Uncertainty filled the tense air while they waited for Kitchi to recover.

A week later, Sunny and Tilly came out of the cave with Supay and Kitchi, sharp and back to full health. Gwada's medicine and Sunny's hands had brought them fast recovery. Kitchi wore new scars from the battle, including a glowing golden gash above his eyebrow. Norah held him in her arms and wept, grateful for his heartbeat.

"Kitchi, you would've died in the circle if it wasn't for your mom's fighting spirit." Eldon smiled and shook his head.

"Mom, you would fight Goliath for your kids." He embraced her and walked over to Peaches. "Your song brought me back, willed me to live."

Peaches blushed and looked down.

Norah smiled at Kitchi. "I am proud of you. You showed mercy on Supay."

"He deserved mercy."

Eldon hugged him. "I thought we lost you. You fought a battle where most men would have died in the first minute."

"Thank you, Kitchi," Theo said, fighting tears as Sunny hung off his arm. "You're my little brother; I wish I could do the same for you."

Kitchi put him in a headlock and gave him a noogie. "Don't worry, you'll pay your dues."

Theo laughed at his beast of a brother.

They filled him in about Gwada and the trepidation of their circumstances.

"We're all together," Kitchi said. "It needs to stay that way."

Another three days passed. One day when they were all gathered around the fire, Gwada walked up and motioned for Seamus to translate.

"Ten-day and nights I have been without food or water, asking the spirits to guide me. They were quiet, angered with me and my stubbornness. Mahara spoke strongly to me; this has not happened in my lifetime, except with my Gwyah, who visited me in my dream. She said, 'Would you not fight for Marama? You old stubborn fool, now go back and stop being a Windaho'—a word for a small weak mouse-like creature. It is over today. We are a family. Thank you, Mahara. Our sons are alive." He lifted his arms in celebration and hugged Kitchi and Supay. "Tonight, we open the cave to see if the gods have spared the woman's life. We will prepare for the celebration."

Marama embraced her father. "Gwyah would be proud."

"Who is Gwyah?" Norah asked.

"My mother. She died protecting me from the Twill when I was a small child. Gwada tried everything to save her, but no doctoring worked." She put her head down.

"I'm sorry." Norah was sad for their loss but also relieved for safety. She returned to the pod for much-needed rest, nervous about the upcoming celebration and the possibility of Veronika being dead.

Eldon and Norah slept in their cozy basket, nestled inside the soft feather-filled wool quilt, and woke to the basket swaying—and not from their doing. Eldon peeked outside to find Nadie pushing the basket. He laughed, jumped out, and chased her. Norah dressed and followed, everyone slowly trickling to the ceremony.

The hot liquid boiled in the cauldron. Gwada was dressed in gold ceremonial clothes. The fabric was different, like linen, and was adorned with embroidered symbols, gold ribbons, and teal fur. He appeared carefree, joyful. The Glidamarus, magically clothed in the same intricate detail, joined hands in the circle, chanting the same line for hours: "Wahu Whau Whau Sepa."

"What does that mean?" Norah asked Seamus.

"It is time to wake."

"I haven't apologized yet. I'm sorry." Her face squinched in discomfort.

"For what? Emasculating me in front of my wife and the entire Glidumara tribe?" His tone was flat.

She looked down. "I'm sorry."

He burst into laughter. "Fuck, Norah, you're too much. It's all good, that used to be sweet talk in the old day,"

She laughed. "Sad but true."

"No one knew what you said. I told Marama you honoured me." He laughed.

Norah shook her head. "I don't doubt that." She was grateful for him, for his ability to let shit go.

Supay passed around a goblet filled with a different liquid, thick and sweet. Norah's mind cleared after drinking it, all distractions gone. Supay kneeled before Kitchi, who sat with his arm around Tilly and Nadie resting on his lap. Supay spoke in Glidu, then handed Kitchi a glowing gold feather and walked away.

"What did he say?" Kitchi asked Seamus.

"He said you are my brother, you showed me mercy, I owe you my life,' and then he gifted you his golden Swillaah feather for loyalty and protection. He's the only one who holds one. Years ago, he found it lying outside his basket, and he considered it an offering from the gods."

Kitchi was honoured by the sacred gift. He walked over and hung it at the door of his basket. They chanted and drank from the goblet for hours.

Gwada commanded silence, and the chanting stopped. He instructed Supay and Sawa to lift the cauldron and carry it into the rock opening. Ollie and Tayo followed. Marama motioned for Norah to join.

The scent of fresh flowers surprised Norah, given how long Veronika's dead body had lain in the small space. The medicine in her eyes had dissolved, but her eyes were still open, her pupils now golden. Ollie kissed her hand. Tayo stood on her other side and stroked her hair.

Gwada spoke in Glidu while Marama gently lifted the blanket, leaving Veronika's naked body exposed. Supay picked up the cauldron, his strong arm shaking from the weight. He emptied the steaming golden lava over her body, starting at her feet and moving up to her head. It poured over Ollie and Tayo's hands but didn't burn or wet them, only left a gritty, sand-like residue. Gwada placed his hand on Veronika's forehead and prayed in Glidu. He sat on his amethyst throne and waved his hand at the others to leave.

An hour later, Tayo came out of the boulder and declared, "She's alive."

Within the same moment, Veronika walked out of the rock, Gwada behind her. Norah pinched herself, thinking she was hallucinating from the drink. Ollie grabbed Veronika and kissed her ferociously.

Gwada walked over and placed his hand on her cheek. "Mohintra, Keeper of Death."

CHAPTER 20

NORAH'S SENSE THAT THERE WAS SOMETHING BETWEEN Freya and Toma was cultivated over the months as Freya and Toma grew inseparable. They tried to hide it, but Norah picked up on the subtleties, like the gentle flirting and the tender moments. Norah thought about Ida, about how thrilled she would have been to see Freya find someone. She would have loved Toma, the funniest Glidumara by far with a devilish grin and light demeanour.

Norah found Freya alone by the sea, her long auburn hair tied in a fur teal wrap, her back leaning against a rock as she gazed at the boundless water.

Norah sat beside her daughter and wrapped her arm around her. "How are you, Frey?"

"Good, Mom," she said gently.

"Do you like it here?"

"I do, do you?"

Norah stared at the water. "I do. I miss the moon though."

"I think that's a given, right?"

"Yeah… I noticed you and Toma."

Freya was silent.

"Sorry," Norah said, worried she had upset her.

"No, no, it's okay." She half smiled. "It's like I can't find words. When I look in her eyes, it's like everything makes sense."

"You know you never talked to me about it?"

"I didn't know what to say?"

"I hope you didn't feel like you couldn't."

"Just felt pointless." Freya shrugged. "No one there for me anyway."

"Makes sense, such strange times."

"I've only ever known these strange times, never lived in your old world."

"Probably better, sweetheart… It wasn't easy."

They sat in silence for a spell.

"Do you think the village will accept us?" Freya sounded worried.

"I don't know, Frey, but we have you're back."

Freya nodded and changed the subject. "I can't believe Marama, she's stunning. Were you jealous at all, Mom?"

Norah found the question funny. "No, I'm happy for Seamus. I mean, she is out-of-this-world stunning, but no, he deserves happiness. I only have eyes for your dad anyway… and Gwada."

"Mom!" She slapped Norah's leg and laughed.

Norah laughed too. "I'm kidding. Better get back to Marama, she has me doing the washing."

"I'm asking her to marry me," Freya blurted. "I'm giving her this." She pulled out a stunning necklace of gold and indigo metal with a glowing teal rock hanging in the centre.

"Did you make this?" Norah asked.

"Yes."

"Freya, it's beautiful. You are both beautiful. My heart is so full for you both." She paused. "Are you going to tell Dad?"

"What was that?" Eldon sat down beside Norah.

Norah smiled. "Were you eavesdropping?"

"Only for a second." He put his arm around Freya. "I like Toma. I'm happy for you guys."

"Thanks, Dad. Hope she says yes." She blushed and put her head down.

"Well, if she doesn't, I'll take her in the circle." He raised his eyebrows.

"Dad! You're threatening to kick a woman's ass?" She rolled her eyes. "Anyway, if anyone's going to kick any ass, you know it's Mom."

He dipped his chin down. "Your mother's name should have been The Emasculator."

Norah smirked. "Oh, stop."

Freya laughed and rolled her eyes. "You guys are ridiculous. I'm asking her tomorrow. How long did it take for you and Mom?"

"To get married?"

She rolled her eyes. "Yes."

Norah and Eldon looked at each other, remembering their wedding, the invitations Maggie made, Ollie's funny poem, and Fatty.

"I can't remember, can you?" Norah asked Eldon.

"Nope." He laughed.

"Do you think your marriage would have survived the old world?" Freya asked.

"You definitely have your mother's inquisitive mind, Frey." Eldon glanced at Norah. "I think so, right?"

"I think so too." She kissed his hand. It made her think about what life would have been like in the old world. In reality, there wouldn't have been a life: their paths would have never crossed, and even if they had, nothing would have happened. Norah had been fiercely loyal to Seamus, even with their problems, and Eldon lived in another world. Without the Shade, their love, family, and life wouldn't have existed.

Freya stood up. "I'm heading back to find Toma."

Eldon and Norah stared silently out into the water, Norah's head resting on his chest while he played with her hair.

"What if Gwada doesn't accept them?" Norah asked.

"He'll have to, there's no choice."

That evening, Norah noticed the necklace hanging on Toma's neck. She and Freya slow-danced by the fire, the first time they had openly shown affection. Gwada walked to his daughter, cupped her head in his hands, and spit over each shoulder. He looked angry.

"What was that about?" Norah asked Seamus nervously.

"He gave his marriage blessing to Toma." Seamus squeezed her hand.

Utter relief waved into Norah's heart.

Gwada gestured to Norah and Eldon, then led them to the rock cave and sat on his throne. He motioned for them to sit and poured steaming teal liquid into three goblets. The liquid warmed Norah's lips; it was sweet with a bitter aftertaste.

"Our daughters wish to marry," Gwada said, then studied their faces. Eldon nodded and took a sip of the drink. "Do you bless this union?"

"Yes," Norah and Eldon said in unison.

"Did unions such as these happen in your world?" Gwada sounded curious.

"Yes, many times," Norah answered. "In yours?"

"No. It is sacred," he replied. "Toma and Freya carry the Tweelah spirit, their blood holds strength and knowledge. Once married, they will be Chieftesses of the Glidumaras."

"Chieftess?" Norah asked.

"They will take Gwyah's home in the trees and hold the same rights as I do. We will rule as three." He sipped from his goblet.

Norah and Eldon looked at each other, baffled. "Have you told them this?" Norah asked.

"No, much preparation is needed. I will honour them tomorrow." His brow furrowed. "Do not say a word to anyone. Leave me now." He waved his hand as if they were peons.

Norah and Eldon walked away silently. Norah struggled with the information. *My daughter, a Chieftess? Could she handle the responsibility? Did she want it?* Thoughts raced. What she did know is that Freya loved Toma.

She drifted in and out of sleep, in a trance, her body feeling airy as if it were levitating off the bed. These rest periods had become synonymous with the liquid from the goblets, altering dream state and reality.

She woke to a light tap on the door the next morning.

Freya stood outside, looking shaken. She squeezed into the basket, sat on the bed, and wept.

"Freya, what is it?" Norah whispered. Eldon sat up in bed.

"Gwada brought us into the rock this morning." She sniffled. "We need to separate for a year before we can get married. He said we would be Chieftesses." She put her face in her hands and bawled.

After another knock at the door, Kitchi squeezed in the basket. Norah worried it might fall from the weight.

"I woke up shaking, Frey, what's going on?" He looked concerned.

"I need to leave for a year, be apart from Toma, or we can't be together." She leaned on him and cried more.

He brushed her hair gently. "Do you love Toma?"

She nodded and sniffled.

"A year will fly by." He smiled.

She cried and whispered, "It's not only a year."

"What do you mean?" Kitchi asked.

"When we come back, we marry and then leave together for a year." She looked at Norah as if she was more concerned about her.

Norah smiled gently at her. "When do you start your journey?"

"After the ceremony this morning." She cried.

The four of them embraced on the bed. Norah didn't fight the tradition; it meshed well in her spirit.

"Freya, do you want to be Chieftess?" Norah asked.

"I want to be with Toma, maybe it's my path." She wiped her tears and grew stoic.

"I think so," Norah whispered, brushing the hair from Freya's eyes. "I think so."

Kitchi and Freya hopped out of the basket. Norah stared at Eldon and then kissed him. The drum beat. They dressed and headed to the fire.

Toma and Freya stood in the middle of the Glidumaras, who danced around them in a circle. Gwada motioned for them to stop and spoke.

"Our daughters, future Chieftesses, are leaving today to find themselves before they marry." He nodded to Sawa, who picked up two bags and handed one to Toma and one to Freya. "In those bags, you will find medicine and stones. The stones will be your food, enough for one year; the medicine will guide you to yourself." He nodded to Sawa again, and Sawa took each woman's hand and guided them in the direction of the circle, the Glidumaras drumming them towards their journeys.

Norah's stomach sank as she watched Freya walk away with Sawa, the small satchel hanging off her shoulder. *Food for a year*, she thought. It didn't make sense, but she trusted Gwada and the ways of the Glidumaras. More importantly, she trusted her daughter's ability to forge her own path.

CHAPTER 21

TIME MOVED QUICKLY UNDER THE SUN, NOT SLOWLY LIKE under the moon. Norah fought her mind's pulling toward incessant worry about Freya and focused instead on her new world for the past year. Villagers had regularly approached Norah to join them on expeditions for protection, and although she found it unusual, she obliged and immersed herself in adapting to the culture and landscape. Feasts now took place around a boulder rather than in a dining hall, and there was still much laughter but it was not the same. Brittany struggled to adapt, but when dark days visited, they reminded one another why they had left.

The village awoke to loud drumming. Norah nearly jumped out of her skin. She knew she would only see Freya for a short time before she left again, but it was enough to just lay eyes on her, feel her presence. She and Eldon rushed to the fire.

The chairs were set in a star pattern around the fire. Sawa walked around with a stone shaker; billowing golden steam poured out of it, and it turned into a fine shimmering dust on their skin. Peaches sang an enchanted love song she had written for Freya and Toma.

Freya walked out from behind the boulder in a simple floor-length golden gown that flowed over her curves; a gold crown rested on her messy bun. Norah wept when she set eyes on her—she looked healthy, shifted. Toma walked out from the other side of the boulder in an elaborate ceremonial wedding dress, long with flowing lace; her lengthy hair was smoothed into two braids woven with ornate golden ribbons. They held each other, weeping.

Brittany squeezed Norah's hand. "Thank you," she whispered.

Gwada blew gold powder in Freya's and Toma's faces. They coughed. He spoke a blessing in Glidu and stared into Freya's eyes. "Have you found yourself?" he asked.

She nodded. He lifted the goblet to her lips, and she sipped.

He stared into Toma's eyes. "Have you found yourself?"

She nodded and smiled at Freya. He lifted the goblet to her lips, and she sipped.

He nodded and smiled. "Now you may find each other."

Toma grabbed Freya and kissed her passionately. Gwada motioned to Norah and Eldon to come forward.

Norah embraced Freya, selfishly not wanting to let her go. Then she embraced Toma. She stared at her family—the faces she adored, her children. "We are here, we are together, and now we celebrate new love," she said. "Our hearts broke when we left our family and now stand strong. Freya and Toma, we love you and bless you into our family with all our hearts. To the ones under the moon, I know you're here in spirit." Eldon squeezed her hand, and she rested her head on his shoulder.

Gwada went to each of them and lifted the goblet to their mouths. Norah sipped the drink, her body warming as it slid down her throat. There was silence for a few moments before Gwada beat his drum twice, then Toma took Freya's hand and walked towards the Swahallah, the Glidu name for sea, not allowed to speak to anyone but each other.

Marama grabbed a handful of talcum sand and threw it at Freya's back; everyone followed suit. Drenched in golden sand, the women headed into their union. The drums continued beating. The wedding guests danced and feasted for hours after they departed.

Norah and Brittany both needed some quiet, away from the celebration. They walked to the sea and found Sunny and Theo cuddled in an abalone shell. Sunny was crying. She looked up at Brittany, startled. "Mom!"

"Sunny, what's wrong?" She and Norah sat on a rock at the edge of the shell.

Sunny sniffled. "I'm pregnant." She looked down at her belly and rubbed it gently.

Brittany teared up. "Sunny, you're going to be a mom!"

Norah stared at Brittany and Sunny; mother and daughter looked around the same age.

"Theo." Norah smiled and touched his leg.

He nodded and nestled into Sunny.

Sensing their children wanted to be alone, Norah glanced at Brittany and raised her eyebrows. Brittany nodded and they walked farther down the shoreline, drums echoing in the distance. Norah curled her arm into Brittany's.

"They've been in love since the second they saw each other," Brittany said.

Norah smiled. "Another grandbaby."

They quieted and watched the Wapado, dolphin-like creatures, splash in the golden water.

* * *

The village gleamed with anticipation of the new baby: the first baby born in the sun. Seamus asked Norah to walk with him after the announcement; he seemed different since he had crossed, serious. He and Norah had spoken little, their closeness naturally dwindling as he spent most of his time with Marama.

"What do you think about Sunny?" he asked.

"I think it's wonderful." She smiled. "Our son is having a child."

"He's young?" His voice sounded like old-world Seamus. The Seamus who could never find joy in anything, even the rarest, most beautiful gifts.

"So?" Norah quipped. "What are you worried about?"

"I don't' know—the responsibility?" He shrugged.

"Seamus, I think you're stuck in old thinking. The responsibility will be shared with the village, they don't need to worry about money or survival. We're having a grandchild. How doesn't that sing in your heart?"

He smiled. "Sing in my heart?"

"Yes," she said with a laugh. "You know, I miss you."

He looked down. "I miss you too. Seems so different. I love Marama, life with the Glids… just miss things sometimes."

"Me too," she said. "I am still here, you know."

"I know, Norah," He put his arm around her. She felt warm, grateful for the conversation.

*　*　*

At five months pregnant, Sunny's belly was massive. Norah wondered how she could continue to expand for the remaining months. Her body was healthy and full of energy, which Sunny attributed to the plant medicines Marama prepared for her daily and to swimming in the sea.

Marama had supported many births in their village. The nearby cave had been used for centuries as a birthing room; Marama said it carried powerful energy, knowledge of what the children and parents needed.

Norah didn't know what she meant by 'what they needed,' but like many things of the foreign culture, she accepted not knowing.

"Mom, get up." Theo shook her basket.

Norah woke, startled. "What is it, Theo?" She rubbed her eyes.

"Come quick, it's S-Sunny..."

Eldon opened his eyes. They quickly dressed and rushed to Theo and Sunny's basket. Fear churned in Norah's stomach, her mind visiting the worst scenario.

Sunny was curled in the fetal position on the bed, face red, drenched in sweat, her teeth clenched down on a pillow as she writhed in pain.

Brittany was beside her, rubbing her back. "She's only five months," she whispered. Panic in her eyes.

"Go get Marama and Seamus." Norah motioned to Eldon and squeezed Theo's shaking hand.

Marama stood at the opening and smiled. "Bring her to the birthing cave."

"She's only five months?" Norah said, trying to stay calm.

Marama nodded. "Yes, time for birth."

"The baby needs nine months, not five?" Norah's voice shook.

Marama put her hand on Norah's arm. "It is five months, Norah, it is different here." She smiled gently and released her.

Over the years, Norah's ability to digest unbelievable information in a short amount of time had evolved. She nodded. "Let's get her to the birthing cave!"

Theo, Eldon, and Seamus carried Sunny to the cave.

"Theo, did you know this?" Norah asked as she rushed beside him.

"I told you, Mom."

Norah scrambled to search her memory. *No, he didn't.*

When they arrived at the cave, Marama put her arm out and stopped Norah and Brittany from entering. "You need to stay outside."

Norah grew angry, tired of being told what to do. "Marama. We're coming in, being with our kids."

Marama nodded.

Sunny's contractions were minutes apart, the urge to push strong. Suddenly, her eyes rolled back into her head and turned black. Powdery black foam bubbled out of her mouth. Her body convulsed. Theo and Seamus held her on the bed.

"Do something," Theo shrieked.

"Get Gwada!" Marama screamed.

Brittany darted to get Gwada. He rushed in moments later and studied Sunny's eyes, then stuck two fingers in the side of her cheek and emptied her mouth of the powdery foam. His face turned white as a ghost, and he put his hand over her heart.

He gazed at Marama. "The Duwan."

Marama gasped and put her hand over her mouth.

Gwada commanded something at Supay, who nodded and ran towards the forest.

"What's Duwan?" Brittany cried.

"It's…" Marama braced herself on Gwada's throne and gasped for air.

Supay returned, holding a goblet. Gwada grabbed it from him and poured the bubbling pink liquid it held over Sunny's face. She coughed, the black foam disappeared, and her eyes returned to normal. She bellowed a scream and pushed, tears and spit covering her face.

A chubby baby girl plopped into Marama's arms and gasped for its first breath. A collective sigh of relief filled the cave. At around fifteen pounds with long, thick golden-brown hair and giant brown eyes, she was the roundest-faced, cutest baby Norah had ever seen. Theo wept and held his daughter.

Sunny's back bent forward, her eyes blackened again, and her face became expressionless, like a marionette. Her body convulsed while black powdery foam spat out of her mouth.

"Another!" Marama shouted, then continued speaking in Glidu. Gwada motioned to Supay with the goblet, who tipped it to show it was empty. Supay shouted at him.

"English!" Norah screamed.

"The medicine is gone, too late," Marama replied.

Sunny convulsed, unconscious, and birthed another daughter. Her body went flat, lifeless, eyes still black, black foam still pouring out the side of her mouth.

The baby was identical to her sister but limp, with no breath. Her sister wailed—not the cry of a new baby but a wailing of loss. Theo held his daughters in his arms: one alive, one dead. Shellshocked, no tears.

Norah, inconsolable, flashed to Tilly's birth and her split-second decision to run to the cave to save her. Broken—she knew that this time. Nothing she could do. Her lifeless granddaughter lay in her son's arms. A vice crushed her heart.

"Gwada, take my daughter into the cave," Theo begged.

"My son." Gwada put his hand on Theo's shoulder and gazed into his eyes. "Your daughter is gone. Sunny will go." He motioned for Supay and Sawa, and they lifted and carried her out.

Marama reached to lift the lifeless baby from Theo's arms.

"No!" he hissed. She backed off gently. Theo slid his back down the cave wall and bellowed a cry the moon could hear.

Norah and Brittany slid down the wall on either side of him, weeping for their children and the grandchild they would never know. Seamus and Tayo joined. The four grandparents broke open as one, staring at the sweet girls.

Theo breathed in deeply. "Help me up," he said, his voice barely audible.

Seamus and Tayo supported him to stand, the babies still nestled in each arm.

Marama waited at the entrance. Theo nodded, and she took the lifeless baby from him. "I will bring her to rest. You will see her soon."

They watched as Marama walked towards the forest.

"What is the Duwan?" Theo whispered as she walked out.

Marama turned back and lowered her head. "A childless female demon. Was once a beautiful warrior, she fell in love with a Drawler from the spirit world. The Drawler's father, Trelah, disapproved of the union. When she became with child, Trelah put a curse on her, brought her into the underworld, smite her child. In her fury, she killed everyone, even the Drawler, and turned into a demon who"—she paused—"steals the breath from mother and child."

Theo looked down at the daughter still in his arms. "This is Luna," he whispered and sat by the fire.

Kitchi embraced his brother while sweet little Luna sprinkled particles of joy into the sadness.

Silent hours passed, except for Luna's cries. The villagers brought Dwar milk in a bottle made from a leathery type of material. Luna drank it with no fussing.

Marama returned and whispered something in Theo's ear.

"Lowah," he whispered quietly.

She nodded. "The spirits are with Lowah. Follow me to bless her as she journeys home."

She led them to a small altar in the forest. Lowah lay in a basket of fresh golden and indigo flowers, her face and body painted gold. A lock of Sunny's hair lay in one hand, and Theo's in the other. She looked peaceful.

Luna had settled, but when she drew near to Lowah, she sobbed, the cries of a broken heart. Theo held her beside Lowah, and her tears fell on her sister's small painted body; five months together in the womb, now left alone to face the world. Theo, incoherent with grief, passed Luna to Brittany, kneeled by the altar, and wept. "I'm sorry," he whispered as he held Lowah's small hand. He kissed her forehead and returned to Luna.

"Baby Lowah will stay here for three days and wait for the spirits to bring her home," Gwada said. "The flowers will keep her safe. You may visit anytime. After three days, we will release her into the Swahallah to be cared for by the Wapado."

Theo spent the following three days at the altar with Lowah and Luna. He played his guitar and sang to them both. Sunny lay unconscious in the cave, desperation blanketing the family. Brittany was near comatose with worry about Sunny and grief at the loss of Lowah. It devastated Norah to think of what Sunny would wake to, but she prayed she would before her Lowah was sent to the Wapado.

Gwada beat his drum and invited people to enter the cave where Sunny lay. Norah went inside with Theo. He sat beside Sunny's body, Luna resting in his arms, and begged her to wake up. Luna flailed as if she was yearning for her mother's touch. Theo placed her in the fold of Sunny's arm, and Luna settled.

Gwada motioned to them. It was time to release Lowah. Theo glanced at Norah, his expression one of confusion laced devastation. He lifted Luna and put her in Norah's arms. She stared at her glorious granddaughter, her heart settled, eyes carrying wisdom. Theo went to Lowah, lifted the small flower basket, and walked towards the sea. The entire village followed behind him in a procession and gathered as he placed the basket at the rock's edge.

Marama carried two baskets, one filled with golden sand and the other with teal petals. She lifted a handful of each and sprinkled them over Lowah, then motioned for the others to follow suit. Brittany raised her hand to release the petals.

A scream bellowed from the village. It was Sunny, running towards the sea.

Theo ran to her and embraced her, whispering something in her ear. She toppled, but he held her up. Echoes filled the village: the cries of a mother who had lost her child. Cries that would haunt a heart forever. Norah wept, watching Theo hold her up as she screamed.

Sunny mustered enough strength to walk. When her eyes met the basket, she fell to her knees and drenched Lowah in tears. She lifted her out of the basket, clutched her to her chest, and wailed. Her arms shook as she laid her back down. She kissed her forehead. "I love you, Lowah," she whispered.

Her legs trembled. Theo helped her stand. She lifted a handful of petals and sprinkled them over her baby. She turned to Norah and gazed at Luna. She brushed her daughter's face with her hand, lifted her out of Norah's arms, and wept.

Gwada motioned to Theo and Sunny and spoke with kindness. "You brought her into the world. You need to send her off." He nodded towards the basket.

With trembling hands, they lifted the basket and pushed it gently, releasing her. As the basket floated into the endless rippling golden water, a family of shimmering Wapado dived in and out of the water, dancing around her. The basket drifted from their vision. Sunny and Theo sat on the rock for hours, holding Luna, staring at the sea. Norah watched them. They appeared so small in the landscape of the sea and sun. Their little beating hearts had been shifted forever. The ripple effect of this loss, like all the losses they had faced, was as vast as the ripples of the sea.

CHAPTER 22

SIX MONTHS AFTER LOWAH LEFT WITH THE WAPADO, THE AIR still swirled with waves of loss and life. Luna was now a chubby, cherubesque six-month-old with dimples embedded into her rosy cheeks. Her teal eyes sparkled, and her skin glittered gold. She walked early for her age, waddling freely around the village, her soft golden curls bouncing with each step. The day she learned to walk, she kept running away from Sunny and Theo. They stopped her, over and over, and finally allowed her to go, following close behind. She ended up on the same rock where Lowah had been sent off and stood at the edge of the sea, quiet tears rolling down her cheeks. The Wapado jumped so close, she could have touched them. She smiled at the small group of people who had followed her. Since that day, anytime Luna was pulled to the sea, they just let her go.

Norah helped Marama hang lanterns around the circle to prepare for Freya's return the following day. She lifted the tiny glowing lights and thought about Freya, all that had transpired since she left, and what life would be like as Chieftess. She heard a rustle in the distance and looked up. The men had returned from a three-day hunting trip to get Dwar for the feast.

Eldon and Seamus, both clothed in the tribe's traditional hunting garb, shared the weight of a Dwar slumped over their shoulders. Kitchi and Supay each carried their own Dwar. They dropped the Dwars on the earth before the circle and left them for Marama and the villagers to harvest.

Eldon winked at Norah, and her knees buckled. He grabbed her, lifted her off the ground, and kissed her neck. "I missed you," he whispered.

She wanted to take him right there but inhaled a deep breath instead, and he released her. "She's coming home tomorrow." She smiled and kissed his cheek.

His face beamed. "I'm gonna wash up." He grabbed her hand and led her to the sea. Luna ran towards him, and he kneeled, scooped her up with one arm, and continued walking.

Sunny smiled. "There you are." She looked at Norah and laughed. "I can't keep up with her." Norah smiled, thinking that if Sunny couldn't keep up with her, then no one could. She lifted Luna out of Eldon's embrace. "Come on, sweetie, time to eat."

Norah and Eldon continued to the sea. Eldon led her around a small bend in the rocks and didn't waste time—he ripped off her dress and ravished her. When they had finished, they jumped in the sea. Norah missed the inlet's effervescent water but loved the Swahallah water; it was soft and left her skin radiant.

*　*　*

The anticipation of Freya's return woke Norah from a dead sleep. Wide awake, she knew sleep would not revisit. This village snored. She loved the quiet of early morning risings. She clutched her journal, hopped out of the basket, and walked to the forest, to the tree where Lowah had lain. Her feet felt light on the earth; it was airy here, without the earth's magnetic pull under the moon. She often visited and sat in the flowers around the tree where the basket had rested. As a grandmother, the loss whispered in another language because she was a mother first, Theo's mother. And his loss weighed down her spirit as no other loss could. She grieved for her granddaughter and son—an unexpected, intense burden. Her grief drowned in the screams of his terror. In front of the altar, these moments were the moments she allowed her grief for her grandchild, which itself shook her to the depth of her core.

She opened her journal and stared at the blank page: nothing, no words. She lay on her back and gazed at the sun, at the birds flying around the indigo stars. She hummed a lullaby to sweet Lowah, her tears absorbed by the warm earth.

* * *

Norah opened her eyes, startled by the beat of a drum. Her hands touched the earth. *Shit*, she thought, horrified she might be late for Freya's return. She hustled to the circle and sighed with relief; the circle was empty, except for Gwada and Supay.

Norah returned to the basket. Eldon was inside, pulling on his Dwar slippers. "I was just coming to look for you." She took her hand.

Everyone was now gathered at the circle. Norah and Eldon sat, and within a moment, Gwada spoke.

"Freya and Toma." He put his arms in the air in celebration, and it was obvious to Norah that he missed his own daughter immensely.

Norah saw Freya and gasped—her skin glowed, something about her changed. She and Toma both appeared full of life, healthy and happy.

Freya locked eyes with Norah and held her heart. Tears poured down her cheeks. Gwada motioned for them to reunite with their loved ones. Freya wept as she embraced Norah, and then she pulled back and grabbed her shoulders and stared into her eyes. Norah tried to fight her tears—no use.

"Mom," Freya said with a sniffle, "I never knew."

"What?" Norah whispered.

"Who you were. I couldn't until I knew myself." She paused. "I saw it—the old world, your struggles. The pain of your heart." She placed her hand on Norah's heart. "I see you, Mom." She embraced her with intensity.

Norah crumbled inside her words and her embrace.

Freya hugged Eldon and cupped his face in her hands. "I'm sorry, Dad. I'm sorry about Nash." Norah could see he was taken back; at hearing Nash's name, tears rose to the surface. Freya pulled him close and released him.

Norah and Eldon looked at each other, shellshocked.

Freya walked to Kitchi next and laughed. They each rested their forehead on the other's and embraced. "I've always seen you. Known you. We share the same spirit."

She went to Theo and Sunny, Luna resting in Theo's arms. "My brother and sister." She smiled and touched Luna's forehead.

"This is Luna," Theo said with a smile, and then he paused. "We need to tell you…" He choked up.

Freya lifted a beautiful package wrapped in embroidered fabric off the ground and handed it to Sunny. Sunny gently removed the material to reveal the gift. The basket. A confused expression covered her face. She and Theo gasped, bombarded by emotion.

"This came to us months ago," Freya said, "with a vision of a magical infant Wapado. The vision showed us she was yours and that her sister resided with you. A message came forth: your daughters are connected, and Luna possesses the powerful gift of the ability to breathe in the water like the Wapado. As she grows, she will be drawn to the Swahallah. Let her dive in, don't be afraid. She will see her sister again." Freya smiled.

"Will we see her again too?" Sunny asked and sniffled, desperation in her voice.

"Only Luna," Freya said, embracing Sunny while she wept in her arms.

Gwada showed Freya and Toma to their new home. A few minutes from the village, it was an elaborate hut built from stone, moss, and hardened talcum-powder sand. Gwada had also tasked his men to build two thrones beside his inside the rock wall: one glowed teal, the other gold. Ornate designs covered the thrones, and Norah was amazed at their carving skills.

Freya was gifted a glowing gold knife with a translucent indigo blade and a woven holder for her dress. Toma was gifted a teal glass sphere on the end of a swirled gold handle. Both gifts signified their standing in the village and carried the final word's weight on any matter.

The village gave Freya and Toma privacy to settle into their new home and regain their footing in the village. Marama approached Norah and invited her to walk.

"Are you content here, Norah?" she asked.

"I'm with my family, so yes."

"Have you ever been content?" she continued as if Norah's answer didn't register—or she knew Norah lied.

Norah tried to think about the question before answering. "At times, I guess."

"No, you haven't," Marama said, a matter of fact.

Norah was mildly irritated. "How do you know?"

"I just know." No judgment in her voice, only kindness.

"Are you content?" Norah asked.

"Yes." She smiled.

Her words shrunk Norah, again faced with the inability to find peace. She believed she had shifted over the years, and she had… but the neurosis persisted—the worry about nothing, the gnawing core belief of not being good enough. Not to mention the sadness of her losses and the foreverness of being with the Glidumaras.

Marama kept digging. "Do you want to be content?"

"Of course I do. Why are you asking me this?"

"Because I want it for you too. You carry the pain of those left behind and those here. It's time for you, Norah. I have a gift for you."

"A gift?"

"Yes. Meet Seamus and me at three waves. Now go get some rest." She left Norah alone and returned to the village.

Norah reeled from the conversation. It brought her down; for some reason, she once again felt guilty for not being able to spin her suffering into something positive. She returned to her basket, curled in Eldon's arms, and told him about the early gift they were to receive.

THE FINAL CHAPTER

NORAH AND ELDON WOKE EARLY. MARAMA AND SEAMUS waited for them by the fire.

"Where are we going?" Norah asked.

"The Gwinhah," Seamus whispered.

Since Norah arrived under the sun, she had heard whisperings of the Gwinhah, the sacred altar behind the mysterious Wahano falls. The Glidumaras worshipped the gods there, but Gwada refused to visit after the Twill killed Gwyah. Still, when the name was spoken, he grew serious.

Marama and Seamus guided them along the steep, slippery, talcum-covered hill, a six-hour gruelling hike. Norah was exhausted, but once again afraid of being like Fatty, she pushed on without complaint. Eldon kept looking back and smirking, which she met with a death glare every time. Seamus caught wind of the joke and asked Norah if she had worn the wrong footwear, her go-to excuse. She laughed, remembering how many times she had blamed her shoes for her being out of shape. Unfortunately, she was currently barefoot, so her old excuse had no weight.

Marama spoke in Glidu to Seamus, and he quieted.

"What did you say, Marama?" Norah asked, breathless.

"I told him to be nice." She smirked. "Norah, tell me about the world before when you and Seamus were one?"

Norah glanced at Seamus, eons from their old life. She thought about the old society, where it had been heading before being swallowed whole by the Shade. The perpetual dissatisfaction. Lies of consumer culture.

"It's hard to describe the old world. Technology was god." She shrugged.

"Technology?" Marama struggled to pronounce it.

"Like feelingless intelligent robots. People were unsettled, medicated, and heavy with emotional and physical pain but numb." She paused. "Life lived behind screens." She looked at Seamus and Eldon for help.

"The planet was hypnotized," Eldon said. "Human beings traded real moments for pretend minutes. Stared at small boxes that recorded their every move."

"Pretend minutes?" Marama asked.

"Like minutes on phones, screens—not with real people," Seamus said.

Marama squinted. "Phones?"

"Marama, it's beyond your understanding. Be grateful for that," Seamus said, shutting the conversation down.

"We did that." Norah looked down and shook her head. "We did that to each other, to Theo; he fought for our attention, we were always staring at our fucking phones. It's like they were a body part. Something we needed to survive."

Seamus put his arm around Norah. "It was a machine we couldn't stop, a never-ending *Black Mirror* episode."

Norah sighed. "I hated it—hated the old world, the fear, the drip-ping ego that saturated the planet. I always used to say it was building up to something."

Seamus nodded. "You did. I was more asleep than you—I had to be, working twelve-hour days just to live in overwhelming debt. If I opened my eyes, I might have killed myself, as horrible as it sounds."

Marama gasped. "Kill yourself?"

"Has no one in your tribe taken their own life?" Norah asked.

"What do you mean?" Marama said, confused.

"It was called suicide," Eldon answered.

"Someone would take their own breath, choose to not live?" Marama fought tears. "Why?"

"Marama, our world was much different than what you know—sti-fling loneliness, heavy minds, sadness, and worry. Human beings lost their way." Norah spoke quietly, feeling guilty about the dark conversation.

"People didn't care about each other or know their neighbours," Seamus said, "not to mention a horrible history that left people hurting and broken."

"Is that why Gwada cried at the stone?" Marama asked.

"Yes," Eldon said with a sigh. "As uplifting as this is, can we carry on?"

"Yeah. Sorry." Norah shrugged. "I haven't thought about how fucked up things were in a long time."

"Yes, fucked up," Marama said.

They laughed, and Marama nodded her head. She guided them to a shelf on the side of a mountain. Eldon helped Norah pull herself up. Her jaw dropped at the view—a richly flowered field surrounded with trees led to a majestic waterfall crashing over emerald rocks, and bird songs echoed off the cliffs. It reminded Norah of the Amazon Forest: dense and rich with plants and wildlife.

Seamus put his arm around Marama and whispered to her.

She blushed and kissed him, then stripped naked and jumped over the waterfall. Seamus followed.

Eldon and Norah laughed, stripped down, and crashed into the clean, crisp water. Norah lifted her head out of the water and gazed around. She was surrounded by a magical cove, where geodes shot out the sides in every direction, the waterfall crashed over them, and the shore was a fine crystalline sand. A firepit, hammock, blankets, and towels hanging off trees made it evident Marama and Seamus often visited.

They stayed in the water for hours; Norah enjoyed a sense of freedom foreign to her. The flesh she loathed was now bare with the two men who loved it the most. They eventually stumbled onto the beach, and when Norah's feet sunk into the soft sand, she felt tipsy from the energy and wrapped herself in a blanket. She lay on the sand, and it contoured around her body like a memory foam mattress. Norah could have lain there forever; never had her body felt more comfortable. Seamus lit the fire. They relaxed and fell asleep on the beach.

"It's time to visit Gwinhah," Marama said, waking Norah.

Norah was surprised by Marama's announcement. She had assumed the cove was Gwinhah. Marama led them to the far edge of the cove and through a narrow tunnel that fit one person at a time. Norah felt claustrophobic, inching through the tunnel on her forearms. But when she laid her eyes on the Gwinhah, her jaw dropped and any fear subsided. The altar was solid emerald rock from wall to wall of the cave, woven with golden roots, and emerald icicle gems hung from the ceiling. Norah's bare feet sunk into tiny emerald glass beads. Three small steps led to a floating emerald sphere.

"If you touch the Gwinhah, memories will flood you," Marama said.

Norah glanced at Seamus. "Have you touched it?"

"I did."

Norah threaded her fingers through Eldon's, and they stretched their hands and placed them on the sphere; a powerful vacuum suctioned them in place. Their minds connected as one, enabling them to read each other's thoughts. Norah looked around and felt dizzy; they were still in the emerald cave, but the air rippled and Seamus and Marama were gone. The air turned into water, and her lungs filled. She panicked and watched Eldon sink down into the water in front of her. She gulped the water and began to drown. Her feet landed on earth.

Hand in hand, they stood surrounded by trees at dusk. Eldon wailed. Her heart plummeted. It was the forest where Nash had been found. A man was lurking over Nash's lifeless body. Eldon ran over and tried to grab him but his hands waved through him as if he were air. Two people walked towards him—his parents. He fell into their arms, like a child. Space narrowed, and Eldon's eyes were pried open, forced to watch the measly coward cover Nash's body with dried leaves.

"Nooo," Eldon wailed, then keeled over with dry heaves. The coward walked away and left Nash's body alone on a pile of dirt and branches. "I love you, Nash." Eldon cried and touched his face.

Eldon blinked. Now they stood in an old motel, vodka bottles and needles scattered about the floor. The murderer sat on a filthy old mattress, looking at an open laptop where young boys' photos splattered the screen. Eldon screamed, lunged at him, and fell through him onto the floor. He tried to kill him over and over. Then he slumped over, helpless, and dry heaved on the floor. He tried to pick up an old needle to rip off his own skin. Norah and Eldon could feel every frequency of one another's pain, but no action would follow. Norah communicated with Eldon through her thoughts; she knew he had to release his son's murderer.

You need to forgive him.

"No!" he screamed at her. He leaned on the wall and sank down on the decrepit, stained motel floor, stuck with the man who murdered his son. He released a writhing war cry and placed his hand on the coward's heart. "I forgive you for murdering my son."

White light washed over Eldon and Norah and released the pain from their bodies. They leaned their heads on each other and closed their eyes.

Their eyes opened in Eldon's old apartment. He watched himself, curled in a ball on the kitchen floor, the guilt ripping out his insides. He kneeled beside himself—he couldn't forgive himself, hated himself more than the murderer.

Nash put his arm around him. *"Daddy, I love you. I miss you."*

Eldon tried to grab him, but he vanished. He tried to leave and find him, but he was glued beside himself, on the floor.

His parents kneeled and put their arms around him. "Son, forgive yourself."

Eldon cried, seeing his own pain. He laid his hand over his heart. "I forgive you." He wailed and gripped Norah's hand.

They fell through the floor and landed in the hospice unit.

Norah saw herself on the floor, one man on top of her, the other watching. She was surprised that the vision had brought her to the attack, sure it had long since been processed, and yet she screamed and tried to beat them. Like Eldon, her hands went through them as if they were air. She followed herself down the hall, the body dragging in the blanket. She sat on the stairs beside the lifeless body wrapped in the blanket, unable to move, consumed with hatred, wanting to kill him, to kill herself. She watched him get up, bloody and mangled, and followed him to the ER where he died. She sat by his dead body and screamed. She placed her hand on his heart. "I forgive you."

Eldon touched her back, and she began to fall, landing by a river in an unfamiliar area. The other rapist sat on a rock, a smoke dangling from his mouth, not feeling an inch of remorse. She screamed in his smug face and tried to punch him but her energy was wasted. He would never pay because he was a broken human with no ability to feel. She placed her hand on his heart. "I forgive you."

Eldon embraced her and they dissolved into the sand and sunk down.

They now stood between the cement lions. They walked inside to find Norah wailing on the floor by the fireplace. Her parents appeared and put their hands on her back. "We're here, Norah, we love you." She stared at them and cried, their faces clear; she touched her mom's cheek—only air. She placed her hand on herself, and her mind flooded with every ounce of self-hatred and pain she had ever allowed. The imperfect human who served a life sentence in her own prison for crimes of unworthiness. She cupped her ears and screamed, wailing in the realization that she had stolen her own years. Overcome with compassion for herself, she said, "Norah, I forgive you."

Eldon laid his head on her. They blinked and opened their eyes— now at the dining hall. Eldon sat on the couch and strummed his guitar, Brittany wrapped around him. Norah entered the room for the first time and Eldon casually glanced at her, then put his head down and smiled—he loved her from the second he saw her.

He turned and hugged her; this time, their bodies connected. They opened their eyes to see Seamus and Marama and the altar in front of them.

Norah and Eldon were both shaking, emotionally reeling from the journey. The rough edges of their humanity softened.

"Thank you, Marama," Norah whispered.

"You had much to release," she said quietly. "You were with the Wahano for two days."

Norah stared at Eldon. It had felt like an hour. They didn't talk on the way back to the village, just silently processed.

Gwada noticed them immediately. "You've been touched by Gwinhah. I can see it in your eyes." He smiled.

Norah nodded, met with an overwhelming urge to be alone. She returned to the basket and grabbed the moon blanket, then walked to the Swahallah. She wrapped herself in the blanket and lay down inside an abalone shell.

Her birthright beckoned into her spirit, a collage of ancestral ties, clear spaces of possibility, and emotion—that which she brought into this life and also what she chose. She now knew peace and her body stilled, at ease with her imperfections and humanity. She wept tears of awe as the sun warmed her into her soul, thinking about her family under the moon, the sun, and the cosmos.

She was her only, her forever. The one constant in her life who would be by her side until her last breath. The one she had visited hell with and returned whole. Her first and last love. She stood at the edge of the sea and stared at her reflection rippling in the golden water, at the imperfect flesh where her spirit resided. Her gifts shone bright. Her beauty glowed. She saw herself how she really was, not the skewed image her mind had created. She kneeled on the rock, overpowered with gratitude for her life and the beauty she possessed. Humbled before life, death, and everything in between.

She dipped her toes in the water, gazed out into the vast expanse, and wondered if her destiny lay in her choices or if she was heading towards an end to which she had no control. Regardless, she was running into an end—a dead end, or a beginning.

THE END